I0831817

The faraway land of the house and two cows

Schott's remarkable book is both brilliant and beautiful, a celebration of childhood and the power of a unique place that gives readers an intimate look at a piece of Melbourne's history that was destroyed. The pulsing community is at the heart of this story as it takes and gives in this suburban cacophony. It is impossible to place this work in a box, for it's a lyrical work of poetics, immersion journalism and creative nonfiction. Dr Schott's creative choice to make her primary characters figurative ghosts channels Australia's first forays from an Anglo-Saxon hierarchy to the multi-cultural society it is today. A must-read for all wanting to know more about Australia from the late 19th century to the late 20th century.
Dr Lynette Hinings-Marshall; Author of *Travel with the Dream Makers*

A fascinating read and thought provoking, descriptions and pictures painted are breathtaking. Monika's visit with my mother and brother as part of her research was the beginning of renewed interest in my family's history. This book is an important timeline and layering of The Farm's history, an unusual history that is part of all of us from Melbourne, Werribee and The Farm. Many names are known, many places have been heard of and visited, others are not part of my story. It makes it personal, and real. I've learnt more of my backstory, parts have been coloured in and vague recollections and snippets have become solid outlines. I now have new imaginings and with that, new understanding and perhaps, forgiveness.
Pam Thompson (nee Sadler); Past resident of the Metropolitan Sewerage Farm

A very powerfully written account describing the tight knit community that worked and lived on the Metropolitan Sewerage Farm. Monika has revealed a time in the history of Melbourne that is largely unknown, with ghosts from the past witnessing the daily lives of people there. Historical facts are woven through the narrative and act as a thread of evidence demonstrating the poignant truth of their lives. This is a marvellously original, researched story that vividly brings the Farm to life and describes how the community's efforts transformed Melbourne into a modern city.
Emma McCarth; Behaviour Practitioner and Educational Consultant

The faraway land of the house and two cows is a captivating and beautifully written book. It is fascinating to learn about life (and after life) on a sewerage farm! Dr. Monika Schott is a wonderful story teller and I can see this incredible book becoming an epic Australian movie one day!
Jo Galea; Interior designer

This is a remarkable achievement that captures in riveting detail a century of ordinary people living extraordinary lives in a little-known corner of rural Australia that's now vanished. Schott has catalogued and distilled in warm, poetic, even microscopic, fashion a thriving, rambunctious troupe of labourers, stockmen, housewives, kids, cricketers, footballers, tennis players and bosses on a giant government farm in an environment peppered by everything from schoolyard snake bites to boozy romantic interludes. Underscoring everything is the pungent odour of ordure, the treatment of which is the Farm's primary task. Think mulberry jam, roast duck and Vegemite, beer, sherry and whiskey. Think cattle, horses, birds and sewage – 38 million gallons a day, and that was back in the 1920s. As Schott reports: "Bloody Norah!"
Noel Murphy; Writer

The ghost narrators are surely as lively and intriguing as characters as the living members of the community. They enable the story to be told across a larger time scale than a single living narrator could. Each tap into an event, a moment or an era, and signify the persistence of those 'times' in the story's narrating present. I particularly appreciated that the community of ghosts included the unborn or stillborn foetuses, and although they don't narrate, Ginger the cat, the white magpie and the dog too. The novel and song stayed with me beyond my reading and listening.
Associate Professor Chris Prentice; University of Otago

A brilliantly written book weaving fact and fiction, providing an extensive historical account told through wonderful and whimsical characters. Intriguing, informative and thought provoking, a great read!
Carolyn Wockner

A brilliantly told story... I was a wreck... I cried my eyes out... it finally got me, all the sadness, emotion, loss, pain of endless change, the desperate ache for what Was ... WOW! WOW! WOW! Thank you!

Who would have dreamt that a tale of such grandeur could come from a load of old sewage?

Monika did, and the Magic of her words create a Time Machine that takes us back to glimpse moments in the lives of a multitude of colourful characters. She puts flesh back on the bones of the ghosts of the past. We experience the lives, loves, losses and tragedies of pioneers, heroes and the occasional villains. We see a thriving community sadly reduced to a land mainly inhabited only by ghosts.

Monika has woven the twists and turns of Life and Afterlife over Time and Tide to share the power of the relationship of the People and the Land. This is about how the Land shapes the People as the People shape the Land. I smiled, I cried. My heart ached for a simpler time when every person mattered.

Michael Young; Writer and editor

The faraway land of the house and two cows generates extended impressions that slowly instil in the reader a nuanced and properly contentious or contradictory mesh of insights arrayed across an emotional 'palette' associated with the sewerage farm community in western Melbourne. Most impressively, this mosaic also has a 'time thickness' to it, granting the reader a sense of the century-long history of everyday lives within the bounds of the 'cordon sanitaire' that has always been cast around the 'abject' townships that serviced the sewerage treatment domains.

Centenary Professor Ross Gibson; University of Canberra

The faraway land of the house and two cows

Dr Monika Schott

Second Hardback Edition

First published in AUSTRALIA 2022
Reprinted 2022 and 2023

Leonie Editorial, Australia
leonieeditorial@optusnet.com.au
Michael Young, AVA ORION Media, Australia
www.AvaOrionMedia.com
www.monikaschott.com

Cover image: Postmistress Mrs Marjorie O'Connor, with the heritage listed 1854 Water Tank over her back fence, 1960s. Photo courtesy of the O'Connor family.
A land faraway song: Elle Murphy, Mitch Rubly and Dr Schott, © 2019.

The faraway land of the house and two cows
ISBN: 978-0-6454754-0-1

A catalogue record for this book is available from the National Library of Australia.

Typeset in Baskerville Old Face, 1952 Rheinmetall, and Courier New.
Printed and designed in Australia.

This book is based on the true story of the community behind the making of one of Australia's most important civic works projects in the 1890s and into the 1900s, who lived and worked alongside paddocks being watered 24 hours a day with Melbourne's sewage. The story combines fact, memories and legendary tales and is told by characters with their own connection to the Metropolitan Sewerage Farm.

Deep gratitude to the Metropolitan Sewerage Farm community, past and present, and in deep reverence to those that passed while graciously giving to the creation of this work. Deep respect to the Traditional Owners of the lands where this story centres and on which we live and work, the Wadawurrung and Bunurong peoples. We acknowledge you and celebrate your enduring connection to Country, knowledge and stories. We pay our respects to Elders of all Aboriginal communities, past, present and emerging.

Aboriginal and Torres Strait Islander readers are advised that this book contains names and images of people who have died.

For Carolyn, an angel

So it came to be

Mavis and Keith Warfe in their home on the 160 Road, Metropolitan Sewerage Farm, 1954. Photo courtesy of the Warfe family.

The faraway land of the house and two cows is a story like no other. Untold and unique, it's the true story of an isolated community once living on a sewerage farm, beside land filtration and grass filtration paddocks being watered 24 hours a day with Melbourne's sewage. And it's told in a way that combines fact, memories and legendary tales by characters with their own connection to the sewerage farm.

It is worth noting upfront, the difference between sewerage and sewage. By definition, sewerage means the entire system used to collect and treat sewage, that of sewers, channels, pipes, pumping stations and other infrastructure for transporting sewage. Sewage is the wastewater from households – kitchen, laundry, bathroom and toilet – and industry. Sewage passes through sewers, channels, pipes, pumping stations and other sewage infrastructure to be sent to a sewerage farm or sewage treatment plant.

The faraway land of the house and two cows comes from my drive to discover and explore our grand world, in all its complexities, noise and subtleties. It was born from my PhD research into communities living in the margins of mainstream society and sewerage town communities in Australia and Europe. It focused on Melbourne's first sewerage farm community that grew on the Metropolitan Sewerage Farm, which was established in 1892 on the outskirts of Melbourne, Australia. Many of those that worked on the sewerage farm lived on-site with their families. The community thrived for around 100 years and was behind the making of one of Australia's most important civic works projects in the 1890s and into the 1900s.

The research used innovative methods to first find the scattered Metropolitan Sewerage Farm community, then capture its social history and industrial heritage through powerful community participatory practices. Research findings were presented as a scholarly analysis as well as the following creative work, for a rebirthing of the Metropolitan Sewerage Farm community and discussion of sewerage ghost towns and their communities, including those that continue to exist on or beside sewerage farms or sewage treatment plants. These communities have a unique set of conditions: those of living around sewage, and the resulting segregation and discrimination because of that. Findings of the research can be applied to any marginalised or segregated community. The scholarly work can be found on my website.

The faraway land of the house and two cows is my creative interpretation of the community once living on the Metropolitan Sewerage Farm. A collaboration to create a new song, *A land faraway*, is also part of this interpretation. The sewerage farm is now known as Melbourne Water's Western Treatment Plant, where it still treats around half of Melbourne's sewage and where today exists an abandoned sewerage town. A sewerage ghost town.

Away from the Western Treatment Plant sees a sewerage town community resurrecting through my research and other work to preserve the Metropolitan Sewerage Farm's fading heritage.

The faraway land of the house and two cows is the true story uncovered during my three and a half years of research. It comes from speaking to many people who once lived on the Metropolitan Sewerage Farm and in other sewerage town communities. Many graciously shared photos, memorabilia and rich memories that some may consider as a subjective remembering of events, recollections and stories of a bygone time. I also undertook vast amounts of archival research that uncovered news stories, maps, photos, reports, meeting minutes, film and much more. Some of these have been incorporated in this book.

The challenge was in conveying these stories accurately yet creatively, to interpret them to evoke the emotion in their truth. I had to think about them and the quirks of memories, the haziness in recollections and romanticised tales, the subjective rememberings, the stories that grow to be legendary because what is truth to one person may not be truth to another. In the same instance, many of these truths are the only remaining truths in existence, truths that vanish to the earth upon the holder's death. Given this, it's vital that they're captured and cherished. And that they're told in a way that gives us understandings on belonging and social cohesion within segregation communities, as a legacy of learnings that are vital for future sustainable urban and community development.

All that aside, telling this Metropolitan Sewerage Farm story in an interesting way is rooted in a writing practice I have developed over many years. It's one that's fused in expressive, avant-garde language and utilises the lavish honesty of Romanticism and Gothic treatment of the Australian landscape. It comes in a layering that stems back to my work as a visual and metal artist where whether painting or creating metal objects, I was always interested in creating texture for movement, expression and emotion. I apply that same idea to language, writing to create movement and texture for an evocative and poetic interpretation of truth. It allows me to portray the Metropolitan Sewerage Farm community and subsequent sewerage ghost town, as one not of death and decay as one might associate with a ghost town, but one full of life.

The Metropolitan Sewerage Farm is not disgusting. It's not fearful, gory or harsh in the European Gothic sense and when I'm down there, I'm more seduced by its wide, dreamy expanse that's tinged in an eeriness of vast open space: sheep and cows grazing in peace under the eye of healthy and bombastic bulls, birds chirping in merry content, and lands of lush green pastures watered in the sewage of a metropolis contrasting with dry paddocks buffering the sewerage farm. It inspires me with the ghostly and ethereal, so light it can't be touched, that it becomes a haunting. This is where I experiment with storytelling to draw out the humanity in the community, where each character has its own unique connection to the Metropolitan Sewerage Farm: now emanating as a haunting in a sewerage ghost town.

As mentioned, my creative interpretation includes a song that takes a nostalgic look at living on the sewerage farm. It was created in collaboration with singer-songwriter Elle Murphy, Mitch Rubly and the broad community through a program of engagement during *Treatment: Flightlines 2017*, a large-scale public-art project curated by Dr Cameron Bishop of Deakin University, who was associate supervisor to my research. It was held in collaboration with Melbourne Water at the Western Treatment Plant over two days in

April 2017. The public art project fostered artists to interpret the Western Treatment Plant through their art. It provided me with an opportunity to encourage the community to share thoughts and ideas of community life on the Metropolitan Sewerage Farm.

Over the two days, I fitted out the Metropolitan Sewerage Farm sports pavilion with blown-up old photos to prompt people visiting to convey their feelings and memories about this past life. The sports pavilion created the nostalgia to help draw out thinking around the sewerage farm community for discussion in a public arena.

I collected the reflections and wrote them into a poetic text that became the basis for Elle and Mitch to compose the lyrics and music. Collaborating was a unique opportunity to bring our skills together to create an innovative response and experience of the sewerage farm. *A land faraway* adds to the historical and haunting interpretation of life on the Metropolitan Sewerage Farm, imbued with a longing spirit and love of living there. The song will be available on my website.

A body of work like this can only be done in the true spirit of teamwork. My gratitude to my Deakin University research team of Associate Professor Patrick West, Associate Professor Cameron Bishop and Paul Balassone from Melbourne Water. Working together allowed for the creation of this rich work. My thanks also to my Deakin University Writing group for the unwavering support, generosity and friendship that has endured beyond our PhD years. I will always cherish our group.

My sons too, for their endless acceptance of me and my rabbit warren research as it ran alongside our happening lives; my family and friends and their staunch support, my pillars of strength at times. Loving thanks to you. To Elle and Mitch, for the chance to create a haunting song together; the field work team with Thames Water, Yorkshire Water, der Stadt Wien - Wien Kanal and Musée des égouts de Paris; the reviewers of this book for taking the time to read it and share their thoughts; and Terry and Jackey for editing my work. Thank you.

My sincere thanks to Leonie, as my friend, editor and mentor for many years, for always guiding me and my writing with insightful and strong, yet gentle advice, while allowing me to keep true to my voice. And my sincere thanks to my patient and loving publishing team: Michael, Chrissy, Susi, Diane and Susan. Without your wonderful support, we wouldn't be reading such a polished book.

A special thank you to all my very special 'ears on the ground' Farm experts for your stories, insights and shared memories.

My eternal thanks to all the Farm people for without you, we would not have captured a truly significant part of Melbourne's history and the Metropolitan Sewerage Farm story. In deep reverence too, to those that passed while graciously giving to the creation of this work. Thank you Deakin University for the opportunity to undertake the work through the generosity of an industry scholarship; thank you to Melbourne Water as an industry partner.

It's been an honour working with everyone.

Enjoy this aesthetic paradox of Melbourne's sewerage farm, one of only a handful in the world, and the haunting truth of the Metropolitan Sewerage Farm community.

Graveyard of yesterday

Cocoroc North State School, December 1970. Photo courtesy of the Sadler family.

Chalky mist absconds from its receptacle of peace,

breathes new found freedom

as the rose of gold spins a forever tune.

What once Was, now Is.

THE SQUEAL OF SWELLING torque. Engines spruik as wild boar fighting for a last piece of carrion. A shot spears through the small bathroom window to the side of the house. Screeching metal rollers drown out the splintering glass showering the gladioli in the garden bed below, now glistening as icicles in morning sun. One less thing for them to smash.

The sullying sour of the enraged beast spews in.

Only a half hour earlier, those chained cogs had ground to a halt. Quiet nothing from the monster menaced over two men dressed in dusty overalls. Spiked in cocky strut and the smug puff of cigarettes, the men measured and marked out the hole to excavate in the aloofness of smug tabby cats.

A few of the local lads peered at the two surveying the land from behind arched, bluestone pillars supporting the iron water tank. A mellowing sanguine sun shining close to the horizon casts long, elongated shadows of the arches. Tomatoes ripened to late harvest this season compared to the tomatoes once growing in the back yard of me. The lads had left half-eaten Vegemite toast teetering on the rim of chipped plates to bolt out the back door as soon as the roar grumbled down the road, leaving the door to slam on the tail of a humidity that's caught between seasons.

The iron water tank was moved from East Melbourne to the sewerage farm here in 1893. That was only a few years before Mr Hickey and the other men built me. The water tank was to be a back-up water supply for the workers and their families living here and was Melbourne's first water supply in the 1800s. We never used it though. The Board of Works, which is what we locals call the Melbourne and Metropolitan Board of Works, MMBW for short, decommissioned the water tank in 1923 as they'd connected the sewerage farm to Melbourne's water mains system. Fresh water came from pipes and through a tap, quite a novel concept in my early years, and for Melbourne.

Rumbling, revving and snarling an almighty roar, the bulldozer blade begins to scratch at the surface grass inside the area marked out, beside the house Wally and Monikas Steinbergs vacated only a week ago. The cream weatherboard, duplex home basks innocently in its staunch years of service to the family, and other families before them. Back and forth the blade scrapes into the dirt, revealing rich red beneath. Deeper and deeper it grates, scooping soil to crown each end of an expanding rectangular hole. The machine's rumble is constant, drowns out the galahs screeching to scatter from the acorn tree by the swimming pool, the tree's leaves on a falling drip. Each engine rev amps up the resolve and snorts smoke from the exhaust. And yet the whistling kite spying for rodents in the paddock opposite, circles in a haughty hush of unperturbed.

One of the lads hurls another acorn. He'd scooped a handful peppering the grass by the pool earlier. It pings off the bulldozer. 'Shit heads,' he snarls.

Chugging groans, clouds of billowing dust.

Another acorn shoots past. 'Bullseye!' A hit to the front window.

The bulldozer hesitates, commands over the hole complete. Until steel tracks coil and clunk, splutter and snort toward the house in an unfaltering intent to flatten and nullify. The wild boar's insatiable for the Steinbergs' home.

It reaches the fence and hedge. Down it goes, as soft butter gliding onto fresh bread, butter once churned in the Steinbergs' shed from the cows they milked. It stampedes through the garden and over the soft, pink tea roses as an arrogant bull charging for the house. The blade spears into the weatherboard façade, blisters through the lounge room window to shatter glass into a million shards.

Cogging, creaking, splintering ... shrills of willie wagtails and squawks of lorikeets mute in the mashing grumble. The lads shove their hands firm over their ears, heads disappear into shoulders. They tear after the machines week after week, they must know the machines are on a merciless mission and won't stop for anything.

Pain pierces me in the asphyxiating tightness of a million castration rings, gnaws at my 80-year-old wooden carcass as termites gorging to their death. I bore my foundations into the nerve centre of sewage treatment, my white magpie mate clawing into my red-bricked chimney edge as he's always done to steady in the chaos squalling in. Another ending for an emergence of the new.

Wooden frames flail as a game of pick up sticks, dust clouds puff from spaces squeezed of love. The tin roof winks a last glint of sunshine before it mangles into a mess of recoiling metal ... contorting anguish drills into the battered and beaten core of me. I writhe in the re-living of my own demise years earlier, my white magpie mate claws into my flue ... Titans battle in an underworld of raging wrath.

Debris slings as crazed fire crackers, the boys flinch and shield their faces.

Beams boom, the chimney crowning the Steinbergs' home crumbles, as the last of the physical is pushed to its death. The family's ardent shelter is now crumpled and collapsed into the crater. Annihilated. A white tail feather wisps onto the pile of splintered and fractured wood and Masonite.

The obliteration is done, the cogwheel of eradication is final. That's how we houses mostly go: smithereened to our death. For almost 80 years I served family after family, the men working in a state most snub their noses to, moving shit around paddocks and channels so people in Melbourne can live with good sanitation. We've come a long way in those years, gee willy.

Alan Croxford was elected as Chairman of the Board of Works a few years ago and has lifted morale. Employee numbers have gone through the roof. Workers began competing in track championships and inter-branch football and cricket games are keenly contested. They're often played at the sports oval down here, home ground to the mighty Metropolitan Farm football and cricket teams until 1964. Even the women played football there in the '50s. The modern advancements are mind boggling. The Board just purchased its first computer and has begun managing data electronically – that's a word we never knew existed when we started sewage treatment here in the 1890s. Back then and for a long time, men moved sewage onto paddocks by lifting a sluice gate from a channel, to allow sewage to flow into the paddocks and through thick grass. Now, telemetry systems monitor and control hydrological operations; people with keyboard and programming skills are in demand. The Board unveiled its new plans for Melbourne last year, to prepare for a four to five million population by the year 2000. They must be dreaming!

Funny thing about the Board of Works' five-year environmental study of Port Phillip Bay. They wanted to understand whether the effluent being discharged into the bay from the sewerage farm here was harmful, effluent being the water we get after the sewage has trickled through the paddocks to come out the other end treated. The study found that the bay was generally healthy and in much better condition than other similar water bodies around the world, until Prince Charles came to Melbourne and swam at Elwood Beach in 1970. Young Charlie drew a crowd, the Royals always do, and compared his dip at Elwood to that of "swimming in diluted sewage". Sent everyone into a frenzy he did. Even critics conceded that the water was "a bit murky at times". The

Board came under further scrutiny over the sewerage backlog and the impact of unsewered properties and septic tanks on rivers and creeks. We had toilets out the back in the township up here. Other homes in settlements across the sewerage farm only had the old pan that had to be emptied into a hole away from the house every couple of days. The government finally stepped in and gave the Board and councils powers to force land developers to pay for water, sewerage and drainage services. Upbeat and optimistic, Chairman Croxford declared that all of Melbourne would be connected to sewers by 1980. As if!

It's all such a glaring contradiction today. 1973 and destruction everywhere. An extermination. There'll be no one left soon.

The bloke in the dusty overalls sitting in the open cabin of his bulldozer is puffing on another cigarette. He kills the butt on the side of his machine and throws it onto the ground as he climbs onto the track pad clogged in muddy debris and timber. He stomps over the mash of mangled mess with no regard, combing it for any old bottles or brass taps, or collectable missed in Wally and Monikas' packing. With nothing obvious for collection, he climbs back onto the yellow Caterpillar and into the cabin, and clicks the engine to a splutter under a rain shower that evaporates before reaching the ground. The bulldozer chomps over the pile of debris, and the concrete gutter into South Street, across into the 25 West Road.

Grumbles grow distant, crushing gravel subsides behind the football pavilion. The engine stops at the workshops.

The old World War II air raid siren whines from the roof of the workshops, shaking its rusting grime. It wails over paddocks sodden in four inches of sewage where the long, curved beaks of the ibis probe the soaking. It swoons my white magpie mate, ever outcast for his wash of white and lack of black, fleeing into a pine plantation over Farm Road. The work day's done.

The lads have taken off down the laneway toward the relic of Wally and Monikas', across the paddock where my stumps once fixed as firm footings, as the homes of Ryans and Camerons and others in between. Love and life, that's all that mattered then. We were family.

'Quick! Stockies are comin'. Hide!' calls the tallest of the boys wearing a brown cable knit jumper covered in little fuzz balls.

The boys tear past the water tank and nursery beside it, across the 25 West Road to an eroding subdrain. They crouch into the grass lining it. Miles and miles of these subdrains crisscross the sewerage farm, channels dug into the dirt many years ago to collect effluent from paddocks. It's part of the land filtration used in the summer and grass filtration in the winter. Both have treated Melbourne's sewage for the past 80 years. It's a natural process where sewage is flooded onto graded paddocks. It seeps into the earth and filters through lush grass to trickle into subdrains of brown earth at the lower end of the paddocks. These grow quick given they're watered with such richness and the only way to manage the lush growth is with natural lawn mowers: cattle and sheep. Thousands of head of cattle maintain the paddocks here, and they grow fat and firm to be sold for a fortune. They help pay for sewage treatment. To manage them requires a team of stockmen who drove them from one paddock to the next; and shearers too, to shear the fleece from sheep.

The littlest lad is beginning to lose his footing down the side of the subdrain. Lumps of soil plop into the effluent flowing within it.

'Shh ....'

'Shush.'

Rain patters into eucalypts nearby, rousing their oils to sweat from the leaves. The rhythmic canter of the horses becomes brassier, their hooves in purposeful clonk to be somewhere. The dogs are usually beside them but instead, pad through the grass ahead, their noses down to a sniff on the subdrain.

'Get those bloody dogs back,' calls Cyril. 'I don't wanna take any chances with the 1080 out, even if they're muzzled.'

Sharp whistles slice over the boys. The dogs dart back in ears spiked to the command of their masters on horseback, to trot side-by-side down the 25 West Road. The stockmen and their dogs reach the other end of the sports oval and the lads scamper back over the road to the garbled pile of brown and cream rubble in the hole. Rain drips from their chins. Lightning flashes greying skies dark mauve. The lads climb in over the hole's muddy edge dotted in cigarette butts, stepping onto an unbroken cream weatherboard. They creep over it to a door leaning on an incline into the hole, and down they slide. 'Weeee ....'

I glide under them in tickling ripples, my white magpie mate flapping his feathers. I keep it steady for the little one though, so he can sidle down safely.

'Woohoo!'

A pink flash, a grumble of thunder.

The lads rummage through the ruins as bower birds picking over remains for the shiniest of trinkets, unperturbed by the storm. One of them walks a plank, 'Ahoy there!' He jumps off onto a small mound of dirt and slips onto his butt.

Giggles skip in the rain.

Trinkets are pulled and piled onto a piece of broken Masonite: a hand-shovel plucked from under a snapped window frame, a half-buried ash tray set in a slice of tree trunk with a bent match box holder attached to it, a corroded bike bell that rasps instead of rings, a lime-green Matchbox car with spoiler on the boot and an old quoit. All treasures to the lads.

'Boys, dinner time!' comes a call from a back fence.

'Boys, time to come in,' comes another.

The rain has stopped and dusk is setting in. The lads collect their treasures and splodge across the laneway through back gates to homes, dripping and splattered in speckles of brown.

THE BRASH OF THE potent push hasn't ended though and the next day, after the home that once Was is dead in its forever hole, the blade is back. This time, to spread the soil from the mountains flanking the dead. Back and forth the bulldozer pushes the earth over the wreckage. Smothering takes little time and the crushed house is visible no more. Burial is complete. Suffocation thrives where breath is void. All that remains is for the grass to grow as the final seal.

The lads are back, walking the levelled ground, sometimes kicking dirt rocks. The few left here on the sewerage farm have witnessed our burials after school and over school holidays for some time, and even while in school. They'd be doing their maths in class in contorting little faces to the smashings and crashings outside. Sometimes they'd sneak a peek at our demolishings at lunch time and giggle at the colourful language coming from workmen after flying house fragments strike an arm or face. One time, the men yelled and scattered as fleeing field mice when realising they'd forgotten to cut the power and water to a house before beginning to flatten it. Would've electrocuted themselves had the bulldozer pushed through a live wire.

Some say this old place is deserted, yet how can it be with the bedrock of yesterday firmly entrenched into forever footings that interweave this land faraway. The Steinbergs' house is still here. Most of the 100 plus buildings that once housed the thriving community of more than 500 people spread across this sewerage farm are non-existent in their physicality. Yet they're all here. We're all in our own tombs of yesterday. Even the handful of homes sold and relocated elsewhere are here because our foundations are cemented here. All the houses of bygone are the homes of Flahertys, Camerons, Warfes, Ryans, Smiths, Pengellys and more ... all of the homes of us.

Our whispers roam free with the bus loads rolling in to learn our story. We weave through treetops to cattle dogs barking, over balls sailing across tennis courts and footballs bouncing the length of the sports oval. Cricket balls are batted, goals are kicked through goal posts to applause and cheers laced in sneaky sculls from bottles hiding in the grass. We breathe endearment into the remnant gardens edging the swimming pool, and the children's laughter and splashing, their racing one another from one end of the pool to the other, then laying on the concrete to warm as basking lizards. The nurture of parents splashing with children in the pool and the sometimes eyebrows raised at young giggles in the change rooms, peering at things they're too young to be peering at.

It's far from an abandoned town. Not with sheep grazing in a haven of always green and a squeeze box lull of *Somewhere over the rainbow* purring from the community hall to meander in and around tea trees exfoliating layers of wafer thin bark. Dances were regular back then, from the time the hall was built in 1903. Then known as the Mechanic's Institute, it lived by the school. For all its years, it was a centre of place, hosting wedding receptions, school concerts, card nights, dances, meetings and all community happenings. In two years to come, it will be moved to sit by the water tank and swimming pool, for a new life.

High-pitched shrills and trills replace the squeeze box, leaves drift on a wafting wind. Under the gaze of the acorn tree by the pool, as sentinel of this land, we gather as the souls of this once thriving place. We're the intrinsic element of people and place that survives in the abandoned, especially strong when a community has bonded tight in this land faraway.

Be in the quiet, of the faint fraying of the old, and soften into us. We imbue corners and crevices, arcs and angles of this vast land, as the sun permeates the musty earth below, nourishing our magnetic pull. Our Life and Soul.

HIS DARK MOUSTACHE LIFTS, accentuating a curling curiosity. It happens at least a couple of times a day, a questioning of whether the kid's paying attention or living in a musing of workshop sneaking to climb tractors and switch on bulldozers and tournapulls. His moustache reminds me of the one Mr Carter groomed to handlebar perfection, as the Lord of me.

He marks a stroke against Pam's name, as last on the roll. She jumps when he slams the grey book shut, his pen sandwiched within. 'So. Our last day today.' He steadies his hands on the desk and lifts off the chair. He's quite a figure when he stands, his height and stature commanding into the space around him and over the nine children in class, three of which are too young to be enrolled in school. Michael and Felicity will begin school next year; Felicity is his daughter and Michael is Paul and David's younger brother. Johnny's the other 'illegal'; he's a year younger than Michael and Felicity and stays with his grandparents, Monikas and Wally, during the week, going home on weekends to his mother. Paul calls by Monikas and Wally on school mornings to ask whether he can take Johnny to school. Monikas gives a shy but pleased chuckle and always says yes. Little Johnny will have a tough life growing up though. And a short one. The three young ones are kept busy with drawing and painting, reading books and building blocks.

That leaves six students officially enrolled at the Cocoroc North State School – Paul and David O'Connor, Damien and James Ryan, and Pam and Barry Sadler. Mr Wally Arnott is their teacher.

'You all know what the last day of school means.' Wally waits for a response. He gets nothing. 'It's clean-up day! And we *all* love clean-up day.' That moustache arcs up again.

'Last day's a no-work day!' sings Damian.

Wally begins directing the six eldest children to empty desks and remove posters from the walls and windows, dust off and wipe down the chalk board, desks, tables and chairs, which are then stacked in the corner. Pot plants are carried outside to sit under the drinking taps at the back of the school, books are pulled from shelves and packed with word cards and maths charts into cardboard boxes, most of it marked for Werribee Primary School.

This isn't simply the end of the school year, it's the end of Cocoroc North School. With six enrolments, the school has fallen below the required number to stay open. Such contrast to when we were booming after the Second World War. We'd had 35 to 40 kids sardined into this classroom for many years. Back then, we were the Metropolitan Farm and somewhere along the way, it was shortened further to the Farm. In the early days, people called the place the Metropolitan Sewerage Farm, until someone dropped the word 'sewerage'.

It's the end of cricket in the yard with Wally, athletics carnivals with Werribee South and Little River schools and wearing black tabards to identify as Cocoroc North School. Wally won't be swinging through the O'Connor's wooden front gate and up the pavement, past Ginger speckled in pink geraniums, to the small Post Office window sitting off the front of the house to collect pay cheques and school mail from Marj. Gone are the Friday afternoons in the school gardens growing cucumbers and lettuce and enough corn to feed everyone in the town twice over, and building scarecrows to protect those crops. Wally would turn the growing of vegetables into a maths lesson and ask his class to measure out plots against the side of the teacher's residence beside the school, where he and his family lived. They'd plant seeds that came from the Farm nursery and if the ground was too hard, they'd ask for help at the workshop and a rotary hoe and tractor would magically appear to dig the ground for planting. There'll be no more extended classroom in Reidy's paddock, or making damper in a hole in the dirt and playing sports out there. Wally and Pat, his wife, won't be cleaning school toilets each week and mowing grass in the school yard, or waxing the floor and washing walls and windows at the end of each school year.

Neither will miss the isolation of this place though. Wally would bound into his car whenever a teacher came to relieve him so he could spend time in another school, and Pat adored the social circle her nursing in the Werribee Hospital offered her, often driving home after a late shift on the unlit Farm Road. One night, Pat sprang from her car after the back tyre lumped over what she thought was a body. Trembling, she lurched from the car and searched with a flashlight to find nothing.

Wally won't miss the school inspectors and their examinations of the school yard, play equipment and behind toilets, even running a finger over the top of the door for dust and kicking at the grass for hidden dangers underneath. What were they thinking they'd find? Sewage? Wally often questioned where the practical help was to support a teacher in an isolated school, or the protocols for emergencies when the school had no phone. Asking Wally to recite and apply Piaget's theories wasn't going to help any child bitten by a brown snake at lunchtime.

'Finish up the mopping, boys,' calls Wally from the mat, where he was reading Banjo Paterson's *Waltzing Matilda* to the other children. 'Then come back to the mat. We've got something special coming very soon.' Up went that moustache to its default position.

The two boys skim their mops over the floor, neglecting sections of the wooden boards. I don't know why they bother. Surely they know this building's going down like the rest of us. They drag the mops and bucket through the classroom, spilling water onto a corner of the mat. They attempt to sponge it up.

'Don't worry, boys,' calls Wally, shaking his head. 'Take the mops out and come sit down.'

The two boys only just reach the mat when there's a chug of a tractor and a, 'Ho, ho, ho ....' The children bound to the window.

'It's the big man on a trailer!' calls Damian.

'Look at him,' laughs Barry.

'Ho, ho, ho, Merry Christmas,' sings Father Christmas, dressed in the obligatory red suit trimmed in white, black belt hanging loosely around his waist and pants tucked into black gum boots. Only his nose and eyes are visible.

'Look at his fat sack in the trailer!' calls Pam.

The kids bound out to the tractor and trailer parked outside the school, cheering and screeching 'Father Christmas' as he dismounts the trailer with his bulging sack. Father Christmas pats shoulders and tousles hair, follows Wally carrying a chair to the shade of the poplar trees by the school boundary.

'Okay, settle down everyone,' yells Wally. 'Give Father Christmas some space so he can sit down.'

'Thank you kindly, Mr Arnott,' says Father Christmas, sitting on the chair. He drops his sack beside him. Beads of sweat pool on the side of his nose; not surprising in the 33-degree heat. Beaming faces crowd him at his feet.

'Lift your bottoms everyone and sit one bottom back,' calls Wally. 'Father Christmas can't move with you all piling in on top of him.'

'Have you all been good this year?' asks Father Christmas.

'Yesss!'

By now, the older boys have arrived home from high school to join the children on the grass. Kath, Joan and John, more affectionately known as Bull by his mates after charging through a fence while playing football for the Metro Farm Herefords, have joined their children. Down the lane is Monikas, with clear sight from inside her fence, always too anxious to move past it.

Father Christmas delves into his sack.

'I wanna be first!' sings Damian.

'No,' says Paul. 'Johnny's first. He's the youngest.'

One by one, each of the children sit on Father Christmas's knee for a chat and present, whether a bucket and spade for the beach, badminton racquets, balls or books.

'Now everyone to the oval for lollies, soft drink and icy poles!' calls John. 'And maybe some sack races.' The children squeeze onto the trailer with Father Christmas and are carted to the sports oval.

Wally has one last task. He carries the chair back into the school and sets it under his desk, taking his time to straighten it. He nudges the top rail of the chair into the tabletop edge. He scans the room. Up and down the walls, the floor, gazes through the three-panelled window into the yard, the glass now clear of red cellophane and drawings of children with their cars and families on bikes. Wally ambles through the small classroom in sometimes scuffing heal.

Whispers and twitters follow in highs and lows, hundreds of us gather. He and we pause and back track, our hesitation in the hush.

Wally finally reaches the white wooden door. He eases it open, struts over the step onto the paved entrance of the school. He turns, kicks a stone in the middle of the pavement into the gap under the door, and pulls the door shut, wedging it firm.

Ghostly giggles of us, interned in the gush.

Wally fondles in his pocket, pulls his keys and rummages for the master, pushing it in to grate into the lock. A click, the lock bolts. Cocoroc North State School No 3230 is snuffed. And the gratitude of one of the best was officially noted in the last school committee meeting.

MINUTES OF MEETING: 30.11.1971, 8.00PM

School committee's book: Cocoroc State School No 3230

Present Committee: B. Ryan, J. O'Connor, R. Sadler, W. Arnott

Matters arising from minutes: nil

Apologies: nil

Correspondence: read and tabled, accepted on the motion of B. Ryan, seconded W. Arnott CARRIED

Treasurer's report: Balance in bank $86.31. Accepted on the motion W. Arnott, seconded B. Ryan CARRIED

Head teacher report: H/T reported on the sports meeting he attended and the excursions to the Museum and the Tullamarine Airport, stating they were a great success. Mr Dunstan, District Inspector, stated that we were not allowed to close anything until received official notice. All money to be spent on children before end 1971.

General business: Moved B. Ryan and seconded W. Arnott that Christmas break up to be conducted on same lines as 1970. 11am start. CARRIED

Moved W. Arnott, seconded B. Ryan that $63 be spent on presents for children. CARRIED

H/T moved that a vote of thanks be recorded for the committee on the work they had done. CARRIED

Chairman Mr.Sadler spoke on the good work H/T Mr W. Arnott had done in his term at Cocoroc School, stating that (he was) sorry to see Mr. Arnott and the school come to an end. The committee endorsed our chairman's remarks.

Meeting close: 8.45pm

Signed: J. M. O'Connor (secretary) and R. W. Sadler (chairman)

THE LADS ARE IN the empty school yard, climbing monkey bars and equipment. Their shuffles echo in the hollows.

'I'm bored. School holidays are boring.'

'Let's get the billy carts.'

'Nah. We need to save the rabbits near the pool. They're going blind.'

'Nah, billy carts at the reservoir!'

The lads sprint home to pull billy carts from sheds. They lug them over the slashed grass and across the road into a thick hedge of eucalypts and wattles, skirt them through the plantation and into a paddock where the reservoir sits. They race one another with their billy carts up the grassed embankment to take off from the top without hesitation, swirling downhill as snakes on steroids, to ultimately slither into a marrying mash of arms and legs and billy cartwheels at the bottom.

It's not long before the boys are stripped to their shorts and climbing down the iron ladder running inside the reservoir.

'Pwoh, it stinks,' says Alan, as he climbs down the ladder.

Damian steps into the knee-high water. 'It's slimy shit.'

'Stop complaining and move over.' Alan nudges Damian forward.

'Hey!'

'Well I can hear frogs and I want them. Where are you my little friends?'

'It stinks like you, Alan!' laughs Damian.

'Shut up, poo-head.' Alan cups his hand over a chunky brown frog in a lump of limp grass. 'Got 'im!'

'Got one too!' says Damian.

They shove frogs into their pockets until they bulge as lumpy balloons. Kids for years have been doing the same things since the reservoir was built. Some rascally boys during the war time, they'd run past me with straws shoved into the bums of frogs, and blow into them. The poor critters would blow up as swollen bull frogs! Kids back then had to make their fun, couldn't go anywhere with all the war restrictions.

The lads climb back up the ladder, shoving one another to be first to their billy carts so they can be first to fly down, until they'd crash under a ghost gum in gobbing giggles. A trail of pungent ick would linger, of being dragged through an anaerobic ecosystem turned septic.

Something's stirring in the dried undergrowth. I blow a whirring gush. Damian peers into the rustling foliage. I blow harder, corkscrewing a pile of parched and decaying into the canopy above to reveal a tiger snake coiled underneath. It slithers past a billy cart wheel. Damian yanks at the billy cart rope. The snake shies away, and I draw my breath of breeze back.

In the dry of a 38-degree day, the lads move to the crowded swimming pool. Damian jumps into the water beside his brother and cousins. All the Farm families are there and other families and friends from outside of the Farm have driven in. Children sometimes disappear across the road for a quick Vegemite or jam sandwich at home before returning. Chicken Sharland, the ever-attentive pool custodian, chats to John by the pale-green, enamelled spotlight, mounted on a tripod pointing down the length of the pool. Another spotlight is at the ready at the other end, both on standby for when day turns to night. A row of older children squeeze in along the deep end edge of the pool, to execute sharp dives into the water as good as any synchronised swim team, aside from the occasional flat belly whack. It's generally followed by a contest for who can sit on the bottom of the pool for the longest. The younger children splash in the shallow end, lay their bellies over its warm edge to kick into the water behind them. Others jump up and down for the sake of splashing and smack the water in clumsy splat to squirt water up noses. Soaked adults lounge by the pool as proud sea lions guarding their cubs, until it's time for their own belly crawl cooling into the water.

Dusk darkens, spotlights flick on. Children climb onto adult shoulders for a leap of faith, some plunge hand stands into the depths for an emergence of chunky thighs to tips of toes swaying sea creatures. Mothers soak their feet in the shallows, some cradle babes in arms. Chit chat brims as beach balls of yellow, red, green and blue lob past signs that read *Throwing of balls not permitted in pool,* towels hang over the wire fence bound by the golden privet hedge ... and there is always someone blowing and snorting a fly tickling trapped up a nose.

It's the epitome of freedom in a place where the troubles of yesterday and fears of tomorrow dare not infiltrate, a place where difference does not exist. Even Joan's lounging on a chair after chasing one of the lads from one end of the pool to the other earlier, for stealing her daughter's knickers from the change room and hiding them. The lad cackled fits of cheeky chuckle the more Joan screeched at him. Those knickers now lay in their own crypt on the Farm, only visible to us above.

HOW QUICKLY THE JOY of then can sour at another ending only weeks later, of what began in 1895. Destroyers plotted and puffed once again, clicked engines to a rumble and snort and excavated to the customary depth of 10 feet, mounds of dirt flanking each end. The clunking over knee-high grass and weeds was quick to come, and brute flattening of wooden fence posts and daisy bushes, and the white building that nurtured the minds of our children for years. Numbers and alphabet, play and stories, 76 years of nurture moans and groans in torturous screech as the school is shoved into its tomb. The first workers at the Farm wrote to the Board a year after families had settled here in 1894, requesting a school be established as more than half the 40 or so children living on the Farm were of school age.

But two holes have been dug today.

Into the second went the push of the teacher's residence, Wally and Pat's home, in the same way as we. Distress and torment, in sympathy we collapse with them into the forever grave. My white magpie mate warbles the death march. Birds fall silent, rodents are still. Galahs line the fence along Reidy's paddock, those gone and others still in the living.

And yet it's not over.

Next comes the blessing of the remains in stinking, spiked liquid. It sears as it splashes in. A small flame is lit, and tossed into the hole by the hand of bureaucratic apathy. Up it wooshes in feverous passion, fuelled in the spiked, to guzzle in the cherish of what once Was.

Sizzling. Hissing insatiable, devouring ravenous on the school and teacher's residence in the rage of a thousand bonfires. The stench of gluttonous digestion menaces in a black smothering of yesterday.

A smouldering satiation ultimately proceeds and the ashen remains sink into their graves.

The engine's roar re-engages and the layering begins, of the smearing of earth upon remains, earth upon dust. Reverence to us. The full stop at the end.

Up here, we greet the smothered.

They sip their beers at wooden tables in smiles at schools of yesterday, lost in a sea of scarecrow and tiggy and schools long buried in lands faraway.

Kelpies yelp to horses giddy ups, sheep graze on stretches of rolling green, half a world away.

They speak of their schools and sewerage farm life as though one and the same, yet unique to them in sacred lands faraway.

The itch is at me again under my rose of gold wedding ring. It's never satisfied, never a gratification achieved and instead, grows with each day and each turn of decade.

What once Was, now Is, in lands faraway.

MARJ GATHERS THE FOUR heavily inked rubber stamps lined on the bench top.

'What on earth are you doing?' snaps the man of prim pretence. His arms fold tight into his chest. 'That's Commonwealth property, madam.' He steals the rubber stamps from Marj, wet ink smearing his thumbs. The buckling hem of his navy blazer lifts higher in the back than the front, sharp horizontal creases in the fabric reveal much sitting.

Marj shrinks into the kitchen, wary of the man stripping drawers of stickers and stamps filed in varying value.

'It's all Crown property you know,' says the other man, his beige suit as insipid as his complexion. 'Belongs to her Majesty.' He seizes envelopes and telegrams from shelves and stacks them into a box with pencils, erasers and pens, and grabs the canvas mail bag for the daily collection to stuff into the box with them. The string on the square lead seal catches on his blazer button. 'Stupid bloody thing,' he snaps, attempting to untangle it.

Marj smirks in the kitchen.

'These boxes are done. They can go into the van,' calls the beige man.

'Yep. When you're ready,' calls the other man. Ash falls from the cigarette hanging between his lips onto his dark trousers. 'Shit. Get me an ash tray will ya,' he snaps at Marj. 'And stop bloody watching me like I'm taking your priceless stuff.' He drops his cigarette onto the benchtop. Ash crumbles from it and the ember of the cigarette burns into the wooden benchtop. Marj slips the ash tray under it.

'Look out.' The man in the sagging beige trousers pushes past Marj.

Paul looks on from the kitchen at the bullish men as they pack every curio, gizmo and doodah from the tiny darkened nook, into boxes, even the ruler he would use to flick soggy paper balls at his brothers. The service window is now bolted shut. That was the first thing the men from the PMG did when they arrived. That's the Postmaster-General's Department to most, the Public Money

Grabbers to some. The PMG built the tiny alcove into a section of the pantry in the O'Connor home to create the Metropolitan Farm Post Office. It built these spaces into the home of the Farm Post Mistress; the job being handed on to another woman upon a Post Mistress retiring.

My white magpie mate calls a lyrical cheer. He's coaxing me to tell you how proud I was, and still am, to have had the honour of hosting the first Metropolitan Farm Post Office. It was built into me in 1914 for Mrs Carter to carry out the duty of Post Mistress and offer postal services to residents and workers. A General Store was later added. She was diligent with her stamps, set them up in pristine order. It was a sad day for me when my alcove was stripped and the title of Post Mistress was transferred to Mrs Taylor eight years later.

Marj with her sly smirk reminds me of Mrs Carter, the way she's clued in to these men. Earlier in the day, Marj inserted five envelopes into the Remington typewriter and addressed one each to her children Paul, David, Michael and John, and one to herself and John: to the Metropolitan Farm P.O, Victoria. 3030. She licked a seven-cent stamp onto each and rubber stamped them with black ink for a post mark that read Metropolitan Farm – VIC, 31JA73. That was the last mail to be sent from the Metropolitan Farm Post Office.

BUZZING BUSY FILLS THE O'Connor home on a Sunday morning months later. While Marj and her sons attend Mass and

John lays face down in hospital recovering from an operation on worn out discs, pixie helpers swarm their home. They pack the kitchen and bedrooms into boxes and lift furniture into trailers and cars, along with John's greyhounds and their cages, even the copper boiler from the wash-house finds a space. Beds and books, toys and tricycles, all are packed up.

Marj arrives home holding her belly swelling with her fifth child. She rests on a box to thank her neighbours and friends for their help, and their foresight to pack the house for their move to a new home in Little River before John left hospital. That way, John wouldn't endure a double move.

We mourn again, we bleed at another departing.

A LAD AND HIS father are driving the Geelong Road out by Moubrays Lane and the Ranch. They've just passed the dreaded stretch of road where the grandfather crashed in front of the Ryan home. The residents from that part of the Farm have moved away, as everyone has. We still gather out at the Ranch, us up here. All who filed through its doors and flounced its paddocks.

'Are we nearly there?' asks the lad.

'Soon,' says the dad, sitting in the driver's seat in the posture of a plank of wood.

'How much longer?'

'Five minutes.'

Five minutes could've been five hours to an 11-year-old, but five minutes later, the Holden rumbles over a cattle grid on the 160 South Road.

'We're here!' The lad peers ahead, as though waiting for the starter gun to fire for the 100-metre race at the school sports carnival. A left into Farm Road, another left into South Street. 'We're home!'

The father stops the car in the back lane, behind cottage 53. The lad's scrutinising the stark empty of the town as he eases out of the back seat.

'I'm going to the shed,' says the dad.

'I'm going to find Ginger.'

'Forget Ginger,' says the dad.

The lad doesn't answer and instead, strides into the backyard. The iron water tank commands in the background over the back fence. All is just as it was that Sunday weeks ago. Lawns tidy, still green, but not in their usual immaculately trimmed edges. Hedges remain neatly clipped and slapdash puffs of pink and red break the bleak of stillness.

'Ginger!' calls the lad. 'Ginger.' He roams along the side of the empty house and into the front garden, scouring the open spaces across Middle Street to the only home left, Jack and Melva Marshall's home. He ambles through the front garden and into the unlocked house.

Floorboards creak in the weary bones of me, rousing my sleeping dust.

'Ginger.' He pokes into the empty lounge room where the family once viewed slides of beach holidays on bare walls, and Sunday afternoons were spent watching wrestling on TV, a religious pastime of many. All are hollowed empty now.

'Lad,' calls the dad from outside.

The lad smears glistening eyes with the sleeve of his navy jumper. 'Ginger,' he only just whispers as he scampers to his bedroom. A times table sheet lays torn on the floor. He peers out the cloudy window stripped of its curtains. 'Ginger! Where are you?'

The fun those lads had in that bedroom. Games of hide and seek and climbing out the window for a sneaky swim in the pool, are now a breath of haunting.

'You've got five minutes,' comes a call from outside.

The lad gulps. 'I'm looking for Ginger.'

'I told you to forget about Ginger.'

'We have to find her!' The lad dashes to the kitchen and Ginger's corner of curling by the window, where she'd spy any huntsman creeping along the ceiling. The cracked soup bowl speckled in dried up food sits empty by the stove. 'Ginger!' sobs the lad. 'Come out before the bulldozer comes!' He bolts to the wash house, mildew lingering in stale damp. 'Ginger!'

'Let's go,' calls the dad from the shed. 'I've got my good leads for the dogs and their vitamin boosters.'

'But Ginger?' yells the lad from the wash house.

'Ginger's lovin' her freedom. She's got plenty of mice to eat here.' The dad's gait down the back path is one of careful step.

A caustic creep in, a veining blue venom. 'I hate you! And everyone that's wrecked our house.' The lad fires a broken stick used to lift wet clothes from the copper. It bangs a hole wide open in the cream wall. 'You and your dumb dogs, I'm not walking them with you anymore. I hate you!'

The lad slides his back down the wall and drops to the floor. 'We can't leave Ginger, she needs me to look after her.' He draws his knees in and buries his face into his corduroys, sobbing. 'I hate your stupid dogs. You love them more than you love me.'

The dad and the lad are at odds, in the eerie haunt of Life. Ginger strays in beside me and my white magpie mate.

BY 1974, THE MARSHALLS are gone and in 1980, the Watkins family living beside the Farm office and workshops on Farm Road leave when Gordon retires, the McPhersons leave in 1984. Some homes were stripped of windows and wood, doors and skirts, anything that could be re-used to build a chook pen or shed before the homes were buried or burned. One police sergeant built his home by reusing much from defunct Farm homes. While some were pushed to their death without any stripping, some were sold and moved off site into Werribee, Werribee South and Little River. Those few are still standing today.

The Board of Works leases a few homes to employees on and around the top of Farm Road into the 1980s but they too are gone in the 1990s – the Melbourne and Metropolitan Board of Works meets a harsh decline at the same time.

A shot bores in the barren of abandonment, pierces the daylight as a diamond-tipped arrow perforates the armour of a RAAF aeroplane whining as the stalwart of the sky.

The rose of gold spins corkscrew taut, at the shot fired.

A slug of lead travels in the drab of weighted despair, bound in a lifetime of yesterdays. It penetrates the eye of the cyclone, bleeds to stillness death.

His life in nil. The Board of Works is no more. The corpse of two and three, the corpse of many.

The whining wavers in moody blue, of the Tiger Moths and Airspeed Oxfords diving over paddocks.

He'd had enough. Work ending, a life breaking. He mourned his pain in private, a termination of a time that's been. His world was ravaged by the revolution happening faster than anyone understood. He snapped, fired the shot near the You Yangs.

There were others too – a gassing, a hanging and another gun shot. All were drowning in the sludging sorrow of no tomorrow.

Winds of change gust in gales, drill into the core of eternal skeletons connected to what once Was, connected in the eternal of the rose of gold.

The people. The children. Schools and homes, all packed up and gone. The workers, their solidarity; departed and disconnected.

His pain was poison. His name was her name and him too. We're all the same, all become the engine out of fuel, nose diving to an exit consumed in quickened pace and fuelled by dollars and savings and corporate restructuring.

Whirring winds elevate, priming to pluck at the essence of the once Was.

The ravens circle, never failing to appear at the expiration door. Their caws mimic the diving of the aeroplanes. More ravens are coming, calling in glooming skies.

Caw, caw, blah, blah, blahhh, ravenous for the remains of the once Was.

Galahs screech, sparrows chirp as a faint chorus. All are here for the shot that's just been. Homage is vast for the final gasp.

He's gone now. So are the other hes. Whispers abound ... who is he, why him, why did he, all the while firing in self-preservation.

He are we, are all of us.

Change flies on its own set of wings to a graveyard of yesterday, the forgotten wasteland. It lays with the homes across the Farm and carries in the glint of glistening rose, just as the fallen by roadsides and in darkened rooms, in a place of once Was.

Rest and repose, a rose of gold spinning its forever tune in the Life and Soul of what once Was, now Is.

'DID YA SEE HIS red eyes? They were staring right at me,' whispers Mark, shining his torch on the kangaroo gargoyle perched on the point of the terracotta roof. My white magpie mate hovers atop the gargoyle's head. The children are at the abandoned, double-storeyed Facey house at the top of Farm Road.

'What're you on about?' asks Karen.

'On the roof.'

'You're off the roof!' she laughs. A super blue moon shadows the gargoyle, boasting the beast.

Mark wanders past the front of the old red brick house, his gaze so fixed on the gargoyle that he trips over the brick garden edging. He glances up at the window beside him. I stir a flurry to shimmy a shadow past the window.

'Wait for me!' Mark spears after Karen, Cat, Matty and Graham, who are climbing through the lounge room window of the abandoned house.

A tawny frogmouth perched in the sparse tree across the driveway, flashes its two amber gems that have caught a glint of moonlight. Its ogling sends Mark scuttling through the window, smashing his knee onto the dusty wooden floor inside.

The children play hide and seek over kiss chasey and scurry in and out of rooms to hide behind left-over boxes and tattered curtains, inside the grimy, snot-green pantry and beneath the matching free-standing stove in the corner. Mark creeps up the rickety stairs. He ducks into a spacious bedroom and up into a fireplace tiled in green foliage, unaware of the soot clinging to the brick flue inside.

My chance for some fun with the young one. I kiss butterfly puffs up the chimney, ruffling a possum resting up high. It comes plummeting, along with choking soot.

'Aahh!' Mark stumbles from the tiled façade. 'Get off me!' he squeals, flicking at his head. The possum scratches over him and gives a hiss before it scats across the room and out the door.

Mark's on his knees when Karen barges in. 'We're going to Dracula's tomb. You comin'?'

'Bloody possum almost got me,' says Mark.

'I'm doing a séance down there,' calls Cat from behind Karen.

'You're séancey enough!' says Mark.

'It'll be cool.' Cat shines her torch under her chin. 'We'll contact the dead, someone from way back on the Farm. They'll have crazy stuff to tell us.'

'Crazy Cat!' laughs Matty.

'And we might be able to contact Dracula too!' says Graham.

The children run outside to the shed and push the dilapidated door open, shoving it off its hinges. They wander into wisping cobwebs layered in dust to an old mechanic's pit.

'The lid's come off the tomb,' quips Matty. 'Dracula must be out partying.'

'Or chasing blood.'

The torches shine into the dark pit. The walls glisten in splattered engine oil.

'Dracula's been redecorating,' says Mark. 'With a blood-on-walls look!'

Stairs at the top of the rectangular cavity lead down into the pit.

'Let's do the séance in the tomb,' says Cat.

'I'm not getting in that grot,' snaps Graham.

'Not a chance in dick-witch I'm getting in there,' says Mark.

'What about over here then?' asks Cat, walking to a corner by a battered work bench, its wooden top jagged and splintered. 'We need to sit close,' says Cat, already on the floor and crossing her legs in the muck.

'Mum's gonna kill me, getting this shit all over me,' says Graham.

'Sit down, whiner,' says Cat. 'And sit close, so we can hold hands. We have to make a five-pointed star, which is what a séance needs.' Cat draws a white tea-candle from her pocket and places it in the centre of the circle. She strikes a match to light the candle. 'Torches off. And hold hands.'

'What?' asks Matty. 'Torches off?'

'Oh gees, don't be such a scaredy-cat. Hold my hand.'

Matty takes Cat's hand, and Mark's hand on his other side.

'Now,' whispers Cat. 'No talking while I call the dead to come forth. I've studied this. I know what to do. The only rule for a séance is that everyone has to believe it's possible, otherwise we won't be able to communicate with the other side.'

'The other rule is no farting,' sniggers Mark. Karen elbows him. 'Ouch!'

Cat sighs. 'Spirits communicate through objects. Who's got something we can use?'

'There's a Tarax bottle on the bench,' says Matty.

'Perfect. Put it in the centre with the candle,' says Cat. She waits for Matty to lay the bottle in the centre. 'Now,' she whispers slowly. 'Please join hands and close your eyes. Thank you everyone for coming today. We're here to welcome any spirits of this land. Please come and join us now.'

'Hey,' says Mark, opening his eyes. 'Who blew the candle out?'

'Mark,' snaps Cat. 'It might've been a spirit.'

'I didn't do it.'

'Stop being an idiot.'

'Shush. Concentrate.' Cat lights the candle. 'Close your eyes everyone. We're here, at the top of Farm Road, and welcome any spirits from the Farm to come forth. Please join us.'

I blow a light breeze that blows out the candle flame once again. I love playing with children. I should've been a grandfather. *Elsie,* I whisper. *Elsie ....* Cobwebs floss over heads.

'Who's Elsie?' Cat's tone is respectful, yet cautious.

'The candle's out again,' snaps Matty.

Elsie .... My white magpie mate flutters his feathers over Mark.

'I'm gettin' outta here,' says Mark. 'Bugger Elsie! Something's touched me head!'

'Wait for me,' calls Matty. He bounds out the shed after Mark and into the driveway onto Farm Road.

Mark turns into his street and as soon as he does, the Farm Night Watchman flashes his torchlight into Facey's house. 'Saved by the bell,' he says to Karen, running in from behind.

More like saved by me and my white magpie mate. With a giggle and a shackle of my doorjambs and windowpanes, I breeze back to my place, my white magpie mate ever with me. We dive past the paddock where Taylors had the Post Office and General Store, past the Steinbergs' paddock and on to my foundations of the home of the Carters and Camerons and the first Metropolitan Farm Post Office.

Three siblings stand in solemn mourning by the roadside, entranced by the billowing mist they've freed from the receptacle of peace, ashes wistful for a resting that only the knowing know. The children yearn for their parents gone.

The dusting flecks waft to where their family home once stood for a quarter of a century, beside the old Farm office on Farm Road. The home rejoiced in being the lone outpost guiding lost strangers on their way to fish or spot birds, and for swaggies searching for work, the frontier to the adrift.

It was home to the father who left in exact time to water paddocks day and night with the waste of a city far away, and the mother who cleaned the offices next door, with cups of tea when done to catch the Farm news.

These ashes, branded with the soul of a lifetime, meander on instinct to join the forever, and rest at their always home.

What once Was, now Is.

The eternally watchful never close their lids, are always discerning the back and forth and round and round in that spin of rose of gold, as the symbol of eternal friendship and love.

Together and everywhere, we're by the workshops, the dog kennels and swimming pool, the homes warmed by families scattered across this vast land.

We guard in a force rooted in tight bonds and only those within those bonds share in the deepest of Farm secrets.

It's an affinity entwined in fibres of together, always together.

Even in the abandonment and scattered remains in knee-high weeds, in the place that once flourished and was far grander than the strewn relics left behind today. There is life.

Soul.

Homes of the once Was, trussed in tight bonds, now rest as sleeping artefacts in an epitaph awaiting unearthing and celebrating once again. We are the ghost town, a place whispering as a landscaped necropolis.

What once Was, now Is. Life above lands faraway.

Pale-blue tiles laid in perfect repetition over steps leading into the pool, once the nucleus of this Life and Soul, now lead to a void of empty where leaves scuff its dusty concrete belly to collect in corners.

The ailing acorn tree looks on, the change rooms beside it in grimy cream layers that peel from weatherboards. Cobwebs cloak inside and out, congealing crumbly in window corners and door frames.

Flapping and scampering under the gutters are the birds and possums redecorating once again. It too will have its day, in years to come.

What once Was, now Is.

What once Was

BACHELOR QUARTERS - DECEMBER 3 1911

BACK ROW. Left to Right. J Morrison, G Wilson, O Kyle, A McCormack Dempsey, S Vinall, F Quinn.

SEATED. J Ryan, T Flaherty, J Faris, C Patterson, P McIntosh, M Ryan, Jack Sheahan.

SEATED FRONT. H Morrison, R Morrison.

Original photo supplied by A Iles

Bachelors' quarters, 1911. Photo courtesy of the Ryan family.

IT'S SUCH A BITCH. This piping hot emblazes my core as a fiend lapping the juices of evil souls. Walter, what's happening to me, where is thy hand? Please hold me.

Damp, beige flannels pat my forehead in a well of care that never runs dry. Shivers come in scarlet waves, dimple over my arms and down the nape of my neck as an angry red scavenge. The cold, the hot, it festers in flushing fissures, torments and tantalises. Dearest Walter, please take my hand, as you did only weeks ago when we stood at the altar adorned in pink carnations and tea roses. Their giddy scent hung in the humidity of March, over our families and friends witnessing our love. My white silk dress trimmed in Maltese lace and sprays of orange blossom, draped in perfect soft pleats over my hips. I clasped my white azaleas edged in fern and tied in tulle, my breath building as an untamed brumby, and only lulling when I could fall into you. Pastor Vickers blessed us and our commitment to a lifetime was sealed with eternal gold bands. Rice and confetti showered us: Mr and Mrs W Cropley. No more Miss Elsie Tinkler.

Whence cometh our children, Walter? Is the nursery ready? We must prepare for their arrival.

My fever runs hot, my throat so inflamed it hinders my breath. A tongue of bogging fur, a mouth lined in a dense coating barrier to the stenching decomposition beneath the bleeding and ulcerating. Membrane upon membrane putrefies. My heart beats at a thousand beats, the pain in my abdomen ....

He's coming, my son is soon to be birthed! Or is it a daughter standing in the corner, a spectre waiting for me? Where art thou mother and father, young child in the corner? I must go to you for a child without parent cannot be. But then there's the son to be birthed, the son my Walter always yearned.

Hot, cold, dabbing at the clammy swathing my body and dampening my bed covers. Where am I, what becomes of me? I'm too young for this, Walter. What of our family together?

The doctor thought I was baring child when I first became ill. The tiredness and lethargy, I was so happy! Then a simple cold and sore throat appeared, thought to be quinsy. I gargled hyposulphite of soda from a glass goblet, and a tincture of iron and chlorate of potash to clear the abscess on my tonsils. Powders of bitter and oils in brown bottles strewn my bedside table.

Bodies of apparition are with me now, in my new bedroom shared with Walter.

How I wish it was quinsy, or even better, that I was with child, instead of tortured by this blood disease. I have the perfect husband. Next was to come the perfect family. I'm only 21. A new bride, married at the turn of the 20th century. This colonial croup will take us all. Why has this happened to me now, Walter, why is death at my door?

My spectre calls me, holds out her hand. I'm coming, my new daughter.

'She's gone,' a broken mother howls. 'My sweet Elsie.'

Who has gone, mother? What's happened?

'My cherry blossom.' Walter sobs.

Why is your hand no longer in mine, Walter? What's happening to us? Walter!

I'm here, Muma. I've been waiting for you.

Walter, what is this spectre from the corner speaking to me? Come near, Walter, you're too far away ....

The daughter from the corner is by my bed. Her hand haunts mine. But she's not ours, not mine and Walter's, not the family we were to create!

Crying rains and hailing tears gush as torrents rupturing from swelling hearts. In solemn regard upon my pale bed, bowed heads choke in collars of lead. I'm by my daughter in the space above, no footing beneath us.

I'm gone, it is no question. My eyes fix on this new daughter, on her most golden mane illuminating the glum of grey.

I've been searching everywhere for a mother like you, ever since I got to the Metropolitan Sewerage Farm.

Her whispers are tinged in the eagerness of a young child.

It was the same year the Hickeys arrived, when Michael started working on the sewerage farm and he and Annie lived with their children on the foreshore. It was the year before, 1897, when sewage first arrived on the sewerage farm and flowed onto paddocks for treatment. Annie was my dream mother, I really wanted her and I waited and waited but couldn't get through her mothering busy. Then I saw you coming, ever so quickly, and oh how happy I was because finally, I would have a fine mother.

I got to the Metropolitan Sewerage Farm because of the same blood disease you got. My mother got it when I was in her belly. She died, and so did I. Then they tossed me into the sewage muck.

MARVELLOUS SMELLBOURNE.

Riverine Grazier, Friday 15 February 1889

(by an original in the Adelaide Observer)

"Bill," said I to my erratic Friend, who's travelled just a bit, "Name the strongest aromatic City you have ever hit."

He bowed his head in silence, and a study that was brown, and when out of reach of violence said, "I name your Melbourne town!"

"William," said I, "thou art witty with the music of thy mouth! Knowest thou that glorious city is the Queen of all the South?"

"Yes," he answered; "well I know it! Heard it till mine ears do ache; and, believe me, gentle poet, still in this she takes the cake!"

Then I asked a chewing Yankee, lantern-jawed and most uncouth, one of that cadaverous lanky sort who always tells the truth.

Wal, Siree, he kinder reckoned Melbourne's people like to blow, so he'd mark her down as second, just to give Port Said a show.

Then I asked one of those who can combine a head and tail upon one poll; one who'd found a way of making both ends meet.

And he says, with laughter shaking - "Melbung smellee welly high!" Others have no chance to win it, for she always comes out top!

HOW FINE IS THIS grand Dame of cities, my Melbourne town. Before 1897, however, when the first sewage flows from the All England Eleven Hotel in Port Melbourne traversed pastures of graded green at the Metropolitan Sewerage Farm, this admired Queen City of the South had a rather unsavoury means for disposing sewage. All liquid waste, which some will call liquid gold in time to come, was tossed into the streets to mix as free as the debauchery at Madame Brussels, in the dim off Bourke Street. My Melbourne town had 'borne testimony to her evil reputation among travellers as one of the unhealthiest cities in the world,' according to one reporter. Such notoriety had spurred him to dub our fair city, Marvellous Smellbourne. Au contraire, a willowy hand to my forehead and clutch of my pearls, not my marvellous Melbourne town.

Slums in Melbourne as far back as the 1850s, spored faster than an orgy of mushrooms steeped in humidity and damp. People lived in squalor, with no bathrooms or sewerage and homes held together on the whisp of a thread. Rooves leaked and drafts blew through holes in walls, people crammed in close and often shared beds. Room to hang laundered washing out to dry was meagre and keeping it clean was nigh impossible. Strolling through streets and children playing outdoors meant an Irish jig within a cesspool of urine, night soil, kitchen and bath water, soap suds from washing clothes, drainage from stables and cow sheds, liquids from trades and manufacturers, and water running off rooves and overland. All would meet in open street channels made from stone that often ran into earthen ditches to become sluggish glob, or collect in pools that would flood and overflow in rain to meander into waterways.

Typhoid and diphtheria proliferated. No one was safe, even when many claimed it was purely in the slums. My bout came from remnant cough bacteria on a pew in church. Come sit with me beside the altar, Dear Daughter, near where my love and I married weeks ago and where I wait for my Walter each Sunday Mass to swoon over him. Mortality rates in Melbourne in 1887 were 86.3 for every 100,000 inhabitants. That compared with 16 in London and 66 in Paris as per same number of people. Establishing a Royal Commission the following year into our fair city's sanitary conditions came when she was gripped by demonic disease. The Commission decided underground sewerage was key to cleaning our city and consulted British engineer, Mr James Mansergh, for his expertise. Mr Mansergh was a straight talker who made no attempt to hide any unpleasant untruths. He was a bit like my Walter in that regard, for which I took great pleasure in listening to him speak about all manner of social issues in our public debating club. Mr Mansergh expressed in quite strong language that our appliances, in the way of closet accommodation, were sickening and disgusting and he had no hesitation in relaying that to anyone he met. He undoubtedly attributed the diphtheria and typhoid epidemic to the poorest of sanitary conditions in a city booming. By 1890, deaths doubled that of the previous year. Marvellous Smellbourne indeed.

He was a slow worker though, Muma, don't you think? He took two years to write the report.

Good things take time, Dear Daughter. He was thorough, and provided eight potential sewerage schemes. Mr Mansergh preferred his M scheme with the two sewerage farms at a most reasonable £4.5 million. And it made perfect sense, dividing metropolitan Melbourne into two by the ridge separating the Gardiner's Creek valley and Port Phillip Bay. Sewage in the east would go to a sewerage farm in Mordialloc and sewage in the west would go to Werribee. Very sensible indeed.

Soon after his report, the Melbourne and Metropolitan Board of Works was established, sitting for its first meeting on Wednesday the 18th of March 1891. The press made such a fuss of the 39 elected members that made up the Board. All uptight and full of self-importance that barrelled from the snout of upturned noses if you ask me! Such a mother's job to wipe those noses dripping in disregard and disrespect.

Muma, I know how to wipe my nose, you don't need to wipe mine.

My little DD, I would wipe anything of you that dripped or dribbled and comb your main most golden. If only I could parade you to Walter, oh he'd be so proud of you. He's not appeared in the congregation yet, but he'll be here.

The Board's Chief Engineer, Mr Thwaites, he could do with a little nose wiping. Politicians and the press assumed constructing the M scheme would begin immediately but our young Mr Thwaites expressed reservations and argued strongly in favour of all of Melbourne's sewage going to one sewerage farm at Werribee. He believed a modified version of another scheme Mr Mansergh had presented could be costed at considerably less. It made no sense to me. Surely taking the sewage across the Yarra River to Werribee meant added complication and expense. He was convinced Melbourne's future growth would be in the west. Truly, an engineer predicting population growth ... not a bright man this Mr Thwaites. Silly little twat.

Muma, you're funny, you make me laugh.

My little, DD. I love your giggles. But pompous fools draw up my petticoat as a ravenous ferret chasing a juicy, fat rabbit. Walter and I saw the same bombastic pretence in debate club competitions in the east, the way they flaunted their affluence with cavalier plums in cheeks. Why does Mr Thwaites not situate a sewerage farm in his own backyard? Probably because he lives in Brighton, near Mordialloc, that's why. There is no doubt where we and our fair Melbourne town would be if the Metropolitan Sewerage Farm and the people that worked it with their families living by their side, did not exist: Dead. Like you and me, Dear Daughter. Dead.

Dear child, you're always giggling.

You're funny, Muma. What are you looking at, Muma? Can you see Walter?

Oh my goodness, who is this divine child sidling up the aisle. Dear, dear boy, he's stood on his lace and tripped. And now he's crying. Poor little dear, let me help you. I swoop down the aisle and dive to urge the boy up from under his arms. I swipe through him instead. The bothers of being dead ... There, there little man.

Dear Daughter swirls around me.

At least he distracts you from Mr Thwaites, Muma.

No, no, not at all. Nothing distracts me from pompous foolery, especially when scant appreciation repeats across the world. And yet in some cities, waste disposal and odour are encouraged. Look at Paris, in the early 1800s. It disposed of faecal matter at Montfaucon with the city's waste, where criminals were hung and their bodies were left to decompose and fall into the waste below them. The stench was never covered up, as a reminder of the fate of criminals. Mr Thwaites claims the Werribee area had the advantage of remoteness, and yet he was also predicting growth in the west? Such contradiction in a head well and truly buried in his snuff box!

Dear Daughter giggles and swirls into a dancing whirly-girly ... come down dear girl before your mane most golden tangles in the rafters.

Yes, Muma.

Mr Thwaites also claimed his preference for Werribee was because of the low rainfall in the area, which land-based sewage treatment needed. He said currents in Port Phillip Bay would carry effluent discharged into it from a sewerage farm at Werribee, out of the bay. If effluent was discharged from Mordialloc it would instead be carried towards Melbourne town. What nonsense, Dear Daughter. Pure codswallop! I saw it immediately. This was about class. Brighton, within a few miles of Melbourne in the east and 10 miles further to Mordialloc, was gentrifying. Au contraire, Werribee to Melbourne was more than 20 miles and Werribee to Brighton, even further!

PEOPLE WE KNOW. -SAYS "Scallway"

Yea Chronicle, Thursday 23 March 1899

MISS SCHWIEGER, one time assistant in Yea School, has been again transferred from charge of Princetown School to an assistantship in the Cocoroc School.

For the information of those whose Victorian geographical education has been neglected "Cocoroc is a small but 'rapidly rising' township between Little River and Werribee, close to the shores of Port Phillip Bay." It is chiefly noted as a health resort, and is guaranteed to contain a more varied collection of germs to the square inch than even Footscray. It is also noted as a haunt of White Knight Fitzgibbon and the Coms. of M.M.B. of Works. Miss S. is fortunate.

Alas, in 1892, the Governor of Victoria, Earl of Hopetoun, turned the first sod in the building of the outfall sewer near Werribee. Purely, no one wanted a sewerage farm in their backyard, not with the extent of the stench that existed in Melbourne town and the high prejudices towards sewerage. Journalists were not shy with their thoughts about that either.

And, and, to my gloomy dismay, the supreme MMBW determined that the one sewerage farm at Werribee would be best without the good manners to elect representation from the Werribee constituency onto the Board. The indecency! Surely that's about class.

Oh I know, Dear Daughter, I can tell you're being patient with me and my rant. But, and here's the golden cherry crowning the pie, the good people of the Metropolitan Sewerage Farm had the last laugh because building and operating the sewerage farm was one of the largest public works undertaken in Australia at the time and provided job security for many workers and farmers during the 1890s economic crash. The good people were lucky to be working and living on the Metropolitan Farm when so many were losing their jobs and homes. They mocked the so called journalist at *The Age* who wrote, 'the Metropolitan Farm is the new euphonic name given to the large area of land acquired at an enormous cost by the Metropolitan Board of Works, between the Werribee township and Port Phillip Bay, and converted into an evil smelling territory. The title of sewage has been discarded, but the filth and smell are there all the same.' Claiming to drop the word 'sewage' for respectability could well make him another twat, Dear Daughter!

THE METROPOLITAN FARM.

The Age. Tuesday 20 December 1898.

The heading of this article is the new euphonic name given to the large area of land acquired at an enormous cost by the Metropolitan Board of Works, between the Werribee township and Port Phillip Bay, and converted into a very evil smelling territory. The title of sewerage farm has been discarded, but the filth and smell are there all the same. There are open "carriers," down which flows with a slowness that adds to the horror, a stream of inky liquid, which, after collection and pump churning, forms the quintessence of Melbourne's human excrescence, and the stench on the lee sides of drains or inundated paddocks is the reverse of appetising.

There are two townships on the Board's map, and a visitor arriving by the first train is liable to be the victim of two delusions. He may imagine that he can widely refrain from breaking fast till he arrives at sewage township No. 1. For a few miles of the journey by the gurgling river, hitherto so loved by the adepts in the piscatorial art, and along by the well grassed paddocks of the erstwhile Chirnside estate, he will be inhaling a salubrious atmosphere, and "anticipation" will "forward point the view" to a substantial meal at some kind of eating house in the new centre of civic life.

To his disappointment, he will find no place at which to refresh the inner man. There is a large corrugated iron shed, a small church, a managerial villa and some workmen's cottages scattered around, but no place of entertainment for a hungry traveller. Even employees have to "batch on their own." This is the more remarkable when it is remembered that thousands of pounds have been spent on a practically useless jetty, where, although the population is next to nil, a hotel licence has been strenuously sought for. But soon all such considerations are abandoned.

On the road from the partially existent sewage township No. 1 to the non-existent sewage township No. 2. situated, according to the map, by the sad sea waves, the des're to partake of food is totally lost. One cannot breathe the atmosphere down there and maintain an appetite – at least, not without being acclimatised. Consequently the visitor is twice deluded. For a time life feels fit to compass the biggest plate of steak and onions, and soon finds that a refreshment room anywhere within the sewage area would be a superfluity and an extravagance.

Perhaps the most disgusting circumstance of all in connection with the farm is the condition of the viaduct over the Werribee River, from which stream water is drawn for domestic purposes. This viaduct is built of brick, is packed with about 6 feet of concrete, on which is carried a large open iron flume, down which the unsavory flood from the metropolis flows. For a mile from the structure the atmosphere is nauseating.

The viaduct itself is a sight to see close at hand as well as something that is smelt at a distance. Its piers are streaked with sewage leakage, its arches are already ornamented with scores of stalactites, some 6 inches long and an inch thick, and in two places the sewage is dripping like shower baths right into the stream on which people are dependent for drinking water.

The sewerage farm comprises 8847 acres. The land had been previously valued for probate purposes at £6 per acre. Mr. Pearson, the Government Agricultural Chemist, analysed samples of the soil on behalf of the board, and valued the land at £12 per acre, but in case it should require treatment with lime at not more than £10 per acre, Mr. Cowderoy also inspected the land on the board's behalf, and he brought its intrinsic value up to £15 per acre. And yet the Chirnsides were paid no less than £17 10s. per acre!

Without any attempt at arbitration in the public interest, they were handed the fortune – tidy even to them – of £155,037 ....

Up to the present date the farm has cost £321,000, and it is officially estimated that the total outlay on it will amount to £592,000! The engineer in chief himself sets down the cost of purchase and "preparation" at £74 10s. per acre; brings the prospective total outlay to £654,678 ....

Looking around to see where the money has gone so far, we observe that there has been a pretty large expenditure, not in clearing the land, for that was not necessary – but in the planting of belts of trees as breakwinds, in the levelling of the ground to make it irrigable, in building numerous cottages for workmen, in erecting head quarters, in making roads, in the laying down of locking channels and distributing carriers, and other work such as properly pertains to a sewage farm. All this suits the residents, who in the main are both tenants and employees. An 18-acre block with a brand new cottage, with a deduction of £25 a year as rent from wages, is attractive enough even on a sewage farm ....

There may come a day when the sewage farm will have to be abandoned as a pronounced failure, and when we will find a better way of disposing of our metropolitan sewage. That consideration, however, is not necessary to emphasise the urgent need there is for an inquiry in the interests of the ratepayers into this department of Metropolitan Board work.

The spending of about £4000 on a useless jetty would by itself justify an inquiry. This marine structure juts into Port Phillip Bay about a quarter of a mile in the very teeth of the prevailing south-westerly winds. Only in very favorable weather can it be used even by an excursion steamer. It was originally intended as a coastal outlet for the produce of the farm. The prospect is that it will never be used as such .... To render it properly serviceable, this wonderful jetty would have to be broadened, lengthened into deeper water, made T shaped, so as to afford some little shelter from the prevailing winds, and a covering breakwater.

As matters stand, the jetty is seldom used, except by some vagrant and venturesome excursion boat. The farmers find other better ways to market .... Had the money wasted on the jetty been spent on making the Werribee River navigable, it obviously would have been of advantage to all concerned ....

By Mr. Thwaites we have been informed in a printed document that the interest on the cost of the farm, and sufficient for a repayment in 25 years of the capital absorbed, would be assured by a rental of £5 16s. 3d. per acre. This is the estimate of the responsible officer based on his own assumption that the cost of the land (purchase and preparation) will be £74 10s. per acre.

According to the most recent return at hand there were 5583 of the 8847 acres let, and the rentals obtained ranged from only a maximum of 16s. 6d. per acre down to 4s. There were 4316 acres let at 10s. and over, and 1267 acres at below 10s. When, if ever, it may well be asked, will Mr. Thwaites's ideal of £5 16s. 3d. per acre be attained? Until it is reached the farm, according to his own showing, must be run at a loss ....

As already observed this is but one department of the Metropolitan Board's operations; as has been previously demonstrated In "The Age" the other branches have been egregiously mismanaged, and yet the representatives of the ratepayers are strangely lacking in that unanimity which the Premier seems to think a sine qua non of any request for a royal commission. The march of events will sheet home the responsibility.

My little DD has gone into her customary whirly-girly, giggling dance, this time above a handsome young boy wearing narrow knickerbockers buckled below the knee and a white shirt with an Eton collar. Beside him must be his sister, a gorgeous little thing in golden locks wearing a crimson dress, ornamental stitching gathering tight pleats from neck to shoulder and again at the waist. The innocence of smocking. My heart is a giddy, doubly so when Walter appears under the wooden buttressed doorway of church. Walter, I'm coming to thee ....

And together, we pray.

MRS BEAMISH IS TALKING to Aunt Issy outside church after Mass, about the claims of stench from drains and inundated paddocks on the Metropolitan Farm, and the stream of inky liquid adrift in open carriers that adds to the horror of the place. Horror, they say! How ill-informed, and most likely from people residing in plush velvet pretence oozing from Corinthian pilasters in Brighton.

'Our Metropolitan Farm will save Melbourne, mark my words, and boost a flagging economy that's slipping into major crisis,' says Mrs Beamish.

'Indeed,' says Aunt Issy. 'Export prices have fallen and our farm is being impacted. We may not get the prices we used to get for our sheep. Stephen's worried.'

'And so he should be. We're in a sorry state. Bankruptcies are increasing by the day and so many building societies and banks have already collapsed. Even the Board had a terrible time securing a loan to build the sewerage farm. In the end, it sought a loan from the British Empire.'

'Oh it's true,' Aunt Issy sighs. 'The depression has shrouded Australia but Melbourne is its epicentre. They're saying at least a third of workers have lost their jobs and are having trouble finding another one, clerks as well as labourers. Wages have fallen and even Stephen can't keep up. He may have to let some farm hands go, which will add to the already thousands searching for work.' Aunt Issy separates the chain handle of her beaded bag to unhinge the brass dragonfly-shaped latch. She pulls out a handkerchief and dabs at her nose.

'And if they're lucky enough to find work, they work for less money. Francis is having to pay his stablemen less,' says Mrs Beamish.

'People aren't spending their hard-earned pennies because they don't have them to spend. My goodness, homes are being lost by the thousands and charities are struggling to cope to help people.'

'Elizabeth!' calls Mr Beamish.

'I know he's serious when he calls me by my full name!' she whispers to Aunt Issy, then turns to her husband behind her.

'We've got to go. I need to get to my stables,' calls Mr Beamish.

Ballarat Star, Wednesday 25 May 1892

Regarding the rush of laborers to the sewerage works at Werribee, an Age telegram dated Monday says;

"Fully 800 men arrived here during today. They are coming from all quarters, and as each train arrives the already large number increases. The men were much disappointed when they learnt that Mr Mixner was not going to commence work till Thursday or Friday next.

As soon as it became known that Mr Falkingham was commencing operations this morning, the crowd, over 1000 strong, marched to the scene of the opening works, and there saw Mr Falkingham, who gave them to understand that he would only employ genuine workmen. After great trouble, owing to the interference of the crowd, he selected about 150, who willingly commenced work on the spot. The others, who were unable to secure work, then marched in a body across the Werribee Park Estate back to the township, where they paraded the main street in files 10 deep.

On the approach of the 2.17 train for Melbourne there was a general rush for the station, and about a hundred of the crowd managed to enter the train; the doors being locked they were assisted through the windows by their comrades, the station officials being unable to control the mob. After the departure of the train they became more orderly, and devoted the rest of the afternoon in drawing up a requisition petitioning Mr G. Chirnside to grant them the use of a piece of ground on which to erect their tents.

There are now about 1000 laboring men in the district waiting for work. They are exceedingly quiet this evening, and have evidently retired for the night."

IT'S DIRE, DEAR DAUGHTER. From the end of 1891 and into 1892, our fair Melbourne town had lost close to 20,000 people. Many returned to a simpler, rural life. Unemployment surged and the rush for jobs was akin to sheep on the Chirnside estate fleeing to dogs nipping at their hooves. Such was the case for jobs at the Metropolitan Farm, which resulted in possibly Werribee's first public march.

The Metropolitan Farm was well on its way at the time. The MMBW had purchased 8847 acres of land from the Werribee estate of Mr George Chirnside, son of the late Mr Andrew Chirnside. Mr Chirnside's acuteness in judgement and understanding of farming is one to be admired, having imported the first Tamworth pigs into Australia. He opened 10,000 acres of the estate for tenant farming, built houses for the tenant farmers and erected windmills and water-tanks on each. He would become Australia's foremost breeder of Jersey cattle. The MMBW would buy more land from other farmers over the next 20-30 years to expand the sewerage farm, including from my Uncle Stephen. His farm sat on the northern edge of the Metropolitan Farm. When the MMBW eventually purchase his land, it will become known as Tinkler's paddock, running along Tinkler's Lane. Mr Stephen Tinkler he was.

Sadly, he and all the farmers had stolen the land from the local Aborigines, as did other white settlers, and wasn't theirs to sell.

Our grand Dame's burgeoning population required an ever-increasing work force to manage the increasing volume of sewage. It meant the MMBW had to build cottages across the vast, uninhabited sewerage farm land for its workers and their families. Travelling by bicycle, horse or foot if living in Werribee as the nearest town, to work on the Metropolitan Farm was nigh impossible when the sewerage farm was more than 20 miles from Werribee at its most western boundary near Avalon, and 30 miles from Melbourne. The MMBW leased the cottages to its workers and their families for a modest rent, along with two cows for milking and making butter, cheese and cream because all services and shops were in Werribee. The cows become so well nourished from feeding on the lush, sewage-watered paddocks that families will share their milk products with neighbours when cows aged and stopped producing milk. And they'll sell any surplus to grocers in Werribee and markets in Footscray and Melbourne. Butter made by the Metropolitan Farm women in their homes will become highly sought after in years to come.

But the MMBW couldn't keep up. Men were employed at a ravenous pace and as they waited for a house, they'd share sleeping quarters with other men or camp in tents on site, going home to their families living in Werribee, Little River or Lara on their days off. Sometimes, they'd live with their families in tents on the sewerage farm until one of these elusive cottages became available to rent.

LITTLE DD, COME. AUNTIE and Uncle are home and I want to show you their farm.

In that touch of no touch where hands cannot clasp or caress, we fly over the chit-chat of the congregation gathered in the church gardens, towards the Werribee River and onto the Werribee Road that began at the Werribee train station. Over paddocks we glide where cows moo with their calves in close and sheep flock thick. The anticipation of Auntie's afternoon baking chasseing out the kitchen window and into the pom poms of wattle flowers lures me into one of Dear Daughter's whirly-girly dances. Even if we smell no more, its lingering memory imbues our veil.

Sweet Aunt Issy, there she is, smearing open scones with plum jam made from the harvest from her orchard, dolloped with cream churned from the milk of her cows. She's sitting at the kitchen table. Still the same nicks carved into its wooden top, one I made when only 12 after slipping my knife while slicing cheese. Eloquent Elsie, she would call me, for all my opinions so well spoken.

I glide in, little DD following behind, and snuggle in beside dear aunt. Scones topped with slices of cheese Aunt Issy would have made earlier in the week, sit on a plate to one side. My hand steeps over Auntie's as she dips for a spoonful of cream so lush, cream I used to help her churn from tepid milk on weekends. Her skin is air. Nothing. She glances my way. You see me, Auntie, do you? Sense me perhaps. A chiselling claw bites in. I wince.

Muma, what's wrong?

I'm okay, Dear Daughter, but for a tentacle of love that never releases.

I have the same sometimes, Muma, and I don't know why. Perhaps it's from the muma I never knew and have searched for everywhere. That's why I hovered over Annie for so long. She's wonderful and cares for her babies like no other. She lives with her children and Michael on the foreshore of the Metropolitan Farm. He has a swooning way with his words, and the children are heavenly. I played with them often before you came. Two of her babies dance with me high above Annie too. Let me take you to meet Annie, Muma. She was the mother I always longed for, caught sight of when I arrived here. Until you came and now you're my mother.

Dear Daughter seizes my hand by will and we glide over the bench top where scones abut on a blue willow, oval serving platter. Their scent is one of virtue, Dear Daughter, one I long to inhale and savour once again.

You're lucky, Muma. How I wish to taste any nourishment at all, know what any scent is.

How blessed you are, Dear Daughter, for that asset of no appreciation of smell and never had to *enjoy* the occasional insensitivity that comes on a southerly breeze, as an earthen pungent of rotting eggs.

We fly over skeletal cracks etched into dusty paddocks, where Merinos crowd hay of poor nourishment on sparse farm land. The carrier flowing in the described inky disdain onto the Metropolitan Farm comes into sight. It's pale in comparison to its exaggerated portrayal. We reach the Head of the Road where the Metropolitan Farm begins and where the cottage of Mr Lester, the General Manager, and his family stands stately off to its left. Three red brick chimneys shoot up from the corrugated iron roof. A veranda propped by turned wood columns with small, winged buttresses, flares from beneath the narrow fascia that skirts two lengths of the house. There's no sign of Mrs Lester today.

The old Mixing Camp appears ahead on the right, established when the Metropolitan Farm first began. It's now as an outcrop of greying wood and iron rooves sprouting from cracked and upturned earth, dusty dry in the midst of a drought and in stark contrast to the lush green of the sewage watered paddocks surrounding it. Some call it the Contractor's Camp, the base for sewerage construction. Tram tracks run intact in front of it, to ferry construction materials to some parts of the huge site. How such tracks were never laid across the Metropolitan Farm from the stockpiles still standing, I'll not understand. Yet it's no surprise either, not with the rumours of clashing egos of the Board, councils and engineers and the bickering that followed and created delays and waste. Claims of misspent money and the Board trying its darnedest to earn revenue to cover the operations ran rife, and continue to do so. The lengths of wood strewn in a haphazard mess across the yard are a sad sight, wood that once rested in stacked piles waiting to be plucked for building. Their exposed tops are damp from overnight showers. Dear Daughter, it's such a waste. A wooden shed with a torn canvas roof, perhaps once a shade house for saplings being grown for plantations across the sewerage farm, leans beside a cart loaded with a small plough. Spokes are missing from its front wheels.

There exists such disparity between the dilapidated in the camp and the six new workers' cottages built beside it in what is proposed as a township at the top of the Metropolitan Farm. The sturdy homes also contrast with those in the slums of Melbourne and are a privilege to acquire in these frugal times. Their infant gardens are watered in sewage to spur their growth, necessary in the windy open plains that dry to the parchest of parch.

The homes of twin-peaks with a passageway running down their centres line a street coming off the main road that stretches north to south through the sewerage farm. Corrugated iron verandas span the front of each house to ripple the sun's shimmy across the front porch. Four squared posts trimmed in wooden fretwork support each veranda. The iron water tank stands on a diagonal opposite, scant rain drops dripping from the dark green base of the tank, past bluestone arches onto the ground below.

Mrs Carter is in the recess off the kitchen in her cottage, at the furthest end of the street. She's sorting letters and telegrams and stacking newspapers and brown packets in boxes for Metropolitan Farm residents and workers to collect. In her haste to finish her postmistress duties before the children arrive home from school, the pocket of her white apron protecting her dark woollen dress catches on the door handle. A powder puff of grime billows from her apron. She loses the few telegrams clutched in her hand, granting a gust of wind much delight in wafting them up the passage and out the front door. They weave into the three-branched forks of juvenile apricot trees planted last winter, now preparing to lose their few leaves. They and apple trees line a path scraped of grass from the front porch to the white wooden gate. Mrs Carter chases after the telegrams, revealing layers of pale petticoats in the breeze. She clamps her skirt down and stumbles over a clumped weed to roll head-first into an apple tree staked to a post. The stake snaps and ricochets into the weatherboard house. Dear Daughter giggles. I can't help but join her.

'Oh, Jane, let me help you,' calls Mrs Engebrigsten from the veranda next door.

'It's okay, thank you. I have them,' calls Jane hurrying to collect the last telegram flapping against the picket fence.

'Come and have a cup of tea, Jane, when you finish,' says Mrs Engebrigsten in a thick northern European accent. 'But it's okay if you have no time. I know der is always work to do wid dis dust from de paddocks. I am always sweeping de veranda and de washing is brown when I take it inside.'

'I will, Mrs Engebrigsten. Thank you kindly,' calls Mrs Carter, pounding up the path.

Frank Pengelly and Son Flaherty ride their chestnut mares alongside George Sadler in his horse and jinker, to Jane's fence.

'Afternoon, Mrs Carter,' calls Frank.

Jane turns back. 'Good afternoon, gentlemen. Come to get your newspapers?'

'Of course, Mrs Carter,' says George. 'As always.'

'Just finished me shift in the stables and on me way back to the Men's hut.' Frank dismounts his horse.

Jane dashes inside to reappear within seconds with three newspapers. She meets the men at the gate.

'I'll take me paper and pick me stuff up, then go home to Phoebs in Werribee to read it in me comfy chair.'

Jane hands Frank *The Age* over the fence.

'There's more chin-waggin' going on about the jetty,' says Frank. 'They reckon the finance committee's gonna recommend blocks be leased for 10 years down the bottom-end.'

'What're the blocks for?' asks George.

'Who knows.'

'It's all to do with the jetty and making money from it,' says Son. 'The Board has to offset the operations here. That's why they got all them tenant farmers down there, to earn some money from their leases to farm.'

'They'll lease the blocks out for anythin',' says Frank. 'Shops maybe, or they might be wantin' a hotel again!'

'Not again,' says Jane. 'A licenced hotel was never a clever idea, whether down the bottom-end or anywhere on the Farm.'

'It'd be fan-bloody-tastic to have a pub here, that's what'd be! Be able to get me grog shit-easy.'

'I've got to go and finish this mail, boys. Talk to you tomorrow night at the Cricket Club Ball.' Jane hurries up the path.

'We'll be there, me and Phoebs. With bells on!'

'Me and Anne'll be there too,' says Son.

BUT I CAN'T MAKE it out, can you? The Werribee farmers they never complain, No matter what weather they get, There's a smile on their face if they never see rain, 'Tis the same if exceedingly wet.

To the cricket contingent that comes from the Farm, A few words of advice I'll confide, Let hope always scatter all cause for alarm, For you ever have right on your side; No, I can't make it out, can you?

'Mr Butcher's in fine form,' says Frank, tapping his foot on the wooden boards of the Mechanic's Institute. 'Come on, Phoebs, let's go for a spin.' Frank holds his hand out to Phoebe.

'It's not time to dance yet, Frank,' whispers Phoebe, pressing her palm to Frank's chest.

'Mr B won't mind.'

'Go on, Phoebe,' whispers Agnes sitting on the other side of her. 'I've got to sneak off to check on wee Francis in his pram too.'

Phoebe takes Frank's hand. Frank leads her in a tip-toe step through the side door to outside. Little DD's following in her whirly-girly dance with Annie's babies above. They swirl over Frank twirling princess Phoebe on the grass.

He's funny, Muma, with his big smile that puffs his cheeks bright red. He would be a good father for me.

Oh, DD, you are the cutest.

And you're my muma, Muma!

Now Everist, the banker, will do nothing rash; And your bills he will always renew, He's placed a good Farmer in charge of your cash – But I can't make it out, can you? Now the cricket club run at the Farm I've been told is badly in want of some cash; And I ask all the tenants to plank down their gold, But I hope they will do nothing rash. If from each but a fiver, 'twill greatly assist, And I'm sure it's the right thing to do; If to hand in a tenner they all should insist – Why I can't make it out, can you?

A peak of pink bonnet by a pram – it's Annie and Muma peering over her shoulder at Ted and Tom inside it.

Debonair in their finery, the two are dressed in English lace collars draped over blazers that shimmy as dew in a freshly ploughed paddock flooded in sunshine. Tom's teeny fingertips peak from the lace-edged sleeve, his arm snuggles in under the embroidered blanket. It probably came in the brown box of beautiful clothes tied in a blue ribbon that Mrs Chirnside had delivered to Annie by jinker. Annie had travelled into Werribee station days earlier with Tom and Ted and happened to pass Mrs Chirnside. She stopped and admired the twins most inquisitively, longingly. She left without uttering a word to Annie. Perhaps she was yearning for children of her own, or aching for the baby she'd lost. It sometimes hovers over the twins with Dear Daughter, lost in an afterlife of yearning.

Beside Annie is Agnes, tucking the patchwork rug made from heavy woven fabric once hanging as a curtain in her mother's bedroom. Francis sleeps cosy inside the wicker basket of the pram on a soft cushion made from the fur of rabbits George had caught on the Farm. The pram gives a dinky jig and scritch of its wooden spoked wheels. At 12 months old, Francis is unperturbed by the singing and dancing, dosing in his place of peace.

'I'd better get to the kitchen quick smart to help serve supper,' says Agnes.

'I'll be there soon,' calls Annie.

Agnes flings through the kitchen door coming off the main part of the Institute to a whirring of women. In a bevy busy, with milk warming in tin kettles to make tea and pointed sandwiches of cheese and ham, cheese and cucumber, cheese and pickles, cheese and all possible fillings lining plates in rows. After all, these sandwiches were made by women from the Farm, and an abundance of the finest butter, cheese and cream.

'What do you want me to do?' calls Agnes, pushing her back against the wall to make room for two plates of sandwiches flying past.

Phoebe prances through the kitchen. 'Start taking these out, lovey.' She hands Agnes two plates of jelly cakes. 'And then come back for the cream lilies.' Agnes skips out to the tables lining the wall at the back of the Institute.

Phoebe cavorts through the kitchen to her own two-step twirl. She reaches for cream lilies overlapping on plates, the pleats in her purple dress wrinkling into the bench top as she leans over. 'The last song's coming up, lovey,' she says to Annie who has slipped into the kitchen. 'We need to have supper done before the real shindig gets going!' She hands Annie the cream lilies. Annie hurries out, balancing two plates down the length of one forearm and carrying a plate in each hand.

The Metropolitan Farm Cricket Club Concert and Ball is held outside of the summer playing season this Saturday night. Son Flaherty's cuddling his wife, Anne, sitting beside him; Michael's holding Annie's hand on his knee and strokes the top of her hand with his thumb. The memory of Walter holding my hand inflames my vacuous hollow. Death is barren.

Muma, how fine are the women, wearing their short, snug plaid blazers. I wish I could dress fine, Muma, instead of being the shiny purple amoebic thing I am.

Little DD, with a mane so golden, you are a unique beauty.

But Dear Daughter is too perturbed. She flies to ruffle gentle ripples into the pretty flags of all colours and shapes hanging from the ceiling and over the walls of the Institute, and lingers undercover, even though invisible to the living. The rope of a flag loosens, sending a string of flags waving down into the audience relishing in Miss M'Cann's heartful rendering of *Hunting the fox.*

'Bloody flags,' grumbles Son, his face concealed by them.

'Let me help you,' whispers Anne, plucking flags away.

The flags and rope fall onto Son's lap before sliding onto his polished, black boots. He stands and kicks them away, only to entangle himself more. In his haste, he falls into Anne and onto the floor.

Little DD giggles from her peeking behind the hanging flags.

'Ssh, manners,' says a woman, sitting two rows up.

Anne and another gentlemen beside her help Son up.

'Stupid bloody flags,' grumbles Son.

'Shush, Son!'

'Let us thank our final, wonderful performer for the evening,' yells Mr Butcher. 'Miss M'Cann!'

Rapturous applause flutter the flags shielding Dear Daughter. The delicate lilacs and honeysuckles and shiny berries of shrubs in terracotta pots on the stage bask in the applause. I hover over them near little DD.

'We're now at the end of our last song at 10 o'clock and it is without exception, the best programme presented in Werribee for years. Even if the program at first, didn't look like much.'

The crowd cheers.

'It's obvious justification too,' yells Mr Butcher. 'That speaks volumes in favour of the proposal to erect a public hall at the Farm that was mooted some time ago.'

Cheers grow lustrous.

'I'll hand you to Captain Chirnside as I'm sure you're eager to extract yourselves from the crammed sardine can we're sitting within!'

Captain Chirnside takes the chair. 'What a stupendous night. It's a great privilege to be here with you. I propose a vote of thanks to the ladies and gentlemen who have contributed to our amusement so ably,' calls Captain Chirnside over an applauding crowd. 'Please dig into the linings of your pockets for our Farm cricket club. We're here tonight to help them. I'm sure you're eager for the dancing to begin so I'll hand over to the General Manager of the Metropolitan Farm, Mr Hope.' Captain Chirnside joins the applause as he walks from the stage.

Cheers accompany Mr Hope. 'Thank you, Mr Chairman. And thank you for your assistance at various times and for all you've given to the Farm and Farm people, and the cricket club by taking them to outside places.' The hall erupts to stomps and whistles.

'Give us a hall at the Farm, Mr Hope,' comes a call from the crowd.

'In due course, in due course,' says Mr Hope. 'Let's first thank the women from the Farm for the supper they've prepared and will soon serve. I can attest it's a most superb supper as I've sampled a jelly cake and can tell you so! And at the end of supper, the hall shall be cleared for dancing.'

'Three cheers for the Farm women. Hip, hip - hooray. Hip, hip - hooray. Hip, hip ....

'Hooraaay.'

'My last announcement, echoes Mr Chirnside's,' yells Mr Hope. 'Please dig deep one and all, to help fund this fledgling cricket club. Collection boxes are placed around the room for your convenience.'

In jovial bob of brimming capacity, men spill from doors to smoke pipes around the fire pit outside while women flock to congregate in clusters around supper. Hoots of Tawny owls, chirps of fairy wrens.

Frank licks a dot of cream from his pinkie finger. 'Your scones are fan-bloody-tastic, Aggie!'

'As always,' says Phoebe, sipping tea from a pale pink cup dotted in tea roses. 'I've not had a bad one in any of our cups of teas.'

'I'd have to agree,' says Annie. 'And we've shared a few in our bottom-end of the Farm.'

Agnes squeezes Annie's hand. 'How else would we keep up with what's going on round the place. The things we know!' Agnes gives Annie a wink.

'Hey, young Engebrigsten,' calls Franks with half a scone in his mouth as the kid bolts past. 'Slow down, ya nearly knocked me tea outta me hand.'

'We dearly need a hall at the Farm,' says Annie.

'The sooner the better,' says Frank, gorging the last of his scone.

'They've got this committee now, after last year's meeting. They're considering the best ways and means for building a public hall at the Farm,' says Agnes, rearranging cheese and cucumber sandwiches that have fallen apart.

'They've interviewed the Board about it,' says Annie. 'But still, we have no hall and we're crowded stiff in this match box.'

'Sardine can,' quips Mr Butcher striding by.

'Yeah, Mr B!' says Frank, stuffing another cheese and tomato scone in his mouth. 'And we need to start clearing tables and chairs outside, so we've got room for some shin diggin'.' Tomato juice drips from his lip.

'You and your scones,' says George. 'You should try these.' George shoves a whole raspberry jelly cake into his mouth.

'George! Manners please.' Agnes swats the top of George's hand.

Annie smiles. 'I'm out of jelly again. I don't fancy doing the 20-mile round trip in and out of Werribee to get some more either. So you'll have to wait for Aub Comben to make his next rounds to the Farm before I can make some more you, George!'

'What about your lovely apple pie, Annie, when are ya making that next?' asks George.

'Next week, George. Just for you.' Annie winks at George.

'We need shops down there like they said they were going to build last year, for the purpose of forming a township,' says Agnes.

Annie sips her tea. 'We do, but people in Werribee were very happy when the motion to lease the blocks near the jetty fell through.'

'My goodness, they should live where we are and with our brood! We're 40 families or so down there already, including the tenant farmers,' says Agnes.

Annie sips the last of her tea. 'They say the tradespeople in Werribee can supply us Farm residents with all our requirements and the Board need not go to the expense of building new establishments on the Farm.' Annie stands and glances over to the pram.

'Codswallop!' huffs Agnes.

George gulps the rest of his tea. 'We don't need shops! We've got the perfect life. Huntin' rabbits, fishin'. Plenty of water and fresh air. Healthy sea air too. We've got a good, clean, simple life. Not like them poor Melbourne mob, with banks going down the dunnekin and people losing their jobs and homes.'

'They're protectin' their interests,' says Frank.

'Who?'

'The shop traders in Werribee, against new businesses setting up on the Farm.'

'Of course they are,' says Agnes. 'But they should come and watch Annie for a day and see all the work she does, and what all the men do down there so they can have proper sewerage.'

'Ungrateful buggers,' says Frank.

'The ten year leases are too short,' says Michael. 'They'd have to erect a building within five years of taking up the lease, which leaves five years to operate. It's not long enough for them to make a profit.'

'Bloody Board,' says Frank. 'Wantin' shops when there's no proper town yet. Bottom-end or top-end, it's all proposed. Nothin's for sure. And expectin' the tenant to pay for property with no return for five years.'

'The place will take off.' Michael takes another cream lily and slurps the jelly oozing from its centre.

'The jetty's set to take tenant farmer's produce to Melbourne,' says George. 'It's cheaper for them to go by steamer over water than by road 'n' rail.'

'They need to lay tram tracks down to the jetty first, so they can move the produce for the steamers to collect it,' says Michael. 'There's stockpiles all over the place.'

Phoebe waltzes out from the kitchen and begins stacking plates on the table.

'Busy in the kitchen?' asks Agnes.

'Been clearing and washing up like a steam plough winding back and forth all day,' says Phoebe, lifting a pile ten plates high.

'And the Board will earn its cut, too right.' Frank shakes his head.

'Of course the Board will use any earnings from the tenant farmers' leases to offset its costs,' says Annie. 'With all the ploughing and building houses for the men, and the sewers to connect homes and bringing the sewage down to the Farm ....'

'Na, Phoebs. Crops are failin' from them tenant farmers. The Board didn't take into account that the farmers wouldn't need sewage on paddocks in winter! They're off their kadoovas.'

Michael and George laugh. 'Bloody Board.'

'Lucerne's not growin',' says Frank. 'There's too much salt in the sewage! Bloody salt scum's spread all over the paddocks once the sewage's dried out.'

'The steamers will bring the people in on the jetty though, from Melbourne. They'll use the shops.' Phoebe continues clearing the tables around her. Annie, Michael and Agnes are doing the same.

'Now that's where the Farm licenced hotel at the bottom-end woulda been good. Bob's your uncle,' says Frank.

'And what about all the visitors that would stop in?' says Annie, collecting Frank's plate and tea cup. 'There'd be people drinking and drunk and falling all over the place!'

'Na, she'll be right,' says Frank. 'And who wouldn't want a beer after work! We coulda had a roast beef dinner there for me birthdee!'

'A boom town,' says George. 'That's what they're predicting with the jetty now built. It's alright for you, Frank, you camp in the Men's hut during the week and go to your quiet home in Werribee after that. It's gonna be the end of our simple life for us on the Farm.'

'Let's get this hall cleared,' says Frank, slapping his knee. 'Me feet are a tappin'.'

SUCH GLEE UP HIGH, through the flags we fly, one after the other, those Hickey babes and I. A Ragtime up and down, lace dress twirls of round and round.

Trumpet lilies of velveteen bloom, stamens glisten in garnish swoon. Fingers unfurl over accordion keys, squeezing a tra-la-la, ra-ra-ree ....

Knees lark, feet tap in jolly jig, a one-step to the Pride of Erin and waltz of two three. Heads kick back, petticoats swirl. A sashay, a Boomah of a Kangaroo Hop, and skip of Polka to a one foot pop.

On we tap, til dawn of nigh.

MUMA, THERE'S ANNIE. HANGING out sheets and towels. They're dancing happy, even on a day so chilly. I want to dance with them.

And off she spins, my little DD, into a whithering dance of whirly-girly glee past the laundered washing and over to Tom, Ted, Nellie and Charlie making circles in the sand. The babies are there too, frolicking in their pretty ivory dresses. The lace trims ripple as frilling seaweed. They're always here by the foreshore, hovering above Annie.

Dear Daughter dances with the babies over choppy waters foaming at their tips in curls of white, churning the darkest of murky waves into shore. They break against jagged and pitted rocks spat out as molten lava millions of years ago that have cooled in pockets of popped air. The water reels in rhyme and rhythm under skies of gluttonous gloom, washed in the plums and mauves of a sun prying for an opening. It lures me to a melancholy bay beneath lacing mist. Distant land in the west is Portarlington and to the east is the Werribee River flowing into the bay, the south of Werribee. In between and along the horizon, is our fair city, grand Dame Melbourne, gilded in silver.

Ice cold flinches off the water spearing in Antarctic emotion, as it skims rotting seaweed edging the shore. It's the kind of chill that finds its way in, biting under any bowler hat or stiff collar to benumb a bare neck. Pretty and pristine, in tints of teal and taupe, but oh so dreary and ever so changeable. The Australian landscape is renowned for its chameleon dexterity, arousing the harsh and extreme in all hues of brazen and blush. Many writers have attempted to capture it in a most lyrical and romantic form. Ion L Idriess will hold a splendid pen in years to come, in the way he will write of distant lands in romantic prose. Such places were only ever in my dreams, until I lived them through his eloquence.

We of Melbourne town say it's a typical winter's day.

Annie's layered in a thick coat over a woollen dress and petticoats, and socks over stockings under long black boots she'd made when machining in her father's saddlery shop in a back street off Lonsdale Street in Melbourne. My dear Walter, he'd be shivering to the bone if he were here now, even wearing his sack coat and the socks mother had knitted him. My love, all I wish for him is happiness. Total and utter joy that I'm afraid he does not yet have.

Annie originally came from Ballarat and Michael was from County Clare in Ireland, migrating via convict ship from England, and so the two must be accustomed to the cold. Yet it's incomprehensible how these dear people manage living within canvas walls in this environment, and to have twin boys within months of arriving here in 1898 to make for a brood of 10 children. Au contraire, if it were I living this way, I'd be in a desperate clutch of my pearls and fading hand to my forehead, searching for a velvet chaise sofa by a well-stoked fire.

Michael scoured for work in the late 1890s. Many men did. The MMBW was the largest employer in Australia at the time, given the workforce needed to build the network of pipes, carriers and pump houses to collect the sewage of our grand Dame city, Melbourne town, and to bring it here to the Farm for treating. Copious numbers of men were required to establish hundreds of miles of connections to sewers, not to mention the main water supply, and to plough and grade thousands of acres of paddocks and build miles and miles of channels to move the sewage around the immense sewerage farm site. And let's not forget the number of men needed to move the sewage over the paddocks once it arrived on the Farm, and the vast numbers of trees to propagate and plant. Sorting Melbourne's sewage was a great undertaking indeed.

Michael's experience working in the timber trade was strongly desired and he was employed to help construct the cottages on the Farm. Annie and Michael hoped that the MMBW would offer them one of the homes Michael was helping to build. Little did they understand however, that it would be 13 years of camping on the foreshore beside the jetty before a house would be offered to them.

'Georgie,' calls Eilly. 'Come away from that water. You'll catch a death.' Eilly chases after her three-year-old brother.

'Ei-lly,' squeals George. In his bliss of giggle, he trips on a rock and immediately howls.

Annie drops the wooden pegs into the woven splint basket and hurries to the water's edge. 'Georgie, what have you done?' She scoops him into her arms. 'Eilly! I asked you to watch your brother.'

'But Ma, he runs away whenever I try and get him away from the water.'

Annie dashes inside the canvas tent with George sobbing in her arms, blood weeping from a gash in his forehead. She snatches a folded piece of white muslin from a shelf and rushes to the water's edge. 'Finish hanging out the washing,' she calls back to Eilly. 'And take out the washing soaking in the wooden tub too.'

Annie dips the cloth into the salt water, squeezes off the excess and dabs at the blood. 'It's a tiny graze, Georgie. We'll fix it. Maybe we sit here by the water for a bit and sing a little yodelling. How about that?' Annie scans the expanse of rocks edging the shell grit stretching across the beach, and perches on a flat surface with George on her lap. She begins tapping her foot to a one-two beat. The two babies hover over Annie, their dresses fluttering and frilling.

'*No, I can't make it out, can you? These things that I see quite mystify me, And I can't make them out, can you? Yodello-ee-ooo.*'

George slows his sobbing. Tom, Ted, Charlie and Nellie wander over to their mother, leaving their shell spirals and sandcastles in the sand. They fossick for small rocks and begin throwing them into the water.

'*Has anyone seen him in Werribee since? Well, I can't make it out, can you? Yodello-a-ooo. These things that I see quite mystify me, And I can't make them out, can you, Yodello-o-a-ee-o ....*'

Annie tunes to the cadence of waves surging and receding. George collapses into his mother.

'Dia dhuit, hello,' sings Michael as he and Harry stride through the sodden salt marsh after relentless overnight rain. They've finished their shift for the day. Michael has moved from his labouring job to become a waterman, watering paddocks with sewage. Harry works with his father. Behind them in the paddock across the road are four Clydesdales being moved into the stable for the evening. They've been drawing scoops all day to grade new paddocks for sewage treatment. A cottage stands by the stable, tenanted farms surround it. Opposite but separated by a freshly sowed plantation of pine trees is another cottage, close to Annie and Michael's camp. Planting thousands of trees along the boundaries and roadsides helped these improve the most monotonous of sparse, flat landscapes.

'Daaa ....' George jumps from Annie's knee and climbs over the volcanic rocks with his brothers and sisters. Annie follows, cringing at George's sometimes unsure footing. They run through the dense salt bush, mud squelching beneath their boots made by their grandfather. Maggie and Bob appear from behind a wooden shelter with three sides covered in sheets of corrugated iron. They'd been chopping and stacking wood.

Food and water were plenty across the Metropolitan Farm, a living off the land as such: fish in Port Phillip Bay and the Werribee River, eels, rabbits and ducks for catching, chickens and their eggs, pigs reared for meat, sometimes sheep too, cows for milking and making cream, butter and cheese, growing fruits and vegetables. Everything is here, even fresh water with water connected to Melbourne's Yan Yean system. It's a life of self-sufficiency.

Au contraire, to be a community isolated from Melbourne and Werribee too, yet connected through the web of sewer pipes leading to channels that meander to this end point here. Their existence relies on our existence, and our existence is dependent on theirs.

'Come, Georgie,' says Michael. 'Let's check the wood pile before we get Betsy in for milking.' George bounds ahead of his father, Maggie and Bob chase after him.

It's not long before Harry comes by with the twins. 'Come on, Georgie,' he calls. 'We'll go get Betsy and Jasy from the paddock.' Harry holds out his hand for George to take hold and together with the twins, they cross the gravel road into the next paddock. Tom and Ted bound ahead after the jersey cows, occasionally stopping startled by a rabbit darting from a bush.

'Come on, Jasy,' calls Ted. Jasy begins mooching towards the road.

'Your turn, Betsy,' calls Tom, shooing her from behind. Betsy prefers to keep eating the succulent grass nourished by sewage. Tom smacks Betsy's rear, giggling and jumping back out of her way. Betsy begins a lackadaisical plod.

Ted and Tom skip and prance around the cows, scatting them to a hurry.

George's attempts to imitate his brothers are gorgeous, shooing Betsy with light taps to her rump. Little DD is as always, dancing whirly-girly with the babies above. Such innocence.

They cross the paddock and reach a track that leads into a wooden-slatted sty Michael and Harry built for milking. Maggie is sitting on a small wooden stool in the corner under a length of canvas stretched above her, waiting with a wooden bucket between her knees.

'Eilly,' calls Annie from outside the tent flap, where she's washing two rabbits Michael had caught and skinned in a bowl. 'Come help with tea, please. I need you to chop onions and carrots for the stew.' Nellie is beside Annie, scraping her thumb nail over a potato to peel the skin from it, a long nail she's groomed just for this task.

'Yes Ma.'

Annie gouges the last of the guts from the rabbit's cavity with a spoon. The handle catches under her wide wedding band. She stops for a moment, rubs at the rose gold that rings her finger. She glances up, searching for something in the invisible.

That razz is at it again, from under the precious adornment of the eternal rose of gold band I wear.

It wrenches inside of me, churns as sour milk.

It comes in a sincerity of cherish and baffle mixed as one.

I double over, gasp. Breathe ... it will pass.

It gets me anywhere, anytime. And without warning. In bed at night, at my desk at work. But mostly, it gets me when I'm on the phone to my sister.

Why this ring, why the rose of gold wedding band. Always precious, always lingering in the sensitive and earnest from a time of once Was.

THE BABIES PRANCE AND pirouette as cheeky elves backflipping and somersaulting in a field of white candy canes and pink marshmallows.

'Ma,' says Eilly. 'What are you looking at up there?'

'I'm not sure, Eilly. Sometimes, it's like something's here, around me. But I can't see anything. And it's always above me.' Annie fidgets with her wedding band, rabbit guts sliming over its rose hue blush. 'It's like I'm somewhere else, but I'm not ... I don't know. It doesn't matter. Where are those chopped vegies?' Annie continues spooning out the rabbits and chopping them into portions, then tossing them with the carrots, onions and potatoes into the deep copper lobster pot her mother and father had given her and Michael as a wedding gift. How I wish to lap at the juices beginning to simmer in the pot over the fire. Rabbit stew was one of Walter's favourites and I would prepare it for him weekly.

Dear Daughter dances with the babies, laughing when they and the Hickey children below them laugh, frowning when Nellie whines at the potato and carrot peel building under her nail. Annie rubs and kisses Nellie's thumb. Dear Daughter's right: Annie's marvellous. She has such love for her children. She's the kind of mother I longed to be to children with dearest Walter. We would've nurtured a wonderful family.

Muma, watch me be a prima ballerina, like Anna Pavlova.

How resplendent, my little DD, as a romantic ballerina of old. And as distinct as Miss Pavlova in her own style of bent knees and misplaced port de bras. In my little DD's case, a style without arms to move from one position to the next.

It's a scene divine, one that would be the extreme in summer with flies lining tent walls in a film of black and gather as a sheath on sudsy water in the wash tub. Sweltering in 103 Fahrenheit in the shade could only mean a cooling dip in the sea under a stark summer sun, or perhaps in the darkness of a waning moon with only a fire on the beach for light.

The next generation of Annie and Michael will ride seven miles on horseback or cycle with a dog running alongside to the top-end town pool. All the Hickey boys but Charlie will work as watermen, little Georgie too. Charlie will become a stockman; Eilly will marry Tom Hallinan, another stockman, and Nellie will marry Eric Forder, to live on the Metropolitan Farm. The twins will marry; Tom to Annie Bensted. A daughter will be born out of wedlock and will be a secret well kept. Nellie and Eric will take in Eric's brother, Frank, who will never marry and work as a waterman before going to the war to come. He'll get shot, return to Melbourne town to recover and go back to the front line, only to be injured again and return in a poor mental state. He'll live in his railway carriage by the Werribee River for a struggling life. Until eventually moving to live with Nellie and Eric and their family near the Ranch on the Metropolitan Farm, until his retirement age. The things I comprehend on this side of the divide.

The winter warmth that comes from a southern hemisphere sun is finally turning on its toast. How I wish to bask in her thaw, have her radiate into my bosom. Winter here is different to anywhere else, different to the Irish winters of bleak and fog tainted in the smog of smoking chimneys that permeates your pores until it dwells in your swallow. The peace, even with a string of mooing content and birds in carefree merry ... it's quite a place to be, a most wondrous playground. The swimming and fishing, freedom to be with eyes of care everywhere. Guarding. Guiding.

The tide's rolling in. Annie and Michael understand those tides, how far they come up and down, where to pitch their camp to be clear of the occasional king tide.

This space of breath is undeniable, an expanse of clarity that exposes the minutest of fractured flaw for all its naked truth. Pristine beauty of perfect imperfection, sharpened to a splendour awashed in a sweeping rain, pulsating through salt bush veins.

Sea birds call on a belly plump, crested cockatoos stream between disrobed trees.

Waders steal over mudflats to a harmonic tide, serenity in the streaming.

Pearling senses gilded in gold, a rose of gold.

The bottom-end township

Losewitz family on the sewerage farm foreshore, 1932. Photo courtesy of the Tate (nee Losewitz) family.

WHAT OF THE 'GREAT future of this city by the sea'? Such high hopes were held with the jetty built in 1897. A quarter mile long, it allowed for 12 feet of water at low tide. If only the Board took note to connect rail lines resting idle across the Farm, with the already laid 7000 feet of tramways on the jetty and along sections of the main road running through the Farm to the railway station in

Werribee. It could have been assembled cheaply and made great ease for moving produce.

Mr Thwaites recommended the jetty works, Muma, but didn't think it through very well. He's off his kadoova!

Oh Dear Daughter, you are a funny one. He may be off his kadoova, as Mr Pengelly would say, but please mind your manners,

SEWAGE FARM A FAILURE.

The Leader. Saturday 02 December 1899

"The Sewage Farm a Failure!"

"Surely not," will no doubt be the response of many who, whatever the blunders of the board in other directions, have always looked upon the sewage farm as something to be depended upon as a solid asset.

Still, the present writer, as the result of a careful personal inspection of the farm, repeats that the farm, for the purpose for which it was originally established, is not only an absolute failure, but has been such for the past three years. The Metropolitan Board of Works insists upon following the impracticable course of managing all the affairs of this property, down to the smallest details, from Melbourne. A resident manager has been appointed, but he is such only in name. He is in the unenviable position of being required to carry out instructions from Melbourne, and in the event of these instructions resulting in expensive blunders, he is accorded the privilege of taking the blame.

Therefore, as the farm was a failure three years ago, and in each succeeding year since then has only been magnifying that failure, the obvious inference is that either the members of the board did not know of the failure, thereby exposing their incompetency, or otherwise that they did, and have kept it quiet.

even if the Engineer-in-Chief is behind another debacle! Members of the Board expressed much disapproval and considered the jetty works unjustifiable. And yet the king of twit-twats pushed it through. Au contraire, Chairman of the Board, Mr Fitzgibbon, could also vie for the title, with his prediction of ocean liners patronising the jetty and conveying produce to the world's ports. His head must be buried in the same snuff box as young Mr Thwaites! The Board spent more than £4000 of our rate paying money and now, the jetty's deserted in not quite 10 years after its construction, eloquent in its silence apart from fisherman flinging their catch from the sea. Dreams to supply Melbourne with produce by water from Werribee settlers, and the Board to earn revenue from carrying such produce, are positively dashed.

But I must concede and give the pompous twit-twats a miniscule of credit, Dear Daughter. Pastures of green stretch as far as one can behold and the drought which proves so disastrous to many, has been a boon to the Board. It has profited from selling sheep fattened on lush pastures at market, profits that have covered somewhat half of the Farm's operating costs. Let's hope the twit-twats don't squander that success and disgrace the entrepreneurship of the Farm's first few years of sheep husbandry.

Remember when I danced over the Chairman, Muma, when he and members of the Board brought a party to show off the Farm?

Of course, little DD, how could I forget! You're always whirly-girling and we giggled to tears. That was the year my Walter remarried that fine young lady from debate club. 1903. My heart both broke at Walter with another, and sang for joy that he was happy again.

Annie's babies were with me, Muma, because the jetty was near Annie and Michael's camp. The men came on the Harbor Trust steamer, *Osprey,* and I dived over the Chairman to woosh his hat off his head. He tried to catch it, like he was diving to catch a cricket ball hit at slip, and nearly bowled the man with the very long beard into the water!

I laughed and laughed, Little DD. They came to spruik their success, which nearly turned poorly! They were right to celebrate the Farm's achievement, after what had been accomplished to clean our fair city of the south. Within a few years of the Farm's beginning, they'd steam ploughed and graded more than 2300 acres of paddocks for sewage irrigation and the intense cultivation of lucerne and prairie grass using teams of four draught horses. They toiled in the rigour of a Bilby on constant burrowing! They fed, watered and cleaned stables of horses, erected a mammoth 109 miles of fencing and laid 540 chains of concrete for carrying sewage, 1054 chains of road and 6213 chains of water pipes to supply this vast land with drinking water. It exhausts me just to say so, Dear Daughter! Work harrowed on, with more than 135,000 trees planted in plantations to beautify land devoid of stick and stone. Naturally, the number of men working here increased, but the Board couldn't keep up building cottages and only 45 were available by these early 1900s to the hundreds of men working at the Farm. Many men had to leave their families in Werribee to bunk in shared quarters and live in camps as small shanties on the Farm.

Some more twit-twats are by the jetty now, Muma. And others are going off their kadoovas in the paddocks.

'ONE. TWO.' NELLIE HOPS over moonstones of jelly fish paced out on their flat underbellies on the sand. Remnant waves ripple in to a reef of cone, conch and pipi shells, tousling them in the flounce of a soft tease. Rounded and dimpled sea urchin spheres dot seaweed of cherry, rust and maroon basking in clumps, some trimmed in translucent green straggles and ruffles. Jelly fish smattering the foreshore are part of the brine and decay, as well as sometimes speckled eggs nesting in large, upturned Mud Ark shells.

'Good girl, Nellie, now hop, hop,' calls Eilly. 'And double jump to the next two jelly fishes.'

Muma, watch me hop, hop like Nellie. Jump, hop, jump; pick up the shell and back again.

Dear Daughter, such mirth in you. In a mane most golden, you are a beauty.

Muma, there's nothing pretty of me. My body of odd banana ill-form, lacquered in a purple tint of shellac, and my tiny hands ... your hand is bigger than all of me!

Little DD, you are beauty in a girl full of heart, even when no heart beats. One not only orphaned, but who has endured a swirling through gurgling, gaseous pipes, to flow into an open channel and arrive here at the Farm. Only to then be flung onto a paddock of swamping sewage as the foetus lost by your poor mother in her death, and searching for a mother since. It's unimaginable, my dear little DD. But I'm your mother now. No more searching. And never forget that I will look after you for all eternity. Come near, my dear.

I stayed in this place of in-between to be near to my Walter. And yet now, in my heart of no hearts I cannot leave. Not when Little DD is here and needs me, not when she has searched high and low for a mother and the chance to be loved, only to find me. That's an honour I hold in respectful gratitude.

'Don't stand on the slippery suckers,' calls Charlie.

Nellie jumps to splayed legs, one foot within half an inch of the curling tentacles beneath the dome of jelly fish. 'Eww,' she squeals.

'Don't move, Nellie. You don't want to fall on that fat jelly finger behind your foot.' Charlie laughs out loud.

'Eww ... stop teasing!' Nellie hops high over the next smooth curve of wobble and tentacle; jelly fish number five. 'It's see-through. I can see shells under it.'

'Come on, Nellie, two more and then pick up the oyster shell.'

Nellie jumps over number six and seven jelly fish. 'Ow, something's bit me. Ouch, ouch, ouch ....' Nellie hunches over in windblown hair straggling into her mouth. 'A shell,' she says, as she eases a broken grey-blue mussel shell from her heel.

'You okay, Nell?'

Muma, Muma, Nellie's only got one more to go! Come on Nellie.

Swirling, twirling tail-end girling, round and round Nellie ... one more to go. Hop, hop, hop ....

'Yeah.' Nellie balances to hop to the last lucent jelly and in bended knee, collects the oyster shell. She hops an about face; then jump; hop, jump, hop, hop back to the start.

'Yay, Nellie-fish, you did it!' Eilly takes Nellie by the hands and spins her until her feet lift off the ground, twirls into baby waves itching to grow bigger. Water splashes her skirt.

I'm whizzing like Nellie, Muma, round and round ....

'Fly me into the water!' squeals Nellie.

'You're flying like a sting ray jumping out the water,' laughs Charlie.

'My turn, my turn,' calls George, splashing at the water's edge.

'Faster,' sings Nellie. 'Spin me into the fairy birds and their spotty eggs.'

'Fairy Terns, you silly-bill,' calls Charlie, laughing into choral bird calls.

'Come away from that jetty!' shrieks Annie from the paddock edging the foreshore. Crested cockatoos flee in screeching fright. 'Eilly, Nellie, Charlie and George. Get back here! Now!' yells Annie, her arms waving in the will of a Fowler 4387 steam engine penetrating compacted dirt for new land filtration paddocks.

Eilly winds down her spin.

'No, don't stop,' complains Nellie.

'We'll come back later,' says Eilly. 'Ma wants us back. And she's not happy.'

Dear Daughter and I follow the children climbing over three-tiered slabs of rugged and ridged warming iron-blue rocks. Back onto the paddock we glide and weave with the fairy terns shimmering in greys and white, gliding alongside them in the breeze of weightless flight.

'In, and stay here,' grumbles Annie. 'Such impropriety is not fit for anyone, let alone children.' Annie shuffles the children inside the canvas home. 'Where's Maggie?'

'Over near the ....'

'Where?' asks Annie. 'Where is she?'

'What is it, Ma?' asks Charlie.

'Such moronic behaviour, and poor Jasy having to contend with it!' Annie shakes her head. 'Where's Maggie?' she demands.

'She's near the jetty with ...' says George.

'George!' snaps Eilly.

'Always my dear boy, Georgie.' Annie dashes out the tent, wiping her hands in her apron dusted in flour and speckled in dough. She'd been rolling shortcrust pastry to bake rabbit pie for tea, and a few apple pies, one of which will go to George. Agnes had given her a cotton sack full of Granny Smith apples yesterday. She bulldozes a path through the paddock of knee-high grass in the charge of a bull at a bright red gate, until reaching the salt bush. 'Mags, where are you?' she calls, as she climbs over slippery rocks awash in tidal seaweed. 'Maggie! I want you home.' She strides onto the foreshore and marches over the shell grit in the crunch of a million empty eggs blistering beneath her boots. She reaches a small wooden shed by the jetty. Squeals and giggles come from behind it.

What's Maggie doing, Muma?

'Oh, Maggie ...' comes a deep voice, and a bang on the side of the shed.

Maggie moans in the lust of intense desire.

What's wrong with Maggie, Muma? Someone's smacking her.

Oh my, Dear Daughter. Stay back. I'm afraid Maggie's squeals may be canoodling shenanigans not fit for your eyes.

'Harder. Oh, Mother Mary ....' Cormorants in elongated necks swoon out to sea.

Quick Annie, go help Maggie.

'I'll give you hard!' yells Annie as she approaches the shed. 'Maggie! Dear God, get that skirt down!'

'Ma!' Maggie forces the man from her and shoots her skirt down over her legs. 'What're you doing here?' Maggie scrambles for her bloomers hanging on a board jutting from the wooden wall behind her. 'Go, go,' she whispers to the man pulling up his strides.

'Shame on you, all that squealing. And with the potty immaturity on the other side of the jetty!'

'What Ma?' Maggie shoos the man. He scrams behind the shed along the foreshore, buckling his belt with one shoe tucked under his chin. A flock of Pink-eared ducks ejaculate in flight. 'We were havin' some fun. Nothing wrong with that!'

'Get home, Mags. Away from the disgusting inebriated.' Annie waves her arms at the jetty and the drunkards swaying on their last leg. 'What they did to poor Jasy. And they wanted a licenced hotel down here! Bloody scoundrels. They could've done anything to you and that young man. You'll be kneeling by your Pa at Rosary tonight.'

Maggie scuttles home with Annie marching on her tail.

'Now you get home and check on the pies baking. I need to see Agnes.' Annie cuts across the paddock to Agnes leaning on a fence by the road. The children linger outside their tent, laughing at the spectacle of police supervision at the jetty, chaperoned by pink-glazed dusk skies tinged in apricot.

The bay of our grand Dame city, Melbourne town, gleams in the sparkle of tourmaline under a sun radiating this late Sunday afternoon. She's unruffled by the commotion before her, as are the red-capped dotterels feeding on a bounty of succulent morsels lacing the seaweed and within the mudflats by the sluice gate and sand spits. It's a stark contrast to the hubbub of drunken men behaving as sullied boys around the jetty, having arrived on the steamer *Derwent,* from Melbourne earlier that afternoon.

'They're a party of choice!' says Agnes.

'Despicable,' says Annie.

'Gotta've been on the hard turps today,' laughs Frank, having wandered over from the stables.

Raucous laughter erupts from a tenant farmer's yard.

'They come ashore and at once, proceed to make things glum,' says Annie. 'Damn fools, riding Jack's horses. He had 'em tied to the fence for feeding and watering. He'll be far from happy when he comes in from the paddocks.'

'We better go break up the drunken bums, or they'll run amuck in Jack's yard,' says Frank.

'Drongos've got too much to resist. They got a scratch race going,' says Agnes.

'Bloody ninnyhammers, look at 'em falling off the horses!' laughs Frank. 'Fallin' all over the bloody place. They'll be sore tomorrow.'

Michael and George approach, having finished their shifts.

'Afternoon ladies and gent,' says George, wiping blood trickling from a cut on his hand after laying water mains pipes all day. 'A welcome spectacle we have here.'

'They're gonna come to blows,' says Frank. 'The old bloke wants ta fist-a-cuff his mate, after falling off the horse and onto him!'

'They'll be in our prayers tonight, Annie,' says Michael. 'Aye, they'll need forgivin'.'

'Especially the swaggie that got excited before and tried to ride our poor Jasy,' scowls Annie. She leans into Michael. 'Not to mention a young miss up to mischief.'

'You should 've seen the foolish man, Michael,' says Agnes. 'Poor Jasy, quietly grazing in the paddock, until a drunkard charged in and proceeded to draw her milk into his mouth. He couldn't kneel for all his swaying and draws not more than an ounce of milk from her.'

'Then,' says Annie. 'Then, he gets on her back for a bit of buckjumping! Good god! Good old Jasy threw him off quick smart, probably most offended by his pungent breath.'

'And then,' laughs Agnes. 'Annie chases him with the dunny shovel! He went charging up the jetty faster than a rabbit being chased by your swiftest ferret, George. And expressing himself in a most choice language! Only to then teeter on the jetty edge and the bugger falls in!' Agnes laughs into her cupped hands. 'Hys-terical.' Tears spritz from her eyes.

'He bloody well deserved it too,' chuckles Annie.

'Abominable!' Michael shares half a smile.

'Looks like the police are finally managing some order at the jetty.'

'That order aint working in the paddocks.' Frank lifts his hat and points to Jack's paddock. He wipes the grime from his forehead with his shirt sleeve. Men are scrambling for ploughs and rakes, broken jinker wheels, bridles and anything hanging from posts and collecting in corners in Jack's shed, to pile them in sloshing swagger into the centre of an adjacent paddock flushed in fresh sewage.

'We need to go and stop them,' says George.

'Why? Let the scoundrels play in the watered paddock,' chuckles Frank. 'A paddock of higgidy-hock. With bloody unhooked draught horses scoffing into chaff and lucerne scattered all over the place, bloody scoops tipped on their sides ....'

'Here come the coppers. Coppers in crap!' laughs George.

The steamer blows its whistle, signalling its imminent departure back to Melbourne. Sharp-tailed sandpipers flee from their perches on the end of the jetty. Men swarm in crooked stagger back to the steamer as mosquitoes blinded in a heady high of intoxicated blood.

'Get me outta this god-for-saken place,' calls one man, jostling in the swarm to the jetty.

'Get outta me way,' slurs another, knocking a man onto the rocks. Blood pools quickly in the red graze on his hand.

The men in the watered paddock drop their utensils to murky splashes. One chap brushes at the mottling brown on his pale grey trousers. 'We're standing in shit!' he screeches, in the blood-curdling call of a vixen fox signalling for a breeding mate. He scrubs his mouth in exfoliating vigour at the germs festering.

George and Michael laugh.

'Bloody ninnyhammers!' scoffs Frank.

'Shit. We're in shit!' yells a man.

'We've been standin' in shit!' Another man heaves.

'Ha-ha, he's chunderin' his guts out, onto his shit stained shoes!' laughs Frank.

The men scram from the paddock as though the Farm's hefty bulls are chasing them.

'The jetty's going to fall into disrepute. It'll be the end of the Farm,' says Agnes.

'It's not used so much anyway,' says Annie. 'It's already doomed.'

'We needed the hotel and shops,' says Frank. 'It woulda worked if we had them, no doubt about it.'

'Rubbish! Not with all the objections opposing the hotel. A lot of councils thought it was questionable,' says Agnes.

'Fitzroy Council didn't object.'

'Yes but most others did. And rightfully so. Fancy having a hotel near the jetty, and us!' snaps Annie.

'Haha, look at him. He's missed his step from the steamer and fallen in the water. And he's taken the fella next to him too!'

Such shenanigans, Dear Daughter. The Board's finance committee tabled a report that recommended a licenced hotel be built on the Farm. They've got rabbit pebbles in their brains if you ask me. Fancy selling liquor on the Farm. Councillor Russell from Hawthorn Council may have questioned the Board's power to build it but ultimately, the Board do a lot of things they have no power to do. Commissioner Cowan moved to adopt the finance committee's report because the lease had been sold in accordance with the conditions stipulated. And of course, he wanted the MMBW to pocket the rent at £23 a year. He knew the lessee had submitted plans for a building which could become a hotel. Such a fool, claiming the Board was under no responsibility and in no position to interfere with the proposal. And then Commissioner Dillon seconding the motion! Pompous twit-twats. The gall to blame the finance committee for not informing the Board when it was plainly in the report. Bugger me, men of so called influence and intelligence who cannot read.

Muma, your language!

Oh I know, Dear Daughter. But their display of such indifference shows they are a law unto their own, 'one of the most insolent nominee Boards which ever ruled in a democratic community,' said a reporter in *The Age* last week. Drive the finance committee to drink they will!

At least Commissioner McMahon had sense, Muma, when he spoke up and said it was bad for the Farm and the Board. Because they said maybe 300 to 600 workers would be employed as the settlement progressed.

Of course it would be bad, Dear Daughter. The working hands of the Farm are located in this bottom-end township, on the boundary along the Port Phillip Bay where breath is clean and air flows clear. The village here constitutes some 40 homes. This compares with the ambitious effort to create a central township to the north, amid the extreme tang of sewage flowing in the Main Outfall Sewer onto the Farm's Head of the Road right beside that settlement. Six houses exist there and more are being planned, with places for sport and recreation, botanical gardens, all that a settlement requires, except the population. The village in the central or top-end township does not compare to the promise of fertile lands for growing crops in this bottom-end.

THE BITTER OF SLEETED stone bites in, scatters ants on the rapid approach of a raging storm. The *Summit* turns into the formidable entry. It cruises behind a black hearse, its windows spotless clean. Wheels grumble into the gravel road, moan into a peal of thunder. Until the wheels halt. Dear Annie's inside, drowning in mother's grief.

The hearse stops. The driver lifts out of his seat, his heel clipping the step of the car. He marches in his satin top hat to the centre opening doors at the back, and opens them.

The driver of the *Summit* appears at the back door, his mourning coat rubbing against the gloss black metal. He twists the handle a half turn. Annie stiffens inside, battles to breathe in the automatic of breath. The door opens, and she's swamped in the emotional turbulence that pounded her earlier in St Andrews church.

A leather-gloved hand guides Annie out of the car. The door bangs shut, echoing into the peal of thunder. Annie gasps, swallows the sour of sorrow in a sea of people shuffling in black suits and dresses of straight and no fuss. Polished boots catch glimmers that don't want to be there. Black engulfs Annie, stares of good intentions scream in charged sombre.

Rain drops of a crumpled life. Her Georgie, his place of hearth when only a child he claimed in the cottage that finally came to the family after more than 10 years in their canvas home. That corner by the fire, 'twas his pride of place. Home is where the heart is, Georgie. You knew that, even in a life cut short at only 22.

A slither of an opening in the sea of darkness reveals a heinous rectangle in the ground. Annie's eyes fix to it: her Georgie boy's new home.

Rain drops stream in icicle spears. Hands grip arms, grab hold of Annie. It's Maggie and Michael, Maggie clutching Clare's hand as the blessed gift she is. A black-gloved hand passes Annie a handkerchief embroidered in lavender. She mops her face stained in grief and places the handkerchief in her woollen coat pocket. Her rose of gold scrapes the black pearl lodged in the point of the pocket. She'd picked it from the foreshore years ago, thought it to be a token of lucky riches. Smooth and lustrous it may well be, but it could also be the darkness that has snatched this soul of innocence. It's said that only those whose birthstone is pearl should ever wear the gem. For everyone else, pearls are for tears and bad luck: back into the ocean from whence it came tomorrow.

First Harry, and now Georgie. You have them both, dam you!

Through a guard of honour they walk, to that place of rest. Most from the Farm stand in solemn head as Annie and her clan pass through to that forever hole. Agnes and George stand tight, Anne and Son, and Phoebe and Frank are beside them. Dearest Michael holds her, the children surround her as the guardians of the Earth. Their love is the strength that props her, and the love of those standing stoic in this guard of honour.

Georgie's in front, in his box awaiting on ropes, topped with a spray of white Easter daisies and yellow chrysanthemums. He'll be with Harry soon.

Father Patrick begins. 'We come to our final farewell ....'

Storming surf batters the coffin, screeching calls of curlew sandpipers soar as Georgie boy lowers into the craggy-walled hole lined in rich, brown earth. Hedged boxthorns puncture in totality, sting ray barbs sear a permanent pain. Her Georgie disappears into his swell.

'Fare Well,' she murmurs.

'Come on, Mama' whispers Clare. 'Here's some petals for you and me, so we can say good bye to Georgie.' Clare places white petals in her mother's palm.

'Georgie boy, why is it so, why did you have to leave? It's not fair that a boy so young and pure must go. Why the need to go, dear God, why on his bicycle, a young man full of love and gentle soul? One so kind and caring who lived each day as its best.' The whispers of a mother in grief boom as a million heart beats. Annie releases the handful of petals into the swell. Her rose of gold twirls its own fondle, its warmth stark against the chill of her skin.

Life without you Georgie boy, is unheard of, is as mysterious as all the universes. Solace is that you're in God's grace. In my rose of gold, the holiness of angels are near.

Splintered and splattered, it's thy love and spirit, the tight weave of compassion and solidarity in all from the Farm that beholds me now. Over lifetimes, hearts of pure never empty, are vessels of boundless capacity. My rose of gold tells me so.

Georgie boy, love is full of thee. I will you back, my Georgie. But for your paradise of love and joy, that is your destination now. The angels are near, to poise your soul to peace. Death and love draw them out as fireflies swarming the warmth.

Death and Love. Two most powerful words in human existence.

Death and Love. A continuum that extends and intersects as an eternal endless, through my rose of gold as the immortal love.

Death and Love, bring anguish and ache, where the dread of endless dire and drone of despair can ulcerate and proliferate.

'Let us bow our heads for silent prayer,' says Father Patrick.

'Mr and Mrs Michael Hickey invite you back to the Cocoroc South School for refreshments. On behalf of the family, I thank you for your attendance today.' Father Patrick's words fade into the whim of a new wind blowing in, a rose of gold whistling its tune.

Why now, in this pearling sea of black and solemn? Faces of grey and skies of gloom, why my rose of gold band must razz me now! My skin heats under it, the band handed to me that only she and me ever wore. It spins in the hot and cold of frenetic fever, and yet in a faith that fills me.

My hand in pocket fidgets my Rosary beads. My breath aligns, and yet this rose of gold spins some more.

My knees are weak. I must sit, even if we're meant to be standing in prayer with Father Michael. I grasp the back of the pew facing me, and drop onto the wooden bench.

The precious and lingering now with me, connecting to her from a century ago through the adornment of eternal.

My rose of gold whistles its forever tune.

DEAR DAUGHTER IS OFF in the curious nature that children hold, toward the men dressed in fine suits on the little bridge at the Head of the Road.

Three men lean over the railing edge. Another is beside them wearing white knickerbockers, hunching over a dark camera with two large reels on its left. The camera sits atop a tripod. The man rotates a long lens that focuses on the sewage flowing in the Main Outfall Sewer, across the road from the top-end township. A waterman is beside them, opening the gates of the deep concrete channel. It sends a rush of frothing sewage through to be diverted via smaller channels to different sections of the Farm.

I hope they don't drop the camera in the muck, Muma.

Now that would be a sight, little DD! The wind's blowing, they best hold their equipment tight.

The men film in a paddock nearby, where a team of four Clydesdales are pulling a scoop to level the paddock in preparation for land filtration sewage treatment. Two men dressed in hats and dusty cream work pants and shirts, vests over the top, guide the scoop. In an adjacent paddock, steam engines pull a plough with a man perched on a stool. He spins a big wooden wheel to steer the plough to break through the crust of the dirt, leaving large broken clumps behind it.

Little DD and I glide over the cameramen as they drive out west of the Farm, to film men sitting on stools guiding horses to scoop up cut lucerne. It's piled into a wooden contraption that uses pullies to lift the lucerne onto the biggest stack five or six men high. Little DD wisps through the mounting stack, sometimes ruffling blades of hay to tickle up the noses of men forking the lucerne on top.

Filming moves to more men in hats that this time wear riding jodhpurs to parade almighty cattle, some of the finest steers and heifers in the country, and men rounding up unbridled horses by the stables. At the 1928 Royal Melbourne Show, the champion bulls in Hereford, Shorthorn and Aberdeen Angus breeds come from the Farm. Its reputation as a breeder of champion bulls soars and it generates much positive publicity. Farm employees are proud as punch of their success. Good golly to them!

This was the 1920s, the decade of building big for the Farm and the Board of Works, who are constructing the Maroondah, O'Shannassy and Silvan dams to hold Melbourne's water. In Parliament, the Government confirms and defines the Board's role in drainage by establishing the *Metropolitan Drainage and Rivers Act.* The Board also purchases land at Mordialloc for a future eastern treatment plant. Finally, noses are clear of snuff boxes to realise Mr Mansergh's plan for the two treatment systems. Alajuela!

The Farm goes from strength to strength, increasing in land size. By 1929, the Board had purchased almost 8000 acres of land west of Little River, boosting its land titles to over 21,300 acres and pushing the Farm's boundary closer to Geelong. Managers are experimenting with grass filtration to help treat sewage in winter and the Engineer of Sewerage travels to Adelaide to review septic tanks, believed to be the radical revolution to the pan system. Mr E.F. Borrie will be appointed Engineer of Sewerage in years to come and in honour of his work on the Farm, the first lagoon to treat sewage will be named after him: Lake Borrie.

With this expansion came the development of services that any growing community required. Since 1897, when the Metropolitan Farm cricket team was established, sporting facilities have developed in the top-end township. A rifle club came into being, as did the Metropolitan Farm football team in 1912, followed by croquet and tennis teams in 1913. The sports pavilion and oval, croquet lawns and tennis courts with club house were all established, as was the Mechanics Institute in 1903. It was later burnt down in 1924 to be rebuilt a few years later as a community hall and library for residents and workers to borrow books. All this in the now thriving top-end township.

The four men filming have parked their black Ford Model T cars beside the hall and the Cocoroc North School, cars assembled from complete knock down kits provided by Ford Canada, at the Ford Motor Company in Geelong. They've already filmed a group of older girls in pinafores and white shirts and boys in shorts, shirts and ties, exercising up and out arm movements in the school ground. Younger children are playing Ring-a-Ring-a-Rosie. As you can imagine, little DD shoots over to dance with them as soon as she sees them. It's as if her veins are dancing, if she ever had veins. I don't have the heart to tell her the real meaning of the rhyme, said to be about the Great Plague in London in the 1600s. The apparent whimsy of the rhyme is a guise for fatalism: the roses being a euphemism for the deadly rashes that came with the plague, the posies suggest a supposed preventative measure, and the a-tishoos relate to the sneezing symptoms. The fact that everyone falls down at the end of the rhyme is supposedly suggesting, well, death. Here she comes, zooming in her girly-whirling.

Muma, here comes Edna, skipping the mile from home along the dusty road, holding her cloche from blowing from her head. She's wearing her shiny black shoes and black cotton stockings. I long to wear those, even though I'm naturally shiny in my young skin of purple. But I'm not pretty, of no comparison to Edna in her green dress trimmed in maroon belt at the hip.

Little DD, your beauty is beyond the material.

You say that because you love me, Muma. Edna looks so fine. How pretty is the matching bow falling loosely around her sailor collar. The sailor neck tie they call it. Every girl wants one, Muma.

Women too, DD, every woman wants one. It frees them to move easily between working in the home and garden to going out, running errands and meeting friends. Its broad opening makes it easy to slip a dress overhead without undoing buttons or hooks. It goes with anything casual in the 1920s and was borrowed from men's sailing uniforms.

A DAY AT THE MELBOURNE AND METROPOLITAN BOARD OF WORKS FARM WERRIBEE

Film produced by Herschells Pty Ltd, 1920s

At this establishment, the sewage of MELBOURNE and SUBURBS is purified by soil filtration. After being pumped from 50 feet below the surface to 75 feet above sea level, the outfall channel carries the sewage to the farm at Werribee.

Distributing sewer channels to various parts of the farm.

Modern implements are employed in forming the channels. A pair of engines, placed about 500 yards apart, draw a two-headed, five furrow plough by steel wire cable.

Lucerne is grown in large quantities.

The sewage of Melbourne is disposed of on the Melbourne and Metropolitan Board of Works Farm. 38 million gallons per day are delivered onto the paddocks.

Shorthorn and Hereford cattle are raised on the paddocks.

Altogether there are about 6,000 head of cattle on the Farm.

There are 160 people employed on the Farm, and 65 homes are scattered amongst the beautiful plantations of gums and pines.

There are 7,000 acres under sewage irrigation. Notwithstanding this, the Farm is very healthy.

Three schools are provided for the children, who are a particularly bright and happy lot.

Sheep fattening is also carried on – 1,000 Comeback Wethers. Maize does well at the Farm.

Commissioner A.G Campbell J.P., Vice Chairman of the Farm Committee and Ex Commissioner E. Naylor J.P.

The great area of country controlled by the Board acts as a purifier, and after the sewage has irrigated the land, it filters through the earth and comes into the channels in the form of clear water, which discharges into Port Phillip Bay.

The end.

Edna's skipping by the iron water tank. I want to skip with her, Muma.

And just like that, little DD's gone again. They're filming from the top of the water tank now, across the rooftops of the twenty or so homes and the manicured gardens at the foot of the water tank.

OL' MELBOURNE TOWN WAS in a sorry state followin' the 1890s economic crash, and now we've bloody been hit hard again. In the 1930s, we got the Wall Street stock market crash hittin' round the world. The Board's gotta cut its works and men by half 'cause they say we're in a Great Depression. And then, bugger me dead, the decade ends with Germany invading Poland, triggerin' World War II and sendin' our home country to fight with Britain in the war against Germany. Fuck-en hell. So much for the war to end all wars from a few years back.

Not only the world's gone bonkers, but our weather has too and is causing devastation everywhere. Skies burn smoky red and our gardens wither 'cause water's restricted when fires raze the forests in Victoria. Call them our Black Friday bushfires they do. They don't bother me much, not when I'm livin' in me railways carriage on the foreshore. Gets a bit windy and wet when the big storms come in and lash Port Phillip Bay but bloody them in Melbourne, they get flooded out.

Disaster of another kind strikes us at the Farm, with beef measles discovered in the Farm's cattle. Bloody hell, that's all we need. It causes more financial strain 'cause the bloody Country-Labour Party coalition, bloody mongrels they are, passes legislation banning all beef sales from the Farm. Scientific reports find there's no outbreak of beef measles and that there's only a small risk to public health. They say good inspections will manage it. Bloody bastards don't listen though, and the ban stays. It's rural politics and graziers lobbying gone mad.

The Board of Works Chairman David Bell, he retires. Poor bloody bugger got sick, and so John Jessop is elected Chairman. He's a bloody gem that young bloke. He changes a few things and adopts a frank policy with the public, encouraging us to send proposals for improving services to the community. He's a bloody ripper. He develops positive relations with councils, the government and newspapers, and praises the workers. He says us public are the masters of the situation and the workers are the servants. People love 'im! A bit of faith in the Board creeps in for the first bloody time ever. Fairdinkum.

These blokes here on the beach are doin' somethin'. A dozen or so stand in a line, poking long wooden stakes into the sand before stepping forward to poke again. Oi, what're you blokes up to? They don't answer me, bloody ignorant bastards, don't even look my way and keep prodding into salt bushes, all cleansed after the storm that raged across the Farm and Werribee last night. It blew sheaves in all direction and over-turned stooks in paddocks. Hail stones battered hay, tree limbs snapped from the Farm's earliest planted eucalypts and pine trees and Cocoroc South School a few chains away, had its bloody roof ripped off. Me hut nearly had a new home in the bay too. Gawe, bloody lucky. Men across the Farm have skipped Sundee Mass in the top-end township and have been re-laying sheets of tin on the school's roof since dawn. Others are in the classroom mopping up. Rain's soaked the floorboards and pooled as puddles in desks. All the kids' drawin's and paintin's, posters of maths, they've all fallen from the walls and clump as water-logged pulp.

These few ol' blokes down here are the only few not repairin' the school. Two of 'em are prying a boulder up by the foreshore to explore behind it. Other men are jabbin' into dense coastal scrub and grassy plains, some over small sand dunes. They get to Tommy Danaher's fishing hut. Tommy comes from Williamstown and lives in the hut by the 55 East main drain. He leaves his bloody fish bait out sometimes, forgets to put it away after he necks a few. The stench mixes with engine fumes from his 26-foot wooden fishing boat and percolate as some kind of pungent fusion of peppery, rottin' aspic of pigs ears and tongues. Bloody rips me guts out. Three kitty cats are sittin' on Tommy's porch, two chooks are basking in a dirt hole in the sun. Confident in their living arrangement, the bludgers would swipe any fish sandwich Tommy would make for lunch. He keeps a whip on the windowsill by his table and when they break such etiquette, Tommy lashes the offending animal out the door with violent curses. They don't care and follow Tommy right back inside as soon as his head's turned.

These blokes, they're poking through Tommy's fishing nets hangin' from a rope he's strung between two posts by the boat. They're in and around his white bath coated in sand and by the bricked copper. One man pokes into the dirt beside the tank of water, tappin' the railin' round his precious mound. Gawe, he's in for it now.

Tommy darts out from his hut. 'What're you blokes up to? Leave me bloody little bloke quiet in 'is grave.' Tommy scratches into his dishevelled hair before reaching for his obligatory morning bottle from the crate of beer by the door. 'Leave a man an' his dog to some peace, will ya. It is a Sundee mornin'.' He knocks the top off the bottle with a bang over a wooden peg jutting from the door frame, and he gulps from the bottle.

'Sorry, Tommy, didn't realise yer old dog was laying there.'

'Yeah, well, he is. So leave 'im alone. What're you blokes doin' 'ere anyway.' Tommy takes another swig of beer. 'I'm busy. Gotta get me fish ready for young Eileen Forder. She's comin' to get some of me catch. And she'll be bringin' me a piece of that best apple pie off 'er old granny, Annie.'

'Joe's missin',' mumbles one of the men through glum lips. 'No one's seen him, Tommy.'

'What'd-ya mean, missin'?' Tommy straightens in the door way to grow his small stature by two inches. 'Joe'll be sleepin' still, from fishin' last night.'

'Na, mate.'

Yeah, because I'm here. You aint gonna find me anywhere but here, no sir-ee. Oi, I'm here.

'What'd ya mean, na mate. He told me yesterdee he was goin' night fishin' with Billy. Flounderin'.' Tommy starts pacing in and out of the doorway.

'He didn't front for fishin'. Billy went lookin' for him at his hut and couldn't find him.'

Yep. They're lookin' for me alright. Popular me. Everybody wants me, likes a chin-wag with good ol' me. And a drink or three. I'm here you blokes. Joe Calis here. Fisherman and good all round bloke. Why aren't they answerin' me? And what are yous two doin' here by the salt bush, dressed in yer finery?

You can see us?

Yeah, course I can bloody see ya. What do you think I am, blind? What're you starin' at?

Nothing, sir. I'm Mrs Copley. This is Dear Daughter.

You're all bearded grey and have messed up hair. You're a bit scary, and look like a mountain goat. If I could smell, I bet you'd reek of someone that's been drinking beer and whiskey morning, noon and night.

Dear Daughter, curb your tongue please!

Leave her go, Mrs Copley. She's not even a kid. Look at 'er, all shiny and primed as a black current boiled lolly. Look at 'er, spinnin' into a willying wind and flyin' away like a spoilt, I dunno, sulkin' embryo.

Dear Daughter, come back! Mr Calis, what have you done. Her ill form is not of her doing. Where is your heart to be so unkind to such an unfortunate soul? I must go after her!

She started it, bloody beggar's kid. Anyway, how'd you know me name, Mrs Copley? And who are those blokes really lookin' for?

You, Mr Calis.

Course they're lookin' for me, everyone loves me. Oi you blokes, I'm here. You aint gonna find me there, no sir-ee you blokes. Oi! I'm here. They're not listenin', Mrs Copley.

Why the search for you, Mr Calis? And more importantly, why are you here with me, why is that?

I don't know, Mrs Copley. Why can't they hear me?

Because you're here with me, Mr Calis.

I bet you got a lovely smile, Els. Come on, Els. Give us a bit of a smile. I can see one creepin' in, might have to tickle yer under yer chin to bring it out. And call me Joe, Els.

My name is Mrs Walter Copley, not Els! And your tickle I'll surely not feel, Mr Calis. Joe. Your tickling delight is nothing more than nothing.

Come on, Els, come here. Let me tickle you, get me a smile up.

I am here, Joe. Beside you.

Come closer, Els.

I am close, Joe. But your touch is nothing. No time, no space. Simply nothing. It must be nothing for you too, Joe.

But Els, why can't I tickle ya?

Oh dear, you poor man. Do you not understand how you know my name to be Elsie when I've not introduced myself as such?

I dunno, Els.

Joe, I'm sorry to have to tell you, but you're dead, Joe.

What'd ya mean, dead, woman? What's goin' on? All I remember is yesterday afternoon, toasting whiskey with Billy after I'd won a fiver at the Werribee races. That's me weekly earnin's, Els! And they got them new totalisators now, makes bettin' shit easy. Pardon me, Els, excuse me language. But they got them at all the tracks and it makes bettin' easy. Then the next minute, I'm here. With you.

Well, I'm not sure what else to say, dear man, but you're dead. D. E. A. D.

So, I'm here with you, which means I'm gone from there? And so ... so you're a ghost? No. Can't be bloody right.

Oh dear man. Joe, come back.

Head spins, sand and water lash ... no, not dead. Not possible. Leaves strip from salt bushes, whip higher and higher into a biting binge, until they blow into a blighting tail of ... blah! Disconnecting, deconstructing, fragmenting. Defragmenting. Dissipatin' into ... blah!

Stop, Joe! Stop your sardonic willy willying. Bring yourself together, dear man.

But they can't hear me, Els, can't see me!! I'm nowhere. And everywhere. Not sure where the fuck I am!

It's okay, Joe. They'll find you, dear man, but not as your human self. I'm sorry, it will be your skeleton in years to come that they will find. They're not searching in the right place now. They've got to go out to your railway carriage hut at Beacon Point, by the succulent samphire scrub. They'll find you there, Joe.

Shit, me bones. They'll find me bones! Sorry, Els, sorry for me swearin'. And me shell grit, bags of it! What's gonna happen to it now if I'm gone? Tom'll be waiting for it, to take it to the glass works at Spottiswood. Oi, Billy! Go take me bags to the skipper of the old *Helen Moore.* He's not listening, Els. Oi, Billy! Bloody listen to me!

Joe, take hold of yourself, I need to find Dear Daughter.

Els, don't go! Don't leave me. Dunno what to do.

Okay, Joe. You stay here and I'll move these men on.

She's bloody gone in the blink of me eye, if it's still blinkin' now I'm dead, diving over them clowns to shoo them away. They head for me railway carriage. Billy's flickin' her! He might strike her! Els, come back, before he gets yer! No woman's ever done anythin' like that for me before. Shit fuck. They're going through me stuff, me ice chest and beer, and me beef I was savin' for tomorra's tea. Me fuel for me boat. Oi, don't you be takin' me fuel, Frankie!

I REALLY AM GONE. I had the best life, even if sometimes lonely. People chancin' by me remote beach, either from the road once they got through the scrub that hid me hut, or they'd boat in at the front, moor their vessel and come up and have a beer with me. I appreciated any company. Why else would I have Bluey, me cats and chooks.

I never found the right woman, able to tame me. Not until now! Nah, back then, chance visitors were me only company. I had a load to tell 'em once I got going, concerning the tides and bay, the always full moon at Easter. Sometimes at night, a black man'd be flitterin' in the Milky Way. I told Tommy once. He said I were nuts, spent too much time on me own. I could never get a good picture of the man, he'd never let me. But I knew him were there. The flitterin' gave it away. Sometimes, the air would go from warm to cold to warm in seconds, or I'd catch the shadow of a spear gliding by when I'd sit on the front porch, mesmerised by the sea. Gawe, that were special. Moon beams on a full moon night would bounce off tides comin' and goin', and the spear would glisten as its own shootin' star. Sometimes if I'd gone flounderin' by the jetty, the eels'd light up in shades of blue and one time, I coulda sworn one of ‘em jumped out of the water and twirled right in front of me. Fuck oath! It hovered for a bit before divin’ back into the water. I flashed me light around but there were nothin’ there. I told Billy that one. He told me to leave the grog alone for a week, to dry out. Fuck not, I said to ‘im.

Now that jetty were a place, and Loosey’s paddock. Old Losewitz and his family lived in the paddock by the jetty and Old Losewitz had the job of looking after the jetty and foreshore. He were the ranger. There he is now, old Carl going out to light the jetty. They call him Chaz though, not Carl. Each day on the brink of twilight, he brings his burning tilly lamp out to light the two lanterns on the jetty. If it’s stormin’ and visibility’s poor, the squeak coming from the sway of the tilly lamp with each of Loosey’s steps tells ya he’s on the job.

There he goes, reaches the first lamp on a pole braced to the jetty railing. He unscrews the lid to open its tank, and tops it up with kerosene. He pumps the tank a few times, to get the kero flowin’ up to the mantle, and lights the wick. He turns the knob and the light slowly grows to a glow. He walks the 1620 feet length to the end of the jetty and lights the second lamp. The large expanse between the two lamps means its centre is pitch dark, unless a full moon dominates a cloudless sky. Old Wohlgehagen, he had the job first, from 1913. Now it’s Loosey that does it, cares for the place, the jetty and its reserve. The place were spotless under his care. Lawns cut, trees trimmed. All green. Picnics always down there, kids' school picnics and sports too. He looked after the Board boat moored at the jetty. Old Loosey'd fish each day and sell his catch to anyone who'd buy it. Musta done alright to support his family and live in a house on the foreshore.

But the jetty dies, as all of us do. Not much ever ties up to it anymore, only official parties mainly. But she were popular with fisherman, shit oath. And on summer evenings, lovers would come out from everywhere and have a cuddle in the dark, a romantic rendezvousing. Shit, it were a place, a special place by the water where me heart cemented.

Twirling, swirling, spinning and furling ... dazzling skies of sapphire dazzle in the virtuosity of Mother Nature.

Higher and higher, over jetty lights serenading waters, and ambers and aquamarines of sea star jewels, tentacles of claret and cream.

Tendrils curl sensuous, of jelly fish and butterflies of the sea, and eels slithering in the flounce of ruffled seaweed, aspiring for that titillating peak that's bigger and brighter than all the sea's bioluminescence. They ride the lustre of a full moon; circling, teasing, until the luminous entwines and grips. Locks in.

Dance jellies, dance staries. Pirouette into the butterflies of the sea, slink into the cerulean skies.

Flounders skate under the jetty and skitter up into flashing arc upon arc, as shooting stars streaking brilliance over dark. The black man flitters in the Milk Way, his spear encrusted in a thousand stars. Banjo sharks, eels and flatheads too, pipis and oysters, the nebulous arms of the octopus ... all in a shimmy of sky high.

Suddenly, curiously, from the joying glee, eyes of jet pierce from skin of blended clay and ash, a transcendence of ethereal beauty.

It's her. Light in her essence, and light in her shadows. Magnetising, hypnotising: complete radiance. Her lure is fierce, hooks me into an embrace anchored to the sea bed.

An entwining bewitches us, of lime-green filigree as the French lace of the sea and iridescent eels in hues of blue. The jellies and staries on the languid limbs of the octopus, and bioluminescence of jewelled transparencies and kelping sea tangle.

In the flounce of frilling seaweed fluttering in salting sea, in the bedazzling carnival of sea confetti, we unite. We are we.

Emmesh in spirit of earth and soul of the sea, she's me gal, Elsie has me heart.

ANNIE LINKS HER ARM through Michael's as they stroll to Eileen, Thelly, and the Locke and Flaherty kids climbing the big ghost gum by Loosey's house. 'We've got lollies and soft drink on the rug,' calls Annie. 'Jaffas and bonbons too, and those new Freddos and Fantales that everyone loves!'

'Graneeee,' sings Eileen from a fork in a tea tree. 'I love your lemonade.'

'Granny has lemon slice too,' says Michael.

'Yum,' comes a call from high up in a pine tree. 'Mum makes it at home,' says the Locke boy.

'Aye, hurry up down, 'fore you miss out.'

'Phillip and me want some, Pop,' calls Thelly, running toward Michael.

Annie smiles. 'There's enough for all of you.' She holds out her hand for Thelly, who latches on and immediately begins fidgeting with her grandmother's wedding ring. Dear Daughter's above, always whirly-girling.

That rose of gold of Annie's is gettin' a twirlin', Els. Annie were a darlin'. You're more than a darlin', you're me gal, Els! She were a wee sweetie, comin' to get fish from me each week. Sometimes bringin' me an apple pie she'd pulled from the oven that afternoon, until she started sending Eileen, Nellie's young one. Those kids are racin' to Annie and Michael's picnic rug. Clare and Maggie're sittin' with Tom and his Annie's there too. Dear

Daughter's followin', the bedragglin' kid she is. Ah but she's a too right sweetie.

'Ray,' calls Agnes as he dawdles last. 'Come to Granny so I can wipe the dust from your face.'

George is sipping a glass of beer and smoking his pipe by Agnes under a pine tree.

'I'll get me cheeky one, Mum,' says Frank, running after Ray. 'Come here you little rascal.' Ray scuttles a few steps, laughing until he trips on a pine cone. Frank scoops his son into his arms before Ray hits the ground and slings him over his shoulder. 'Gottcha!'

'No, I want lemonade!'

'It'll be lemonade *after* we clean your face.'

Isn't he adorable, Joe, with his chubby red cheeks smudged in dirt, and his drooling dribbles. He's a mess, but so adorable. I always wanted my own.

He'll be a good young bloke that Ray. Fishin' and snaggin', trappin' rabbits and shootin' ducks. He'll be a goer that boy Sadler, bagging that much tucker. Good fresh tucker too. He'll work on the Farm, marry, have kids here and retire from the Farm as a research engineer.

My friend, Lottie, and her mob did a lot of that, fish in the Werribee River. They'd throw a net downstream then when the birds settled on the riverbank, they'd clap and hoot to scare them off. They'd cause such a ruckus that the fish would swim straight into the net.

Big word, Els, ruckus. And a clever lot, your friend's mob. The Sadler kid's a clever one too. Him and young Phillip Flaherty, they'll pry mussels off the jetty piles and bag pipis by the dozen when they get a bit older. Tommy Hickey's young girl'll follow, wantin' in on the adventure. They'll tell her to rack off, but she won't listen. Has her own mind and all, just as a certain lovely someone by me right now, with that slayer smile of yours. Wish I could hold you in me arms, Els.

My flutter will have to do, Joe, and my coy smile for you.

Me Els takes off after Dear Daughter, and I go after them. Over salt bush and seaweed trailing the shoreline, past million-year-old boulders splashed in salting water that whispers an effervescence that was me seafaring lullaby, me reminder of life. It got into me bones and each strand of me. Me sensations may be no more, but the scent of seaweed never disappears when it catches up your nose hairs, bounds up in yer forever.

Over the school tin roof we hover, me little family of three. The Sadler kid and young Phillip'll cook pipis and mussels over a fire beneath a sheet of similar tin. They'll finally let the Hickey girl stay and she'll shuck and eat mussels with the boys, downing the opalescent morsels quicker than the blue buggers'll open up. She'll eventually go back to her nan and pop's for tea, stay the night there and recite the Rosary with them, knealin' by their beds. The boys'll wander down past subdrains and the sluice gate dischargin' them effluent waters into the bay. The gate will be lost to the tides one day, along with the pylons of the jetty. Those kids'll cross Little River and pass settlin' pits, scrub and swamp land to finish at the highwater mark in Murtcaim. Dusk will approach and they'll camp in the bough of a mulberry tree to sleep overnight. The possums will make room for them, no bother to that. Nothin' better than catchin' that wisp of wind comin' off the bay on a balmy summer night, with stars a-bright and water a-plenty, flounder and rabbits to catch and cook over them coals. Ray'll get a personal best and hit 72 of the cotton tail buggers with a stick on a Satdee afternoon. That was before the myxomatosis war to come.

They'll be safe for the night alright, nowhere safer than this Farm, with eyes of nurture wide open, protecting as a Hereford heifer protects her calf. Bob's your uncle, billy's for tea.

I wanted my own kids, Joe. Lottie would always say the same. She cursed the squatters just before she died because she was robbed of having children.

Stinkin' squatters. Despicable mongrels they are. They had the cheek to bloody complain to me dad when the Aborigines killed the sheep they put on the Aborigine's huntin' land. It was land for huntin', Els! And they put sheep on it and expected the Aborigines not to hunt the land anymore. Makes no sense to me.

Lottie had it rough, Joe, that was obvious. Her whole Wadawurrung mob did. If I could get my hands on those squatters

... I've seen some twit-twats in my time and I can tell you, those bastards take the cake! Au contraire, they were bastards. Mongrels.

Els! Never heard you speak such language. But you're right, they were bloody mongrels. If that weren't bad enough, they put arsenic in bags of flour and left them out for the Aborigines to take. Poor buggers had no clue there were arsenic in them bags. The flour cooked good, bloody good alright. Until they ate it. Then it were blowin' through all of them, and they were pissing blood and groaning like wild pigs, spittin' yella from the mouth and arse at the same time. Stunk of rotten garlic and shit.

Lottie said her brothers and sisters were crying until they couldn't cry anymore, and starved to death. Poor little Susi, I was cradling her in my arms when Lottie lost all her strength. Kids and babies were crying, poor little darlings. Lottie would say she was drowning in their squealing, with a head that killed and mouth that dried as paper bark. My stomach still twinges for her, pain memory doesn't go away, Joe. Those bastard squatters wiped Lottie and her mob out overnight. Excuse my language, Joe. Some say it was the Chirnsides that did it, others says it was other farmers. And some say it never happened! One things I do know, Joe, is that Lottie died. And she didn't get caught in the in-between like us.

We're not caught in the in-between, Els. We're here for each other, and Dear Daughter. You know that.

I do, Joe, I do know.

Come close, Els. I'm with yer forever.

Els slides down the angled bough of the pine tree to sit close to me.

I feel yer, Els, even when I can't. I, I ... I bugger me words when you're with me, Els.

Your touch is my touch, Joe. Always.

Shades of blue shimmy translucent, cherries and greens tangle in the sea kelp with jellies and staries too. A spangle of pipis and octopus, and filigree of French lace of the sea. Waters enchant skies in the lustre of pearls.

WHAT A SIGHT, ELS. Christmas tinsel in the trees and round the table, dancin' in me sea breeze, and the red and green baubles glitterin' in the sun. Annie and Michael with all the grandkiddies, and their kiddies all grown up. Tom's courtin' his girl, Annie like they're still datin', Thelly holdin' onto her granny's finger and always twiddlin' that rose of bloody gold.

I adore the Flaherty kids, Joe. Salt of the Earth they are.

Their grandfather, Son, he's a bloody character, him and his horses. He was a well-known jockey. Saw him ride the winner of each race in a seven-race programme at Myrniong one time. He had this champion horse, Roisel, down here at the Farm, always grazin' happy in the paddocks. I backed young Jack when he rode the gelding and won the Australian Hurdle and Australian Steeple races. Bloody legend horse. Got caught in a fire down here at the Farm and survived. Bit of a rumour he were in a Melbourne Cup race. Son drove the horse team that ploughed the dirt for the main sewer drain down here in the first years. Here's a story for you, Els. Son's dad, Patrick, who Son was named after to be Patrick too, he were shot in the mouth by Andrew Chirnside!

Those Chirnsides again, Joe! Mischievous critters.

Andrew Chirnside though, he bloody claimed he let the gun off to frighten boys from a mulberry tree and it accidently got Patrick. The real story goes that Chirnside were jealous of Patrick. Bloody drongo in his spiffin' daks, jealous of Patrick! Poor bugger that Patrick, he attempted suicide a few years later. Threw himself across one of the train lines when the midday train from the metropolis was approachin' Werribee Station. The station master and a couple of bystanders dragged the bloke off the tracks and onto the platform. He didn't tell them why he did it and then fought them to try again!

Poor man, with all that torment. And poor Anne.

Heard some other stories too, Els, about one of the Chirnside blokes lovin' blokes! Blow me down – that story aint fit for your ears, Els.

There's Son down there, talkin' horses with his Jack. The Losewitz people, they're good bloody people. Chaz and Betty're already cleaning up, and Betty's givin' Issy's young Phillip a piece of strudel. Dear Daughter's havin' a bonza of a time with so many kids to play round.

Where you goin', Els?

I'll be back, Joe.

There goes me Els, tusslin' her auburn waves into the trees of whispering leaves. She cruises to the top of the ghost gum that cloaks the east facing parlour window of Chaz and Betty's house, her translucence casting crystal shadows onto the tree's pale trunk. She's jim-dandy dreamy, I'm fuck oath lucky to have 'er. Loosey and his family won't be so lucky during the second war, when they come under surveillance because of their German heritage.

This mob picnic into the late evenin' sun, with a southerly coming off the bay and breezing over paddocks. One of me favourite times of the day it is. Until baskets pack into jinkers with kids and their pressies of rag dolls and wooden locomotives, embroidered handkerchiefs and a football or three. Some of the little ones are holdin' the ever-popular *Gumnut Babies,* and some of the older kids have started reading the fantastical adventures of Bunyip Bluegum and his friends Sam Swanoff and Bill Barnacle in *The Magic Pudding*. It'll be a classic one day. "Eat away, chew away, munch and bolt and guzzle, never leave the table till you're full up to the muzzle."

Joe, you would've been a good dad.

Shoulda, woulda, coulda, Els.

I need to round up little DD, Joe. I'll find you later.

Els lights up before fading into the trunk of the ghost gum and I take off over the jetty. It'll be gone soon. Any amount of serviceable timber in it will go to fencin' on the Farm; piles of ironbark will go to the carpenters' workshop for repairs and new buildings. The decking is redgum and the hand railing is oregon; 90 per cent of it is serviceable. Even the 200 tons of dunnage left after its decommissionin' will be used for firewood or rough temporary work on the Farm. We all have a second life, even Chaz Losewitz.

WERRIBEE LANDMARK. METROPOLITAN FARM JETTY DEMOLISHED.

The Age, Thursday 8 Aug 1935

The Werribee jetty at the Metropolitan Farm, one of the oldest landmarks on the Port Phillip Bay foreshore, is being demolished by the Public Works department. The jetty was built more than forty years ago, and when the Metropolitan Farm was first opened up it was used by the Metropolitan Board for the shipment of goods and material to and from Melbourne. All the material required for the construction of the 100 dwellings now used by the workmen at the Metropolitan Farm was landed from Melbourne at the jetty.

Years ago, Bay steamers also made the jetty a periodical place of call, but it is more than twenty years since a steamer called at the pier. That was the paddle steamer Weeroona in 1914, the occasion of the annual farmers' picnic, but so much difficulty was experienced in berthing operations that it was decided to discontinue the service. Of recent years it has been a popular weekend holiday resort for visitors from the metropolitan area. In the holidays, as many as 200 people have camped on the beach near by. It has also been a popular rendezvous for school picnics.

At present a party of unemployed men is engaged in the dismantling of the jetty. It contains a large quantity of durable timber, and this is being shipped to Queenscliff for the repair of wharfs and piers there.

He finishes his ranger duties in 1946 and his life comes to an end only three years later. Call his name and he'll come a-comin', forever here by his beloved jetty.

'BOB,' SAYS VIOLET, RAY sleeping in his mother's arms with his head on her shoulder. The blanket Phoebe made drapes over him. 'Why don't you go with the kids outside? They're over on the tennis courts. Take Mary with you.'

'Yes, Mrs Sadler.' Bob gets up off the school step as a 90-year-old bloke with a hunched back. He's only bloody nine. Poor kid.

'Go with Bob, love,' says Violet to Mary, who remains on the step, her elbows propped on her bony knees to bolster her chin. 'Go have a play with the kids round the back.'

Mary says nothin', but gets up an' follows 'er brother down the side of the school. Poor bloody kids, their mum dyin' and all. And what a way to die, being dragged by a horse after it shied at the white-wash sign promoting the dance in the Mechanic's Hall. Near Brophy's Crossin' it was. It bolted and broke the harness, draggin' the woman outta the jinker and along the road. Two of the bloody kids were in the jinker too. It slammed into the tree with them in it. Poor bloody kids. Her soul, it tells me she's okay. The pain was excruciating, ripped into 'er skin and tore 'er insides up. But her soul is pure and she's protected. She's with her mob. Her time was up.

Violet's going back inside the school house now that Bob and Mary are gone. She sits in a chair and feeds Ray spoonfuls of soft pumpkin. Bob and Mary's older sister, Pattie, shuffles here and there, serving plates of sandwiches and cups of tea. People keep bailin' 'er up with their condolences. She's hatin' it, always tryin' to pull away to the kitchen as soon as someone pats 'er arm or rubs 'er shoulder. So much goes on in the Cocoroc South schoolhouse. The dances and committee meetin's, Belle of Balls. This place is their place and they're bloody proud of it. Can see it in their ripper gardens.

COCOROC SOUTH SCHOOL'S DOUBLE SUCCESS.

Werribee Shire Banner, Thursday 26 April 1934

Two awards have been secured by the Cocoroc South State School as a result of the attention given to the school garden and its environs.

The first of these awards is that presented annually by the A.N.A. Board of Directors for the school in the Geelong inspectorate adjudged to have the best improved garden and grounds.

At the presentation of the A.N.A. prize last week, Mr. A. Campbell, chairman of the farm committee of the Melbourne and Metropolitan Board of Works, stated that only a few days previously it had been decided by the judges to award the farm committee's prize, given annually, to the Cocoroc South School for being in possession of the best school garden on the farm. Mr. Campbell offered hearty congratulations to the teacher, pupils and school committee upon this double success.

Big difference to a week ago, Els. We were two and four steppin' through the wooden girders above this lot as they were treading the school floorboards to celebrate young Loorham's 21st. Blood oath, the dancin' and merriment, neckin' a few beers out the back 'round the fire. I was tonguin' for a lick of that creamy froth dribblin' down the neck of the bottle. Be droolin' if I could. Some blokes were blind as bloody hell parrots and they'd skedooddle back inside as soon as Annie started yodellin'. Bloody hell, that woman can yodel her lungs out. And the old man and his Mrs dancin' in that same centre down there, laughin' and kissin'. It's a stark contrast now, Els. He's sittin' on a chair in the middle of the crowded room, spotlight on him and yet lost in the depths of a dark Milky Way. Bloody poor bugger. He's an empty shell, scarcely fittin' into his baggy suit. His eyes are so far away. Empty they are.

Clouds will brew in, Joe. Clouds that will grow and grow in years to come, and meander as a mass of violent venom.

'HE'S COMIN'. HEARD HIS jinker up the drive. Hide!'

Footsteps scram. A bolt to the potato box in the food pantry; flip the lid to climb inside. The crouch is low, the lid's shut. Panting into the potato grime dark, with little breath to draw to feed the pounding in a chest cavity. The stench of potatoes rotting is rank and only a slither of light from the tilly lamp on the kitchen table spears through tiny timber slits.

'Where are ya, brats.' Stamp and tramp, clomp and clump. 'Where's me tea? Better be rabbit stew, like ya bewdiful Ma used ta make.' A shoulder into the kitchen wall, shuffles across the floor. 'Bastard. Where are ya, brats?' A slump into a chair at the kitchen table. Then quiet. Maybe he's nodded off.

No. The chair scrapes across the floorboards. More stomps become louder, heavier. A shuffling scuff of a boot ... a banging fist. The potato box trembles. The pounding now pelts.

'I know you're in there, ya little bastard.'

Panting quickens, becomes a heavy wheeze. The lid hurls open, and a lurch through the air as a terrified frog lunging for a lily pad. A snatch of the hair ... miss! A grab of a potato, and a hurl at the scampering. Clomp. It stings the scamper in mid-air flee, and drops the scamper in the thud of a 20-pound sack of potatoes hitting the floor. 'Ow ....'

He staggers to the injured writhing, smirking as the feral cat honing in on the neck of a Pink-eared duck. A boot drives in. 'Weak as piss.' The writhing groans. Another boot kicks in.

'Stop.' Gasp.

'I'll stop al-right, when I think you've fucken had enough.' A kick in the guts. He grabs the hair to lift the head, stumbling in his stagger. 'You shoulda been home when I fucken told ya.' He hammers the head into the floor. It bounces on the bare boards and knicks a corner of a well-worn rug in the kitchen doorway that leads into the living room. Blood seeps from a cut. 'Ya little cunt.'

'Gawe. I'm so ... I'm sorry. I won't ....' Gasp. Cough. Spluttering red mucous.

'Daddy! Nooo!' comes a scream from a sister running from under a bed. 'No more hurting! In the basket, there's fish he caught for tea. He's done nothing wrong. He went fishin' for our tea, 'cause we had none.' She reaches her father in the living room.

'You tellin' me a father don't provide for 'is fam-ly? Are ya?' The hand of a broken man prepares to strike.

'No, Daddy, I wasn't!' A head ducks under a swinging arm.

'Go, run!' she screams to the writhing. But the writhing is nothing but gasp and cough.

Flailing arms and hands of the she. 'Daddy ... stop!!'

Moans and cries, screams of blue murder. Hearts drub, drown in blood, smeared in the dread of the dead.

'Go.' Gasp, cough from the gimping kid. 'Run. Get outta here! I shoulda, I shoulda been home. It's my fault.'

The boot goes in again.

The writhing is none.

Arms of fearing muscle swing and swipe as wild lions ravaging for the last hunk of meat, knocking the tilly lamp on the dresser to spin on its side. 'Stop daddy, leave him alone! She hits a folded newspaper at the fire lighting the dresser, until the father staggering in drunken swagger draws near again. She bolts through the living room, swiping the mother's shawl from her once armchair, the same shawl the father drapes over himself to sleep most nights in a blubbering mess of despair. The burden of grief, more powerful and heavy than the day of death.

'Yeah, go you dumb fucker. Go to ya dumb fucken sister, probably rootin' in the paddock. You betta run outta here.' The drunk of staggering swagger has no idea whether son or daughter has just bolted from him. He tumbles over the side of the tattered couch, fraying in cherished fibres of fine. 'Ya weak as piss, good for no-thin'. You should be outta here and married ya frig-id bitch.' He heaves himself up and staggers back to the writhing curled up ball on the floor.

Boot, kick in the back. 'Dad,' comes a withering whimper.

A punch into the Masonite wall. 'You're lucky, ya scrawny cunt. Next time it won't be the wall.' He staggers to a chair outside on the porch. And cries into his hands. 'Where's me fucken shawl. Ya bitch!' he screams.

The fleeing and the writhing, oh dear Lord, he's dealt his hand.

NO ONE HAS MUCH durin' the Depression, even if the Farm people have the Board's cows for milkin' and the few bob they earn from workin' on the Farm. But some have less, especially when a broken man drinks away the money he's earned and his kids have to cut a pencil in half to share between them in school.

Lucky, if you can say they're lucky, they have a bounty load of rabbits and fish to catch for tea, pumpkins, tomatoes and marrows to pick in the paddocks, and the freedom and space to roam and be alone in this vast back yard. Although the old man never hit them kids, he gave them more belt ups than anyone knew, drove more boots into 'em than into a football in a winning playing season. They were gonna be chucked into a home somewhere early on, until the older girl told the Welfare Department she'd take over the house and care for the family. She saved those kids.

The years pass and those kids got away and the writhing is now seventeen and a half years old and says ta-ta, bye-bye to go to war, to get out of his dark hole. The old man retires and is daily at the pub, becomes a full alcoholic.

Those kids weren't reared, they were dragged up. And if the writhing one stayed, he mighta done more than hit the old man. He mighta shot him.

'OI, TWIT! WHERE ARE the kids gonna go to get their education?'

'Settle down, Jack,' says Issy, yanking at his coat.

'He's a bloody drongo, Iss. Their stiff collars are chokin' their brains dry. And their suits are that bloody crisp they might snap if they bend too far.'

'The odour from the sewerage is far too great. It's not healthy for the children,' says the suited man. His crocodile-scary eyes peer over the top of a cream cotton mask concealing his mouth and nose, with ties over his ears.

'Can't hear yer, drongo, for the bloody mask you're wearing!'

'And it's sewage that flows, not sewerage!'

'Whatever you call it,' he yells. 'It smells worse than one hundred buckets of prawns sitting in the sun.'

The crowd erupts into laughter.

'Bloody drongo!'

'Odour, shmodour!'

'It's turning my stomach as we speak,' says the taller man, rubbing at his nostrils.

'Ya dick-head, with bloody cotton wadding up yer nose.'

'Ya weak bastard!'

Old man Gebbie's firing up, Els. Fancy bloody wantin' to shut the school down. Bloody arseholes. The school's been here for 45 years, since 1906.

Oh I remember, Joe. I was here when Cocoroc South School opened, the same time as Cocoroc West School up near the Geelong Road. All these good people got their education here, stupendous people – the Hickeys, Flahertys, Gebbies, Sutherlands, Loorhams, Girouds and Lockes.

Was all a sign of the Farm's growth, Els. Four bloody schools on this Farm, all overcrowded at times. And now, these mongrels wanna shut the bloody place down because they reckon it's too smelly! Dickheads. Typical bureaucrats in the Education Department, sittin' on their fat arse all day and thinkin' they understand all the things of this world. Sorry, Els, gotta be careful of me language. They're up-their-arse arrogant.

'The intense odours are a major health concern for the Department, akin to the Diphtheria epidemic here some years ago,' says the man through his mask. 'You should be very concerned for your children's health.'

'Diphtheria epidemic my foot,' calls Jack. 'The two McLellan kids died from someone like you visiting the Farm who had the disease. They went into someone's house down here an' coughed their bastard lungs out all over their home and made the kids sick!'

'The local health authorities shut the school and fumigated it to prevent it from spreading,' calls Issy. 'Doctor Prouse took swabs of everyone who visited the Farm and found the carrier. He was from outside of the Farm!'

Old man Gebbie throws his fist in the air. 'We rallied when those kids died and helped Mr Vincent get the school up and running again. And we're rallying for our kids again now.'

Go Mr Gebbie! I like him, Joe. He knows how to tell them, a bit like my Walter would do. You tell them, Mr Gebbie.

And in a flash, me good woman, Els, is shaking her fist over the top of the two suits.

'The smell's no problem for anyone but you. Go and educate those kids you're supposed to be educating rather than having a go at us working at the shit-face, us working class!' calls Jack.

'Nothing wrong with our kids,' calls Issy.

'The offensive smells from the Board's property have increased over the past week, and have been unbearable at Laverton and Point Cook. There's no question that it's causing harm to these children.'

'We wrote to you, the school committee wrote to you,' says Issy. 'We told you there was no problem with odour. We don't smell it.'

The crowd's thick, Joe. People are spilling from the schoolhouse onto the grass outside. Some aren't able to get past the hedge and kids have to push their way through to get to the tennis courts out back.

They're loving their bloody day off too, Els. Good kids they are, they deserve it. The Warfes and Orams from up the 160 Road are here. And Hazel Moore's here next to her parents. She gets up to a bit of mischief that young Hazel in the Head of the Road township, when her parents are out of the house. The Kings and Maynes from up there are here too, beside Tom and Ted Hickey who've come in from waterin' the paddocks. Thelly's here, who's holding onto her granny Annie's hand. They've come from all over the place, even that bloody bastard wife basher from over the road's here. I'd fucken bash him if I could. 'Scuse me language again, Els, but he's a fucken scoundrel that bloke. As a matter of fact, he's no bloke. I mean what man bashes a woman. He was yellin' at 'er in the kitchen last week, slammed inta 'er another night. Mongrel bastard, I flew me own punch into him once. Disorientated him for a minute, but it didn't stop 'im shovin' her into the cabinet.

Despicable man sends my blood cold, if I had any. What sort of man does that to a woman, tells her he loves her and makes a lifetime commitment before God, to protect and cherish her, then bashes her.

Bloody right, Els. You've got that gleam of a glint comin' on, the one you get when yer all riled up. You'd send me blood hot, Els, if I had any.

Oh, Joe, you'd send me blushing if I could.

Me Els flutters over the blackboard and spins a string of pirouettes through the girders. I go after me Els.

Ted Sutherland rushes past the tea-tree hedge at the school's entrance, slowing to navigate the crowd before reaching inside the schoolhouse. 'I got these reports,' he calls, waving two pieces of paper above his head. 'Here, read these.' Ted shoves the papers into the chest of the taller of the bureaucrats, the one drowning in cologne. 'Tells you how good our health is, us people who aren't concerned for our kids! They reckon it's higher than the surrounding districts.'

'Read it out loud!'

The man clears his throat. 'It is perhaps appropriate, to record that a former Medical Officer of Health to Werribee Shire

Council testified before a Royal Commission some years ago that the standard of health among the residents on the Farm was the best in the whole Shire.'

'Yeah, stick it up ya!' Jeers coming from outside drown him out.

'Dumb bastards!' calls Issy.

'Read the other one!' calls Ted.

The man clears his throat again. 'Ahem-em.' He attempts to smooth out wrinkles in his suit that don't exist, and catches a finger in his coat pocket. 'It may be stated that the standard of health of the residents of the Farm is, at least, the equal of the remainder of the Shire of Werribee, which comprises an area of 271 square miles with a population, at the 1933 census, of 4,369 persons.' The man glares at his colleague, his mouth gaping.

'Yeah, onya Ted!' calls a deep voice from the back.

'That was only a few years ago, dickhead!'

'Go back to ya sterile office, yer sterile prick!'

'We've got a brilliant school here,' calls Issy to cheers all around. 'Francis McGarry's done a colossal job with our kids. We've won awards, our children receive scholarships ....'

'Yeah, my Ray got a scholarship here,' calls Frank, having come in from checking on his men watering paddocks. 'Twelve pound, ten shilling for four years he got, and went to Geelong Technical School with it.'

'My girl too!' calls old man Gebbie.

'Read the other part of that report,' calls Ted.

'Shush!' comes from the back, followed by a piercing whistle.

The tall man reads from the paper. 'In order to provide additional accommodation on the Farm, and at the same time enable the residents to enjoy more modern conveniences, the Board is now considering proposals for the establishment of a model township designed in accordance with the best ideas of housing and town planning. It is hoped to make a commencement on this work shortly.'

'If there were odour problems here, the Board wouldn't be considering expanding.'

'Go back to yer offices, drongos!'

FAMILIES COME AND GO and Cocoroc South School will see many teachers swivel through its doors, especially in the soon to begin Second World War when securing teachers will be difficult with men going to war. The school will finally close in 1963, after the Rye family leaves the Farm and school enrolments drop below the required number to keep a school open.

All families will leave the bottom-end in the years to come. Some will be reluctant to go in the early 1970s, even with the chance for homes with electricity, toilets inside and telephones in bustling Werribee. The Gowlers and Mockridges will loath to depart; some people never do.

Not in this place where pink petunias and purple pansies stretch as an endless sea of pretty. Along the fence line and beside the channels they flutter, beneath burgundy heads of dahlias soaking in a mellow sun, and where red ranunculi and blush tea roses waft in bygone bliss. Delicate petals wrap snug around a centre devoted and precious, in a field brimming in the tender nurture of down south.

It's here by the subdrain at the 160 and 95 roads that more flying flecks will flitter in endless day and night, with Mr and Mrs Towers always among them. Their finery is her and him, amid the cotton-tails scampering in paddocks and quack-quacks flying in honking horn. Sipping tea from fine porcelain cups painted in pale blue forget-me-nots, they relish in raspberry jelly cakes sprinkled in Easter daisies and pies made from apples grown in backyard orchards. They chuckle and laugh, chin-wag over beers around fires and toast in the whiskey of mates past and present.

It's her and him, Mum and Dad, unwavering in the hydrangeas that tinge and wilt under a harsh reality, and yet colour in enhanced beauty.

Her and him fly in adorning eye, in heights over gladioli rivalling to be the finest curling lip puckerings, and lemon chiffons of heavenly jonquils.

Gardens will be abandoned to make way for a vast expanse of sewage ponds. There'll be no more pretty mugs of coffees when the day's tea quota has been reached, no more chocolate hedgehog and cream puffs bulging in Farm whipped cream, or singing at dances and rosaries in school.

And yet her and him, they'll always be here, with the fuchsias flowering and twirling as ballerinas in tutus on the gist of gardenias. Her and him will be forever free in the garden of this bottom-end town.

Head of the Road

Head of the Road, date unknown. Photo courtesy of the Pengelly family.

FAIRY LIGHT SPRINKLES SHOWER the windows of the lone weatherboard building. The mauve-grey sky greets low today, welcoming the murk of mustarding waters that are devoid of air but brimming in critters gorging in souring stench. Bubbles percolate from the water's depths. Yet the misting rain can't penetrate the taut surface of the olive and brown flowing steady and silent in the deep open channel. A tree barren of leafing life stands at the head of the concrete carrier, steam evaporating from its scabrous crust. Its leafy grandeur of once was, is now lost to the dire of dry.

Drizzling rain on any Melbourne summer's day can grow to spits and splatts and lashings of sheeted rain. It now hammers into plantations and onto wooden railings and gates surrounding the building. Stomps of hairy hooves halt, clanking wood and wincing chains grow silent. Men in wet rumpled hats and dusty trousers half tip a bucket of scraped soil before scattering for cover in a plantation of wattles and gums. They hold brims of hats over faces dribbling in water that marbles their skin in the dust of this land faraway. More men in a paddock nearby scurry from two steam engines where a steel cable stretching between them draws a two-headed plough into the cracked and puddle-pooling earth. Clouds concede to the wet, spilling from their heavy blanket.

Joe, something disturbs my heart cavity, there in the main carrier. A poor blighter is bouncing in bobs of ups and downs in this tangy bouquet.

Blimey, Els, somethin's comin' in alright. Better get the kid away.

It's not a blighter, it's my kinfolk. I'm not going anywhere!

DD, come away from the edge. Those waters of olive and brown will gurgle under gates at this Head of Road, excited to go this way or that, and could take you with them!

But Muma, it needs me. It's more ill formed than me. It'll get caught in the gushing of olive and brown.

Gurgle and guggle, eww ... salted sewage. Sniffle and snuffle. Achoo!

Muma, it's sneezing the icky water from Melbourne town that's flowing fancy. We have to catch it before it goes west.

The poor blighter's disappeared inta the muck!

It's gone under – Joe, please help it!

Droplets morph into globules, lustre as opals sprinkled across a subterraneous blueprint of channels, pipes and paddocks. The white magpie mate perches afar on the red-bricked chimney of the Carter home, distant to the magpies and ravens sheltering in trees that sometimes brave the wet to dive for a morsel in the frothing atop the mustarding waters of olive and brown. They waver as a distortion of black and fading grey, of those gone and those of today, to diffuse in the shimmy of sunshine bursting from a clouding restraint. It's as if a flushing blush saddles both worlds, where no chill can infiltrate the warmth of yesterday or today, to become a harmony of its own nature.

We're the almost babies, Muma, craving for that something we knew was coming but never did. We lust for the umbilical of life, the nourishment of all nourishment smothered in a mother's compassion. Nurture. Together in our place of rest on this Farm, us kinfolk have something. We have each other and those that saved us in death. Hundreds of us are here, huddling along the steep embankment rising from the main carrier and lingering in the gums and pine trees lining the channel. Our eyes are fixed on the mustarding waters of olive and brown that have travelled from our grand Dame city, Melbourne town. We survey in the spitter and spatter and spattering spits, for the one in the bobs of ups and downs, hovering for the poor blighter to appear from under the arch. Come from wherever you are, poor little blighter.

As if honing into our call, a black half oval ebbs through the arch. It's not the blighter though, only a heel of a shoe. Behind it floats a branch lumped in festooning faeces and pulping paper, and a tumour of black. It's a cat, one so fat and feral that's fallen in while reaching for a rat, and one who now prowls in spirit with us.

Muma, there it is, behind the cat! The blighter's gasping and spluttering some more.

Arms with hands of pin-needle size and those with stumps or no arms at all, some with thumbs suckled in mouths ... all are frantic to draw the blighter from the flowing of olive and brown. It's no good though, we can't take hold for our swipe is clear through its sheer veneer.

Muma lunges for it to lift it free, Joe dives into the mustarding waters of olive and brown to boost it out ... both only skim through the bobs of ups and downs.

The poor blighter disappears again, vanishes for a long time, and us kinfolk gather in teetering toe, swirling into its flow. It resurfaces where the carrier begins heading out west, to more coughing and snuffling. Us kinfolk flock over the swirl that's starting to steady with the lulling rain. It's becoming clear now, the poor blighter is so ill-formed and has only one stump of an arm and no hands at all.

Two stockmen appear on horseback at the top of the channel with their kelpies strident alongside. They've finished their hustle of steers in a paddock nearby and are trotting back to the stables. They stop near the blighter bobbing in ups and downs. Their chat is brief and the shorter one dismounts his chestnut mare. Dusty water pools over the rabbit-felt brim of his Akubra. He dashes to a pine tree nearby and collects a fallen branch with four small pine cones still attached, and thrusts its forking end into the mustarding waters flowing in the western carrier. The taller stockie has dismounted and is by his mate, holding a forked stick into the water too. They swirl and swill their branches around the poor blighter. Us kinfolk gasp in bursts. Mr Stockmen, please fish our kinfolk out!

The two branches come together and snag the stump. The poor blighter summersaults and disappears into a spin. The curve of a butt breaks the mustarding waters of olive and brown. The poor blighter ... he's a boy! They stir their branches once again and this time catch him under his chin. The two stockmen ease him out onto the dirt beside the channel. They stand silent over our boy in the grey dull of day: a torso with one stump for an arm and no legs at all.

The taller stockman taps his friend on the arm and suddenly the two move in quick motion. The shorter stockman pulls a towel from under his horse's saddle and lays it by the boy. He scoops the boy in his steady hands and wraps him gentle but snug into the towel. He cradles the wrapped boy in his arm and hoists himself back onto his horse with his free hand. His stockman mate has mounted his horse and the two shorten the reigns to turn their horses left. No words are spoken. They walk along the top of the channel to the main carrier at the Head of the Road, their kelpies still by them. The rain now drizzles and us kinfolk twirl in tumbling delight, at what these stockmen are about to do.

Once they reach the Head of the Road, the taller stockman dismounts and grabs a shovel by the gate. He digs a hole near our place of rest, the kelpies sniffing up at our hanging presence. We gather close, whispering in hushes of what's to come. The hole is soon deep and wide for our boy so small and the shorter stockman rests him gently inside. His mate shovels soil back into the hole and as the layers build, a light begins to emanate from the boy's place of rest. It grows in brightness, until his hole is filled and the light drapes the small mound. We spin a bobby dazzler – he's coming, he'll be with us soon!

The shorter stockman breaks off a branch from a wattle tree and takes it to his horse. He rifles through his saddle bag and pulls out a spool of twine and pocket knife. He trims stems of flowers from the branch and begins shearing it into two sticks, then binds the two sticks with twine to form a crucifix. He walks back to his mate, still the two have not spoken, have not connected in eye. He hammers the crucifix into the mound with the back of his shovel while his mate lays wattle flowers at the base of the cross.

Our boy illuminates from his place of rest, grows as bright as Sirius in the Milky Way! Come our boy, come flock with us.

The boy's radiance is undeniable and as he makes his way to us, a band of Archangels hum in the nobility of a million king proteas and queen of the night flowers, higher than us kinfolk ever dare fly.

I'm here, speaks from our shiny opalescent boy, in eyes drilling from his egg-shell skin.

Nothing but head and torso, I was surely gone to those critters who would've gorged on me in the souring stench. Then they caught me in a grip so fierce and now stand in heads of bowed grace, with hats in hand under drizzling rain. By golly, they saved me!

Thank you Mr Stockmen, thank you for your kindness and compassion. Thank you Mr Watermen and Mr Sludge Cleaners, Fence Builders and All who have done for us as your Mr Stockmen mates.

Thank you.

We linger and struggle, suffer our loss of nurturing life. And then you give us the courtesy of a place of rest, for our souls' peace. Thank you for caring, thank you for respecting us and uniting us kinfolk.

Under your cloaking dust and layers of grit, in the bitter cold and rain when all and sundry take shelter, and when shoulders burn under a harsh summer sun, you give us the grace of peace. You slosh through paddocks of sewage and gum-boot trudge through piled up sludge to take on the waste of this grand Dame of cities, our Melbourne town. Digging and scraping where many scowl in pegged nose, trussing and baling, opening and closing sluice gates with shovels as your extended arm, we humbly and gratefully thank you.

For your care and the dignity we could never imagine, thank you for the repose and rest, and giving the time in your day of busy to allow us our humility.

Thank you for your consideration of us so unfortunate and ill-formed, for reverence to our mothers and fathers.

Thank you.

Our debt to you is forever, from these mustarding waters of olive and brown, laced in the precious of liquid gold in time to come, on this land so far away.

Thank you, our guardian angels. We trust in your honour and pledge to protect you in return. In unending gratitude, from us kinfolk foetuses.

A KINFOLK SWIRL IN Sunday sunshine, a summersault spin over Edna approaching the white weatherboard church beside the new community hall. The church is owned by the Methodists but today, the Presbyterians will deliver a service after Sunday School. Next week it will be the Anglicans to hold Mass there. The Methodists use it the first and third Sundays of the month while the Catholics toff their noses at sharing a church with anyone. The poor Catholics from the Farm must make the 15 to 20-mile round trip into St Andrews in Werribee for Mass. Farm people teach Sunday school each week for all children, no matter their faith.

Edna flies through the church front door. 'I'm sorry, our dinner was late.'

Elsie Taylor stands at the altar with Bob and Bessie Hayes, their bibles open in their hands. 'Come in, Edna. It's no bother. Mum was late with our dinner today too,' she says. 'She started cleaning out shelves for the newspaper deliveries tomorrow and found ants, and of course went into a cleaning frenzy!'

The children giggle, all 16 of them spread across three pews with bibles open. How elegant they are in their simple lines of delicate dress and waved short hair. My mane most golden is out of place here. Even the boys are in their Sunday best, of carefully knotted ties and shirts and pleated woollen trousers.

Edna scuttles to the front of the church, collecting a bible from the pile by the altar. She opens it to page 55. Us kinfolk cram into the crevices and corners of the tiny church, some hang wistful by the cross hanging over the altar. That poor blighter boy is nowhere to be seen. We listen to their bible stories until the hour is up and the Farm congregation begins filing in for 2 o'clock Mass. Edna makes her way to the organ and begins tapping keys.

The Angel Gabriel from heaven came, his wings as drifted snow, his eyes as flame; 'All hail,' said he, 'thou lowly maiden Mary, most highly favoured lady.'

Gloria!

The archangels shimmy their usual heights while we sing and swing to the hymning inside and the trilling of sparrows and wattle birds outside.

'MY SUPER DAD!' SAYS Edna. Issy's sitting beside her on the edge of the croquet green. The cast iron water tank in the background complements the manicured lawns and flowering plants, and spectators wearing their Sunday best. Husbands are standing by wives with cups of tea and orange pound cake, children lark in games of chasey nearby. It's the epitome of a grandiose English garden party. Beside the tank is the nursery where trees are grown for planting across the Farm, and flowers too for decorating tables in the office when higher-ups visit from Melbourne. So lavish are the stupendous blooms grown that in years to come, they'll go into the Board of Works office in Melbourne each week. That's when transport improves and cars take over the roads.

'He's going to knock the watermen out of the game!' says Jack. He and Issy have not long arrived with Frank and Violet after staying late at the football dance last night, where they celebrated Metro Farm winning over the INF. That's the Irish National Foresters to those uninformed.

'No one's going to beat Dad,' says Edna, in the smirk of a fox that's feasted on a hundred chooks. 'We sometimes go on the train to watch Dad play at Brighton and Sandringham, and at the Werribee Croquet Club.'

'Golly, that's a long trip for croquet,' says Jack.

'He's a fine player, your Dad,' says Issy.

'Our best,' says Annie Taylor, honorary Secretary of the Metro Farm Croquet Club for 15 years.

'Bloody fine player,' says Frank. 'And a bloody fine way to end his carpentry years here.' Frank and Phoebe sit with Frank junior and his new wife Ellen, as well as Frank's brothers.

'No more twenty past seven starts and five o'clock finishes for ol' Fred,' says Frank senior. 'No sir-ee. They were long days when he was working miles away on the other side of the Farm. He'd leave an hour before on his bicycle to be out west to start on time. Thank Christ the Board had the sense to introduce a bus to pick us up from around the Farm and Werribee, and drop us off at our work posts on the Farm. Made bloody good sense with the size of this place. It's a long way for us workers who live in Werribee to ride our bikes out here and then back again each day. Hey, Phoebes?' Frank rests his arm over Phoebe's shoulder.

'It was far better for you to stay in the men's huts back then,' nods Phoebe.

'Are you comfortable there, Ellen?' asks Issy. Ellen's squirming in her seat while holding her expectant belly. 'You can have my chair so it's more comfortable for you.'

'I'm okay, dear. Thanks for asking.'

'There he goes,' says Annie Taylor. 'Fred's going to knock the game on its head with a four-ball break.'

'Too right.' Frank rests both hands on Phoebe's shoulders. 'He's gonna stroke that pink ball into the middle of the lawn, right near the bloody last two hoops, and then run 'em both.'

He's a clever one that Mr Hanson. Not as clever as my Pupa, Joe though. Him and Muma are the best. Mr Hanson's examining his alignment and the hoops on bended knee, preparing to hit the ball through three hoops in one stroke. Us kinfolk gather over Mr Hanson practice swinging his wooden mallet. He steps up to the ball, lines his mallet behind it, and ponders. Us kinfolk whirl willy around the mallet, whipping our momentum as Mr Hanson taps at the ball. We sweep into the mallet to edge it wobbly. He curses. The shot's gone off course and the ball rolls east instead of west.

A shiny dapple comes from behind the wooden lattice façade of the nursey. It's a bespeckling of opalescent egg-shell. The flash is quick, but it could be 'him'.

Us kinfolk draw back on instinct and we plunge the green as excited baby bunyips gleeful in the splash of a freshly watered billabong. We swoosh the ball with all our might, arcing it as Mr Hanson had intended. It hurls through the hoop, nicking its edge to ricochet right to the next hoop and knocking another ball out of its way to skim the green onto the centre peg.

'Woo-hoo, he's done it! Pegged out both balls for 26 points.' Fred's carpenters drop their mallets and rush to Fred, lifting him on their shoulders. We cartwheel a merrymaking mirth.

For he's a jolly good fellow.

For he's a jolly good fellow.

For he's a jolly good fe-llow!

They march Fred past spectators clapping and cheering.

'Onya Fred,' calls Frank. Violet sits in front of him holding baby Ray.

Which nobody can deny.

Which nobody can deny.

'Admirable, Mr Hanson,' sings Nellie from her chair, now married to Eric Forder and with babe in arm.

For he's a jolly good fell-ooowww ....

Which nobody can deny.

The carpenters and watermen teams lead the procession past the nursery, where that opalescent egg-shell appears stronger through the lattice squares. It *is* him. That boy. My main most golden shimmies fancy-free. Come out, don't be afraid young boy. The pearly blush darts away.

The cortege below weaves as a garland of spring blossoms. Of Nellie and Eric strolling with Annie and Michael, the rose of forever gold gracing Annie's finger, a rose of gold that will span lifetimes. And Jack and Issy, Frank and Violet, pushing babies in prams, and Son and Anne strolling. The Pengelly brothers and their wives, delighting in witty banter, the endearment of blossoming garland carrying into the leafy tree tops, drawing us kinfolk in its bloom. I'm ever wistful of a whiff of eucalypt, or chomp of nuts that the boys and girls pry from pine cones as they dawdle in the tail-end of the convoy to the hall. The boy's following now, but always darting to hide behind the next trunk or tuft of red flowering gum.

The two hundred or more are deep in jovial chatter. They come from across the Farm as far south as by the jetty and as far west as Murtcaim. The convoy passes the bluestone arches of the water tank, and the home of Elsie Taylor and her Annie's Post Office and General Store. It finally reaches the white picket fence fronting the hall nestled between the church and school. People squeeze through the gate in twos and threes, one man catching a blazer pocket on a Gothic spire atop the gate post. Mr McKee is by the side of the hall, slicing a piece of flesh from the pig roasting in dripping juice over hot coals.

Long trestle tables inside the hall are spread in an array of stewed, baked, pickled and curried rabbits, chickens, ducks, pork and eels; roasted vegetables and bread, and pile high plates towering beside boxes of cutlery and napkins. And if there's room left in bellies, there are sponge cakes and apple pies, cream lilies and jelly cakes by the dozen, and scones topped with mulberry jam and rich Farm whipped cream. Kitchens would have been in a flurry in preparation for Mr Hanson's retirement today. It's mostly women and children serving themselves a plate of food. The men sit under trees outside, guzzling beer from bottles sitting for hours in long grass or behind trees.

It's a picture perfect, sunny Sunday kind of day.

Edna begins playing the piano and children leave half eaten plates of food to twirl to her tunes, women sashay a two-step as they scrape plates into small pails. Us kinfolk skip through the rafters and woosh over tables, longing for the aromas to infuse us. Most are here now from our place of rest. That boy too, is in playful pace in corners and doesn't dart away when I approach him.

Your colour is most splendid, Mr Boy, so shiny and creamy. You're so much more developed than me.

I may be more developed than you, but I'm with these defects you can see: bald, not like your glorious main most golden, and with a stump for an arm. My mother got a virus they call German Measles, and had a mild fever and rash when I was at three months gestation. The doctors didn't understand, until I was born dead like this.

German Measles is a new disease, Mr Boy. Doctors are realising the link between pregnant mothers infected with the virus and infants born with cataracts. Mr Boy, you're staring at me. Stop, why are you staring?

Your mane most golden ... you're taking on a blush of sweet cerise.

No, how can that be ... I spin and swirl, a new something in me.

Come down from those dizzying heights, Dear Daughter. That's your name isn't it?

I spiral back down to Mr Boy's eye. Call me, DD, like Muma and Joe. Isn't the music that Edna plays so fine, Mr Boy? Muma says I'm a whirly-girl dancer and can't help but spin to a tune, like I did to the soprano tones of young Gordon and Gwenda not so long ago. We gathered to celebrate the opening of this new hall after the Mechanic's Institute burnt down, with all its fine books for reading. Even when reading over their pages, I'd be whirly-girl swaying.

Shall we dance, DD? I offer you my stump.

Yes please, Mr Boy!

We weave sways of embrace and kick Charleston steps forward and back through the party in the hall. The pale egg-shell of Mr Boy shimmies an opalescent mauve. Men have followed their noses to feast on the banquet inside, and our kinfolk are here too. Some are winged in arm or webbed in tiny feet, others are with hands protruding from a bloated belly, their undernourished umbilical still hanging. We're all in our own amorphic form, content in glee.

'Ethel, love,' calls Nellie. 'Bring it here. We can squeeze a plate in here near the roast duck.'

'There you go, Mrs Forder,' says Ethel, handing her a plate of pork and crackle.

'Tell your father to have a wee rest,' calls Issy. 'We've enough food in here to feed all of Werribee.'

Ethel bounds outside, sidestepping the queue for food and dancing merriment.

Because the breeze blew sou'-by-east across the China Sea;
Or else, because the thing was willed through all eternity
By gods that rule the rushing stars, or gods long aeons dead,
The earth is made to smile again, and living things are fed.
Mile on mile from Mallacoota
Runs the news, and far Baroota
Speeds it over hill and plain,
Till the slogan of the rain
Rolls afar to Yankalilla;

Wallaroo and Wirrawilla
Shout it o'er the leagues between,
Telling of the dawning green.
Frogs at Cocoroc are croaking,
Booboorowie soil is soaking, ...

'I never tire of *Song of Rain* by C.J. Dennis,' says Issy.

'Me neither,' says Phoebe, tapping her foot on the floorboards. 'How can we when our marvellous parish of Cocoroc is captured in time.'

Issy contemplates the tables of food lining the walls of the hall. 'I'm not sure we'll need to place any food orders with Aub when he calls by tomorrow, not with these leftovers.'

'I still have a few things to ask of Aub. I need some salt, sugar and lard by the time he delivers on Tuesday. And I've got blocks of butter to sell him,' says Nellie.

'I'll need bread from Mr Coombs,' says Issy, clearing plates from the table.

'I must get a piece of corned beef this week. God bless the butcher calling by with our meat,' says Nellie. 'And the greengrocer from Lowman's shop in Werribee. His beans are snap fresh!'

'What a thrill it was when Mr Bill made his deliveries while we were at school,' says Edna, savouring a bowl of her mother's trifle. She sits beside Issy. 'He'd always come round at playtime and we'd rush him with our three pence or six pence to buy sweets. Sometimes we even had a whole penny to spend on lollies!'

'The Indian hawker's one of my favourites. He's an interesting gentleman with an assortment of lovely linen to sell. It's good quality too. And his socks and trousers are as good as any you'd get in a high-end shop in Melbourne.' Issy licks the jam dripping from the scone onto her finger.

'Miss Hanson, Miss Hanson,' call children rushing to Edna. 'Play *Waltzing Matilda* for us, please? Pretty please?'

Ooh, a favourite of mine, Mr Boy.

Mine too, DD. Shall we?

Mr Boy motions me in bowed head, as the young gentlemen he is, and we encircle one another to *Up jumped the swagman* .... I sometimes twist behind me in a senseless search of his stump pressing into my back. Hundreds of our kinfolk are here dancing. Muma too, with Joe by her, and Joe's dog, swinging and swaying, flowing with the jellies and staries and butterflies of the sea.

Sheep flock in chiffon sheer, heifers float in flights of liberties, cows for milking and others with eye and skin disease. Bulls in bombastic chin-chop parade with stockies' dogs, energetic once again after rustling into their last days. Horses gallop behind in virile vitality of peak droving years. All prance in pomp and pimp, gallop between rafters and roof, past walls that hold endless stories. Out into the eucalypts and pines they go, in the jewelled transparencies of kelping sea tangle.

The Archangels vacillate at elevations beyond clouds. As above, and so below.

THE WAR

Farm Committee Minutes.

(Sgd.) F. H. Vincent. Farm Manager, 25/8/42.

Additional members of the Farm Staff enlisted during this year for service with A.I.F. or the R.A.A.F. So far it is pleasing to state there have been only a few minor casualties amongst the men enlisted from the Farm. Apart from the above enlistments several Farm employees were accepted for service with the A.M.F, whilst a large number was compulsory called up in their age groups or with the militia.

A further considerable number of men left to take up work in Munitions and other protected industries.

One of the Assistant Engineers was co-opted for Defence work with the Department of the Interior.

With its thus depleted staff the Board was called on to assist the war effort by carrying out a number of important Defence Works, chiefly on aerodromes, necessitating the use of the whole of its earth moving plant, machinery and transport, and at times over 100 men and many horses.

This left the Farm with barely enough men to carry on from day to day such work as could not be deferred without seriously interfering with the disposal of the sewage in Melbourne. Consequently, such work as drain and carrier cleaning, road maintenance, and fence repairs had to be held in abeyance until such time as the urgent defence works were completed, or well advanced.

At the same time it was gratifying to be able to assist the national effort at such a critical time and to know that the knowledge and skill of the Farm staff in this direction have been so eagerly sought and appreciated by the Commonwealth authorities.

No fencing material has been obtainable for many months, and it is becoming increasingly difficult to maintain existing fencing in a stock-proof condition.

'THE ONIONS ARE GROWING thick,' says Doug, inspecting the plot of onions beside Sunshine Cameron's cottage.

'The Board's sent two tonne over to England for the war effort, with some of our beef too,' says Jack, leaning on the wooden picket fence fronting Doug's cottage.

'Three of the township blocks'll be planted with Farm-grown onions this season and we can cultivate our own vegies on the land that's left,' says Doug.

'Look out, here comes trouble,' says Jack, nodding towards Issy, Jean and Dot.

'G'day young ladies,' says Jack. 'How are you on this lovely day? Mrs McKane, Mrs O'Connor? And my lovely dear wife?'

'Full of charm, aren't ya, Jack!' says Dot, with a cigarette-lazing-between-the-lips smirk.

Jack winks. 'Always, Mrs O'Connor.' He tips his hat to Dot.

'Gentlemen.' Dot draws on her cigarette. 'Mick's got the same hat as you, Jack, *The Wyndham.*'

'You betcha, Dot, a Maurice Rushford exclusive.' Jack tips his hat to Dot. 'We were just discussing, as gentlemen do, how much land we've got to cultivate.'

'Seven blocks were set aside to grow onions for the War,' says Doug. 'But they don't have enough seed to plant all the blocks and so the Board's given us the other four to plant for ourselves.'

'As long as we donate the profits of one of the blocks to the Comforts Fund,' says Jack.

'Sounds fair to me,' says Dot. 'We'll do potatoes here, half beans and half peas over there.' Dot waves her arms as she marches towards the vacant land.

'I do love you living here in town, Dot,' calls Issy, scuttling after her friend.

'Keep up, dear. We've got some work to do.'

'Jack! Doug!' calls Vivian from beside the water tank. He waves the two men over. Young Beryl's running around her father and laughing as she pulls his shirt tails.

She's a fun girl, Mr Boy. And so lucky to have a father like that to play with.

Mr Boy sighs.

What's wrong, Mr Boy? Your sigh is wistful.

I have no mother or father, DD. No one but you.

Well you have someone then, Mr Boy. Someone who'll be with you always.

The two men stroll across the road into the park, and up to the water tank. 'What's up, Viv?' asks Jack.

'Did ya hear about the new swimming pool? Bloody good old Jack McKee got the ball rolling and sent the Board a letter, he did,' says Vivian, turning behind to a daughter full of cheeky grin. 'Okay, that's enough,' he says to Beryl. 'I want to talk to Mr Flaherty and Mr McKane for a bit.' Vivian kisses the top of his daughter's head. 'Now go off and play.'

Beryl skips to the Flame bottle tree nearby, sometimes stopping to peer at trainee pilots flying their Airspeed Oxfords overhead. Naturally, I whirly-girl dance round and round over her with Mr Boy, who's becoming quite an accomplished dancer too. We fly into trees preparing for their annual winter's sleep, diving and dodging one another in the speed of the aeroplanes above. We turn and barrel roll to aeroplane hums and throttles, sometimes skimming each other in quaking quiver. It's not possible in our state of life, but oh so real for me.

'Bloody Jack, in his capacity as Secretary of the Combined Schools Committee, sent the Board a letter. He refers to their proposal to establish a model township down here after the War, for the predicted population boom.'

'That model town's a ripper,' says Jack. 'They want the front gardens to be open and not a mere decoration and fenced off like ours. Fancy that, no bloody fences! Bloody hell, what's the world comin' to! They're planning for two churches, and a shopping centre. Me Pop said they were gonna build shops down the bottom-end years ago, but never did.'

'Jack tells the Board he's enquiring whether the swimming pool could be constructed before next summer,' continues Vivian. 'Cause the war restrictions don't allow us to go for a swim. And it's part of the planning design for the model town anyway. He tells 'em he could get volunteer labour from us residents to construct the pool if the Board supplies the design, materials and engineering supervision.'

'Too right we'd volunteer,' says Jack, kicking a tuft of dried weed from the dirt. 'The whole Farm would.'

Mick walks over after taking wood into Dot, adjusting his grey hat trimmed in tan. 'Bloody pool's a bonza of an idea.'

'We need volunteers though,' says Jack. 'It'll be bloody tight for the Board to build it with so many men off for the War effort.'

'We'll get the volunteers, no trouble at all. Dot'll round 'em up,' says Mick.

'Daddy,' calls Beryl. 'I've got a splinter.' Beryl flashes her finger to her father.

Vivian nips the splinter out in a flash and kisses Beryl's finger. 'Off you go.' He turns back to Jack and Doug. 'And they're gonna add play equipment for the kids. They'll love it!'

'Vernon and his mates will love it too, all the kids will,' says Doug.

'We'll get everyone from the Farm swimmin' up here,' laughs Jack. 'What a shindiggin' that'll be!'

THERE'S 375 MEN EMPLOYED by this time and cottages are built in four main settlements across the Farm. A hundred families live here. There's a school in each settlement and they're places of teachin' and bringin' the good Farm people together. Grocers are

PROPOSED SWIMMING POOL AT THE METROPOLITAN FARM.

Melbourne and Metropolitan Board of Works. Development of Scheme.

J. McIntosh, Acting Engineer of Sewerage. 25.8.1943.

The general scheme for the future township, which was prepared by the Consulting Architect, Mr. L. M. Perrott, in connection with the Board's officers, and subsequently adopted by the Farm Committee, included the provision of recreational facilities, comprising a swimming pool (110′ x 60′), bowling green, and tennis courts, all to be located in the park adjacent to the existing sports oval. The general lay-out only was agreed on, details being left for investigations at a later stage.

Earlier this year, a Committee for the Farm residents, having heard of the proposal to establish a new township after the war, wrote to the Board pointing out that the present restrictions on the use of motor cars practically precludes them from bathing in either the Bay or the River, and requesting the Board to consider the possibility of proceeding at an early date with the provision of a swimming pool. So keen were the residents to have this put into effect that they offered to provide volunteer labor for the purpose if the Board would supply the materials and supervision …

The capacity of the above, calculated on the basis quoted by the Department of Public Health, is as under:-

Wading pool	55 children
Swimming pool (present)	35 persons

It is proposed that both these structures be located on the eastern side of the elevated tank. For the dressing sheds, fibrocement construction only is allowed for at present. This would be replaced by a permanent structure as soon as circumstances permitted.

COST:- £3,350

deliverin' goods now and the General Store's gone. The Post Office is well established and the church continues to be shared; the community hall, park and sportin' facilities for football, cricket, tennis and croquet draw a crowd from all over the Farm and Werribee too. Only the top-end township has power and all others rely on candles and kero lamps for lightin', ice for refrigeratin' and wood fires for stoves and heatin'. Bloody fuck oath better than me rail carriage.

'MARY ABBS!' CALLS ELLEN from the side of the pool. 'Come here, love, and I'll fix your strap.'

Mary walks the four shiny-tiled steps out of the wading pool, over to Ellen standing by the wire fence. 'Thank you, Mrs Pengelly. It won't stay up,' says Mary, pulling the thin red strap over her shoulder.

'That's because the strap's been torn off your bathers, love,' says Ellen. 'How'd that happen?'

Mary stares plain-faced at Ellen.

'Let me guess, one of my boys ripped it. Right? No need to answer, I know they can be mighty rascals.' Ellen loops the strap through a small hole in the back of Mary's bathers and knots it three times. 'There,' she says. 'It won't fall down again.' Ellen smiles at Mary, before looking over to her three sons in the pool. 'You boys be respectful,' she yells. 'And don't play rough with the girls!'

'They keep you on your toes, Ellen,' says Doris, standing on the outside of the pool fence. 'And you've got another on the way!'

'Afternoon, Doris,' says Ellen. 'Come for a peek at the new pool? Thought you'd be baking for the boys tonight.'

'I am, but I had to check on the kids. And I wanted to sneak a peek at our glorious pool. Bloomin' fantastic isn't it. Good old Board.'

'You boys better not be up to your tricks again,' calls Frank, coming across from the stables.

'Hello, love. Finished for the day?' asks Ellen, as Frank reaches the pool fence.

'Yeah, heading over to Sunshine's to check out his air raid shelter. Him and Dave next to 'im have built shelters in their backyards. They dug 'em out and lined 'em with bags of sand, then covered 'em over with tin and spread dirt over the top. They've even got gas masks in there, just in case! So I'll leave you to it, love,' says Frank. He kisses Ellen on the forehead before walking across the park and over the road to Sunshine's home.

'Mum,' calls Beryl, smacking at the water in the deeper pool. The splashes hit Margaret and her brothers. She's a head taller than most of the children around her.

'Hello, Mrs Gillet,' calls Margaret, waving madly. 'Watch me kick. I'm good at it.' Margaret lays on the tiled pool edge and kicks into the water as a motor boat powering on. Her brothers squeeze their eyes tight and smack into the water near her.

Doris waves to the children as she continues to Ellen, 'Being over the other side of the footy oval doesn't let me see all that's going on, but I hear giggles and laughter. It carries in the wind and across the oval. Puts a smile on me face. And I want to check on who's heading over to the aerodrome with me tonight to feed the boys.'

'It's not me,' says Dot. 'We've got our euchre night on and I'm going over early to meet with Issy and Violet about the school bazaar. That's coming up soon. My turn tomorrow though, and I've already got an apple pie baking in the oven.'

Mick walks across the mowed lawn, having finished watering for the day. 'These kids of ours must be here, Dot,' he says, scanning the swimming pool. 'Bloody oath, there they are,' he chuckles. 'Look at 'em, they're lovin' it. What a sight.' Mick beams from under the shade of his hat. 'Who'd 've thought we'd be able to get a swimming pool during these meagre times. Bloody fantastic Board.'

'They love it,' says Doug, striding behind Mick from the mechanic's workshop. 'Splashin' and jumpin' all over the place.'

'Dad!' calls Vernon. 'Look at me.'

Doug waves to his son curling his toes over the edge of the swimming pool. In bended knee and arms spread wide, he leaps into the air and whacks the water, belly first. He knocks into the backs of Kevin and John, sending the boys gurgling under.

Jean wanders over from across the road with a towel draped over her shoulder, wiping flour caught between her fingers in her pink apron. She leans in beside Doug and hangs the towel over the fence. 'Vernon forgot his towel in all his excitement to get over here,' she says.

'You baking for the pilots tonight, love?' asks Doug.

Jean nods. 'Got a few scones and slices packed in a box. My turn to go out with Doris and give the boys some supper while they do their night flying training. What about beach patrol, who's on roster for that?'

'Not sure. It aint me,' says Doug. 'There's a rumour going round though, that someone mighta seen a Jap plane flying over last week. But I reckon they were on the turps! No one else's seen anything on their patrols. But maybe the Jerry's are spying on Loosey down the bottom-end, who knows.'

'Yeah, I heard that one too,' says Jean. 'Gotta go, love, and get back to the kitchen. Got a few vegies to prepare and some cream lilies to make for Mr Vincent and his visitors tomorrow.'

'I love your cream lilies,' says Tonti, flying past after her brothers. 'But I love this pool more!' She leaps from the pool's side mid-stride into the water, her knees tucked in close, and douses all near.

'Hi, Ma,' waves Noel.

Kath waves back.

'May I have my towel please, Mrs Ryan?' asks Phillip. 'From under your arm.'

'Yes of course, young man,' says Kath, lifting her elbow. 'You have such lovely manners, Mr Flaherty.'

Phillip wipes the mucous dribbling from his nose, then runs to the centre strip separating the wading and deeper pools. He lifts his arms above his head and brings his palms together, bends his knees and drops into the water, hands first.

'Come swim with us, Charlie,' calls Tonti, sitting on the edge of the deep pool.

Charlie's heading for football training at the oval. 'Quick one,' says Charlie from outside the pool fence. 'Just for me baby sis!' Charlie drops his boots onto the grass and slips his thongs off beside it. He hurdles the fence. 'Incoming bomb!'

He soon resurfaces, shaking water from his face and hair.

'Where are you, sis? I'll give you a heave up.' Charlie holds out his upturned hands with fingers weaved tight and waits for Tonti to climb on. As soon as she does, Charlie hoists her into the air to send her flying, and plummeting into the water.

Bob Gebbie from the bottom-end leans over the pool fence. 'Bloody good pool. But we've got to get to footy training, Charlie, before we get extra laps for being late.'

'Comin', Bob.' Charlie hauls himself out of the pool and hurdles back over the fence to Bob waiting.

'Don't wanna be late, bloody hell the extra laps will kill me. I've only been to training twice so far,' says Bob.

'Yeah, poor bastard Ernie last week, first training and he's 10 minutes late, had to run eight laps.' Charlie slips on his thongs and collects his boots from where towels and thongs scatter the grass. 'Didn't matter that he had his school to clean and lock up. Bit harsh if you ask me. And he weren't far behind the blokes comin' in from over the Ranch.'

The two men roll into a casual jog across the grass to the oval.

What a fine sight it is from atop this tree, Mr Boy. How the Board built this glorious swimming pool when the workforce is so depleted is beyond my understanding. The Man Power Authorities have demanded all men up to 41 years of age are released from work for the war effort. Mr Vincent spared all the men he could for defence works and the War, as well as horses and most of the Farm's mechanical equipment. The small number of men left, work hard and only tend to essential sewage treatment tasks.

The Board pay the shortfall in the wages of their workers going to War too, DD, so they can continue to provide a home for their families living here. The Board refuses women to do this dirty work and I would whole heartedly agree, even with maintenance falling into arrears.

I would do it, Mr Boy, I would do this dirty work. It's not fair that old men in retirement are called back to work on the Farm.

No, it's not for women. The Board knows what it's doing, DD.

Muma would disagree with you, Mr Boy!

Knowing your Muma, I'm sure she would, and she'd argue with anyone that says otherwise.

I love my Muma! And I love this magnificence before us, Mr Boy. It's all part of the plan to house the much bigger workforce needed to treat the increase in sewage from good old Melbourne town's predicted population boom. The model town plan will triple the size of this township.

It's a place of respite, DD. Anywhere with you is respite for me.

Mr B ... come swimming with me, the water's calling us. Annie's babies will be here somewhere too, they're always at water and love children just as much as me. Come swim whirly girly with me.

Under leaves staining butter and cherry-red, I skim the pristine water dappled in sunshine lace. Mr Boy's on the tail of my mane most golden, over steps of white hexagon tiles speckled pale blue and curved at their edge, into the spritzing wading pool we dive to whirly-girl dance into the bliss. Stroke, breathe, bathe, twirl .... Through pillars of happy feet we swim, to surface under the mottling canopy of the young Oak tree. Sprays of slender leaves flutter from branches weeping from the white, silken trunk of the ghost gum behind it. Standing tall, as air marshal of the sky, the eucalypt commands well before the first sod was turned for this swimming pool.

Mr B, where are you?

Sloshing beside you, DD. What a place!

Mr Boy's opalescence tinges bronze, capturing the sun's rays. A blush of pink washes over me, radiates from my lacquering purple once again.

In gloating giggles and glee, we and our kinfolk slice through the water to Avro Ansons and Airspeed Oxfords training in the skies above, sometimes tickling past boys and girls that adds to their giggling joy.

Purity of poise, levitating in flotation ... nothing and everything.

PILOTS AND SOLDIERS FORLORN and frayed, arms and legs in halves and missing. They walk weary, disheartened in a stain of grey-blue blood. Khaki uniforms mute in air, land and sea. Some wear dog collars and steel discs stamped in service number and name, their blood type and affiliated religion. Others wear life jackets inflated and not, bomber jackets ripped and breathing apparatus still covering cut and bloodied faces imprinted in shock and horror. Mr B, what is this abstraction?

Mr B doesn't answer.

This benumbing smears us, could suffocate us if we had breath. Of aeroplanes in wings shorn off and tails bombed in jagged shred. Some are studded in exploded shrapnel and others are split in half, pilots mangled of recognition are still strapped in seats.

It's a bleak scene in the airfield at the top of the Farm, a satellite aerodrome to Point Cook and Laverton air force bases.

Detached from the bleak and abstraction are aeroplanes flying overhead, looping and turning, taking off and landing one after the other from no clear designated runway and with only a windsock blowing a direction. Fuel pumps refuel planes from tanks buried underground, leaking flammable liquid into the grass and soil. The air is drenched in a fusion of kerosene and oil. Men run between hangars carrying bundles, some in youthful haste. Others are in the abstraction, worn and tired in an age that has no number, they speak and smile and have a colour of ghostly shade, transparent grey. Army tents line the roadside, guns lean on logs and fences, and more tents congregate on the Werribee Racecourse on the other side of the railway line. It's a webbing network that only a million spiders could weave.

Doris fiddles with her tilly lamp on the table. 'Those boys will be working hard tonight,' she says. 'I hope we've got enough sandwiches and tea for them. Seems to be a few more than usual. I know they need the night training, I mean how else will they learn to penetrate our enemy territory at night. But it's down-right dangerous, Jean.'

The two women have set up beside the administration building, between the living quarters to the south and the hangar in the upper corner of the aerodrome. Four other hangars are spread along the boundary of the airfield.

'I brought extra,' says Jean. 'And I have two full milk churns for any of the boys wanting a cup of milk instead of tea. If one of my boys was training and I couldn't be here to feed them, I'd hope someone would be feeding them. Some of them are so young, barely have a whisker to shave.' Jean rubs her hands together. 'It's getting cool.'

'Ellen's sent a bucket load of sandwiches,' says Doris, unpacking them from a bag and stacking them on the table. 'Poor Ellen. She takes off with the kids to the plantation when the planes fly over and the winds are blowing westerly. She says they shake her house! She's sent a few scones and slices for the boys too, and put herself down to make some more to give to Mrs Locke and Mrs Searle for organising tomorrow night's supper.'

Jean kicks her shoes into the ground. 'The cold's coming alright. Lucky Doug and the kids, they'll be in bed all snug and warm.'

'My lot too,' says Doris. 'But Viv'll be back to pick us up later and take us home.'

'Heard about young Bob the other day, coming home with coffee and cigarettes? He dropped some cream, butter and eggs to an officer up here and the officer gave him coffee and cigarettes in exchange.' Jean laughs. 'Bob thought he'd struck gold!'

An American pilot jogs over to the table. 'Don't you love these Airspeed Oxfords.' His toothy smile lights up the darkness. 'The best twin-engine monoplane ever!'

'Sandwich, dear?' asks Jean.

'Yes please, ma'am.' The young man accepts a round of cheese and tomato sandwiches, his grin now wider. 'They're for training mainly, ma'am, the Airspeed Oxfords. In navigation and radio-operations. We use them as air ambulances in the Middle East too.' The young pilot looks at the milk churn. 'Is that milk from a cow down here at the Farm, ma'am?'

'Yes it is, young man.'

'I'd be most grateful for a cup please. It was creamy gold last time.' His baby blue eyes out shine his smile.

'Come on, mate,' comes a drawl from behind, his accent more nasally broad. 'Us blokes are hungry too.'

The two women speak few words between them and only focus on the trainee pilots streaming in two lines in front of them. The young men are on a quick break after a swanning sequence of take offs and landings in their Avro Ansons and Oxfords. Jean and Doris serve sandwiches, lemon slice and scones, cups of milk and one cup of pale tea after another.

CRASH! HE'S DOWN! HE'S just finished his cup of milk and sandwich, Mr B, oh my dearie me! My tail's a flutter. He's down, they've come down together!

They've burst into flames! To an explosion and a massive ball of orange-tinged, smoking plume.

Both Oxfords are down, Mr B. They crashed together! Into the trees in the top corner of the airfield.

DD, it's okay. Come close, to ease your jitter.

Your steady is strong, Mr B. Dearie me, one taking off, another landing ... and the two crashing.

The pilot coming in to land came in too fast and nose-dived in. His plane shook, DD, his wings weren't able to steady and balance.

'Get the fire trucks out there! Quick.'

'Where's the ambulance?'

'Poor bloody bloke, he was coming in on his side and clipped the tail of the plane taking off! It was his bloody mate too, flying the other plane. A bastard tragedy.'

People run in frantic flee, in a flurry of burning black. Desperate and yelling, screaming for the pilots to be saved.

Trucks and jeeps racing over but they're all too late. Those boys are engulfed in flames.

Where are you going? DD? Wait, wait for me!

Those two boys, their rise is instant. They're already in the trees. Oh those dear boys, dearie me. One is in vibrating shock, that baby-blue eyed American. We must help him, the two of them, help their souls to steady from their earthshattering end.

A carnage of flames devour, spitting and hissing a venomous smog that leaches into the dawn.

HERE'S A BIT OF history for yer, history I witnessed in me life after me railway carriage life. It was February 1940. The Commonwealth Department of Air asked the Board to lease Farm land for a satellite aerodrome. The Board said nah, yer not havin' it, not when the Commonwealth asked for land the year before. Then the No. 1 Flyin' Trainin' School at the Point Cook Air Force base needed more space for its trainee pilots. They said land south and west of the Farm near the Werribee River was perfect. The bloody Board had no choice but to comply because of the need for war trainin', and so this time, the Farm Committee agreed to leasin' land to them at £2.10s. per acre per year, for the duration of the War.

More land was needed after the United States entered the war in December the followin' year, for aircraft and personnel. The Australian Air Force planned to increase its strength from 32 to 73 squadrons. Bloody shit load number that is. The Board leased a further 70 acres in 1942 to the Commonwealth and the Allied Works Council, and the Civil Construction Corps built five hangars of a trussed timber design from the Yanks. They finished bulidin' 'em in March 1943, along with administration buildin's, workshops, storage tanks, armament stores and accommodation huts.

Flights takin' off from the Werribee Airfield are a regular part of life at the Farm. Aeroplanes fly overhead day and night and aeroplanes crashin' weren't uncommon. Pilots stationed at the airfield often went to Dot's card nights in the hall. I'd peer over one Yankee's shoulder 'cause he always had good hands and I'd be burstin' to bet on his hand. Don't know how he bloody did it. They do a bit of machine gun trainin' and bombin' practice at a range built along the foreshore of the Farm too, sometimes gettin' a bit too close to me old home. Men workin' on the Farm sign up to a volunteer roster to patrol the beach in search of Jap aeroplanes.

This airfield'll have a second use after the war.

MR B, HOW FUN! I want to run and scream and go whooshing mad like them. Yankee doodle dandy that smiles with the eyes and his shadowy mate are soaring with the Mayne twins and Vernon, diving and twirling in and out, between the boys and girls.

They never got the aeroplane out of them, DD! More pilots too, are flying in and around the children, who're going crazy mad. They're hitting tins with sticks and running around the streets, yelling and holding up cardboard with PEACE blocked in black paint on it.

I'm going after them, Mr B, to whirly-girl dance with the girls and boys charging the streets like bucking bulls. Yankee doodle dandy that smiles with the eyes and his shadowy mate are popping nails from fence palings as they zoom over them, and the kids are pulling the pickets from Jim Harton's fence and Mr Lynch's next door. My mane most golden is flirting free again, free in peace.

'War's over!'

'Peace! Pe-ace, pe-ace.'

'The Japanese've surrendered! War's over!'

'We won, we won!'

'Victory – Hitler's dead!'

'Prime Minister Ben Chifley announced the news in a radio broadcast this morning, at 9.30! The War's over!'

Les Giroud's chasing Davey Mayne and Mervin Smith, Ronnie Pengelly is hurtling about with Alec and Andy, screaming it's over. Shirl's there with best friend Sunny, and Vernon, Tom and Larry too ... all the girls and boys are running amuck, the dogs in their kennels are barking to the commotion. Hands pound the air, pound pots in smiles and laughs, past the water tank and around the pool to smack the pool fence with sticks. The noise, the laughter ... the raucous song of rejoice!

The adults are out too, singing in too-ra-loos. Frank dashes across the football oval from the carpenter's shop to smack a kiss on Ellen's lips. Dot and Mick are holding hands on the front porch, the ever-hanging cigarette pursed between Dot's lips and hat on Mick's head. Issy and Jack are by them. Frank and Violet, the Lynchs, Smiths, Ryans and Loorhams are in the streets cheering with the kids. Jean and Doris are all smiles with Belle and Ellen, the Giroud sisters are cheering, laughing at the pandemonium. Men have come in from watering the paddocks and stables. Sunshine and Bessie have the nine-gallon keg of beer tapped, making good on their promise for when the war would end. People file into the Cameron's backyard, which is soon chock-full of people celebrating with a beer and sherry and food brought in on plates by the neighbours. All the children are out of school, Billy's running around wearing the gas mask never used and Shirl's playing guitar with Brian Lethers under the peppercorn tree. Roy and Sunshine share horse stories with the Ryans and Forders, of the horses they trained for the army. The drollery and buffoonery that's here now, that would be on the airfield too. The elation and tears barreling into a future secured, with that rose of gold spinning within it.

It's a soaking of peace, Mr B.

With your mane most golden more shimmering in this hour of peace.

IT'S A FUCK OATH day to remember, Wednesday 15th of August 1945. Just days after the US dropped atomic bombs on Hiroshima and Nagasaki, the Japs surrender to the Allied powers. The War's over and with it, six years of wartime hardship. About 34,000 Aussies are lost. From the Farm, all who went to the War, return. Thank Fuck.

Boom times after the war

Women's football team with Ted Whitten, Charlie Sutton and Bill Collins from Footscray Football Club, 1951. Photo courtesy of the Hassett family.

BOYS AREN'T ALL THAT skilled at playing Jacks, Mr B. Ray's throwing them too high and they're bouncing off the back of his hand. There's a knack to catching jacks, Mr B. You've got to be light and relaxed when tossing them up, so they can land softly on the back flat of your hand. Mr B? Are you listening to me? Mr Boy!

Those boys are highly skilled at rolling their marbles, the way they flick them hard or soft depending on their strategy. If only I could roll a marble.

Mr B, I'm rambling and not paying attention to your blight. I'm most sorry for not thinking before I speak.

Thank you, DD. I must say, I admire young Tonti who rolls a marble as good as her brothers.

'Photo time everyone,' calls Jean. Her cream skirt catches on a money bush growing under the kitchen window as she hurries into the backyard. 'Line up along the picket fence. Tall children at the back would be best.'

Vernon kneels in front, with Barb nestling in by him; Kevin, John, Murray and Ron kneel on the other side of Vernon. Dottie stands behind them, beside Ray and Keith, Alec, Davey, Mervin, Les and Andy. All of Vernon's friends are at his party.

'Smi-le, say cheese.'

The boys and girls smirk and smear all sorts of crooked grins and zigzaggy squints, while shooing flies in the afternoon sun streaming into the McKane backyard. Vernon props a salute to his mother.

'Time to sing happy birthday to Vernon. And have cake.'

The children rush inside for one of Mrs McKane's cakes. She has quite a reputation for her cooking. The Board has expanded her kitchen and installed a fancy big oven so Mrs McKane can cater for Mr Lock's meetings and visitors to the Farm.

Three course dinners of soup, roast beef and vegetables, and desserts of golden syrup dumplings or jelly cakes. Morning and afternoon teas were regular too. However, her cream lilies ... every single person wanted the cream filled, sponge delicacy. Even me and Mr B!

CREAM LILIES

3 eggs

Small cup sugar

1 cup corn flour

½ teaspoon bicarb soda

Beat yolks and sugar together.

Beat egg whites until stiff.

Fold in egg whites and sifted flour into yolks and sugar.

Put dessertspoons well spaced on a greased tray. Bake to pale brown in a moderate oven for 10 minutes.

Remove from oven and while the cakes are still hot, fold into lily shapes with fingers or over a wooden spoon as quickly as possible before they start to cool. A good idea is to place the end of the lily in the mesh of the cake cooler to keep its shape as it cools.

When cool, fill with whipped cream and top with a streak of jelly, so they resemble arum lilies.

'RABBIT IN THE SEAT,' yells Les. 'Let's get 'im.'

Les and the boys take off to the paddock where a rabbit sits quiet in the grass. Tonti and Margaret chase after them.

Les hurdles a channel to the paddock. 'Shit,' he laughs. 'I fell in the shit drain.' He climbs out of the waist deep sewage to chuckling around him.

'What's new!'

'I was in it last week,' laughs Davey. 'Surfin' the western carrier on a sheet of tin. Got a red raw sun burn too! Me and Alec.'

'Ya dills!'

'We took that tin ya bent up to the reservoir the other day, but we didn't fall in like you!' laughs Mervin.

'I was catchin' eels off the subdrain near the reservoir to sell to yer mum, Marg. Threepence an eel she gave me,' says Les.

The boys and girls creep towards the rabbit sitting quiet, gathering wide of it.

'Watch 'im,' whispers Margaret, eying the rabbit off.

The rabbit fixes wide-eye and cautious on the strangers. The boys and girls begin jogging together around the rabbit lapping it and inching that bit closer with each lap.

The rabbit never lifts its eyes from them.

'Faster,' says Les. 'Gotta run a faster lap now.'

Quicker and closer they spiral in. Mr B and I loop above them, with Yankee doodle dandy that smiles with the eyes and his shadowy mate always in acrobatic flying loops. The rabbit follows each tight circle. It sways a wobble, gives a wiggle. The children run their circle closer in, now within 10 feet of the rabbit. The fine fluff edging its ears flutters. The rabbit woozy-doozies to lose balance and the children lunge for those ears. We dive into their huddle following the jet stream of Yankee doodle dandy that smiles with the eyes and his shadowy mate.

'Got it!' yells Les, clasping its ears. He snaps its neck; death is instant.

'Another fur for selling in Footscray,' cheers Margaret, patting Les on the back. Her brother, Kevin, cringes and shuns away.

The children march back to the village, Les still in firm hold of the rabbit's ears, its limp body swaying with each step.

'Quick, Ronnie Sharp's at Loorham's!' says Davey, spotting his horse nibbling on grass by the roadside gutter. 'Ronnie's last delivery in town. Gotcha!'

'Let me drop me catch off first,' says Les. He dashes into his backyard and hangs the rabbit on the fence; he's back in an instant. 'Gotta get Mum some kindling on the way back home,' he says, panting.

Margaret and Tonti shoot off down the laneway. 'We're going to the pool.'

'I'm coming too,' calls Kevin.

The boys run in the other direction and crouch into the grass by the hall, peering at the horse and covered wagon loaded in goods.

'Now we wait for his horse to nibble its way down the street,' says Mervin.

'He never ties the bugger up,' says Les. 'Lets it snack on grass while he has his own little snack inside!'

Davey giggles. 'They'll be havin' naughties.'

'In the nuddy!'

Mr Sharp has the fruit shop in Werribee and delivers fruit, vegetables, lollies and lemonade each week in his horse and wagon, to the Farm people. He leaves his delivery to the Loorham household for when Mr and Mrs Loorham are out working. DD, your flush is shimmying under your shine of purple.

Mr Boy, please! The shenanigans partaking inside. I wrap my mane most golden around me.

And still you glisten, DD.

The boys wait in the grass until the horse reaches the end of the road, to be near the Farm hall.

'Let's go,' whispers Les. The boys follow him out of the grass to the wagon harnessed to the horse. Les lifts the flap and the boys begin their pilfering from the back of the wagon, stuffing their pockets with lollies and hanging liquorice straps around their necks, carrying lemonade, apples and oranges, and the peachiest of peaches.

It's late afternoon by the time the boys have finished gorging on their delights in a paddock nearby.

'Who wants to play cricket?' asks Davey.

'Gotta get Mum some kindlin' for the stove first,' says Les. 'Who's comin' with me to Harton's? He's got a barrel full,' smiles

Les. 'We'll get it from there and then we'll have more time for cricket.'

'If he catches you ....'

'He won't catch me, Mervin. I'm too quick for him.'

The boys load up on kindling and drop it a few doors up onto a heap at Giroud's, then head off to play cricket in the laneway. There are enough children to play eight a side, with the Pengellys, Sadlers, Girouds, McKanes, O'Connors, Maynes, Smiths and Kings making up two teams. They bat the tennis ball into paddocks and channels, over fences into gardens, including over Mr Harton's fence into his yard. The older boys try to convince the younger ones to retrieve it, assuring them that Mr Harton won't be so harsh on them. But no one wants to be privy to Mr Harton's wrath.

'I'll get it,' says Les finally. 'You bloody bunch of scaredy cats. I'll jump Harton's fence and get it in a snap.'

No sooner is Les in the forbidden domain when Mr Harton flies into the backyard.

'Get outta me yard, you bastard kid. Get out, ya mongrel!' He chases after Les with his stockman whip. Les is too far from a fence and scrams up a gum tree in the yard. 'Get outta me tree, you shit-house kid.'

Les perches in a bough of the tree. He has nowhere to go.

'Come down. Now! You'll cop a fuckin' hidin' when yer do,' yells Mr Harton, cracking his whip onto the tree's trunk.

Les shudders. Mr Harton goes inside and Les sits on the thick branch, until dusk approaches.

'Tea time, Les,' whispers Mervin from the darkness behind the fence. 'He's gone.'

Les says nothing and climbs down the tree. He scoots over the fence to Mervin. 'Thanks, mate.'

'You better get home for tea. Your dad's on the war path.'

Les dashes home, the stockies' dogs barking from their kennels as he passes by. He creeps inside, only to be greeted by his father with hands on hips, formidable in the hallway.

'Mr Harton says you stole his kindling.'

'No, Dad, no way.' Les fidgets with the flap torn from the pocket of his shorts.

'Mr Harton says you did.'

'No, Dad. Harton's got it in for me,' says Les, peering up at his father.

'Mr Harton to you.'

'Sorry, Dad.'

'Go eat your tea. Quick smart.'

Les slides by his father, certain his father could feel his heart beating in its chest cavity.

I'D NEVER HAVE BELIEVED it after the frightful, grim war, but the 1950s are boom times for Melbourne. We get the Olympics in 1956 and people are in love with the car, which is beginning to choke the city. Of course I have my own love now, my DD. She lightens me, although I'm not sure how much lighter a ghost can be. I'm happy I suppose, and with this sense of belonging somewhere. She won't leave her Muma and Joe, and I won't leave my little DD. We're all connected to the Farm somehow.

We've got freeways and urban sprawl in Melbourne's outer fringes, and suburbs expanding rapidly without regard for basic infrastructure for water, sewerage, drainage, roads and footpaths. The Board struggles to keep up with the pace and develops a Master Plan for Melbourne. They start to set controls on what and how land is used and provide open reservations of land for the public. The number of unsewered properties more than doubles in five years, from 20,000 to more than 51,000. Septic tanks are installed to help reduce the expanding sewerage backlog. Even with 400 workers on the Farm and laying hundreds of kilometres of sewers each year, it's not enough to keep up with demand from the post-war building boom.

Financial problems hit the Board because it doesn't charge enough for services to reflect increasing property values. For the first time since 1893, it raises excess use charges. That's no increase in more than 60 years! Prices go from one shilling per 1000 gallons to one shilling threepence. It's not enough though and as DD's Muma says, heads are well buried in snuff boxes once again.

The Farm and pumping station at Spotswood struggle to cope with sewage flows, especially when it rains and adds volume to the flows. Plans are developed to build a new pumping station at Brooklyn and enlarge the Main Outfall Sewer, allowing more sewage to be carried to the Farm.

Mr Ronalds becomes Engineer-in-Chief. He reorganises the Water Supply and Sewerage Division to create three new groups: Design; Construction and Maintenance; and Scientific Services. It's the first major overhaul of the Board's structure since it began. A dinky-di long time, Joe might say.

'BLOODY BALTS ARE AT it again.' Bill scratches his head. 'Rain, hail or shine, the heat sends them battier than a dog chasing its tail when it has none. Eighty degrees on Satdee at midnight and with a few drinks down the hatch, they bung the place up to shit.'

We not all do that. He wrong that Mr Speckman.

'They're always fightin',' says Vernon. 'And then we're always busy Mondees because we're here fixing holes they make from their weekend brawls. The amount of furniture they break, it's criminal, Mr Speckman.'

'It is, son. And as you know, it's a weekly occurrence in this camp. There's a couple of holes in the shower block that need your patching up too, son,' says Bill.

'Yes, Mr Speckman,' says Vernon.

'You're doing well with your apprenticeship, young Vernon,' says Gordon. Vernon smiles. He walks inside the dining mess, looking for rubbish to take to the tip. 'What'd they get up to this weekend?' Gordon asks Bill, his arms folded across his chest.

'The usual. Card games and getting blotto. Poor buggers. They're all strugglin' with their war horrors,' says Bill. 'We all are.'

He know the mans struggles, and he knows they lonely. That's why they go to Dot's card games. She kind and look after them, feed them cakes and talk to them, even when they not understand English.

'At least they don't run riot when they go across to Mrs O'Connor's euchre nights,' says Vernon. He looking at the broken legs of three chairs in the corner of the dining mess.

'They'll need fixing too, son,' says Bill.

'No worries, Mr Speckman.' Vernon rifles through his tools and pulls out his hand drill and bit brace.

'I wouldn't want your job, Bill,' says Gordon. He stand far away from Bill, who also folds his arms in his chest. What wrong with these two men?

'Some of them went to the movies in Werribee,' calls Wally Steinbergs from the kitchen, where he stewing mutton in a big pot on the stove. His thick Latvian accent is good here in the camp, it like everyone's accent. He flee Latvia with his wife, Monikas, and their children, and come to work here at the Farm. His family, they stay at Bonegilla while Wally work here but soon, they come to live on the Farm and stay here until 1971. Sheesh, they must like it here. That a long time. They will be a last family to leave the Farm.

Voldemars is Wally's real name. The Aussies call him Wally for short. All Latvian names have an 's' at the end: Monikas and Ventis and Juris, the sons of Monikas and Wally. Steinbergs too, where Steinberg has no 's' in German spelling.

Wally tips the edge of his chef hat to sit higher on his head. He sharpening his knife on a stone on the kitchen bench. 'They go to the movies to see *Dream Girl* with Betty Hutton and Macdonald Carey. They say it's a comedy, but that's not true, not if they come out of the picture theatre angry. They start a big fight with knives because somebody call Adomas a stinkin' Balt.'

'All bloody hell broke loose!' says Bill. 'Come'n Gordon.' Bill strolls towards the door. 'There's a mound of broken chairs beyond repair and a table snapped to bits for you blokes to take.' The two walk outside to wooden crates full of broken beer bottles and furniture, and hessian bags filled with pieces of wood, cardboard, paper, and hundreds of cigarette butts. They two walk across the wooden floor with much distance, a truck can drive between them. I heard the rumour that their battalions fight during the war. But they not speak about it.

MANY DISPLACED PERSONS COME to work at the Farm and live in the Balts Camp. Balts are Latvian peoples and when the Soviet Union takes over Latvia after World War II, many Latvians escape to Australia. They are homeless and have no country.

Sometimes, when country borders change, persons can become displaced too.

This story I tell you, for it is not for the young ones like Dear Daughter and Mr Boy, even if they think they know everything, like all young ones think they do. Coming in on Annie's rose of gold, it's the same with children in the millennia.

I'm not a displaced person but I'm from Germany and I'm here because of the War. I live in the Bonegilla Camp. My friend, Wladyslaw, from Poland, he live there too. Wladyslaw was a teacher and officer during the War before he come to Australia. The German army catch him soon after the war start and make him a prisoner in a camp in Bavaria until 1945. He learn to speak English there, and he meet his wife. He always tell me, all his body sings when he first saw his beloved, across the village platz.

'She was always smiling,' say Wladyslaw. 'And she have a gentle angel smile.'

'Oh mine god, Wladyslaw,' I say to him. 'You tell me this all the nights when we lay in our army beds!'

'Ahh, but this woman, as soon as the war ends and after six years of no woman, oomba-boomba,' say Wladyslaw. 'I could not keep my hands from her!'

'That's enough, Wladyslaw! I no want to hear anymore,' I say. Secretly, I want to know more but that his wife now.

'She was the same with me, always want me. Oomba-boomba. We have our daughter very quickly, and then a son and then we must run from Bavaria with them. It was impossible to live in Germany or Poland after the war because the countries were enemies. We have no choice but to run away.'

They come in Melbourne on Christmas day in 1949, same as me on the same ship. We stay on the boat because no one was working on Christmas day to take us off. We have lunch and their children could not eat it. It was a single lettuce leaf, a slice of tomato and a small piece of meat. I remember that because Wladyslaw's beloved, she so sad, and Wladyslaw say his beloved's always-smile fades because a cloud passes over her. The next day, they put us on a train to the camp at Bonegilla, along the border of Victoria and New South Wales. It was such a long trip, oh mine god, we were going to nowhere. Villages at home were only two miles apart but travelling to Bonegilla, we saw much nothing, no villages anymore. Wladyslaw's beloved, she cry for her family and the children hug her on the train.

We come to Bonegilla and still no nothing; no trees, no flowers, all hot and dusty and a barbed wire fence all around it. Oh mine god, it remind me of a concentration camp. On hot days, we must take buckets of water inside the barracks and tip it on the floor to cool down.

From the first night in the camp at Bonegilla, all the families are separated. Wladyslaw's wife and the children stay in one part of the camp, and Wladyslaw has a bed near me with the other men.

The Bonegilla Camp started two years before we arrive and is full of people with no home. We not pay to come to Australia but we must work for the Australian government for two years. That was the immigration contract. They give us jobs from the Bonegilla, to help Australia rebuild after the war. That was the government program and displaced persons were not in competition with the Aussie workers. Some of them go to build in the Snowy Mountains, that was big work.

Many Europeans who lose their home are very scared of being catched and tortured because of their politics and religion. More than 170,000 displaced persons come in Australia from 1947 to 1952, and nearly 20,000 are from Latvia. Many Latvian refugees work at the Farm and live in the Balts Camp.

Balt, it is such a bad word. The government, they try to forbid the word and say, 'These people are innocent victims of war, displaced from their homes and homelands, and now, as Australia is the land of resettlement for them, they are no longer displaced persons.' He use a lot of big words but I say he is right. No matter if some call it the Balts Camp or the Migrants Camp, or the New Australian Camp, any way you want to call it, the camp on the Farm is for us migrants. I call it the New Australian Camp and they make it in the barracks left on the Werribee Airfield after the war, near Farm Road.

Here he comes. As soon as you say airfield, the Yankee doodle dandy that smiles with the eyes and his shadowy mate fly in.

You're speaking about my home, sir, our barracks during the war. The Australian Airforce and Army, and the good ol' American Air Force built those barracks. We had a shower and toilet block outside, a kitchen and dining mess. It was a fine place indeed, with all the whining wavering of the Avro and Oxfords diving over paddocks. Music to my ears they were.

The armed forces, they go now, and all the old aeroplanes are resting. They taken apart and their pieces are sent around the world. What is left, goes in the smelter on the airfield for melting. The aeroplanes, they not really resting, mine god no.

No-sir-ee, they're not, not us pilots either. We fly our loops in fine acrobatics. The Aussies say we lark in loops because we sometimes fly pranks. DD flies with us when Mr Boy is able to be without her. We fly and circle together. She's a darling gal that DD, a fine flyer in her mane most golden. Speaking of which, I've got to take off. Until next time, good day to you.

Yankee doodle dandy that smiles with the eyes and his shadowy mate fly away, always flying, flying. Anyway, I was telling you about Bonegilla and how the government visit Bonegilla Camp to find workers and in January 1950, a week after we get to Bonegilla, the Farm Manager, Mr Lock, he come and offer Wladyslaw a three-year contract. He say to Wladyslaw, come and fix fences on the Farm, be a labourer. I was so happy for Wladyslaw. But I was very sick by then. My stomach is sore. It not liking the fatty mutton they cook for us. Wladyslaw was a kind man, he bring me tea in bed. He look after me, sometimes he bring me toast mit marmalade too. He was my only friend in Bonegilla.

I die when Wladyslaw leave Bonegilla because no one look after me anymore. So I follow my friend here, to live in the New Australian Camp on the Farm with him and the other migrant mans. His beloved wife and children stay in Bonegilla while Wladyslaw searches for a home for them in Werribee. It take him four months to find a very nice house for his family.

It was hard for Wladyslaw at first. He not good at fixing fences when he not use a hammer before. And staying in the New Australian Camp, he miss his family very much. But what choice does he have if he want a new life. People always say to him, 'don't tell them you are a teacher, Wally, or have an education because they only want manual workers, labourers.' The Australians, they must like the name Wally and call Wladyslaw, Wally too, like Voldemar. And so we have two Wallys in the camp.

Wally has to make his hands hard when he starts on the fencing gangs and the Union say he must join the trade union because that's the rule if you working here. The mans are scared, oh mine god, because they think the union is mit the communist party and they just escape from the communists in Europe!

The governments in Australia was preparing for thousands of new houses they need to build after the war. Oh mine god, up to 12,000 houses a year. This big population would make problems because much more sewage would go to the Farm and the Board of

Works need more mans to clean it. So it plan for Melbourne's big population and get many workers to help treat the sewage. But they not have enough houses for all the workers and the big architects of Melbourne, they make a report to build more houses in the Head of the Road township. The report say such things as planting trees and the gardens, the materials and labour to build the houses and all the things for a nice life. They make very fine drawings too.

FARM MINUTES - MIGRANT CAMP

The severe labour shortage experienced throughout the country after World War II affected labour at the Farm, where numbers had been greatly reduced and some 500 new employees were needed.

Between 1949 and 1953, huts on the site of the old RAAF base were used to accommodate some 100 migrants, who in turn were required to remain in the Board's employ for 3 years.

Due to a shortage of New Australian labour, the camp was used as single men's quarters from 1953 until 1956 when it eventually closed down.

Mans stay working on the Farm for short times and long times. Some go to other government work and some, they stay and work on the Farm for many, many years after finding a house here, or in Werribee or Little River, and they catch the bus to work at the Farm. Wladyslaw grow to love the Farm and stay working here for a long time. He was one of the lucky blokes, as the Aussies say. He escape the Germans to make a new life in the lucky country.

When Wladyslaw move into the New Australian Camp, Bill Speckman was managing the kitchen and Wally Steinbergs help old Bill cook in the kitchen. By 1950, it become too much for Mr Speckman. Poor old Bill, the mans from the camp complain that the food is very bad too. So old Bill retire and he ask the mans, 'Who wants to help in the canteen?'

Of course, my friend Wally, straight away put the finger up. 'I will do the kitchen,' he say to old Bill.

'I think you'll be very good in the canteen, Wally,' says Mr Speckman. 'You speak very good English too, and most men in the camp don't.'

A week later, Mr Speckman say to Wally, 'The Farm bosses want to change the job, Wally. They like you to manage the canteen as a business.'

'That's a big difference to only doing the cooking, Mr Speckmen. I'd have to leave my labouring job on the Farm.'

'And that will be okay, Wally. It still falls under the immigration contract,' says Mr Speckmen. 'But Wally Steinbergs will have to go back to labouring because the kitchen will be yours to manage.'

It funny because the two Wallys, they swap jobs! It now 1951 and the kitchen belong to Wladyslaw Roper, Wally Roper as the Aussies say.

For the next four years, Wally do the kitchen with his days starting at 3am. He ride his bicycle one and a half miles from his home in Werribee to the New Australian Camp every day. The mans there, they pay for Wally to make the breakfast, lunch and dinner for them. I think the Aussies, they call dinner, tea. The mans live well, better to some of the other camps where displaced persons work. Conditions there, oh mine god, are very bad. They sleep in tents in freezing cold, and work and live in mud to build roads with picks and shovels, and drive tip trucks in sandstorms along dangerous tracks.

The mans here in the New Australian Camp, they have good beds under shelter, good food and good working conditions. A young church woman, Mrs Scully, she come from Werribee one night a week to teach the mans English. Wladyslaw has good English but no time to teach. He try to help the mans by buying soaps and the cigarettes, washing powder, some razors, and special drinks like lemonade, and they pay Wladyslaw for them.

Wladyslaw, he feed 100 men every day. He make the breakfast what old Bill made, bacon and eggs. And he make sandwiches on a big bench. Three sandwiches for each man, in the beginning for 20 people but now, for 100. One sandwich with cheese and two with sausage, which are tastier than the grey fatty mutton sandwiches Mr Speckman made. He has a little bag and puts one spoon of tea in the bag and a spoon of sugar. He wraps it up and when the mans came to get their breakfast, they take the lunch and the tea with them to work. It was a lot of work for Wally and once he and his beloved's children start school, his beloved would walk to the camp to help Wladyslaw in the kitchen. His beloved is Wladyslaw's only helper. He always thanks her, and kisses her and make her a cup of coffee and a biscuit when he go home from work.

Wally make soup for the dinner and fry the meat and make a sauce with it, and sometimes spaghetti. His pudding with fruit from the tin on top was fantastic. The mans eat it in four spoons. His beloved, she peel many potatoes and pumpkin, and slice the bread and put it on the table with the butter. Sometimes, they have bosses coming from Melbourne to visit the Farm, some vets too, and they have lunch at the camp and Wally's beloved serve them.

The visitors, they say to her, Mrs Ropa, your accent, where are you from? You speak so soft and soothing, like sweet cordial. She not know what is this cordial, until Wladyslaw make her some. She smile and say it is delicious, like the raspberry syrup her mum make. Wladyslaw, he say to his beloved, 'Gertrude, you charm everyone with your sunshine smile.'

Gertrude say Wladyslaw is always a wonderful man. He place food orders and clean the kitchen and dining room while the mans work. He have a big trough for all the plates and he clean them and wash them all, fill up all the bottles for sauce, wipe the tables and mop the floors, and come back home at seven o'clock. He do the kitchen, seven days a week.

When Gertrude help Wally, their children ride the bikes to the kitchen after school. They have a cold glass of milk from the milk churns and milk arrowroot biscuits while the parents work. Sometimes, the children ride to the village to swim in the pool. Oh mine god, they love swimming there. Gertrude must fight them to go home when she finishes helping with the dinner. Sometimes they take a ride home with the Farm boss when he pick his son who make university, from the train station.

The mans leave the camp slowly and there is less and less. Wladyslaw say, 'I can't do it anymore, I must do the same work for a hundred people that I do for 20 people and 10 people. It is not a good business anymore.' He finish the kitchen in 1954.

Everything change now. People living on the Farm start to leave to live in new homes in Werribee, Little River and Lara. They buy cars and the Farm bus picks them up to bring them to work. This model town of the future is never built because the Board of Works not need more houses for their workers anymore. Some people whisper that the Board of Works want people to leave their house on the Farm because they scared of inbreeding, like when cousins or second cousins marry and have babies. Gertrude, she make her eyes and smile upside down when she hear the whispers. She happy people are moving from the Farm. Gertrude would make her whole head upside down and run like a chicken with no head if she hear the other whisper, of the teenager who rub the young girl in the swimming pool. Oh mine god. We not know where the boy touch her but it is somewhere very private because the girl, she run away from him and cry to her mother and the boy, he stand at the swimming pool and laugh at her. The girl, she never, never, never go back to the swimming pool. Oh mine god, if Gertrude know this when her children were swimming there.

The Farm bosses, they think Wladyslaw is a very good man and they say to him, 'Wally, you come take a new job and look after security on the Farm.' Wladyslaw, he take this job because he know Gertrude misses her family and he wants to earn money to send her home to visit them.

Some people, they scared of Wladyslaw when he become security man. Not me. I not leave my best friend. We have funny times together in his new job. Sometimes, mans with their children not from the Farm come here to catch rabbits. Wladyslaw is good at security, he hide in trees and sneak up on them, and drive fast to catch them when they try to run away from him. Sometimes, they disappear in the bushes and Wladyslaw, he not see them. So I blow in the trees to shake the leaves and still, he not a good detective and not see them. They laugh when Wladyslaw drive away. I laugh too.

The Farm become special to Wladyslaw and he care for it very, very much. He work at security for more than twenty years. He retire from the Farm at 65 years old.

SHE LINES THE WORN burgundy ball in front of the goal posts, clutching it firm in her hands. She takes a few steps towards the goals wearing her brother's boots from years ago. Her momentum gathers in a few strides and she sinks her boot into the ball to kick it towards the goals. High and straight it sails, through the centre of the two tall posts. I twirl after the ball and Yankee doodle dandy that smiles with the eyes and his shadowy mate barrelling loops in front of me.

'Go, Mon!' yells Margaret.

Cheers and applause from the four-deep crowd jostling at the oval boundary, a standing ovation from those in the timber grandstand. The roar soars into the trees fringing Chirnside Park and even the fronds of the Bunya Bunya Pine seem to revel in the appreciation. Mr B lingers in the honouring of the River red gum on the bend of the Werribee River, a distance away.

'That's my friend, Monica Miller,' says Margaret, rushing past Linda Tetsil, sticking her tongue out for added gloat. Shirl, Sunny, Mary and the other girls in the team swarm Monica. 'Best drop kick in Werribee!'

Linda stands with her hands on her hips as Monica receives one pat on the back after another. 'Shit.'

'Okay, back we go, girls,' says Monica, her tone always subtle. 'And let's do it again.' Monica claps the girls and sends them back to their positions. She jogs to the centre square, past Linda snarling.

'Best drop kick or not, you won't be doing that again,' snarls Linda.

Ted blows the whistle and bounces the ball in the centre circle. Beryl leaps up and taps the ball toward the Services goals.

Linda's not watching the ball and instead, is eying off Monica. The two women hip and shoulder one another.

'Captain-shmaptain!' barks Linda, shoving Monica to the ground and sending her sliding across the dewy grass and onto the pitch still recovering from cricket season. Monica jumps up, blood glistening over her mud-streaked thigh. She dashes after Margaret who is bouncing the ball on the run.

'Marg,' calls Monica.

Margaret hand passes the ball over Loris's head to her captain. Loris charges for Margaret even though the ball is well gone. She shoves Margaret into the ground. Margaret rolls twice to finish flat on her back and Loris jumps on top.

I roll and roll, waving to Mr B still perched afar. He waves his short stump at me.

Monica marks the ball and hand passes it to Sunny. It bounces into her shins. Shirl's by her, as always, and scoops the ball on the rebound to kick it to Mary. The kick's too long and glides over her head. Beryl's behind her though. Go Beryl! She hoists her arms up and marks the ball over Mary's head in her ever-unfaltering grin. I shoot up to mark my ball too – go Beryl!

Yankee doodle dandy that smiles with the eyes and his shadowy mate zoom by and I'm whisked into their jet blast.

Shirl runs onto the goals and calls for Beryl to kick it to her. Linda rushes in and knocks Shirl head first onto the wet grass.

Sunny's cheeks flush in the colour of her hair and she charges for Linda, steamrolling her into the ground as a prized Farm bull. The two women scuffle on the ground; I dive in to help Sunny. Yankee doodle dandy that smiles with the eyes and his shadowy mate rocket past with Mr B and suck me into their jet stream once again. My mane most golden tangles into a tease.

DD, why the need to be such a tomboy all the time!

And why do you have to be such an upturned stuffy stiff! Leave me alone, Mr Boy. I barrel in summersaults back to the coach's box where I know he'll dare not enter.

Ted runs to the women on the ground and blows his whistle. 'That's enough, girls,' he calls.

The crowd cheers as corellas screeching at raucous galahs.

'Teddy's got his job cut out for him,' says Charlie in the coach's box. Apples Preston stands by him in folded arms. He's coached these mighty women for the last two years and arranged for them to play their first match at the Footscray ground in 1951. After which, Margaret and Monica invited Charlie Sutton and Ted Whitten to be involved in the match today.

'No more than he gives,' laughs Charlie. 'His fondness of back-chatting gets him into all sorts of trouble with the umpires.' He slides his hands into his woollen trouser pockets. 'Bit nippy today.'

'Fondness! I'd say it's a volatile back chatting,' laughs Apples.

Ted pulls Sunny from Linda. The two women are panting with scratches riling red on arms and legs and hair pulled and plucked into battered birds' nests. Ted smirks a smile of hard knocks after he debuted in VFL football this year for Footscray and came up against Mopsy Fraser of Richmond. Ted politely offered his hand before the opening bounce of that game, only to receive a sharp kick in the ankles in return. Undeterred, Ted goaled after marking early in the first quarter and Mr Mopsy, ooh-ee, he retaliated in such a way that sent Ted to a hospital bed. Wound-up Mr Boy says such stories are not for women, and he dislikes women playing football altogether. Stuffy old stiff. Not me, Whirly-girl chasing after the ball flying down the ground is, is ... well it's the complete opposite of being as insipid as a limp lettuce leaf sitting in a hundred degree heat!

'It's gonna be a bloody ball up again. You girls are playin' that bloody hard. Make some room,' says Ted.

The girls spread out, pushing and shoving some more. Ted tosses the ball up. Beryl taps it on to bounce at Teresa Green standing clear at the opposite end of her goals. She picks it up, tucks it under her arm and runs. And runs some more along the wing towards her goal without a bounce, and some more again past the 50-yard line, as the heron that's stolen the prized mollusc. The girls on both teams laugh, Sunny and Linda included.

'Let her go, let her go,' laughs Ted, swinging his arms to motion Teresa forward.

Teresa dashes towards the goal, still smirking with her prize. She's run 50 or 60 yards without a bounce.

'Kick the ball now, young Teresa,' calls Charlie from the side.

Teresa reaches the edge of the goal square and drops the ball to her boot, kicking it to skim past the goal post. The crowd cheers and whistles, claps as the girls from both teams run around Teresa giggling and laughing.

Charlie takes Apples' hand and shakes it. 'We've done a fantastic job training these girls.'

'My oath,' laughs Apples. 'Seriously though, Charlie. These girls love their footy. Twice a week they're at training through most of the footy season, rain or hail. We're up one end of the ground while the boys are up the other. Keen as mustard they are.'

'Dedicated women, that's a certainty,' says Charlie.

The siren wails. Shirl runs for Sunny. 'Winners!' The two huddle. Ted walks over to the sideline to Apples and Charlie, leaving Beryl and three other girls to haul Margaret onto their shoulders. I whirly-girl dance above them with Yankee doodle dandy that smiles with the eyes and his shadowy mate flying in loops, steep turns and barrel rolls, finishing with a downward bomb burst that I can't help but plummet after.

'Three cheers for us!'

'Bloody good girls,' says Charlie. 'They've done a sterling job, and they understand the game better than a lot of blokes.'

'Bloody oath!' says Ted, pulling on a woollen coat to cover his bare arms and legs. 'Up, the nay-sayers.' Ted shoots his thumb up. 'The bloody toffs'd be turnin' their noses. The girls did good.'

'Come in girls,' calls Apples from the boundary. He turns back to Charlie and Ted. 'Improved a heap since their first game here.'

Ted smiles. 'They've invited us to pie night next Thursdee, you and me Charlie.'

'No worries, I'll be there.'

'The girls've raised £2000 already! That's a shit load of money from donations and women making and selling chutneys and sponges.'

'And don't forget the entry fee to this game. Bloody good girls they are. More than half of them come from the Metro Farm too.' Apples walks to the women strolling into the boundary.

'Too right. And all to raise money to build a new hospital in Werribee, and for the Children's Hospital!'

THE WOMEN PLAY FOOTBALL in Werribee to much admiration from 1951 to 1954, at the Metro Farm, Geelong, Footscray and Chirnside Oval grounds. Some turned up noses to it and considered it unladylike. Unfortunately, I was one of them, and considered bathing in a tub of lemon juice after receiving a million cuts to be better than sitting on the sideline enjoying a women's football match.

Yer had the wrong end of the pineapple there for a while, young Mr B.

I know, Joe, I see the error in my ways now. I'd hide in the River red gum when DD and Yankee doodle dandy that smiles with the eyes and his shadowy mate flew over the women coming down the player's race to go onto the ground. The women would giggle and glow red, be daunted by the huge spectator crowds that gathered for their games. It was DD who taught me to understand and appreciate the game.

You mighta been jealous, matey.

Perhaps, Joe. But as games were played, I began to watch more closely and appreciated their skill. A 'Best Farm Team Ever' was assembled in 1954 and the women wore the infamous red jumpers with white 'V' of the Herefords, the Metro Farm men's football team. They wore them puffed out proud and I blew puff and proud for them. The women also got to wear the Hereford burgundy team blazer to pie night after borrowing them from the men's team. The women's team had nothing and would borrow football boots and shorts from brothers and friends and make the rounds of shops in Werribee, asking for donations of oranges and chewies.

The women had much support and recruited special football guests to their games. Bob Davis was involved in the Geelong game. The Werribee women played that game at the invitation of the women in Geelong who wanted to raise money to build a hospital in their town too.

Carlton player, Chooka Howell, and Footscray player, Jack Collins, umpired games. Bruce Comben, the son of Aub Comben, the grocer delivering to the Farm's residents, played football for Carlton and was supportive. He helped Monica and Margaret set up games and find jumpers when they were needed and arranged for donations too. Bruce encouraged the women playing to mob Mr Chooka at the end of a match and tear off his shirt. Charlie Sutton from Footscray coached both women's teams one year.

Me and Else were at that one, when Chooka went runnin' off the ground with his torn shirt hanging by threads. You were scoffin' at that one, Mr B, if I remember correct, and tried wavin' DD away from the ground. A few bloody men and women were shaking their heads that day. Bloody toffs.

You recall correct, Joe. And DD, what a ray of sunshine. She was so busy laughing and sailing with the ball through the goals with Yankee doodle dandy that smiles with the eyes and his shadowy mate, that she didn't notice me calling her away. That was when I realised her true beauty, her comfortability in who she was, in her shiny purple amoebic form. She told me later that sailing through goal posts was one of her most funnest things to do, and especially through the Farm goal posts because they were crowned with ventilation holes and she wished a whiff of the sewage odour seeping from them. These goal posts were connected to underground pipes and were ventilation columns as well as goal posts.

Old before yer young years, Mr B. I'm happy you've loosened up a bit, you needed to.

My perch from the River red gum gave me good sight and I most enjoyed DD's revelling in cheeky Mr Whitten whispering to the women, to push and shove when they played, to make the game bigger and something to be remembered. He'd tell them the crowd would love it. And the crowd did, cheering and yelling whenever the girls scuffled. Nobody was ever hurt, not really, not unless Linda Tetsil pushed someone. I must say, even I was scared of her. She was so big. Sometimes she'd sink her claws into the jumper of a girl running past and whiz them through the air as an upside-down cake pan. They'll call them Frisbees in time to come, the plastic version of the cake or pie pan throwing.

Linda and Sunny would fake fights in games but never come to fisticuffs. Loris got Margaret once with a most grand push. She was a bitch.

Mr Boy! What's come over you, buddy?

Sorry, Joe, hush my tongue. She stole one of Margaret's boyfriends once. And Linda, she gave Monica such grief when she pushed her onto the cricket pitch. It slit Monica's arm. She had to take a week off from working in the clothing factory because of the poison in the material that could seep into her wound. That was a week without wages.

All for the cause to raise money to build a new hospital in Werribee and for the Children's Hospital in Melbourne. Fundraising was important to the Farm people, from growing onions to feed men and women at war, to raising money for the Farm football, tennis and cricket teams and all four Farm schools. It started early, was instilled in the young ones. And continued even when the good Farm people leave their homes, where the Farm workers raise money through their social club.

LETTER TO MISS ISABELLE MAYNE

From the Children's Hospital, Carlton, 1946

Dear Miss Isabelle,

I am informed by Mr. Mason, the Headteacher of your School, that you and Miss Kathleen McKee have raised the sum of £9 by a bazaar organised for our Hospital Appeal.

I want to let you know how pleased I am, in the first place for your kindness in thinking of the sick children, and especially for the very splendid amount which you have raised. Your action is certainly evidence of your sympathy for the sick children, and I can assure you the amount will help us in our efforts to restore them to health and strength. Yours faithfully,

V Barrett, Manager.

'OKAY YOU BLOKES, GET into groups of six for line work.' Les stands on the flank of the Metro Farm ground. 'Last game we played against INF was piss weak. I want aim and I want goals.'

Digger, Noel, Frank, Texas and Vernon hurdle the fence to make a group. Bull charges behind them. The other half dozen players form another group.

'And let's do it properly. The women played better footy than you blokes on the weekend,' calls Les.

Dot leans over the white fence railing with the usual cigarette pressed between her lips, the ash about an inch long. 'The women did well on the weekend,' she says to Gordon beside her.

'Yeah, not bad at all. And they raised a heap of money,' says Gordon.

'We'll be raising a bit more too with our card game on Mondee night,' says Dot. 'Money to buy sports equipment for our schools.'

'Swap,' yells Les. 'Left footers go right, right footers go left.' By now, Les has joined the second group to warm up.

'Pick up the bloody ball and stop yer fumbling,' calls Gordon. 'The kids did a better job picking up beer bottles after last week's game.'

'They got 10 pence a dozen too,' says Dot. 'Blimey, they're havin' trouble holding the ball tonight. The heavy dew's got them stumped.'

'We'd have a swig of Whiskey at half time when we'd play in this cold,' chuckles Gordon.

Dot laughs. 'You'd be runnin' round and you need warmin' up!'

'Yeah, who am I kiddin'. Some blokes would turn up and play pissed as.'

'Well I reckon one or two of them out there tonight might be half tanked, the way they're fallin' all over the place.'

Gordon laughs.

'Got the ad in the Werribee Banner,' says Dot. 'For our dance an' euchre party in two weeks' time. We'll get a few come to that, and raise a decent pot for the Herefords. Our card games've been a good fundraiser for years.'

'The blokes last Mondee shoulda led with a singleton off-suit ace,' says Gordon. 'Coulda trumped the ace.'

'Then they spent the next half hour dissecting the hand,' laughs Dot.

'I dunno how you keep up with all the fundraisin' you do, Dot.' Gordon kicks into a tuft of grass, the top half of his shoe wet after walking across the paddock from his home by the office. 'Close game last Satdee. The boys on their own ground are hard to beat.'

'A 13-point win against Altona isn't good though,' says Dot. A plume of smoke escapes her mouth. 'Altona aren't much chop.'

'Yeah but geez, they turned on some fast footy.' Gordon leans over the railing. 'Good one, Vern. Solid mark,' he calls onto the field. 'So you got enough coming to the euchre night on Mondee, Dot?'

'Yeah, got a few. Maybe 15 so far, and a few will come across from the Balts Camp.'

'Better tell Mick not to stoke the fires too much and make you too comfortable, not like a few weeks ago when you girls pulled an all-nighter!'

'Bloody good game of cards that was. Edna Sadler and Eunice McKane, shit they played well. Edna should've played the clubs and she would've won the pot!'

'And the dance after the game this coming Satdee, we've got that sorted I think.' Gordon doesn't shift his eyes from the men training.

'Just need a load of saw dust from the carpentry workshop dropped over to the hall, so we can scatter it on the dance floor. Can't sashay the Modern Waltz without it, Gordon!'

'Or the Foxtrot.'

'Too right.'

'We'll get a few in there on the Sundee for a good clean up after it to make sure it's spick 'n' span for your card game Mondee night. Leave it with me, Dot.'

'A president's job's never done, Gordon.' Dot stubs her cigarette into the wet grass and slips the butt into her apron pocket. 'Me and Mick'll be there to help ya, we'll get a few others over to tidy up. And we'll have to start planning Guy Fawkes night soon, after footy finishes. Mick's got some fireworks already stored.'

'I'll start organising wood to build the bonfire so we can make it as big as last year. The kids loved it, and settin' off the crackers.' Gordon yells onto the ground. 'Pick up the ball, fumble fingers!' He still doesn't shift his gaze from the ground. 'The food's all sorted, the band too.'

'Yep, everyone'll bring a plate. Jean's on cream lilies and sponges, Kath's on jelly cakes and Ellen's on lemon slice. Issy, Violet and Doris're makin' sandwiches. Sonny Hassett's playing accordion.'

'Nell's makin' sandwiches too,' says Gordon.

'Yep, she's on me list, and Bessie Cameron's making sandwiches. Got a couple of apple pies comin' and I'll make a few scones.' Dot studies the dark sky. 'I better go, Gordon, before me tea dries up. Stewed eel tonight and a bit of leftover plum pud. Need to check on one of me cows too if Mick hasn't already. When the kids went to block eight to call them in, one of 'em had a red right udder. Probably an infection. She came into the yard okay but she's swollen. Margaret loves callin' in the cows. She's always asking how they know which yard is theirs, how they wander in for milking without anyone leading them into the yard.'

'Yeah, Dot. You better get goin', it's startin' to rain.' Gordon pushes his hat firm over his head and lifts the collar of his coat to shield his neck. 'I'll be off soon meself. Nell's probably having a cuppa with Doris after she and the girls've finished cleaning the office.'

'Bloody good old Board,' says Dot. 'Giving Doris a cleaning job so she's got the house to live in after Viv died. She woulda had to find a new home if she weren't workin' here on the Farm. I still have a giggle when I think back to how scared she was to flick the switch for power, after movin' into the cottage up here and not havin' electricity in Murtcaim. Took her years to get used to using electricity.' Dot fiddles with the lid of her cigarette packet in her pocket.

'She worked hard to look after those five kids after Viv died. Ironed and cleaned for the mangers and still used the flat iron when she had electricity for an electric one!'

'The girls helped a lot. They had to.'

'Not sure how much me young Eleanor's helpin' clean over at the office!' Gordon gives a chuckle. 'She'll be soaking up all the juicy news those girls'll spit out. And I'll bet you a pack of cigarettes they'll be talking about Beryl's boyfriend, Don Breguet, from over Murtcaim.'

'Beryl's a good girl. She stepped up when she was only nine years old, took on all the outside chores before and after school while the older girl helped Doris inside.' Dot pulls out a cigarette from her apron pocket. 'Good old Doris, she got her licence a year after Viv died, learning to drive in a Whippet. And then Beryl'd crank the handle on her mother's car to start it. Such a sturdy lass, and yet so softly spoken.'

'Some mornings when I'd be up early taking a pee, she'd be swingin' that axe like a professional wood chopper, cuttin' wood for the stove and copper to heat the water. Splinters never bothered her.'

'Splinters. I'll never forget Mick having to take a splinter out of young John's willy after he slid down the ramp in the sheep yards.' Dot chuckles. 'I had to hold John while Mick pulled it out. At least half an inch long it was. Poor bugger. He ran around confused about God for a while, couldn't work out why God had punished him for being a naughty boy when he hadn't done anything wrong.'

Gordon scratches his head. 'Bloody hell, Dot, poor kid. Brings a tear to me eye.'

'Yeah, poor bugger was on his best behaviour after that. Well, for a bit of a time anyway.'

Les blows his whistle. 'Five laps of the oval boys!'

'Girls and their boyfriends, we might have a couple of weddin's coming up, Gordon, what with Beryl and Donald and me John and his girlfriend, Marjorie. There'll be a lot to do to get them organised, and the hall's the perfect place for a wedding reception.'

Gordon nods to the cigarette Dot holds between her fingers. 'Another one, Dot! You said you were going.'

'Yep, you're right. Better go. They'll be finishing soon anyway. The fog's rollin' in, they'll be blinded and end up kicking balls over to the workshops!'

'And you might fall in a drain, Dot!'

'Yeah, on me way now. Mick'll be waiting. Toodles, Gordon.' Dot takes off across the grass, towards the swimming pool.

'Hooroo, Dot.'

METRO. FARM

Werribee Shire Banner, Thursday 17 July 1952

Another scalp to their belts the Farm boys seem to be proving themselves real mudlarks. However, the big test is next Saturday, wet or dry. Any way, the boys will be triers.

Congratulations to Jack McKee and his wife on the arrival of a daughter. Club officials, who were hopeful of another footballer, are, however, slightly disappointed.

A ripping time was experienced by one of the regular players at Laverton last Saturday. He is now being measured for a new pair.

A much stouter figure was seen as goal umpire last Saturday, Jack Dowling being away on holidays.

Members are pleased to hear that Les Weatherly and Vernon McKane will be back with the club next week, following release from an ankle injury and the army.

They are also pleased to see Brendan Thompson still with the club. It is rumoured that he's going home to Western Australia on leave. The hope is that this will be delayed a bit longer.

The "garden" seems to keep a well known committeeman very quiet at the week-ends nowadays. Hope everything is blooming.

Lovely weather, particularly for a prominent member of the team who got water in the distributor of his car last Sunday afternoon.

BANG! 6.45PM. HIS WATCH now fixes in 1959.

Straight up the backside of a truck with its rear-end parked two feet on the road.

Bang. Smash. Driving his new Morris Oxford. It was instantaneous, on impact. Right out the front of the Ryans'. His willowy ascension was instant too.

A fleeting moment is all it takes. As is the instant of he's for her and she's for him. Bang. It strikes in a moment of sudden, as a drunk driver thuds up the arse of a truck.

It was his birthday the next day. He was to turn 53. He snitched work to celebrate, left his watering of paddocks with the sewage of our grand Dame city Melbourne town, to drink for hours in the Little River hotel on the fatigue of night shift. Beer after beer got him by the short and curlies. He drove his new engine down the Geelong Road, swerving in his lane. He misjudged how close he was to the back of the truck jutting out. How could he not in a drowning tiredness of grog.

His leg and nose were broken, skull fractured. His internals pounded under a sternum damaged beyond recovery.

People knew before her. They waited at the gate with friends, for the Constable to get to the home.

They thought at first that it was the son of the one lying dead because of the letter in the glove box addressed to him, and went to the son's new bride with a knock on the back door to deliver the news that her young husband was presumed dead.

The son answered the door. 'How can this be if I'm here,' he said. In that moment of sudden, the penny fell a million stairs to hell. The news was not of the son. The news was of his father who lay dead, the son now having to tell his mother that *her* husband was dead.

The tears, the howling. The dread.

THAT INSTANT OF HE'S for her and she's for me, that giddy in the tummy that grows to a dizzy on ten glasses of sherry. Who would've thought a chance knock on a door at night would land him to her, or that she would want to sit by him with Humphrey Bogart on the big screen. The electricity, the magnetism, the instant recognition in eyes afar. For him, the trump card is the black Austin A40 convertible with white wall tyres; for her, it's her kindness in the curtsy of her curl and pink puckered lips. Resistance is futile. Connection has its own will.

Love and loss are reluctant partners, come sealed as bride and groom in white virtuosity that bleeds a virgin weep. Whether in boundless breath beauty that shines from deep within, or the enduring sturdy of souring stench, they come together in the dualism of yin and yang.

In sacrifice and compromise and no judgement most of all, with patience and humility that's encircled in that rose of gold spinning a forever tune. A circle of no beginning or end with a centre as the gateway to something new. Rings of twisted and braided sedges and papyrus, rings of yellow and white and bliss and bling that heighten as she cushions her hands under his jaw and glazes his lips in the floral of carnations. It's the kind of exchange that exudes nurture and care and mutual absolutes until dying death. The kiss is gentle, yet ripe with what's to come.

It's in the one and only ever unity in the Farm church and in the many wedding receptions in the Farm hall. Eating and drinking joyful and jolly, on long tables that stretch the length of the hall, adorned in the splendour of white daisies and roses and pink points of chrysanthemums from the Farm nursery.

Families and friends, Issy and Jack, Beryl and Don, Marj and John; the Mckees and Smiths, Ryans, Hesketh s, Porters, Pengellys and McDermotts, we sing and dance and fill in the gluttony of more. Of roasts and Murray Lawson's piece of corned beef, 10 pounds broiled. Beer and sherry, trifle and pavlova; the guitar, piano, accordion and three-tiered wedding cake, tinkle and toll.

Any way you have it, anyway the sun streams in, the deal's done. Sealed. With that kiss, now sultry and gasping for more.

The euphoria of weddings, in a bubble of squish and squash and marshmallow more, soaked in brandy and laced in sherry. Leave your shoes at the door and revel inside, away from the harsh reality of yesterday to be in the deity of the day. And where the havoc of tomorrow is not welcome.

FROM THE BLISS OF wedding to the dread of farewell. He's gone. And so is the partnership of the bride and groom.

The altar is sombre in slate and stone, and lilies languishing in mournful weep. Motions in the belly waver in weighted dross and sludging dense, fuelling the gamut of gushing disregard and restraint. It fights uncontrollable and unreasonable, whispers a beasting breath and the only way forward is over parched lands studded in splintering glass and riving rocks. Darkness becoming darker, blacker, deceptive in groggy vertigo.

Until in the black, it emerges. That epicentral orb of family. Farm family. Its strength is in its ability to penetrate the dull of dread, as the sun infiltrates to suckle the earth. It spreads its tendrils in a web of silence, buttressing to carry the weight into a public procession. Solemn in no smell, solemn in sobriety. Farewell.

The dress of red and white check sits on the bed, unworn. He bought it for her to celebrate his birthday in the colours of his beloved Metro Farm Herefords. She won't wear it now. Not when his funeral replaces his birthday, not when people will come and go and offer all they have: food from the Farm ladies, and another broiled corned beef, time to sit with tea and jelly cake, time to be. Time for everything but him.

And still, tears brim for a best worker and father and husband. Sitting in the kitchen for days and nights, unable to go to the empty bed. Even the dog and cat hang in the dread, howling all night and not eating a morsel, until his jumper is given to them for their bed.

More cleaning, more organising and fundraising to do, for the zoo picnic and movies and books for the kids. More card nights to run, this time without the groom. More scones to bake and plum pudding too, rabbits to skin, pelts to sell, chickens to rear, butter and cream to make ... always more, always nourishing in the nurturing. Maybe it keeps her going. Until it doesn't, and a stroke hits her core.

Life's whammy of love and loss, weddings and funerals. They give us the extremes of elation and jubilation, and the destruction and explosion of the cyclonic and demonic. Happiness and hurt, anguish that bites as the antithesis to bliss. Of course, one must be stripped bare to attune to the extremes and to give without expectation. Unconditional. It's who we are on the Farm.

STINKIN' FICK'N SEWER RATS!

'At least I don't reek of sweaty arse!'

Terry Foote's belted him! In the full forward. And it's only the bloody first quarter, bloody bastard. Ventis was kickin' his fifth goal.

The umpire's taking his number. And so he should for that bloody dirty play. Mongrel!

Ventis is gettin' up and walkin' away. Good on 'im for not retaliatin'. Bloody, I would.

The half time siren's gone. Blokes have stopped mid stride, got hands on hips, puffin' and pantin'. Some are wanderin' to their rooms under the grandstand: Metro Farm left and INF rivals right. Captain-coach Mick McDermott led the Farm boys to a premiership in 1940 over INF and as he led his blokes down the player's race onto the ground, two women whacked him with their umbrellas. Turned out the women were sisters of his mother-in-law who barracked for INF and demanded that Mick play for the right team!

Ned O'Malley, the INF head trainer, is stompin' into the middle of the ground. He's making a bee-line for Ventis with a scowl so dirty it makes the sludge drying pans appear pale. Ventis is dawdling from the pocket, Digger Pengelly's beside him.

'Ned's lifting his wet towel. Blood-y hell. He's clobberin' Ventis with it!'

Terry gets stuck into Ventis again and Ventis retaliates, his patience no more. Digger grabs Terry but an INF player's plucked him by the jumper and thrown him onto the grass beside one of the Cooney boys. Charlie's throwing punch after punch and players are running in rabid mass.

'Sewer rat!'

Whack!

'Crawl back into ya shit pipe!'

'Go rest in piss, dickhead.'

Whack!

The other trainers join in, some punching, others pulling players apart. Noel's swingin'; Tex's draggin' his brother out of a huddle. Bull's copping it one minute and chargin' players the next.

'It's a fuck'n frenzy. Punches goin' to fuck'n Timbuktu.'

'Poor bloody Tiger Ryan's waitin' on the edge for casualties to patch up.'

'Get 'em Ventis, fix the fucker up!'

Spectators hurdle the fence and swarm the ground as seagulls amassing the main carrier on a hot, still day.

'It's an all-in brawl!'

'They're bloody goin' hammer 'n' tongs!'

IN THE END, THE Irish National Foresters win by three points. Terry Foote and Ventis are banned from playing football for seven weeks and four weeks respectively. Ventis and Terry become friends and in years to come, will recount the fight whenever they meet to quips of, 'the Corbet brothers are at it again!' – named after English boxing champion brothers from the 1920s.

The Metro Farm Football Club has much success and fields junior sides too. Three of the five leading players in the most popular footballer competition in 1951 come from the Metro Farm team: J. O'Connor, F. Pengelly and P Flaherty. Premiership wins are a plenty and stretch back to the club's early years. The club folds in 1964 however, to merge with the Irish National Foresters,

Services and Werribee South to become the Werribee Football Club the following year, based at Chirnside Park.

Metro Farm plays its last game to a final siren wailing in heavy heart after losing to Werribee South. Players come to a huddle, the crowd cheers a solemn song. They hoist the captain, coach and president upon shoulders. Tears brim.

Come on, oh come on boys and play
Come on we will thrash that team today
Team work and fighting spirit will bring the flag to the red and white
Premiers that's just what we will be
Premiers oh just you wait and see
Team work and fighting spirit will bring the flag to the Metro Farm

The team walks a lap of the oval, players lifted in rotation onto shoulders. The crowd's thick. Dot's holding onto young Paul while John drops by home to check on Marj and their newborn son, Issy and Jack ever by Dot. Gordon with Nell and their children are there, the Breguets, Gilletts, Pengelly boys too, all the good Farm people and friends are gathered. Many are glassy-eyed, unable a mutter of the club song.

Celebrations continue in adulation of friend and foe, in a Club Ball that rivals all Balls. People dance and sing to the accordion and piano and feast on friendship supreme, reminiscing into the early hours over beer after beer, whiskey upon whiskey.

Werribee Shire Banner, Thursday 11 September 1919
FOOTBALL. METRO. FARM BEAT WYNDHAM.

The matches in connection with the Werribee and Lara District Football Association last Saturday week were played at the Farm and Lara, in fine spring weather.

FARM V. WYNDHAM.

The above match was played in the presence of a large crowd of enthusiasts, the beautiful day enticing many to make the trip to the Farm. The game was fairly fast, and stubbornly contested, the Farm eventually winning, and securing the premiership. Umpire Hart (according to some of the barrackers) made several mistakes in his decisions, which caused them to get a bit out of bounds. The following were the teams:

Farm - Aitcheson, Hickey (3), Miller, Morrison, Chamberlain, Losewitz (2), Peacock, Sewell, Smith, Prentice, Moore, Flaherty, Bretherton, Stewart, and Wallace.

Werribee - Hogan, Palmer (2), Small, Wills, Lee (5), Harding, Mowat, Anderson, Burrowes, Ashby, Newton, Abbs, and Densley.

The final scores were: -

Farm - 5 goals 7 behinds (37 points.)

Werribee - 3 goals 3 behinds (21 points.)

For the Farm, every man did well, but the most conspicuous were Peacock, Moore, Morrison, Miller, and Wallace, whilst Sewell, Hickey Bros., Bretherton, Prentice, Aitcheson, Stewart, Flaherty, and R. Losewitz are also worthy of special mention.

PREMIERSHIP LIST.

	Played	Won	Lost	Pts.Sc'd.
Metro. Farm	12	9	3	36
Werribee	12	8	4	32
Lara	12	6	6	24
Little River	12	1	11	4

Best friends Shirl and Sunny are there, Beryl and all the women footballers. Sunshine Cameron and his friend Roy, Margaret and Monica with their Stan and Nobby, and Vernon and Tonti now married too. Trophies are handed out and players are recognised in a friendly roast, the club song is sung over and over until hoarse voices sing no more.

WHISPERS NOW CIRCULATE ON the street and in the Post Office, of people needing to move out of their Farm homes. It becomes clear that the Board of Works made the decision to shift people from the Farm some years ago. Better communication and transport allow people easier access to their work, and all must leave.

The exodus is unstoppable, not even a rose of gold spinning its tune can stop it.

Us up here, arrivals grow by the day.

Out west: Murtcaim, the Ranch and Moubrays Lane

Cocoroc West School pupils, date unknown. Photo courtesy of the Warfe family.

GLEAMING TOWERS OF BURNT orange contrast in the black of night, hunger in peaks over the You Yangs to dip into its curves. It's as if the devil himself has risen from hell, to terrorise the living and prey on the pretty, duping them vulnerable in the dark of damnation.

The incinerated cavity of a garage exploding in the inferno sweeping through is apocalyptic bleak in the ghosted landscape. Burnt tin sheets hang from poles that once supported them, a pile of tyres secretes thick black plumes constricted in soot. We'd stopped there earlier in the day to fill up on fuel, on the way to Torquay Beach. Surrounding the garage is a vast patchwork of white ash scattered in smouldering black, of stumps and the metal frames of drays, their cargo now gone, in an empty void of grasslands devoured. The ravenous beast is racing for the airfield, en route for Murtcaim at the Farm's boundary, where it got me and my family.

In speeding haste in my sandalwood Kingswood station wagon, I veer in and out of smoke billowing grey and tinged in orange, struggle to outrun the rampaging massacred madness that's spurred by a frenzied wind capering over the road from Geelong. Relentless seas of smoke and flames, embers glistening in shooting sparks cross-hatch the thick and ubiquitous. The road is barely visible five feet ahead. I clip the side of a sage green Vauxhall, swerve and screech to a halt. Doors fling open without words spoken, children and adults flee in frantic fright from cars onto softening bitumen excreting the toxicity of crude oil. Within seconds, the windows of both cars shatter into blistering shards, giving flames free reign to breathe inside in boastful breath. Smoke all round us, I can't see the children in the crackling and hissing of distressed dire.

Outrunning the hoggish inferno is beyond doom and we and the children still wearing bathers, bolt not more than three yards when the devil's wand taps the tops of innocent heads. Screams and squeals, running in firing fluidity ... falling to the bitumen in flailing arms and legs on fire. Hungry, peaking curls of orange engulf us. Mothers and fathers, children ... we anguish in the abominable and abhorrent.

Another wave of the wand and the screams cease. Nothing but the deafening of cackling and spitting flames, the devil's devouring of emulsifying bubble and squeak. Bodies coil in mounds of musky myrrh, scorched and blistered on the highway. Mounds of last gasps.

I rise with my girls, but not my son. He lays partially covered in a picnic blanket by a boulder, exposed skin red and blistered. Torment pierces in the point of a searing knife, bleeds me to weep when pain and blood have evaporated. The distance from him is growing and yet I can't leave him in his time of need! My wife drifts with my daughter to that other place. I can't go, not with my son breathing in hacking wheeze. I gasp with him and try to hold him, but can't. Not when I am gone.

A man in a blue Ford panel van parked a hundred yards ahead, pushes on the chest of a boy laying in the car's back seat. Flames hopscotching the road halted their route to hospital, the devil spreading his tentacles afar. The boy fades as the man increases his compressions to the boy's chest, to slowly rise in smouldering flesh to follow my girls ascending in stops and starts. The man peers up from the body of no life, as if the boy beseeches him so. I fly in amped melee over and around the man, swoop him to entice him to my son. He finally glances toward my car and the boulder, and dashes on my tail for my son.

Beside me now is the boy so blackened that ascends in stops and starts, peering at me from a face of seared and charred and hot pink wounds weeping withery. The boy from the Ford panel van has doubled back to follow his father, who is now with my ailing son. Love we cannot abandon unites the boy and me, a sorrowing father and a blackened boy damned in the devil's taunt.

HORSES STAMPEDE, NEIGH AND nicker, dogs bark and howl in blustering blab; cows billow, bulls bellow, sheep squeal in baa-baa blather ... flames engulf paddocks in a combusting inferno, deafened in a firestorm spewing yelps and yawps, crickey and caw. Flesh burns crisp onto bones, the black of death saturates as pervading repulsing perversion.

Inside homes, curtains are drawn, wet blankets drop over them. Eucalyptus oil sweats from wooden drays burning outside to leach through the minutest of cracks. They sit and wait in quiet whisper, until the time to flee is now. A grab for photos, grandmother's crockery, the children's baby keepsakes. It's too hot to sit in the dam or Lollypop Creek – quick, get in the car! Call Bluey and the cat, bundle them in. Keep the ash and smoke out of lungs and for heaven's sake, heads down! Lean into the wind if you must, it might be the only way. Nostrils burn in light breath, hacking choke as the devil's breath shrouds the land.

Four doors slam, wheels spin into the gravel; the car takes off to flames leaping over the house as 12-foot waves crashing over surfers at Bells Beach. The house is engulfed, explodes in a blaze of fury.

The bad angels are behind, chasing for more wolfing and greedy scavenging. Run from this hell, end of the world!

Ian speeds up the driveway, his face dipped into his navy work shirt. He leaps from his ute with the motor still running and ducks his head low as he dashes past the cypress trees spritzing in tindering cinder. A glow more orange surrounds the Holder home and sheds on Beach Road in Murtcaim, as fires speed across grasslands from Avalon airfield in a trailing black, a fire beelining for the house. He scoops the black cat into his arms and rushes to the two cocker spaniels to unhinge their collars from the chains. The dogs run for the water troughs and dive in to submerge until only their snouts break the water's surface. Ian springs up the steps and bangs on the door, belts in.

'Where are you?' yells Ian. 'You gotta get out!' Phyllis and Dawn are in the passage.

'You broke the door!' snaps Phyllis.

'The fire's comin' straight for the house!' shouts Ian.

The two women stare at him.

Ian yanks Phyllis by the arm. 'You gotta get out! Dawn, follow ya ma out! And tuck ya heads into ya dress.'

'The fire wasn't here 10 minutes ago!' yells Phyllis, her voice hardly audible over the rapacious roar. 'How can it be here already.'

'Dunno. We just gotta get out!'

Ian drags Phyllis to his ute under a blizzard of squalling ash. He throws the cat into the back of the ute and shoves Phyllis and Dawn into the front seat. A furious rainstorm of gusting embers shoots into the swirl of sooting fog as a mass of frenzied fireflies. Coughing and gasping, Ian spins his wheels to bust out of the driveway and hurtle down Beach Road. The Holder home explodes behind them, to a backdrop of hay bales burning as huge bonfires, a mini fireworks display.

'Where's my Terry, and Claude?' screams Phyllis.

'They're okay,' yells Ian. Soot smears his face and hands. 'Terry's been fightin' fires in Truganina but had to leave to get Bev from home. Little River's under attack too.'

'And Claude?'

'He's musterin' the stock with Barry and Reg and the other stockies.'

Ian races down Beach Road, makes a wide left to rumble over the cattle grid onto Grills Road and almost takes the wooden gate with him. He speeds over gravel roads through the Farm, swerving to miss flying fire balls shooting from hay bales.

'Where's everyone?' asks Phyllis as they pass a waterman's hut beside subdrains collecting effluent from lush land filtration paddocks. The contrast of green to the blackened outskirts of the Farm is as brazen as flood and drought.

'Everyone that can fight fires has gone out. The maintenance crew from the Western Carrier, Wally from school, the watermen, carpenters ... everyone's out.' Ian reaches the Head of the Road where the workshops are a central point of safety and respite for all the Farm workers and their families. He stops at the workshops. 'Everyone from Murtcaim and up near the road to Geelong are either here or at the refuge centre in the hangars at the top of Farm Road. They're waiting it out. You go inside and have a cuppa. There's a few in there servin' food and drinks. I gotta get up to the McLarens and help 'em.'

Phyllis and Dawn amble dazed into the workshop. Mrs Pengelly greets them. 'Come in dears, you're shaking.'

Phyllis and Dawn sit on a vinyl chair each. Phyllis surveys the workshop. 'What's happening with the McLarens? They're so close to the highway.'

'No one's entirely clear on what's going on, Phyllis. Everyone's just going wherever to see who needs help. Reg was on the stock but he's gone now with a few men to fight the fire round his place. It's roarin' in on Paradise Road. Greta's got the two boys swimming in Lara, but not sure how safe they are with the fires hammering Lara too.'

'Men are fightin' fires and tryin' to save the stock,' says Mrs Ryan, approaching with two cups of black tea. Other Farm women strut between serving sandwiches and filling cups with tea from a large urn, and walking across the grounds to check on Mrs Arnott and the children taking refuge in the swimming pool. Soot and ash layer the water and each time a child breaks the water's surface, they come up in a fine veneer of speckling soot.

The grass fire began yesterday afternoon, after a smouldering burn to smoke out rabbits was never snuffed out. No rain last summer and oppressive 116-degree heat has given gusting northerlies of 60-70 mile an hour free reign to fan flames ferocious and billow smoke iridescent apricot. The wind swings light poles to scatter them as my girl's pick-up sticks. Some lay flattened across roadways with bases licking orange and wires laying submissive to the brute. Flames soar to ignite one tree after another in blazing dazzle and strike hay bales into baguettes of fiery amber. All disintegrate back to the earth in a whoosh of no return and fill skies in a dread, that shrouds the sun into an unassuming yet mocking pink disc, deriding in a haze of death as if in cahoots with the devil.

THE YOU YANGS SMOULDER in the numb of a widow veiled in her husband's death. Pale dust powder layers a nuked landscape that summer had already dried to a frazzle. Smouldering mounds and carbonised tree trunks only three-feet tall pepper the landscape. Some horses escaped to the You Yangs, others lay with the hulled carcasses of sheep, cows and kangaroos, and echidnas sensitive to heat stress that did not burrow quickly or deeply enough for safety.

A day of century heat, 60mph winds – and carelessness

13 KILLED IN VICTORIAN FIRES.

Canberra Times, Thursday 9 January 1969.

MELBOURNE, Wednesday. – Thirteen people have died and at least 110 houses have been burnt in bushfires sweeping through Victoria.

Hospitals in Geelong and Melbourne have admitted 27 persons with injuries and eight of them are listed as serious or critical. Hundreds more were treated for burns at city and district hospitals.

At the township of Lara, 36 miles south-west of Melbourne, 10 persons have died and at least 41 houses have been burnt.

Six of the victims, including two children, died in three cars when 40-foot flames jumped the Melbourne-Geelong highway.

Seventy-six major fires and countless small outbreaks – the worst fires in Victoria for 25 years – struck as the State was having its hottest day this summer with above century heat and wind gusts of nearly 60 miles an hour.

The chief officer of the Country Fire Authority, Mr A. G. Pitfield, said late tonight the situation was still extremely dangerous with several big fires still out of control.

He said the fires should never have happened and blamed careless persons who failed to clear and burn-off their properties for 99 per cent of the outbreaks.

The State Government has declared Lara a disaster area and relief workers were on their way tonight. The six persons who died near their cars are believed to have alighted and to have tried to run from the flames.

Around 300 people that police evacuated from the Little River hamlet are returning to disintegrated homes to salvage anything that may have survived inside the fire's vortex of heat and oxygen. At the small Werribee Hospital, weary fire fighters line the corridors and more than 100 people have been treated so far. The farmer who jumped into the middle of his flock of sheep and crouched low to protect himself from radiating heat and sparking embers, miraculously survived. It's believed the thick wool of his sheep provided the ideal fire retardant and he is being treated for only minor burns and smoke inhalation. Police at Werribee, Lara and Bannockburn are busy shooting sheep and cattle that are dying from the effects of the fires. My son's stable in intensive care, but not yet out of danger. I'm by his side constantly, with the blackened boy by me, terrified of being alone yet pacing to get back to the Farm to search for his father. I'll take him back to the road out west of the Farm once my son is out of danger.

Miraculously, not one head of livestock is lost from the Farm. Stockmen worked with their dogs in blinding smoke and heat to herd them to safety from around the Ranch and near the stables in Murtcaim. Such is the faith they have in their loyal companions' abilities to understand the animals' distress, that the stockmen sent their dogs into paddocks of heaving and helling and sang commands and piercing whistles to them to round the animals up. It's in these stables that Vivian lived when he cared for the horses, where he and Doris lived once they married and had Beryl and her sisters. Beryl would always cackle when a horse would poke its head through the kitchen window. That was before Farm Manager, Mr Vincent, realised the Gilletts were living there. As soon as he became aware of the oversight, he immediately moved the young family into a home at the Head of the Road. That was Boxing Day just after the second world war began.

The McLarens are surveying the rubble in the light of today, of their sheds that once stored their car, wood and tools and where they milked their cows. Their faces are hollowed in fine charcoal. The stainless steel buckets that carried chaff for the cow to feed on while being milked, sit on their side, now dull grey. They were lucky to save their home, with only a few holes burnt into the veranda and laundry outside. The Holders however, they lost everything. Their entire home and belongings went up in smoke. They're now staying with Terry and Bev in Little River and are receiving generous donations that magically appear on Terry and Bev's doorstep: pots and pans, pillows, underwear, cutlery, crockery and more, left by friends and neighbours from across the Farm. They'll never return to the Farm.

The fire leaves nothing but thousands and thousands of acres of ash slabbed as confetti upon a day of apocalyptic magnitude. In all, 17 people died in the fires and 48 that were seriously hurt, recover in hospital. Over 200 buildings are soot and cinder – homes, sheds, schools, churches and factories. Some barely stand as rickety skeletons of mangled metal. Smoke leaches from skin and hair for days, no matter how many times one washes, and etchings of soot in skin remain as the stubborn reminder of the day the devil raged its wrath.

The doll of yesterday is hairless, faceless and shapeless, the wooden train engine is a warped wheel resting on a small pile of ash; other toys are rebirthed as blobbing, discoloured plastic and nuggets of alloy. Cypress trees soaring in flames yesterday are now but a haunting eerie of flimsy frame, glass soft-drink bottles have melted as globs beneath them. Bank books and birth certificates and forefather's trinkets, clothes and his father's war memorabilia, her rocking chair and family photos ... they've returned to the earth as dust, but for the gold rings that fuse into lumps around diamonds, the precious gems withstanding the devil's fury.

Even the bodies that yesterday screamed and shrieked unto death, of the mums and their children and the dads attempting to shield them from the fire storming through, my wife, the children ... they're gone, but for the blemish of bubbled and burned now blotched as permanent shadows onto the bitumen between Geelong and Werribee.

The devil may rejoice in the return of his juicy dues, but he'll never infiltrate the memories and kinship of linage across generations, the deep rose of gold that spins a forever tune of love so strong. Nor break the comradery of this land faraway.

I hunch over my newspaper on a stool at the table abutting a ceiling-to-floor window, sipping a dark latte from an insulated glass. An exposed sliver of skin coos in the cool as my grey T-shirt rises over my faded jeans. I sometimes glance at the passing city foot traffic in the lane outside. A woman in red speeds past, the café door remains shut.

When the door finally swings open, my knee bounces, until it's not her. A customer approaches the counter instead, asking for a long black and a toasted focaccia to go. The barista moves in speedy hustle, coffee machines grind Ethiopian beans to a hiss and steam. I relax back, and wait some more.

A couple at a corner table wearing black suits chat in dynamic pitch. Hands wave and heads nod over a frothing coffee and tea stained by a drop of milk in a mauve cup on a yellow saucer. They're oblivious to anyone or anything, immersed in work ditherings.

Another sip of coffee, a swipe of my moustache laced in milk. After the umpteenth willing of the door open, I leap from my stool. She glides in. Deep lines of smiles, the joy of her.

Eyes sparkle, her rose of gold spins on her middle finger. She hurries to me in unruly locks that part to the sides, her toned legs accentuated in skinny jeans.

Although there's no skin-to-skin contact, that quintessence of zest and zas within each of us meanders and entwines in unwavering pull. Until arms wrap and yearning embodiment bolts into a rose of gold spin, chests and thighs fuse, pieces fit in perfect puzzle. The connection is sealed.

Then comes the kiss, of deep longing and linger, a diamond beacon in a tiny, black-tiled Melbourne cafe.

Upon release, I pull a stool and take her hand to guide her to sit. We chat in smiles. She relaxes one hand over my knee, and I rest my hand on hers, twirling her rose of gold. It quivers a twinkle, shimmies a bygone love. She clutches my bicep and leans in. Faint creases radiate from the corners of her eyes. She kisses me.

A waiter brings a coffee in a long glass topped with whipped cream, and a slice of Linzer tart on a plate with two forks. She breaks a piece with her fingers and feeds it to me, kissing my lips to catch the falling crumbs.

She sips her coffee, scoops at her cream. I sweep a falling curl behind her ear, then break a piece of buttery tart to ease into her mouth. She savours it. My hand on hers, her rose of gold warm in its spin.

City busyness passes by the window but we two entwined are oblivious to anything but one another.

AROUND ME, THEY CONGREGATE. The rose of gold draws them out as a lighthouse shining in stormy seas. Dear Daughter and Mr Boy and their kinfolk, Yankee doodle dandy that smiles with the eyes and his shadowy mate, Joe and Elsie, the jellies, staries and flounders, and the black man flittering in the Milky Way with his diamond shimmying spear. Dogs with their horses, prized bulls, cows and sheep by the thousands. The Carter home and white magpie mate perched on a girder, other homes bulldozed to collapse. Banjo sharks, eels and flatheads, pipis and oysters, the nebulous arms of the octopus, and office lovers secretly rendezvousing in the plantations on the 29 Mile Road and on the foreshore at dawn and dusk, an orgasmic luminescence sky high.

No matter how many we are in the growing solidarity of our caught in-between, sorrow still engulfs me. I cannot bleed and yet bleed to no end in this limbo-land, separated from my love and daughter who are now at the light and from my son recovering in the living plane. The boy so blackened is constantly by me. We all have a connection to this place that's too strong to leave. Mine to my son, and Blackened Boy to me as his companion and the roadside where separated from his father, in constant search of him. We're caught between the two worlds, and segregated from both, 'existing' as ghosts can in a strength that's ever growing atop this Farm while the community below diminishes.

Melbourne's moving through a period of profound change, with new social attitudes and technological advances. Better communication and transport sees more and more families departing the Farm. It's not been an easy decade for the Board of Works though, with three of the four wells carrying increasing sewage at the new Brooklyn Pumping station, flooding to more than 100 feet. It's a year before the wells drain and work continues. We've had water restrictions due to dry summers and two years of severe droughts.

The Board of Works is building to cater for the continuing urban growth in Melbourne's south and east, with a population predicted to double within the next two decades. It has just begun constructing Cardinia Reservoir and is steaming ahead in connecting properties to the sewer system: Melbourne is 80 per cent sewered in comparison to Sydney at 67 per cent and Brisbane at 43 per cent. The Board restructures sewerage so there is a west and east sewerage catchment. The Farm in Werribee will treat sewage for the west of Melbourne and a new treatment plant at Carrum with an ocean outfall at Cape Schanck, will treat sewage in Melbourne's east. Alan Croxford is now heading the Board after giving up his city law practice to become Chairman three years ago.

Him, Sorrowing Father, he's as crooked as they come! By golly, his shenanigan ways will be exposed to all and sundry!

Elsie! You surprise me.

Mention the Board, commissioners or a chairman and me Els is never far away!

My dear man, men, he is a crook! So much for being a lawyer. He will inseminate his own cows with the sperm of champions bulls bred at the Farm. He'll get caught, mark my words, and will stand down in a few years' time while an inquiry into his personal land dealings and acquisitions takes place. That Mr Arrogant will be cleared of any improper behaviour but mark my words, he is as crooked as a swaggie's unfortunate set of teeth! Controversy will erupt too, over the Board's secret plans to discharge effluent from the new eastern treatment plant into Port Phillip Bay instead of into the ocean as they announce. And where do you think that backflip comes from, Sorrowing Father? Joe? Crooked Croxford, that's where!

The 1970s will see much change, Els, all the bloody economic, political and social change will hit us. The Australian Labor Party will come into power after 23 years. Young Gough Whitlam will lead the party. He'll be a beauty and will bloody dismantle the White Australia Policy that excludes non-white immigrants. There'll be protestin' all over the world too, about the Vietnam War and the violence against America entering it and the fucked up, distorted facts about how it started, bloody hell. In Northern Ireland, they'll protest against British rule. Bloody wars and protestin'. And then the bloody fancy bell-bottoms will come in and the young ones will dance the fancy-pants disco. Shit, now I've done it. Here she comes.

Dance? Fancy dancing for me and Mr B? And the mutt. He likes twirling with us and jumps around like a little puppy even though he's 12 years old.

Little DD, there'll be much more dancing for you in the future. My daughter used to love to dance, like you, and I imagine she's dancing in the light right now.

And there they go, doin' the Loco-motion and mashed patata. The crazy mutt's followin' like always, frolicking his black and white Border Collie coat free.

Dear little things aren't they, Joe.

And always with the dirt smeared nose from all his diggin', like my little mutt, Sandy. She didn't get caught in the between with me though, died way before me and got over to that other side.

Such progress to come will take time to reach the Board. They'll be their usual anachronistic selves, particularly with employee matters. Women will be required to resign and give up their superannuation entitlements if they marry. What rot! So much for women's liberation. This has much to do with Crooked Croxford. Leadership comes from the top. A female employee will be sacked for not wearing her navy and orange uniform and it's because of him. Fifty of her colleagues will immediately ban uniforms in solidarity. Stuffy-nosed twit-twat. Nothing's changed after 70 years! Croxford's threatening dismissal of male employees who wear their hair long. The Municipal Officers' Association describes it as unwarranted interference with personal liberty. And so it should!

It's not all bad, Elsie. The Government asks the Board to extend the Metropolitan Planning Scheme, and they'll do it well.

Board-shmoard, Sorrowing Father. Do not fall victim to the mentality of the Board. Why, they couldn't organise a, ahem ... in a brothel with a fistful of dollars!

Els! That's bloody harsh.

Codswallop. They'll incur the wrath of Premier Bolte when it asks for the ban on the use of water from Big River to be lifted. Premier Bolte will try and reign the Board in by appointing eight Liberal MPs to investigate options for making the Board more accountable. The faceless eight won't eventuate though, not with Crooked Croxford at the helm.

Look what it did out here in Murtcaim a few years ago, Els, got a new school organised for the kids, near me old railway carriage too.

That's true, Joe. The Board supported a school out there and converted a hall to start them off. It took parents teaching the children themselves and lobbying for eight years to get a school down there. The Education Department kept insisting on the need for more pupils to justify a school and appointing a teacher, which it finally did in 1939.

They had bloody good teachers out there for the kids. Mrs McLaren, she were a goer. Head teacher she were. The mutt loves roamin' over the little ones out there, between Murtcaim School and Cocoroc West School. It's where he grew up, with his man on the stock and chasin' his tail around the Ranch. Loyal to buggery he were to his man. Shit, pardon me language, Els.

Thank you for the apology, Joe. You're a sweet man and I love you as you are.

The two are off in a wink, probably out to the plantations where office lovers roam by the dozen. It's where the white magpie mate takes refuge sometimes, when not with the Carter home. He sought protection there in his living years after being cast out by his kin for his lack of black. His difference. Until swooping in to land one day against a plantation of bottle green pine trees, grown for sewage treatment experimentation, accentuated his angelic plume. A magpie struck him in pointed beak, and others joined the attack until he was paralysed and died soon after. He now roams with the Carter home, knowing he's protected there. It's a stark contrast to the other fadings on the Farm: the paddlings of small pink-eared ducks and their pert little quacks from square-tipped bills, and the foxes slinking in packs, still sly on their prey even though incapable of delighting in a catch. Behaviours are hard to change, as are prejudices.

The mutt's been back and is gone again, this time sniffing around Lollypop Creek on the way to Murtcaim School. Blackened Boy skipped after him without uttering a word. He won't be gone for long though, not after I promised him another fly over the Geelong highway in search of his dad, near where Cocoroc West School once stood.

MURTCAIM WAS ONE OF me favourite places on the Farm, with the lush grass filtration paddocks all around. That was for winter sewage treatment. The stench of souring eggs evaporatin' off them would shoot up me nose and latch onto the hairs inside. I'd be scratch, scratch, scratch until me nose streaked red raw. Didn't seem to bother the kids. They'd be too busy playing. That was many years ago now, when Murtcaim School was still open, when the tiger bit me at the Ranch. Rustling bulls we were, me Mann whistling me here and there. Loved working for me Mann. I was paralysed on the ground after the darned snake sunk its fangs into me ear. Me Mann didn't know until I stopped responding to his whistles. 'Whisky,' he was calling me. 'Whisky, where are you?' I was desperate to get to him but it was the beginning of summer and the snake's venom glands were full. I was a gonner in minutes. Bloody thing. Me Mann knew there was something wrong with me because I always responded to his whistles. I love me Mann, would do anything for him. That's what I was doing at the time, chasing the snake away from him and his horse so they wouldn't get bit.

Me Mann was good. Strict. He told me to wait at the gate one time after rustling cattle all day. So I sat, always did what I was told. And I sat and sat, keep sitting all through the night. He never whistled for me because he had too many beers and whiskies that night and forgot to call me in. I wasn't going to budge until he did, no chance of me movin'. I'd do anything for me Mann, even chase the blasted wind away if I could.

We'd get these winds gusting down this way in winter, lash the hair of the young lassies across their faces as a cat o' nine tails, and whip up coats to bite in the bristle of a thousand tea-tree needles. Brrr, that Antarctic chill blew a wild howl. It speared me ears to full mast and lashed that souring of mustarding waters into all eternity. It don't bother me anymore though, not since I crossed the divide, well tried to. I couldn't quite leave me Mann.

The little ones would be warming by Mrs Gillett's fire on their way to Murtcaim School in that weather. She'd be offerin' them hot cocoa, cold cocoa in summer, and toast to help them thaw out. Hmmm, toast grilled over a stoked cooker, soft and warm on the inside and crispy outside, smothered in gooing butter made from Daisy's milk and mulberry jam. Me mouth's watering, even when it's not. A triangle of toast would fall onto ash flaking from the bottom of the fire and I'd frisk and flounce, nudge me nose into the dirt to lift it up and eat it. But I could never get the darned thing and ended up chasing me tail in circles instead.

'Don't worry, dear,' Mrs Gillett would say to little Brigita. 'There's plenty more bread coming in with the mail today. Might even be in the box on the fence post right now, with my meat.' It always came wrapped in newspaper and Mrs Gillett would store it in the ice chest. I'd be eggin' to get at it!

The rain would spit in and Marjie would be tucking into a piece of toast smeared in the dark stuff. I'd pant and prance, Vegemite was me favourite! I'd swish me tongue at a triangle of toast on her lap and me licks would always swipe through. It's a darned thing bein' dead. She'd shoo me with a flick of her hand that would wave through me. Little tackers could always sense me around.

One day, we were havin' Anzac Day commemorations, a few years after the second world war, and Mrs Gillett hurried the kiddies along, reminding them that Mrs Mac had been working hard to organise everything so they couldn't be late. Rain pelted as pebbles that morning and the little ones snuggled in, away from the veranda edge. The fire hissed when water spat down the chimney. The rain would've stirred the souring of mustarding waters from the grass filtration paddocks and a freshly graded paddock adjacent to the Gillett home turned to red mud. The gums clustering its boundary faded into the downpour as pale ghost gums. It gave the white magpie mate the best camouflage to roam free! The office lovers seemed to giggle more boisterous that day.

In pinky fingers poised high and last gulps of Mrs Gillett's hot cocoa, lips of purple-grey had softened to rosy pink. The downpour stopped and after a few swipes with coat sleeves at dribbling noses, the lassies and laddies skipped across the road clasping posies of flowers wrapped in alfoil. Me lovely Mann was over the road sittin' proud as punch on his chestnut mare that day, with three other stockies and their dogs. I panted and pranced in ears cocked to the heavens, chased me tail in circles. They tipped their hats to Mrs Mac, who already had the flag flying half-mast. Ventis and Terry were carrying chairs out to the flag pole. I wagged me tail in no tomorrow and sniffed round the pole, hopin' to catch a whiff of who'd come before me. Rain or sunshine, I loved a pole, and still do.

The young ones took their flowers to the flagpole and laid them at its foot. They took a seat and Mrs Mac began the service. Me Mann was there, head bowed and hat in hand. I hovered beside him, trying to lick his hand but only swiping through.

UNDER THE FLAG POLE heavy in gloom, is a sea of poppies and Easter daisies and dahlias in full bloom. In the years after the war's end, thanks be, for we are the lucky country.

Thanks to the men and women from the Metropolitan Farm who fought in wars and supported the war effort, all who volunteered and laboured in defence works, all who gave when there was little to give.

Soldiers sing their triumph, march the muddy track in rows of six in khakis tucked into water-logged boots. The synchronicity of voice and arms swing in unison as the symbol of proud solidarity. Whether land, sea or air, in Egypt, Crete or Tobruk, each triumph mattered, each defeat an unparalleled modesty when thousands were killed. Their combat and tireless toil to save the wounded, sick and malnourished, risked one's life in the brutality of war. The inspiration of their selfless ways, inspiration of legendary acts.

Silence. The bugle swoons.

They shall grow not old, as we that are left grow old:

Age shall not weary them, nor the years condemn.
At the going down of the sun and in the morning
We will remember them.
Lest we forget.

'WHO WANTS TO GO to the beach?' asks Shirley.

'Yeah I do, but I want ice cream first,' calls Ted, cycling ahead of his sister.

School's finished! I pant and prance, chase me tail a few rounds before bounding after Ted riding down the 29 Mile Road, towards the Dando home. The Smith boys are following, Stan too.

'You're lucky you've got electricity,' says Faye.

'We're the only ones in Murtcaim that have,' says Shirley. 'That's why Mum can make ice cream, 'cause we've got electricity for a proper fridge.'

'Our fridge runs on kerosene,' says Faye.

'Mr Thomas in the fishing hut who comes down on weekends and fishes with Dad, he built us a windmill to make electricity. He works for Ansett, and flies aeroplanes all around Australia. He made the windmill and he made it so big that we have enough electricity to light our whole house. No more tilly lamps for us!'

The windmill in the backyard comes into view. Makes me dizzy it does, the way it spins and spins, all the time round and round. Can put me to sleep. Me Mann was good at sleeping. He'd tumble into his jinker after a night at the Racecourse pub and tell ol' Peggy to take him home. He'd be dozing to Timbuktu in seconds and Peggy would gallop him through the gate back home on the Farm. One time, some naughty boys smacked Peggy on her rear end and sent her back to the pub. Off Peggy galloped at a hundred mile an hour and didn't return until the next morning. I was waitin' and waitin' for me Mann to let me out of me kennel and as soon as he come steering up the drive way, I barked and barked for him to get me out. He was cranky and as dishevelled as an old swaggy comin' out of bush diggings. He let me out with a huff.

There's Mrs Dando, waitin' with bowls of plum ice cream on the porch. She must make the best ice cream by the way those kids scoff into it. I sit on me backside like a good boy, nice and straight with me ears cocked and tongue floppin' out the side of me mouth, waiting for a creamy drop to drip onto the floor. It never did. I'd do that by me Mann, sit up straight and keep me eye on the prize as he waved his toast left and right. Me favourite was rabbit stew. I'd sprint to the kitchen door when it was cooking, chase me tail in circles then sit still on me butt. Waitin' and waitin'. Until me Mann would give me a taste and pat, 'Good Whiskey boy,' he'd say. I'd sit and wait for some more, but I only ever got the one taste at a time.

The young ones finish their ice cream and are swimming in the bay in no time, splashing and crawling along the water's edge, dodgin' the straggles of seaweed rotting under the sun. Cormorants perched on the old jetty pylons of the sluice gate nearby barely flutter a feather. I'm sniffing the foreshore like a dead dog does, in dry paws that should be wet and among shell grit that should be scrunching under me paws.

That woulda been my shell grit for baggin' and sellin'.

Joe, you're here again!

I'm always by me bay, Whiskey boy. Can't get the water out of me veins, or leave me railway carriage home. Why would I want to, with no one around and all this peace. It's fairdinkum bliss.

Me tail stiffs to a point, ears spear up to the sky. What's that sneerin' behind yer, Joe? Who is it? Front up.

Grrr comes through gritted teeth.

That's me dog, Bobby. He's me old mate from when I lived in me railway carriage. The bloody loyal bugger found me and won't leave me side. Together once again!

Grr yourself, dog, I've got me Mann. So rack off! Stay away and we'll be right.

Plovers are squawkin' to buggery, ever protective of their eggs. The kids are emergin' from the water, laughin' and yellin' to go pick mulberries from the tree.

Food! They're getting' food!

Whiskey's off with the kids, to the tree edging the paddock by the foreshore. His long coat flounces free and happy.

Mr Bean's down in his fishing hut. He's still buying butter and cream off Mrs Dando. She's now comin' along, with Mr

Dando. He's finished his feedin' and waterin' of the Clydesdales after their ploughing. A bunch of others are with them, with tea. Mrs Newton's there with her knittin' bag, always knittin' to raise money for something, for the war or new hospital, the school. She buys the wool from money raised at card games to knit and then sells what she's knitted to raise more money.

There's roast duck in that heavy bag, gotta be.

Whiskey's back in a flash wherever there's food. Your nose for it hasn't left yer.

It's me sixth sense, Joe. Mrs Dando might've fried up the flounder Jack and the kids caught last night. Wouldn't mind getting' me lips round some of that too if I could.

THE MURTCAIM PEOPLE WERE as tight-knit as any of them across the Farm, with its dances in the shearing shed and celebrations in the old hall and Murtcaim School. The Board looked after them as it did all the Farm people, and would send the tramways bus to collect the children and take them to the pool at the Head of the Road for weekly swimming lesson.

I was there when the school came of age with its 21st anniversary. The once youngsters were there, all grown up and working: Beryl and Don Breguet as husband and wife, Shirley as a spiffin' good lookin' married young woman, Bill and John Day, and Stan too. He'd graduated from school to be a Farm billy boy, then a shearer, one of many needed to shear the thousands of sheep on the Farm. I'd bark over the top of him and the sheep, itchin' to round the darned things up. A few other Newtons and Dandos were there for the anniversary, the Ryes, Gilletts and Jenkins. They all went to the dance that followed that night, and the Belle of the Ball in the Wool Shed. Lovely Shirley won Belle of Belles in the bottom-end dance a few years ago, with Ronnie Rye as her partner. What a belle she was, in her dress of pale blue chiffon, hemmed by her old dad.

They had an official guest party for the Murtcaim School's 21st anniversary with Mrs Randall, Mrs Searle and Mrs Forrest. They were pinnin' small posies of daisies to their floral dresses as they sat on vinyl chairs outside, pine trees all round them that would've been oozing in possum piss for sure! Chased me tail in circles when the front tubular steel legs of Mrs Forrest's chair started sinkin' into the grass. She was on such a lean, she looked like me Mann after 10 whiskies. Mr Forrest dashed to his wife and held out his hand to help her stand. He pulled the chair from its sinking bed and sat it on sturdier ground. Such a gentleman bloke. Mrs Holder and Mrs Beard were behind them, stacking jars of pickled onions, tomato chutney, plum and mulberry jams and handmade aprons at their stalls. Me mouth woulda drooled if it could.

Mrs Newton snapped at Mrs Beard, caught me by surprise. 'Careful with your ash!' she snarled, flicking smudgings from a pile of embroidered hankies on the table. The ash had fallen onto them from the end of Mrs Beard's cigarette.

'Sorry, dear,' said Mrs Beard, very sheepishly.

Mrs Newton shuffled the baby beanies and booties she'd knitted over the past weeks into neat piles beside the hankies. Mr Gillett was at his stall alongside them with bottles of Tarax and Coca Cola for sale at threepence each. All money raised would go to buying new sports equipment for the school.

Mr Forrest spoke well, called everyone to attention. 'Welcome everyone. Come in close please,' he asked, fidgeting with the knot in his tie. The crowd softened its conversation to a whisper and the Murtcaim class sat on firewood dumped near a tree, starin' at Mr Forrest like he was some kind of alien beast. 'Before I hand you over to Mrs McLaren,' he said. 'Who she herself as many of you know, was part of the school's early life when she taught after the War, then as Miss Nichols.'

'Greta lived with us back then,' called Don, standing behind a seated Beryl, his hand over her shoulder. 'Boarded with Mum and Dad, she did.'

'Well, they must've done alright by Miss Nichols because she fall in love with the place and Reg McLaren, to finally marry him!' The crowd chuckled. 'And so today, Mrs McLaren is with us and this time, is being paid to teach her own two boys at school! Which I might add, is thriving thanks to Mrs McLaren and her love of literature and all things Australian.'

Murtcaim State School 1939-1960

21st Anniversary Souvenir ~ 1/-

OUR DEVELOPMENT

About 30 years ago the tenants on the south west corner of the Metropolitan Farm felt the need for a suitable building in which the people could meet together in social activities. Approaches were made to the Melbourne and Metropolitan Board for a site of land on the twenty-nine mile road for the removal to that site of a very large hut that was lying unused at the old Red House. Working bees were arranged and with the helpful co-operation of the M.M.B.W. a hall was established ....

Meetings were held, petitions were signed, approaches were made to the Metropolitan Board of Works to make the Hall available and representations were made to the Education Department of Victoria to establish a School. Although all parents co-operated in the venture a special tribute is paid to the untiring efforts of the late Mr James B. Lindsay who argued, coaxed and cajoled until,at last,the school became a reality.

In March 6th 1939, Mrs Murtagh (nee Miss Ryan) became the first teacher in the Education Department's newest school, State School No 4375, Murtcaim. Eleven children were enrolled on the day, but, by the end of year, twenty children were attending.

During the last twenty-one years fifteen teachers have taught at the school and the School Register records 128 children have been enrolled.

Small rural schools such as this play an important part in our Education system. The prosperity and progress of the country areas rely on them to an extent almost as great as it did fifty years ago. Looking back, we can feel that the efforts of those parents of twenty-one years ago, have been well rewarded.

Only those who have the patience to do simple things perfectly ever acquire the skill to do difficult things easily.

John and Max grinned in the spotlight that day. Their mother taught into Murtcaim School's last years before movin' on to teach at Werribee State School and retirin' to become a volunteer tutor to children livin' on outback stations in the Northern Territory. So much for retirin'!

She thanked Mr Forrest respectfully and jumped straight into the celebrations, with the youngsters singin' the national anthem, *God save the Queen.*

IT'S WARM FOR AUTUMN. Sometimes we get that. There's been no rain and we're still in drought across Victoria; paddocks are dried to washed out frizzled expanses of ochre. Unless you live on the Farm, near flourishing green paddocks watered in sewage and gardens well-tended and watered with as much effluent as they desire so they pop in pinks and blues and all hues of the colour wheel. My wife would appreciate it, she loved her garden. She's been gone three months now and I've settled into the Farm with Blackened Boy, blotched in red wounds that glow from his charred little eight-year-old body. He still says very little and we still search for his father when he's not playing with Whiskey near the children. Whiskey's a good looking dog, immaculately groomed, and with such a friendly demeanour. He hovers over the young lad in his herding and protective way, even at the beach while the boy floats transparent winking as shimmering crochet in the salty bay. It's a curious translucency.

People had kept metal knapsacks filled with two or three gallons of water and a wet hessian sack in their home when the fires raged out west. These were to put out minor fires usually lit by sparks coming off steam engines back in the day. Those knapsack tanks melted into lumps in the heat of the fires and the wet hessian sacks went up in cindering tinder.

More people than ever from across the Farm and not just Murtcaim are moving away and making new homes elsewhere. It caused school enrolments to fall and the Education Department shutting Murtcaim School a few years ago, in 1965. Cocoroc West School had been shut many years before that, in 1948. Whiskey starts panting and prancing.

Lucky there's a few Farm youngsters at Cocoroc North School at the Head of the Road to play with, they're not all gone yet.

And the boy loves going with you too, Whiskey. So few homes are left and to many, the Farm may appear as a ghost town. We know better though don't we, Whiskey, about how accurate they really are!

We do, we do ... I chase me tail in circles.

While fewer people live on the Farm physically, up here, we thrive. We're all connected to this place in some way and those who have had their ashes scattered here on the Farm upon their death, take prime position as elders among us. It's why we're caught in the divide and can't reach that other place, because our attachment to the Farm is too strong. I'm desperate to be with my love and daughter at the light and yet unable to leave my little man, even when he has recovered from his burns and is living with my brother and his family. Then there's Blackened Boy, endlessly searching for his father out west of the Farm – I can't leave him.

The stains of those burning bodies on the highway from Geelong remain these months later and drivers sometimes stop to lay flowers at them. We shouldn't have run from the car. The government is saying that now and is attempting to teach people not to leave their cars if caught in a fire. Ludicrous really. No one has the ability to outrun the ferocity of fire that's spurred by the devil himself.

A few cottages around Murtcaim, Moubrays Lane and the Ranch have been lifted off their stumps and loaded onto the back of a truck, to be relocated in Werribee and Little River. The Ryan house from Moubrays Lane, the one the Wallace family lived in for a time too, that's been moved to Mambourin Street in Werribee. Sunshine and Bessie's grandson married a loving girl and together they renovated the house into a home oozing care and warmth. It's still there today and is somewhere I sometimes visit to reminisce about my home and soak in the essence of family. It's a parallel of lifetimes that the rose of gold intertwines Farm love to radiate across eternity. In years to come, Charlie Hickey's house will move over the road from the Farm and the Gillett house will go to Little River to offer accommodation to travellers. Holidays are over for me. As are beach swims at Torquay with the children and kissing their little peanut foreheads good night. Grief bleeds from me some days when I bleed no more.

Blackened Boy is off again, eyes glistening from his seared and cindering, after Whiskey bounding in lithe and agile stride. He wags his tail with such might that if the boy was of any substance, the mutt's tail would knock the boy to the ground. They'll be disappearing to Piggy Hughes' hut at the bottom of the 280 Road. Don't ask me why they call him Piggy, especially when he breeds silky terriers and has a pet cemetery by the row boats he stores for fishing. Whiskey'll be playing with his silky mates, before prancing and panting all the way to Cocoroc North School, to be engrossed in the Sadler, O'Connor and Ryan children, Texas Pengelly's boys too, even though they live up near the Ranch. The boy and Whiskey will play above the children, follow them to the dam and the water tank. They're a happy lot, finding amusement in much around the Farm.

Tex Pengelly's boys would've gone to Cocoroc West School if it was open, in the west of the Farm near the Ranch. The school taught children for 42 years, including religious education given by a visiting priest. Cocoroc West School was originally situated near the Princes Highway on the 160 South Road and moved 10 years later to Moubrays Lane, which was more central for families living in the area. With enrolments always on the increase, a bigger school was built with concrete tennis courts and gardens. The old school remained for storage. Mrs Hill taught first, then Miss Edwards came along, until she married Leo Toohey late in life.

Whiskey, you're back!

Yep, Blackened Boy too. He knew you were near the Geelong Road and came zooming over.

Of course, his father. The boy's already flying small reconnaissance, with one eye on us. I was reminiscing about Cocoroc West School and Mrs Toohey's smoking out the back away from the young ones, puffing away on her *Kool* cigarettes.

But they all knew she smoked because whenever she leaned over their shoulder to correct their work, they'd screw up their button noses at her pongy breath. Mrs Ryan came after her and Ernie Best taught during World War II. That's when he played football with the Herefords. And little Faye Oram, she was the last kid ever to enrol at Cocoroc West School.

I loved lunchtimes at Cocoroc West School. Those darned rotten banana sandwiches made me churn upside down. Would swap it for peanut butter if I could, like the young ones always did. Peanut butter was another of me favourites! I frisk and flounce, pant and prance.

You and food, Whiskey!

It's me favourite! What can I say? So's Vegemite, and mulberry jam, ice cream, roast duck ... all food's me favourite! Except for banana. And followin' the youngsters round school was one of me favourite things to do too. I'd be chasin' me tail in circles as soon as Mr Best would yell at the kids. One time, he was battlin' Alfie to sit back in the chair because Alfie was fightin' the visiting dentist!

'But Mr Best, Mr Best,' Alfie would cry. 'I'm scared of the needle!'

Kids'd be cackling their little hearts out when Alfie fled out the window, and every time Noel'd climb out too. He'd dash through the school yard to play tennis. I'd bark and bark, chase me tail in circles and sometimes, I'd be rolling in the dust when Noel's brother Frank would fight Arthur in the school yard. He'd be punchin' the kid all over but would avoid his snotty nose. Noel'd play tennis whenever he could, with his brothers and sisters and the Warfe youngsters too. Those Warfes had their own tennis court in the yard at their home by Lollypop Creek, which was by me old home with me Mann. We had a tennis court too.

The old school almost closed down once, until the Board asked Mr Wallace to enrol little Allan at the school. That got enrolments up and saved it from closing. Allan was number 11 in a family of 14 Wallace kiddies. Bloody Norah, that's more pups than me mum had! Bloody Norah too when Allan would come to school on a cold rainy morning in bare feet. I'd pant and prance, tryin' to get warm for the kid! He'd say that he left his shoes at home so he could jump in puddles. His older sister, Joan, married Mr Best and in Grade 6, Allan won a scholarship the Farm manager was handin' out to kids in the Farm schools. It was worth 50 pounds over four years and got Allan to Werribee High School.

You've been around a while, Whiskey. Why you still here, in the in-between worlds?

Me Mann. Can't leave me Mann. He might not live here anymore, but he works here and I've only ever known him in this place.

Many men here are like you – born here, lived here and only ever worked here.

It's in us, branded in us from a young age. Boys that grew up here on the Farm often landed their first job here as billy boys at 14 years old. They'd boil billies to make tea for the men working in the field and when they weren't doing that, would cut thistles and chop trees. It was the usual job start for boys on the Farm. Did you know Frank, the eldest of the Ryan boys, was a billy boy? At the beginning of the war, John Castell weighed him and being a wiry thing, pressed his hand on Frank's head to tip the needle on the scales past six stone, so he was big enough to get the job. A few months later, Frank moved onto the stock and eventually, joined the air force. He returned to his job after the war and a home on Moubrays Lane. The Board always had the men's jobs waitin', those that went to war.

Just past the school over there near the highway, was where the little tackers would play *Run the Rabbit.* Darned funny game that, I was with Joe one time, pantin' and prancin' with the kids.

Run the Rabbit, Rabbit in the Seat ... these Farm kids make the best games out of the simplest things.

SHIRL LOOPS AND LACES rope to the old handbag. This is the other Shirley, the Shirley Cameron Shirley, Sunshine Cameron's daughter. She tightens the last knot to fasten the rope to the bag's handle. 'There you go, Bernie.' Shirl hands Bernie the bag.

'Why's it always me?'

'Because you're me greyhound fast brother,' calls Noel from the branch of a pine tree.

'And we're up in the trees already,' says Billy perched in the tree beside Noel. Kath's there too, with Leo.

'You're the best at runnin' the rabbit,' calls Noel. 'The fastest.'

Bernie takes the bag reluctantly and starts runnin' through the thicket of sheoaks and bottle brushes. He swills past dry grass reachin' his knees and pinches between the wire cabling of the fence to drop the bag onto the edge of the Geelong Road. He draws the rope attached to it back under the fence and over the kangaroo and spear grasses. Wish me Els was here, she'd be loving this mischief.

I'd be in heaven if I could catch a whiff of that grass, Joe. It'd be drenched in fox and feral cat pee. I pant and prance, chase me tail in circles over the grass while Bernie takes the rope to Billy in the tree before dashing to Shirl and Kathleen squattin' in tufts of grass.

And there they wait, for the inquisitive and unsuspecting to take the bait. It's the usual crew of kids, sometimes a few more, sometimes less.

'Someone's comin',' calls Noel.

Shirl giggles.

'Shush,' calls Billy. 'The car's stoppin'.'

Haha, cheeky kids, peerin' as perplexed possums at the car pullin' into the service lane. It stops at the bag. Two women leap from car doors and scuttle to the bag. The shorter, plump woman dressed in a lemon chiffon dress bends to pick the bag up. Billy tugs at the rope. The bag slithers from her grasp to a string of giggles. She crawls after the bag, hunched over. A curl from under her lemon pillbox hat falls over her eye. Billy tugs again, draggin' the bag to the wire fence.

'Oh my,' mutters the other woman in the pink lamp shade dress followin' her friend. Her matchin' hat blows off into the grass.

'She's got boy's hair!' laughs Shirl.

'Shhh!'

The woman in the pink lamp shade chases after her hat.

'I'll get that bloomin' bag,' shrieks the round lemon. The woman trots after the bag's slitherin' creep towards the fence and scoots down to pick it up. Billy's quick and yanks the bag through the fence. 'Bloomin' bag!' she squeals as she attempts one last snatch. The round lemon loses her balance and rolls face first into a clump of tussock grass. Her petticoats fall over her head, revealing a sateen girdle with garters hooking her lemon stockings. Bloomin' hell!

I bark and bark, pant and prance and roll in barrels like a mad dog scratchin' dried mud off me back in the grass. The bloody kids are holding back giggles that are desperate to erupt.

'Oh, dear,' cries the pink lamp shade, skittering after her friend with her hat in hand.

'That bloomin' bag!' growls the round lemon. 'Blasted kids'll be behind it!'

The pink lamp shade helps her round lemon friend up by the elbow and brushes away grass and twigs caught in the flimsy fabric of her dress. The two women wander back to the car, cursin' and complainin' before drivin' away. They sound a bit like me Els when she's on her high horse about the Board. The kids emerge from their hiding, in hysterics. Whiskey's above them, still rollin' and pantin' like a mad dog.

'Bloody funny,' laughs Noel.

'Classic!' Billy snorts, as if blowing milk through his nostrils. 'Bugger, me, dead!'

'You're naughty, Billy!'

The youngsters cackle as kookaburras in a gum tree.

'Let's go again,' says Noel. 'Go on, Bernie, run the rabbit back to the road.'

'It's always me,' whines Bernie.

'Told ya, you're the best.'

Bernie takes the bag while the other children sidle into their positions. He's easing between the fence cabling when the warning comes.

'Down!' calls Kath.

Bernie drops flat into the grass, unable to escape into the bushy trees and shrubs. A good-lookin' big black Ford Custom in shiny chrome bumper and grille cruises past.

'It's gone,' yells Noel after a time.

Bernie gets up. 'I'm not doin' that again, someone else's turn.' He stomps into the plantation.

The children emerge from the trees and grass.

'Nah, yeah, you're alright mate,' says Noel.

'Yeah, you're good, Bernie,' says Kath. 'It's gone now.'

'You're the quickest outta all o' us,' says Noel. 'Come on, let's go again. How funny were the ladies, especially the fat one fallin'!'

'Come on, Bernie. Go lay the rabbit.'

'Fine.' Bernie takes the handbag and skulks for the road while the others sneak back into their positions.

He's through the grass and fence and is at the roadside layin' the handbag when the Ford Custom appears again. It stops dead. Whiskey's ears cock to the heavens. A six-foot four burly bloke jumps from his wide open door.

'Shit!,' whispers Noel. 'It's the copper!'

The copper's shoes clip the bitumen in flogging swift. Bernie dashes to the fence and flies between the wire cabling. The brute's after him, strides over the fence and is two steps behind the young kid. The copper only needs to extend his arm and he'd reach Bernie. There goes Whiskey, blowin' and breezin', divin over the copper in circles. The copper flinches, slows his stride. Bernie bounds ahead. Noel's right – the kid's greyhound fast. Whiskey leaps into the copper's face. The copper flicks at him as though shooin' a pesky fly.

'Oi, ya bugger!' yells the copper. 'I know what you're up to!'

Bernie runs to the boys nestled in discreet forks of the trees. 'Piss off, don't stop here,' they whisper. 'Keep goin'!'

Bernie dashes off. The copper's catching up again, his breath heavy and quick on the tacker's neck. Just as he's about to throw his hands out to catch the boy, Bernie bolts past the gnarling trunk of a River red gum soaking up the wet from Lollypop Creek. The copper loses his footing in a muddy hole and splashes into the creek. Bernie doesn't stop and bolts past the Ranch and the winding wheel of the Hammer Mill pounding grains for the animals. Cascading neighs from mares, foals gather jittery. Whiskey's pantin' and prancin' to whoosh Bernie faster! He shoots towards Moubrays Lane, the copper catchin' up to be a few soggy steps behind the kid. Bernie races along the road and up the driveway of home, through the back door and into the front room, towards the bedroom.

'What the hell's going on, Bernie?' snaps his mum.

Bernie slides across the wooden floor to land well under the bed. The chenille bedspread drapin' down its side shields him, but not the thumping from his chest onto the floorboards. Whiskey slides in with him and crouches beside the boy.

Kathleen parts the curtain to peer out the window. 'Why's Constable Semler marching up our driveway? What have you done, Bernie?'

Bang, bang, bang!

'Mum, make him go away!' cries Bernie.

'By the way the Constable's bashing at our door, you're in some trouble, young man.'

'I'm not gettin' outta here,' sobs Bernie.

Jim comes in from the vegie garden and he and Kathleen listen to the Constable's heavy berating of their son's scallywaggin'. They're only kids havin' a bit of fun. Bastard copper I reckon my Els might say.

THE NEXT DAY, THE children giggle in the schoolyard about the escapade but are too daunted to play *Run the Rabbit* again, not for a while at least. Instead, they decide to meet at the Ranch after school.

The Ryan boys and Alfie take off for home by Moubrays Lane for a quick snack, Shirl and Billy are already at home doing the same. Leo and Margaret skip along the dirt road together, until Margaret turns into the driveway of her and Leo's Auntie Elsie's home. Margaret's stayin' with their Aunt and Uncle Charlie for the week. Leo glances at the apples and strawberries he often pilfers from Aunt Elsie, and the apricots that stockmen sometimes stop for juicy sampling. His aunt and uncle live next door to his home. Margaret's a Bensted, and so is Aunt Elsie. Charlie's a Hickey, as is Nellie, Leo's mum. Thellie's a Bensted too, until she marries a Fitzgerald. Nellie married a Forder, Eric Forder, who is Leo's dad. Charlie and Nellie are the children of Annie and Michael from the bottom-end. Eilly Hickey marries a Hallinan, Ryans marry Smiths marry Castells marry Pengellys marry Hesketh marry Ryans ... it's hard to keep track of who's related to bloody who on the Farm. The rumours about inbreedin' might not be rumours.

Nellie's preparing apple pies with Eilly, Leo's sister, according to her good Ma's recipe. Her fascination for patterns she once delighted in making in the sand as a kid on the foreshore of the bottom-end, now echoing in her crimps, ripples and rainbow edges of her shortcrust pastry pies. Bloody I remember those apple pies like it were yesterday. Young Eilly'd be bringin' me a piece of that best apple pie off 'er old ma, Annie, whenever she come and got fish off me at me railway carriage.

Leo bursts into the kitchen, pantin' like Whiskey. 'Can I've a scone before I go to the Ranch? Please.'

'No hello first?' asks Nellie.

'What's the hurry, Master Forder?' quizzes Eilly.

'Nothing,' smirks Leo. 'We're going to the Ranch and then I'll go visit Uncle Frank before tea.'

'Poor Uncle Frank,' says Nellie. 'He's still struggling after the war. He doesn't go to work some days and sleeps for hours in his caravan. I was there the other morning and found him fishing by the river with a few empty beer bottles in the grass next to him.'

Leo gobbles his scone and sculls half his milk. 'Goin' the Ranch,' he calls, dashin' out the back door. He pecks a fleeting kiss on the forehead of his horse tied by the water trough before hurdling the back fence.

GOTTA GET TO THE Ranch! Me Mann's there. With Keithy and Franky, and all the blokes! The kids are there too.

Whiskey's out at the Ranch nestled off Old Boundary Road in seconds. The Ranch hugs into a windy curve of Lollypop Creek, which meanders over the western side of the Farm into a subdrain that carries effluent out to the bay. It were sorta near me railway carriage where I caught fish feedin' in the nutrient rich water enterin' the bay.

Leo's lurking by a gate at the Ranch. He quietly unlatches it and eases it slightly ajar, smirkin' from ear to ear as the cat full on 20 mice. He sneaks in twinkle-toe to a fence post and climbs up to perch on its top. A bull nudges the gate open. Leo's smirk grows to a cheeky smile as the bull mosies through. Other bulls follow and quickly begin stampeding into the dip of Lollypop Creek. Black ducks scatter from their feeding, quacking into a symphony of squawking parrots and magpies and reed warblers galore.

'Bloody kids!' yells Frank from his horse.

Leo jumps from the fence, his woollen jumper catchin' on splintered wood to pull a stitch. Frogs call in the croaks of slow and low oscillation, in unison with the bulls mooing on a mission.

'What've they done?' yells Roy, tightening his grip on the reins of his chestnut as its tetchy hooves dance into the dirt. 'What're the bloody bulls doin' in the yard? They'll go straight for the cows in the next paddock.'

A hammering echoes from a fencing gang fixing fences. Tractors chug, harvestin' paddocks for Lucerne needed on constant feed at the Ranch. Three Clydesdales stop with a dray piled in hay for unloadin' at a Rupert Bunny haystack in another paddock nearby. Fine hair flows from above their hooves, bit like when Whiskey bounds his puppy dog ways. A worker on the crest of the haystack leans on his fork, his wristwatch gleaming sunbeams; another stands high on the ladder planked against the haystack. A nearby paddock has been slashed and men donning Akubras and blue and brown vests pile the slashed grass sweetenin' mellow in the sun, into mounds awaiting collection. Everything comes to an abrupt stop, to the shoutin' and yellin' in the yard at the Ranch.

Eleanor's climbed the front fence at home to see what's happening. She and Archie next door will be off in the stealth of rabbits outrunnin' a fox once the men finish their day's work at the

Ranch, to play and build cubbies into the hay. Until then though, the order from dad is to stay at home.

The commotion hasn't stopped the office lovers though, dozens of them in their moans and groans and giggles and more, in unison to the moos and coos coming from the Ranch. They're always on the move between haystacks, plantations and the office, always in the hand of no hand and the kiss that sealed them in the lifetime before.

Two-year old Hereford bulls are runnin' amuck, chasin' the heifers up Lollypop Creek. Loose skin hanging under their shoulder swings in swaying delight. The heifers are runnin' frenzied and rampant, bloody hell, crashin' into a labyrinth of fences. The head of one cow catches between two fence slats, giving a chocolate brown bull with white underbelly and face, time to jump her from behind. She squeals in a distress of no end. The children are bewildered into silence.

Mud and cow dung kick in brown glob, pointed horns agitate, push into cows' red rumps. One charges past the silo full of oats, taking out the siphon pipe carrying the feed to the loft where cattle are fed from. Oats pile onto the grass. The loaded feeder grinds to a halt halfway along its track in the stable.

They need me down there, Joe! I'd round those heifers up in a few quick whistles from me Mann.

They got good dogs down there already, Whiskey. But the mutt's off pantin' and prancin', friskin' his fancy coat free.

'Leo!' yells Roy. 'What the bloody hell have ya done, son!'

Frank takes off after a cow charging through a wooden fence. He whistles for his two dogs to follow.

Leo giggles wide-eyed from the fence post. Billy and Shirl are with him in gobsmacked awe, perched on a wooden railin'.

Whiskey's here and there, boundin' in stunning stride over his Mann on his horse in ears cocked to the skies. He pants and prances, chases his tail in circle after circle, stoppin' after each two or three for a glance at the bombastic bulls taking over.

'Get home you bloody kids,' snaps Sunshine. 'Bill. Shirl. Get moving to yer ma!' Sunshine gallops with Reg after half a dozen heifers runnin' towards the Geelong Highway, where gum trees and melaleucas line the road edge. They'll need to break past the maze of wooden fences three and four horizontal slats high first, fences that have been bolted into lengths of rusted rail tracks, five foot high.

The kids scram to their homes. Birds sing in colourful choral, frogs baritone into the sonata of Lollypop water. Pert willie wagtails jump from nests woven in neat grass cups, encircled in fine silken webs that glimmer in sunshine rays.

Roy eyes four heifers in a panic, their hooves gluing more heavily in the mud in their desperation to escape the bulls on a mission. A fifth cow is cornered between a gate unhinged from its sturdy fence post. The bull takes his opportunity and mounts her in an air of aloof nonchalance.

'Get that fucken bull off 'er,' yells Roy. He shoots a long whistle. Whiskey sprints in frisking circles, barks after Red and Mick roundin' up the squealin' cow and bull in stone face taut on the taking. 'She's not ready for inseminatin'!' He cracks his whip into the ground. Whiskey yelps, Red and Mick bark at the bull's hooves in a dance of get-off, until the bull stumps back to four legs.

Texas and Keith flank a small herd of cows collidin' and stompin' onto backs and shoulders, knocking into horror-stricken white faces with bulging dark eyes. Whips sling in hoops of up and down, side to sides. Whiskey leaps over them in acrobatic finesse. Commands are whistled to dogs that yelp and rustle the Herefords, to legs that skip and kick into the mob. In flies Clancy, circling them, barkin' and usherin' them towards the race for single filing into a holdin' yard bounded by a wooden fence, three slats high.

The cows are gathering, yet they're still agitatin'.

'Texas!' yells Roy. 'Go get 'er.' The expert horseman clicks his heels into the horse's side and shoots off after a stray. His back straight and powerful, his centre of gravity unmoving as he leans forward and back, pulls the reins left and right. His horse responds, pre-empts each command to move here and there in a tail of flurrying joy. In a whirligig of muck and slush, he rounds the outside of the cow and in one last bolt of chase, Texas draws his reins back to steer her back to the herd. The horse slows, heifers are gathering large. Bulls snort of bother and balls.

Me and Red and Mick, Jet and Clancy, the Coollie dogs in their crystal-clear blue eyes, we're holding this mob together. Chuckles on the breeze up Moubrays are calling though. The girls are callin', who taught me much of me acrobatic tricks, the girls of me Mann.

'AHH, THEMS ME GIRLS,' smiles Roy. He and Keith are riding home, their trousers and Driza-Bones layered in a mottle of mudding muck. 'They're giving me trapeze a good ol' go.'

'Ripper set up you got there, Roy, with that rope strung between the peppercorn and gum,' says Keith.

'The girls saw the trapeze at the circus on the weekend. Me old mate Billy, who I travelled the circus with, he got us in for a matinee show on Satdee.' Roy pulls his chestnut short.

'Bloody tiger on the road,' calls Keith, stopping by Roy. His horse gives a niggle, and stomps its dark hoof into the dirt.

'Hold 'er tight, Keithy,' calls Roy.

Bloody tigers! I'll get her away from me Mann, snap at her 'til she's gone.

Whiskey! Look what happened to yer last bloody time you tried, look where you ended up.

I'll chase it in me best growl ever this time! Nothing's gonna hurt me Mann, or me girls.

Whiskey's off as a shooting rocket.

'The old mutt died by one o' these.' Roy unfurls his whip from his saddle, circles it above his head to whip it into a crack of the fine leather strap. It snaps onto the snake and splits it in two. 'That's for me old Whiskey boy.'

Roy glances to the two girls, and Whiskey hovering a fading of black and white above them.

Do ya reckon he can see me, Joe? Do ya?

The two girls stop their twirlin' on the trapeze from inside the front gate. 'Pop!'

'It's alright, me girls,' calls Roy.

The two girls have a knee each twirled over the bar of the trapeze.

'I make a big noise so you know I'm killin' a snake,' calls Roy.

'Okay, Pop,' says Faye.

'That's why you're never to come past the front gate. Where's Mother and Margie?'

'Mother's inside readin' and Margie's just got home from work,' says Faye. 'Can we get down now, Pop?'

'Yep. It's safe to get down. Peggy'll be taking me into town before tea,' says Roy, now at the front gate. 'So off ya go and play.'

Hope he remembers Red and Mick before he goes, and it's not a repeat of when he forgot to call me in!

Faye and Susi hop and skip along the driveway to the back of the house. 'Come on, Speedo,' calls Faye. 'Let's get some rabbits.' The slender whippet bolts from the back porch after the two girls. 'Mother's got a stack of skins to sell at Kirk's bizarre. We'll get 'er some more.'

Faye and Susi scoot past the clump of trees, Speedo flies out over the sludge drying pans for his first rabbit. Quick as any whippet, he's got the rabbit by the neck. There's no struggle, only a limp rabbit hanging from Speedo's jaws.

'Speedo, bring it here,' calls Susi, in her sweetest of sugar voice.

Speedo drops it on the spot.

'Oh no,' complains Susi.

'Speedo! Bring it back,' yells Faye. The dog is as deaf as a lamp post and instead, dashes after a scattering of rabbits. 'Now I've got to get the bloomin' thing.'

Crikey, here she goes again. Little Faye's always crawlin' after the rabbits that Speedo catches and never brings back, over those darned sludge drying pans behind their home that cook in tops of crusty cracks. You never know how sloppy or podgy the blasted sludge is underneath. Men pump the sludge from raw sewage into open tanks and after weeks of bugs and critters gorging on it as a natural digestion process, the sludge is then pumped into these drying pans. It slowly dries out under the sun, but you never can really tell how long it takes. And that's what little Faye's crawlin' over now, drying sludge!

Bloody crikey, the crust's movin', wobblin' under Faye's knees. She's goin' slow, she understands the perils. I bark and bark, chase me tail in circles. Susi looks up at me. Want me to help yer sister, Suse, don't yer? You know I will. Always have! I bound over little Faye and bark and bark, chase me tail some more. I nudge Faye's backside with me nose. She scratches at me nudge. Slowly does it, Faye. The crusty sludge top sways. Break through and you'll drown in that sludge, little Faye, and end up with me! They'll never find yer in there!

They never find a lotta bits 'n' bobs thrown in there, like old car number plates and wads of stolen money from criminals, and probably some murdered bodies too. Bloody crikey, safer for them to be playin' tennis. They play a bit of tennis, these Oram girls, with the Warfe kids next door. The boys are always in and out of one another's homes and Keithy's takin' Margie out for a bit of kissin'. They're the only two homes within a quarter of a mile of one another on the 160 Road. Until the Days move in to the Warfe's after old man Henry retires, then the Oram tackers have new mates to play with.

Hurry and get that rabbit, little Faye. But slowly and safely. And before yer Pop catches yer!

HE'S STEADY IN HIS Akubra, shirt and tie, boots resting in stirrups polished shine high. Chin staunch, back straight in shoulders thrust forward, he's primed in his tanned saddle lustring in bees wax. The Australian flag of blue, white and red flies from a pole slipped into a strap tied to his saddle, alongside his whip curled by his leg.

He led Melbourne's Moomba parade that replaced the marches celebrating the eight hour work day, an Aboriginal man at that.

That was nearly 15 years ago. In the years since, a pilgrimage of Farm stockmen and their horses have shipped into Newmarket to ride the Moomba Day parades: Roy with Frank and Texas, Terry and Bernie with Cyril, Harry and Murray and more, together they marched under gleeful eye of children and family.

Whether performing in travelling carnivals or shows of the Wild West, boxing in bouts of win after win or riding rodeos in the charisma of the travelling showman, he's one of the greatest horsemen in town. He holds that grace in the sashes awarded him and in the scarf of constant wear, his prize for winning the rodeo for Australia against America. Much to the delight of fluttering female lashes, much to the delight of me. He was me Mann.

That was before he came to the Farm in the 1940s, to work as a stockie and break horses in at the 80 Yards for the army during World War II. He'd travel with them to India on a passport few Aborigines held.

He was strict and commanding, of high ethic and esteemed by all. I sit to attention, ears reaching for the skies. He was me Mann: Mr Roy Oram.

BLACKENED BOY SOARS BEHIND Whiskey striding his skilled agility and yet no matter how far ahead Whiskey may be, he always circles back to ensure Blackened Boy keeps up. The boy almost always does nowadays. He's far more buoyant and exudes a soft burnished lustre when flitting over grass plains outlying the Farm that germinated after the fires, as though emerging in rebirth.

Below us, the mischief and mirth diminishes, where scallywags scrammed through bottle brush and rabbits were caught from wavering seas, their skins sold on the roadside with peas and mushrooms picked from paddocks and bagged in cloth, some bags filled halfway with horse dung and topped only in a few mushrooms. It was a freedom to be without fear.

Snatching bags is no more after the Constable laid down the law, and Hiekeo is finished, the game of kicking a tin can or hitting it with a stick. Ryans, Wallaces, Smiths, Forders and Days, the Dandos, Holders, Breguets, Newtons and more ... all leave Murtcaim, Moubrays Lane and from around the 160 Road and 80 Yards, the Ranch too.

Generations across the Farm have gone, of children and adults riding on horseback, hitch-hiking or cycling eight miles to and from work and school. And hats taking collections for anyone without or to help a mate with no car or little for dinner. Time is vanishing. Always does. It's one of the few inevitables of existence, with life and death as a three-way tie.

Bachelors bunking together, women and their cottage industries, ice boxes and kerosene fridges, tilly lamps and little boys that sit in my gut. The devastation of him and them, running and fleeing, sorrow in innocence lost, in spirit quashed.

The Farm is changing, its light is dulling.

Twenty-firsts, dances, weddings and wakes, parties and presentations; card nights, Christmases and concerts in the Farm hall, schools, family homes and shearing sheds. They were the places to be and of being together, and that other place of beating heart where cannon balls splashed and learning to swim was a rite of passage, even if thrown in with a rope tied around a little belly. Men and women's football – credit to the gals – tennis, cricket and croquet. Rich milk coffee steaming in copper pots, shuffling boots on sawdust covered wooden boards, a one, two jig to Alf on the squeeze box and five, six waltz to Mrs Beamish on piano. Roy's in his element, humming a pitch through his gum leaf as a soft bugle stretching east to west across the Farm.

Emotion seeps in tentacling web, fuels endorphins into the Farm's core, and us above.

Police visiting to check on the untoward, uncovering beer to confiscate and drink later at the station, or deciding to drink it on the spot with the Farm men. That's if those mischievous little boys spying on the men stashing their contraband in bushes and tractor buckets didn't get the beer first and conceal it in channels or hay bales, then hide and spy in giggling merriment at the men searching for their precious stash. The jovial, the cursing and occasional full-as-bull brawls after those beers that spill into the school grounds and spear at homes, rattling baubles of roses and hydrangeas fertile in hope. The sometimes grief sinking into sludge pan sorrow, but always in the freedom to play and wander, to explore and be in the vast expanse without fear.

Bands played, couples danced in the lightness of silken thread wisping on the gist of spring, until the music stopped and the MC called to disperse to a corner. An empty bottle spun, chancing its long neck to point to the group next excluded from the dance floor. Until one couple was left and crowned winner, awarded a teapot or cup and saucer. Belles of Balls too, attracted young women and eligible partners far and wide, opening themselves to scrutinising judging of dance, dress, gloves, etiquette and posture. A winner crowned at each ball was awarded a sash and moved to the next Belle of Ball until finally, a Belle of Belles was crowned, just as Sir Dallas' daughter had judged before.

All is fading now, the lights are dimming in this land faraway.

Until you hone in for our whispers echoing boundless, catch our giggles in the trees, the galloping and yelping with the moos and coos and baas aplenty. Cobwebs clump secrets in corners, mustarding waters sour its distinct bouquet. The mettle of yesterday is pristine today.

All good things must come to an end, exceptional things too.

In its place is a warmth brewing in our divide, our deity of the day. Familiarity and friendship, affinity and affection, it grows in disintegration and death. In Elsie and Joe, Dear Daughter and Mr Boy, the Yankee doodle dandy that smiles with the eyes and his shadowy mate. The Carter home and his white magpie mate, the constant reminder of outcast and segregation. And Blackened Boy and Whiskey, with me as three.

We dance in the jellies and staries, pirouette with the butterflies of the sea before slinking into cerulean skies. There's a comfort in the hundreds of foetus kinfolk, with the flounders skating and skimming as shooting stars streaking light over dark, and the black man flittering with his diamond encrusted spear in the Milky Way.

Luminescence of electric blue, brilliance of white, more incandescent with the lost and disconnected on a quest for a place of no place. They seek our warmth: the inquisitive boy falling into a street drain and washing into the sewer to be caught in a grid on the Farm; the disappearing weather presenter and her belongings dumped here and never found. And the man of discontent who flees the Little River pub after an alcohol infused bender, arriving here to shoot himself by the river. They're all here. Even those lost in a stranglehold of torment who will suicide in the years to come following the Board's turbulent demise, where their dark cloud is intrinsically woven into the fabric of safety and kin within this place today.

Under a rose of gold sun is the warble of unperturbed, is the feeding, watering and branding, heifers with stillborn calves and granddaddy pine trees at least 60 feet tall. The wisp of sheoak and wattle of feathery frond, gathering butterflies fluttering in the present and past. On the breeze is the whisper of ghosts gone, of horses and frogs, lizards and snakes, the reservoir and church and Cocoroc North School to come. Farm family and kin hover in that rose of gold of yesterday, today and tomorrow, in the gleam of gold that never dulls.

While they leave down there, we grow up here in the sublime of the underworld, where home and hearth breathe beneath the earth to dream in tombs of yesterday. Archaeologically, a sleeping beauty awaits her Prince Charming's awakening.

Cheers to a life in lands faraway. In an honouring that's caring, appreciating and trusting, padlocked in a tiny box of jewels of the most precious ... the jewel of the crown is life on lands faraway.

A living ghost town in a life at honey speed, a calm and peace unwavering in the howl of withering leaves. Crested cockatoos shrill between trees, a flush of begonias hang as buxom chandeliers beside glamorous hibiscus in extrovert parading ... all hinge in a haunting of melancholy, beguiling ghosts to rejoice in veiled, century-old tales.

Listen carefully for our lifelong gloating in the rose of gold gilded over lifetimes, in this space of breath as a vast expanse of clarity, a bounty of beauty in perfect imperfection.

The air below chokes in asphyxiating abandon, with families and kin gone and most houses and two cows and gardens well-tendered disappearing from lands faraway. Jewels may fall from crowns, but they never fail to sparkle in the brilliance of the most brilliant, multi-faceted gems. Whether in a white, yellow, green or rose of gold setting, they shine into forever.

Cheers to a life in a living ghost town, in a life at honey speed, wistful of what's to come with a house and two cows and a land faraway.

What now Is

Jetty pylons at low tide, 2018. Photo courtesy of Dr Schott.

Ambling honeysuckle, laurels of lavender,
Mother Earth imbued in spring.
A blossoming new hope in the now Is,
of twenty-first century faraway lands.
Ashes of the once Was scatter across the Farm,
reveal a resurrection of what now Is.

'You're a shit player from the shit farm.'

'At least I'm not a shit person.'

– Player exchange, under 18s football match, Werribee, 2016.

NO ONE LIVES ON the Farm today. No residence stands, although the stables at the Ranch still breathe, albeit in layers of asbestos. Nothing remains in the bottom-end but the tea tree hedge once fronting Cocoroc South School, now growing wiry wild. The Cocoroc South School still exists and is now the Werribee Girl Guides Hall. Jetty pylons and the original sluice gate from the 1890s can be seen when they're exposed at unusually low tides, where shell grit bathes the foreshore to share a million stories with the rise and fall of oceans. Only one fishing hut stands and that's along the Werribee River, which many of us office lovers venture into to rattle and roll its shanty foundations. And sadly, disturbingly, prejudices remain.

The Farm hall was moved in 1975 and now sleeps peacefully by the swimming pool, change rooms and water tank, four hearts beating as one. Those once working in the Farm office at the Head of the Road, moved into this building of modernity at the top of New Farm Road in the same year, where me and my love are today. The randy of us, lovers frolicking and romping above the beavering below, stirring glances of curiosity in the always rumours of office lovers. Rumours that are true, many times over.

Me and my guy are in the boardroom, waiting for the members of the Friends of the Metropolitan Sewerage Farm to make their coffee and tea, before talks begin with Melbourne Water about the fate of the Farm swimming pool. He's hovering above the freshly brewed coffee steaming from a thermos in the small kitchenette, shooting me that devilish look he knows I can't resist.

Workers of the Farm are on the move again. They're returning to the Head of the Road into new offices just built, where the water tank continues to bask in morning sunrises. Its viridian green tank is iridescent pretty. Beneath it has been cleared out and refurbished as an exhibition and performance space. It's where red-head artist, Fiona, brought guitarists together to strum electric riffs that reverberated into its bluestone base and core of the empty tank. Heavenly it was, hovering in the haze of neon with my sweet guy, sometimes adding our own bass of riff. *Treatment,* they call it, a public art event. Here he comes, my sensual Eros, knowing my thoughts before I release them.

What a time that was, my Aphrodite. You and me, bolshy in the musty haze, our desire as strong as when we first met.

That was so many years ago.

1957 if I remember correct, which I always do. The last cricket match the Farm played. I don't remember much of the game after my eyes caught you.

You in your dashing whites on the pitch, playing for the Farm team, having walked out of the pavilion in your cream blazer for the last time.

I flush my champagne blush and flee into the alcove kitchen. He's following me, corners me. Our kindred spirits enmesh in an arousal that never mellows.

What a boom time those 1950s were for the Farm, a stark difference to its demise 40 years later and the radical change of extreme consequence on the good Farm people. It tested the Board of Works motto of 'Public health is my reward', and the strong culture and pride in our work and life here. A prouder workforce I could not ever find anywhere. We worked diligently and the Board left us to do what we had to do, had faith in us to get the job done. Melbourne would not be a city of such standing and have gained the reputation of being one of the world's most liveable cities in the world had it not been for the staunch reverence of us Farm people. I saw it daily. Anyone I met that knew the Farm, loved the place. It wasn't unusual for your washing to magically come in off the clothesline if rain was approaching and you were out, or for a child to be rescued from falling into a drain and taken home.

You're such a softy for an engineer. It's what I love about you.

And I love you. Working here was powerful and we bonded outside of work also. The social club kept the momentum up after people moved off the Farm, organising many functions and Friday drinks after work, with quite a few in this boardroom and theatrette off the foyer.

Until corporatisation blew in, my love, and the Farm came tumbling down. We were quashed, our sense of pride was destroyed during the transitioning from Board of Works to Melbourne Water. Massive restructuring forced redundancies in an ever revolving teary-eyed, slammed door, one after the other told their job was cut. Many had links to those who first worked and lived on the Farm. They were born and bred here, went to school here and had their first kiss in the Farm playground, got a job here, married and had their reception in the Farm hall, to start the cycle all over again and make a home and life on the Farm. Our Utopia was gone.

I know, sweet man, how could I ever forget your glitching of blue-print-blue, as a slide show of your engineering breakthroughs in sewage treatment. First, people were asked to move from their homes, which many did reluctantly, then they were made redundant and forced to leave their jobs. They were shattered. I would've been too had I worked here.

My erratic flicker, that was beyond my understanding. Hundreds left over a few short years and so many were devastated, their umbilical attachment to the Farm had been severed. Many men suffered mental ill health, some wallowing in pubs for days on end and never venturing back to the Farm. Men who lost jobs, took their own lives. Suicided!

Come close, my shattered man.

Until that one down there came along and brought some of the men back here for the first time since they got the boot all those years ago. They cried, spilled their tears to her about those harrowing times.

They laughed about their blissful days of working and living here too. The women also. She down there noted it all down, got this group working together to create the Friends of the Metropolitan Sewerage Farm. Sadly, some men haven't recovered, some tears continue to fall.

But the organisation has recovered and Melbourne Water works to social and environmental values, and economic needs. That's good business.

The bureaucracy never leaves my sweet man bureaucrat.

After working for the Board of Works for 25 years, it's hard not to think like a civil servant, my love.

Treatment, the art event, got people here over the last few years, people came from across Australia to see the Farm through artists' eyes. She down there was part of it, created a song from her involvement in it. The gold glitter spraying from a heavy duty sewage diving suit near sewage lagoons tickled me no end.

That's where *he* was.

He? What are you on about?

You were over at *his* meetings, no need to hide it. You probably followed him to the methane gas plant when he was meeting contractors there. Farm managers are always meeting someone. You're a sucker for blue eyes, always have been.

Blue eyes? What's got you going?

Him, sitting atop the boardroom door, smirking as the feral cat content on a hundred sewer rats. He's perving on you.

That blue-print-blue flicker is blinding you, sweet man. Can't you see the fondles between he and his love. Those two have been roaming these corridors for years, always together in the ardour of office lovers. Honestly, come here my Eros.

Hmm, how about a visit to the bird hides by Lake Borrie after this meeting? Perhaps we can do some of our own research and development, and slide into a cuddle and caress.

My old engineer, you. Stop with that always devilish look and roaming hands. They're coming!

They're too busy to notice us. Let's have a little roll on the boardroom table before they start their meeting.

No, they'll know. That Diane will sense us, from the Friends group.

I want you, to intertwine divine ....

Stop will you! Or I'll whisk away.

Go on, let's go to the ornamental lake outside – I dare you!

Shush. They're coming to the table with their cups of tea. There's cute baby John, now all grown up and six foot something. He was a newborn when Marj and John left the Farm.

It would be a miracle if Dot wasn't nearby, wanting to dote on him.

John's going to sit next to Flossy and her brother. They're the great grandchildren of Agnes and George Sadler from the bottom-end, Pam and David. And Pam being of the underwear stolen by that cheeky Paul, John's older brother! Paul was part of the Friends group in the beginning, but didn't continue.

They're marching about as proud troopers, and so they should after working so hard to establish the Friends group. Most are original family and kin. Eleanor's there, the Watkins girl.

Eleanor and her brothers scattered their parents' ashes up near where they lived at the Head of the Road: Gordon and Nell Watkins. They'll be flying about to no end, probably with Mr and Mrs Towers whose ashes were scattered on the Farm too.

Terry's here, one of the last to leave a Board of Works house from the small cluster at the top of Farm Road. Such a quiet achiever of much greatness for all that is the Farm, in engineering, heritage, the environment and more. Those last homes were sold off to develop the Riverwalk housing estate when Melbourne Water was born.

What's wrong, sweet man? Your eyes are glassing over as a faraway fading. Where have you gone?

Back to the transitioning days. The pace of change was relentless. Privatisation was bullshit government cost-cutting, masked as supposedly good corporate business. It merged the

Board of Works with local water authorities and split the lot into five: three retail water companies, an organisation to manage parks and public open spaces, and Melbourne Water to manage sewerage, bulk water supply and the waterways. In four years of restructuring, the Board of Works went from 6,500 employees to less than 560 with Melbourne Water. They renamed the Metropolitan Sewerage Farm to the Werribee Treatment Complex. All was done by 1995.

Renamed by an engineer by the sound of it.

You are such a cheeky minx, it's a fantastic name! That was when the earliest black plastic membrane cover was installed over the first pond of the 115 East lagoon, a marvellous piece of state-of-the-art technology to capture methane to generate electricity.

The visiting education groups would walk on the cover with raw sewage percolating underneath. Drove security nuts! They were terrified someone would fall through. I'm no engineer but even I knew it was reckless to have the public walking on sewage.

We had a swinging time just before Melbourne Water was born.

We did. The Farm's centenary to celebrate 100 years since Board members sat for the first time was a fantastic time. You shone as the consummate rose among the thorns. Thousands flocked in to celebrate and view the paintings, collage and photographs hanging in the art show. You were a vision and I chased you under the glass ceiling in the foyer and outside to the trees surrounding the ornamental lake. Ohh-la-la, that lake....

I loved that exhibition because outsiders got a glimpse into the aesthetic of the Farm. She was part of that too, that one down there, asked artists to come onto the Farm and interpret the place through their art. *Treatment*'s the modern adaptation of it. Maudie Palmer from Heidi Art Gallery came and awarded prizes for best art works. The elegant pencil and watercolour wash of the Ranch still hangs on the wall outside the boardroom. You're staring at me again, burning into me. And I'm blushing over my colour of champagne.

You're more sultry-steamy to me, effervescent in a flush of pink diamonds.

And there it is, that which catches my insides. I'm without words and instead, sweep over the long oak table laid in cheese and grissini sticks and parmesan sprinkled zucchini slice. He's on my skittering tail, always is.

'Where's that breeze coming from?' asks Diane, glancing our way.

'I'm not sure. None of the windows open in this meeting room,' says Paul, sitting by the Farm manager with his notes at the end of the table.

'Okay, shall we start?' says she down there. 'It's five past five already and we need to start.'

They're all a bit tetchy. Going over notes and doing a terrible job at holding back scowls. David and Pam are talking through brother and sister glances. John's pondering out the window and only brings his attention back when the Farm manager speaks.

'Melbourne Water will continue with its plan to fill the swimming pool so that visitors can interact with it in a safe way. Safety is paramount and interpretation is important for all of our visitors.' Staunch shoulders, upright and uptight.

'They can't interact with it if it's filled in. It won't be a pool anymore!' Eyes roll.

'We'll fill it to just below the pool's rim so that kids can sit on its edge and dangle their feet in the pool, so to speak. It'll be part of their experience to interact with it. The pool needs to be safe.' Stiff and rigid.

'And then you'll plant it out to make it into a rain garden! Really? A rain garden in this wind swept place? We're under a rain shadow here, on basalt, dry plains.' Eyes roll.

'The pool's redevelopment into a rain garden is part of the stormwater management for the site.' Stiffness gets stiffer.

'It won't look like a pool. How's it supposed to be interpretation if it doesn't look like a pool?' Eyes roll the other way.

'We're taking the pool from a decrepit state to something that is preserved for the future. We can undo it later if we want to. The redevelopment of the pool is focussed on interpretation, we have to remember that. Doing nothing is not an option.' Breathe deep.

'The garden isn't going to do anything to preserve the pool, OR interpret it. Filling it with dirt for the roots of plants to grow and damage the pool!' Huffing and puffing and hands that want to bang tables.

'The team thought about turning it back into a pool but it needs too much work to meet current pool guidelines. It'll be more detrimental to the pool if we did that.' Stiffness becomes taut tight.

'The pool could be made into a play space, maybe with a Perspex deck built over the top so the kids can see into the pool, to understand it and get a sense of what it was.' Feet want to stomp with fists that want to pound.

'The pool is being redeveloped not just for children, but for a range of visitors.' Breathe something, anything.

'The pool is the whole history of the Farm, the focal point of our life. It's important to preserve it as it was the centre of our lives here. You're destroying that.' Steam blows from the nostrils of a bull snorting in a paddock on a frosty morning.

'What we've come up with is a balance we need to strike between operations, heritage and the environment.' Breath in slumped shoulders.

'Once the pool's filled in, it'll be lost forever. The cost will be too great to return it to its original state. It'll never be unfilled.' Deep sigh.

'Melbourne Water has a strong commitment to heritage.' A stream of sighs.

'You're killing it, burying it just like you did with all the homes.' Despair.

'Swimming pools are always the centre of communities, we understand that. We're a long way into our work to relocate the administration building and education services to the township. Master planning, concept design and construction documentation were all completed some time ago.' Slumping sighs.

'As a group, please think about what's proposed for the pool and respond to me with what you like and dislike. What's acceptable and not for you and any further ideas you may have.'

Huffing and puffing, sighing and discontent. Hearts are yanked from chests. Again.

They'll end up incorporating blue glass aggregate in the top layer of gravel mulch once they've filled in the pool. It'll resemble shimmering blue water. It's a good addition. The pool has to be safe and what they're doing is a good solution. They'll reinstate old markings, such as 'No Diving', along the external pool walls and install signs similar to what was there, such as 'Throwing of balls is prohibited in the pool'.

Always the engineer. People won't be able to understand the meaning of the pool though, won't be able to see it. That's important for people like me because we learn visually.

It's a pool. What's to understand?

Its heart! It's much more than a simple stinking pool.

The room begins to fill. The white magpie mate perched atop the chimney of the Carter home, Dear Daughter and Mr Boy and the hundreds of kinfolk behind them. Sorrowing Father with Blackened Boy and Whiskey, Yankee doodle dandy that smiles with the eyes and his shadowy mate, Elsie and Joe, dogs and cats, cows and their calves, tiger snakes and horses, staries and jellies and butterflies of the sea ... we hover in the resurrection of cerulean skies.

THAT WAS THREE YEARS ago. The decision to fill the swimming pool remained: to line it and fill it with dirt and scoria to become the rain garden the Friends group opposed. Set up to advocate and actively preserve, capture and promote the culture and heritage of the Metropolitan Sewerage Farm, the Friends group was incorporated in 2019.

The global pandemic has eased and school children can visit the Farm once again, no doubt taking their lunch break in and around the pool space. They won't understand that they're sitting at a pool with such depth of meaning, not when plants grow inside it. Blackened Boy will glide above them with DD and Mr Boy and their kinfolk, swoosh into the children's games of chasey. Yankee doodle dandy that smiles with the eyes and his shadowy mate will fly in barrelling formation and aerobatic flair with other pilots, flying low to skim the children for added tease. And the resident possums will adore the feasts the children will leave behind.

Wyndham Council now owns the 1970s administration building at the top of New Farm Road and me and my sweet guy, we continue to romp our sexy jaunts through it, as well as the rafters of the new office building back in our beloved Head of the Road. We've had two new managers since the hunky blue-eyed Farm Manager. Both women. Shame it took more than 125 years for women to have the chance to manage the Farm. My sweet man would glitch shades of blue-print-blue when I glinted an eye at the hunky Farm manager back then. I followed him to the pool one time, the Farm manager, being the sucker I am for blue eyes. Ooh-la-la, what he could do to me!

But I'm only really into my sweet Eros and we continue our delicious rendezvousing all over the Farm, even in the musty workshops nearby. That place was a favourite of ours when the workshops buzzed back in the day and our trysts there would sometimes stir the workmen. The blur between them and us can be thin and squints our way were not uncommon, especially when the amour between us reached swirling heights that sometimes sent men outside, as the two that left for their own privacy one time, into a waterman's hut unhitched beside the workshops.

The original weatherboard change rooms beside the pool were pulled down last year to ghostly cries of mischievous boys and girls and no, Pam's knickers were never found underneath. Public toilets for visitors to the Head of the Road were built in its place, as a replica of the original change room building. The new toilet block, will never have what the change rooms had though: heart and soul. That only comes with people and emotion, experience of life. It distressed me no end when the remnant gutters along the roadside were dug up to build new roads as part of the redevelopment of the area. They were memories exhumed, of young girls and boys skipping merry along them or sobbing broken and battered on the gutter's side, and men tripping over them in befuddled booze. They'd have had a story or two to tell. Everything has a life. The Farm hall, thankfully, has been saved and was refurbished into an education centre.

The tennis courts may be covered over and the croquet lawn has disappeared beneath overgrowth upon overgrowth, but the sports pavilion and oval remain, even if smothered in a dense cover of grass and weeds and ramshackle trees.

Life goes on in the space of in between, that transcends the up and down, even for my broken-hearted engineer after I left for the light to be with my son who died in a car accident. My Eros was inconsolable, until Sorrowing Father stepped in.

And so today, I'm blissful with my son beyond the clouds, above the walk on the Farm foreshore, more than 125 years after the Hickeys and Sadlers first came to the Farm. Three enthusiasts from the Friends group, one being the Sadler great grandson, stroll over shells that blister under each safety-boot step. They walk kilometres under a warming sun to discover the remnant jetty pylons inclining into Port Phillip Bay, and the 1890s wooden sluice gate built to carry our Melbourne's effluent into the bay, its wooden boards worn by the lapping salt water. Both can only be seen on a very low tide.

And all while that rose of gold continues to spin its forever tune. Now in Werribee, it graces the finger of Annie's great granddaughter as the enchanting enigma never revealed.

Jewels never fail to sparkle in the brilliance of the most brilliant, in a rose of gold that shines a forever shine.

Cheers to a life in a living ghost town, in a life at honey speed, of a house and two cows and a land faraway.

A land faraway

Swimming pool, date unknown. Photo courtesy of the O'Connor family.

Time unmoved in a land far away,
living in a life of honey speed
waves are walking in curls of white,
moving over me at honey speed

I can hear their voices calling out, calling out
I can hear their laughter running free, running free
I can hear their voices mm-mm, mm-mm
I can hear their voices mm-mm, mm-mm

Pastures of graded green,
Stockmen on horses, strongest of forces
Bound by isolation, power and freedom,
I can still see them

I can hear their voices calling out, calling out
I can hear their laughter running free, running free
I can hear their voices mm-mm, mm-mm
I can hear their voices mm-mm, mm-mm

In a ghost town running wild,
I've got memories on file, moving on, moving out
Swimming pools hold cannon balls and yearning hearts hold stories,
Of what we had before, torn down in a blaze of glory

I can feel their voices calling out, calling out
I can hear their laughter running free, oh running free
I can hear their voices mm-mm, mm-mm
I can hear their voices mm-mm, mm-mm

To hear the song, visit
www.monikaschott.com/publications-books

Annie Hickey. Photo courtesy of the Hickey family.

History of the Metropolitan Sewerage Farm community

1891	The Melbourne and Metropolitan Board of Works (MMBW) is founded.
1892	Work begins on establishing the Metropolitan Sewerage Farm on the outskirts of Werribee; workers begin living on site.
1893	The MMBW starts building cottages in the bottom-end and top-end townships; families join workers to live on site.
1894	Jetty built in the bottom-end township and the MMBW Board considers a proposal to build shops and a licensed hotel alongside it.
1895	Cocoroc North State School opens in the top-end township.
1897	The Metropolitan Sewerage Farm community establishes a cricket team; the first sewage flows reach the Metropolitan Sewerage Farm.
1903	A Mechanics Institute is built in the top-end township to also act as a library and community hall.
1906	Cocoroc South State School opens in the bottom-end township and Cocoroc West State School opens in the north west of the Metropolitan Sewerage Farm, along Geelong Road near the Ranch.
1912	The community establishes the Metropolitan Farm football team.

1913	The Metropolitan Farm croquet and tennis teams are established, as well as a rifle club. The sports pavilion, oval, croquet lawns and tennis courts with a club house follow in the top-end township.
1914	Around 27 cottages stand in the bottom-end township and 20 cottages stand in the top-end township. A postmistress offers postal services to residents and workers via the Metropolitan Farm Post Office in the top-end township; a general store follows.
1924	The Mechanic's Institute burns down; it is rebuilt five years later and becomes the community hall.
1939	Murtcaim State School opens in the far west of the Metropolitan Sewerage Farm, near Avalon.
1943	375 men are employed, cottages provide homes for around 100 families and grocers deliver meat, bread, haberdashery and other goods to replace the General Store.
1944	The swimming pool is built in the top-end township.
1948	Cocoroc West State School closes.
1950s	Women from the Metropolitan Sewerage Farm and Werribee come together to play football; the population of the Metropolitan Sewerage Farm peaks at more than 500.
1960s	The community begins disbanding; houses are buried, burnt down or relocated.
1963	Cocoroc South State School closes.
1965	The Metropolitan Farm football team folds; Murtcaim School closes.

History of the Metropolitan Sewerage Farm community

1971	Cocoroc North State School closes.
1972	The last family leaves the bottom-end township.
1974	The last family leaves the top-end township; all four settlements are now abandoned.
1975	The community hall is moved to sit beside the swimming pool.
1984	The last of the homes scattered across the Metropolitan Farm is vacated. A few employees live in a small cluster of houses on the boundary of the Metropolitan Sewerage Farm and Werribee River, at the top of Farm Road.
1990s	The homes at the top of Farm Road are vacated.
1992	The MMBW becomes Melbourne Water and the Metropolitan Sewerage Farm is renamed the Werribee Treatment Complex.
2015	Reactivation of the Metropolitan Sewerage Farm community begins through the public art project, *Treatment.*
2016	The Metropolitan Sewerage Farm community begins reconnecting through the research into its social history.
2019	The Friends of the Metropolitan Sewerage Farm is incorporated.
2022	*The faraway land of the house and two cows* is first published.

Images

Hand drawn and painted map of the Metropolitan Sewerage Farm in 1907. Map courtesy of an anonymous donation.

Phoebe and Frank Pengelly, date unknown. Photo courtesy of the Pengelly family.

Jim Bensted outside the Bachelor's hut, date unknown. Photo courtesy of the Hickey family.

Mixing Camp, also known as the Contractor's Camp, 1891 - 1893. Photo courtesy of the Public Records Office of Victoria.

Cottages at the Head of the Road, 1895 - 1915. Photo courtesy of the Public Records Office of Victoria.

Farm jetty, early 1900s. Photo courtesy of the Sadler family.

Grading paddocks, Metropolitan Farm Manager, Richard Philippe, 3rd from left, 1909-1926. Photo courtesy of the Phillipe family.

Ploughing land filtration paddocks, 1912. Photo courtesy of the Sadler family.

Metro Farm Manager, Richard Philippe (2nd from right) & Earl of Stradbroke, Governor of Victoria (5th from left), early1920s. Photo courtesy of the Philippe family.

Making hay, date unknown. Photo courtesy of the Warfe family.

Hickey family, 1922. Photo courtesy of the Forder family.

Cocoroc North Sunday School, 1925. Photo courtesy of the Fisher family.

Metropolitan Farm football team premiers, 1931. Photo courtesy of the Edwards family.

Workers taking the tramways bus to the west of the sewerage farm in Murtcaim, 1934-1962. Photo courtesy of the McLaren family.

The Losewitz family in Loosey's paddock, 1932. Photo courtesy of the Tate (nee Losewitz) family.

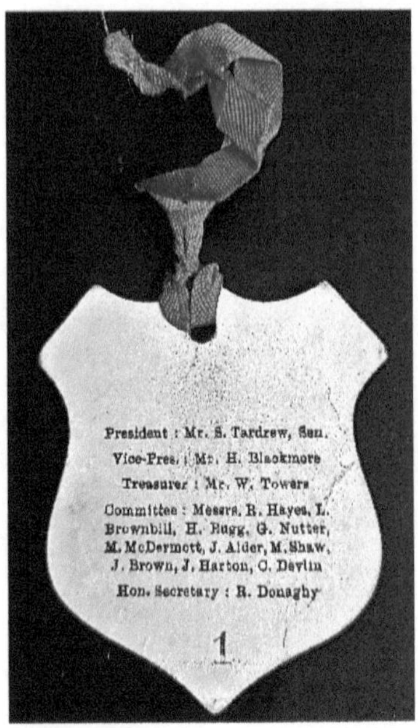

Metropolitan Farm Football Club Gent's Ticket, 1940. Photo courtesy of the McDermott family.

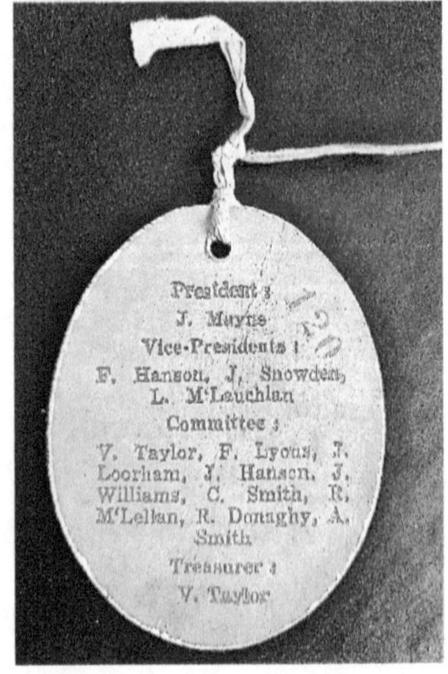

Metropolitan Farm Football Club Lady's Ticket, 1934. Photo courtesy of the McDermott family.

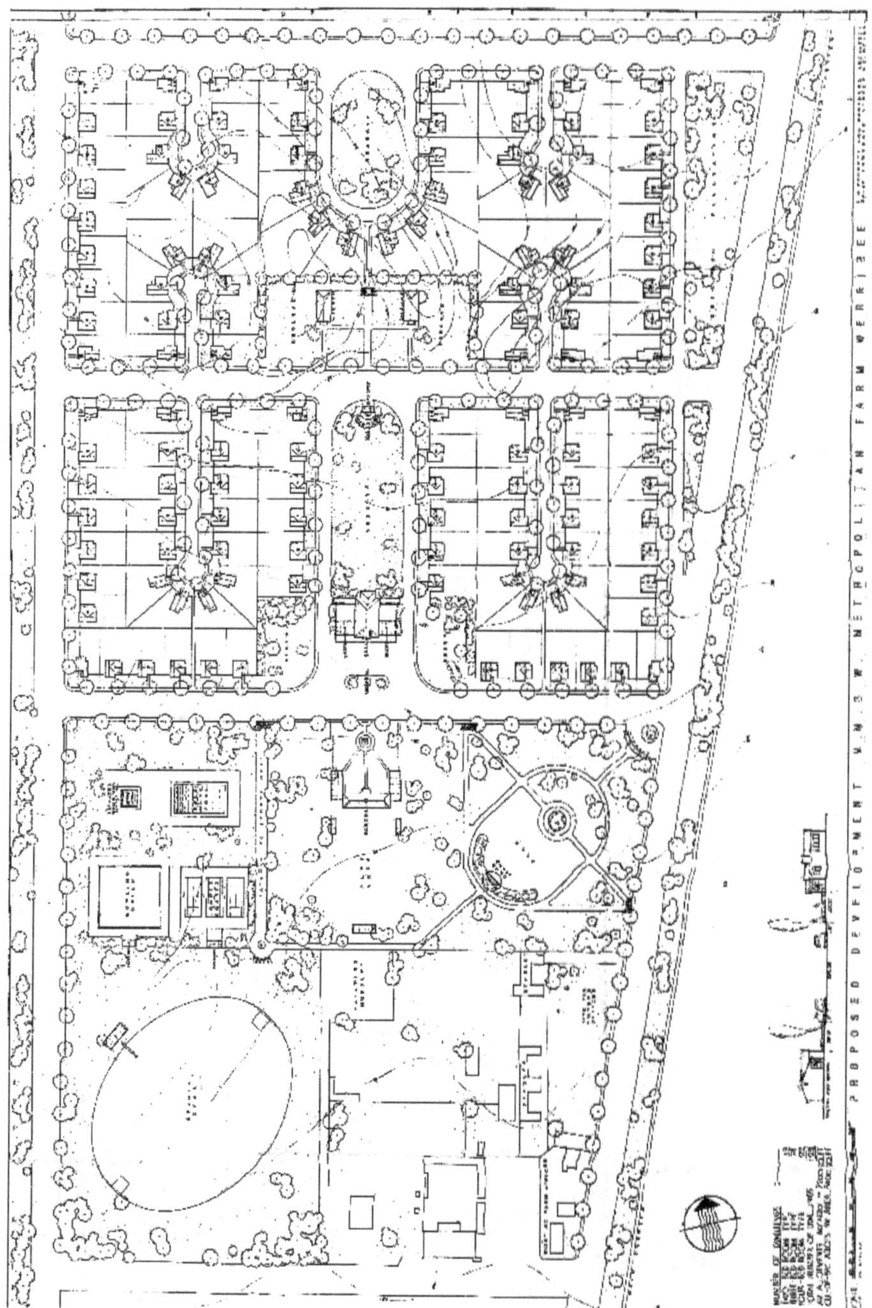

Proposed New Township M. & M.B.W. Farm Werribee, 1942. L.M. Perrott & Partners Architects.

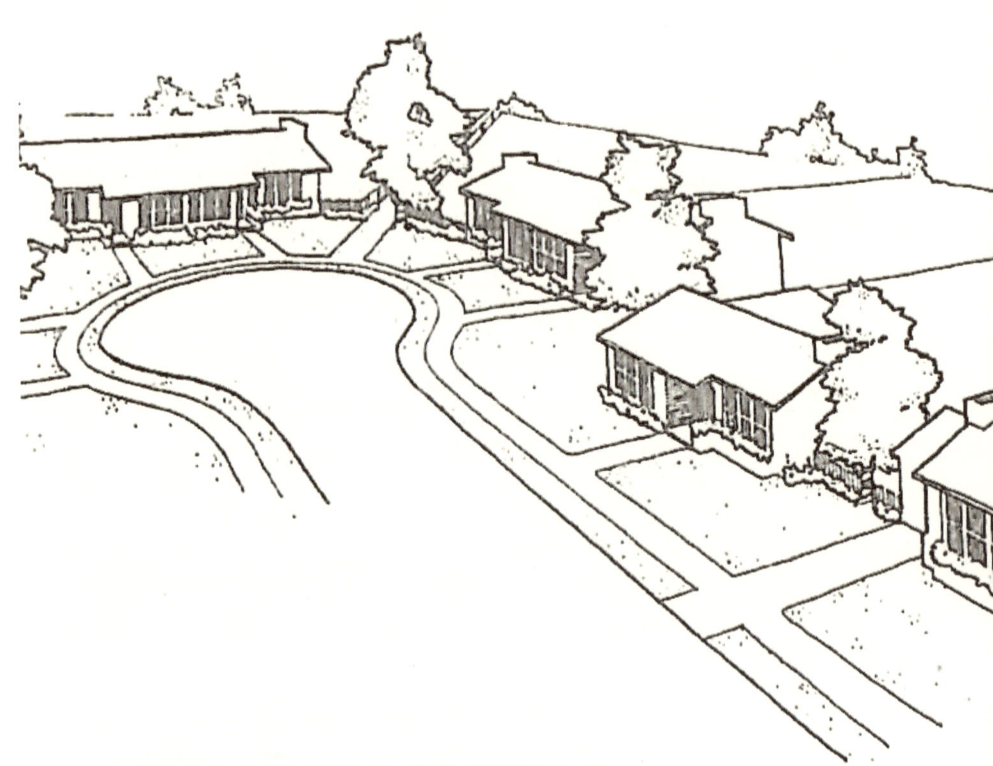

SKETCH INDICATING THE EFFECT OF PLACING A PAIR OF HOMES AT THE END OF EACH CUL-DE-SAC IN PLACE OF TWO INDIVIDUAL HOMES. SHOULD THE DECISION BE SUCH THAT THE BOARD TAKES OVER ALL GARDENS, WE WOULD ADVOCATE THAT THE TREE-PLANTING IN THE CUL-DE-SACS BE KEPT BACK TO A LINE BETWEEN THE HOMES . . .

Plan for open community living, part of the Proposed New Township M. & M.B.W. Farm Werribee, 1942. L.M. Perrott & Partners Architects.

THE MODERN PLAN

The Modern Plan, part of the Proposed New Township M. & M.B.W. Farm Werribee, 1942. L.M. Perrott & Partners Architects.

Cocoroc West State School, 1945. Photo courtesy of the Ryan family.

Cocoroc South School, date unknown. Photo courtesy of the Sadler family.

Cocoroc West School teacher, Ernie Best, 1943. Photo courtesy of the Ryan family.

Bill Ben outside the New Australian Camp, circa 1950. Photo courtesy of the Ben family.

The Rovers Metro Farm Tennis Club run by H Warfe, date unknown. Photo courtesy of the Warfe family.

Metropolitan Sewerage Farm stockmen, 1948. Photo courtesy of the Ryan family.

Dot O'Connor lifting the washing on the Metro Farm, 1950s. Photo courtesy of the Hassett family.

Farm office in the top-end township, 1952. Photo courtesy of the Breguet family.

Heritage listed water tank, date unknown. Photo courtesy of the Pengelly family.

Murtcaim State School, 1954. Photo courtesy of the Steinbergs family.

Bill Cameron with Metro Farm prized cattle at Melbourne Show, 1952. Photo courtesy of the Cameron family.

Roy Oram leading the Moomba parade, 1955. Photo courtesy of the Toohey family.

BEST FARM TEAM EVER 1954

TOP ROW. Left to Right. Nancy Gillett, Doreen Rye, Beryl Gillett, Patricia Haverd, Margaret Hart, Lois Gillett, Lena Morrish, Valerie Reeve.

CENTRE ROW. Pamela Miller, Lorna Towers, Melva Welsh, Edna Hampton, Freda Hampton, Margaret O'Connor.

BOTTOM ROW. Marlene McGrath, Shirley Reidy, Pauline Wallace, Elaine Wolters.

Best Metropolitan Farm women's football team, 1954. Photo courtesy of the Breguet family.

Women's football team celebrating a win, with Maragret Hassett carried on shoulders, 1953. Photo courtesy of the Hassett family.

Women's football team pie night with Charlie Sutton, 1952. Photo courtesy of the Carlton family.

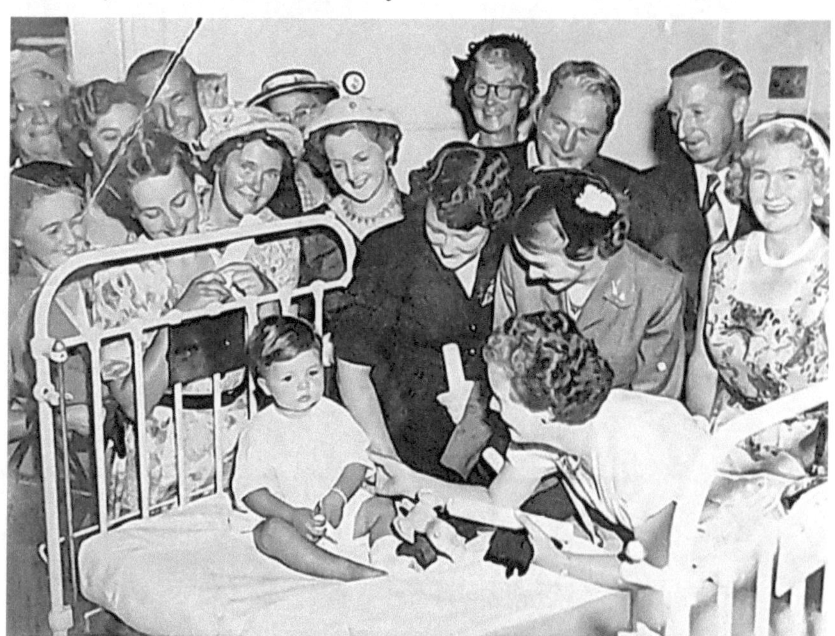

Women's football team donating money raised from their football games to The Children's Hospital, 1953. Photo courtesy of the Carlton family.

Jim 'Snowy' Miller and Charlie Hickey, date unknown. Photo courtesy Pengelly family.

Margaret O'Connor milking a cow, 1954. Photo courtesy of the Hassett family.

Rabbiting, date unknown. Photo courtesy of the Warfe family.

Murtcaim State School class of 1960. Photo courtesy the McLaren family.

Back row: G.Watkins (President), L.Doolan, B.Lee, V.McKane, D.Law, L.Smith, E.Pengelly, W.Day, T.Brown.
Centre: B.Cooney, L.Weatherly, J.Mayne, K.Ryan, L.Ryan, F.Pengelly, S.Porter, B.Thompson, L.Farrell.
Front: F.Ryan, E.Henderson, R.Pengelly, L.Plumridge, L.Parker (Capt.), J.O'Connor (V.Capt.), K.Eales, L.Danaher, C.King, G.Nutter.

Metropolitan Farm football team, 1956. Photo courtesy of the Ryan family.

Metro Farm football team, 1959. Photo courtesy of the Steinbergs family.

Metropolitan Farm football team playing on the Farm oval, 1963.
Photo courtesy of the McKane family.

Murtcaim School fete, 1959. Photo courtesy of the McLaren family.

Tex Pengelly at the Ranch, 1961. Photo courtesy of the Pengelly family.

Cottage 67 on the 160 Road, 1962. Photo courtesy of the Steinbergs family.

Postmistress Mrs Marjorie O'Connor, with the heritage listed 1854 Water Tank over her back fence, 1960s. Photo courtesy of the O'Connor family.

Swimming pool, 1969. Photo courtesy of the O'Connor family.

Metropolitan Farm Post Office in the O'Connor home, 1967. Photo courtesy of National Archives Australia.

Metropolitan Farm swimming pool, 2015. Photo courtesy of Dr Schott.

One of the last homes at the Head of the Road, 1972. Photo courtesy of the McKane family.

Murtcaim hay bale, date unknown. Photo courtesy of the Pengelly family.

Sheep being moved through the Head of the Road, 2018. Photo courtesy of Dr Schott.

Inside the Ranch, 2018. Photo courtesy of Dr Schott.

Cocoroc South School, relocated off the Farm to become the Girl Guides Hall in Werribee, 2022. Photo courtesy of Dr Schott.

1890s sluice gate once carrying effluent into Port Phillip Bay, exposed at low tide, 2018. Photo courtesy of Dr Schott.

1890s sluice gate exposed at low tide, 2018. Photo courtesy of Dr Schott.

Stables at the Ranch, 2018. Photo courtesy of Dr Schott.

Swimming pool, change room, football pavilion in background, community hall and water tank, 2018. Photo courtesy of Dr Schott.

Metropolitan Sewerage Farm with residents in 1951. Original map courtesy of the McNaughton family.

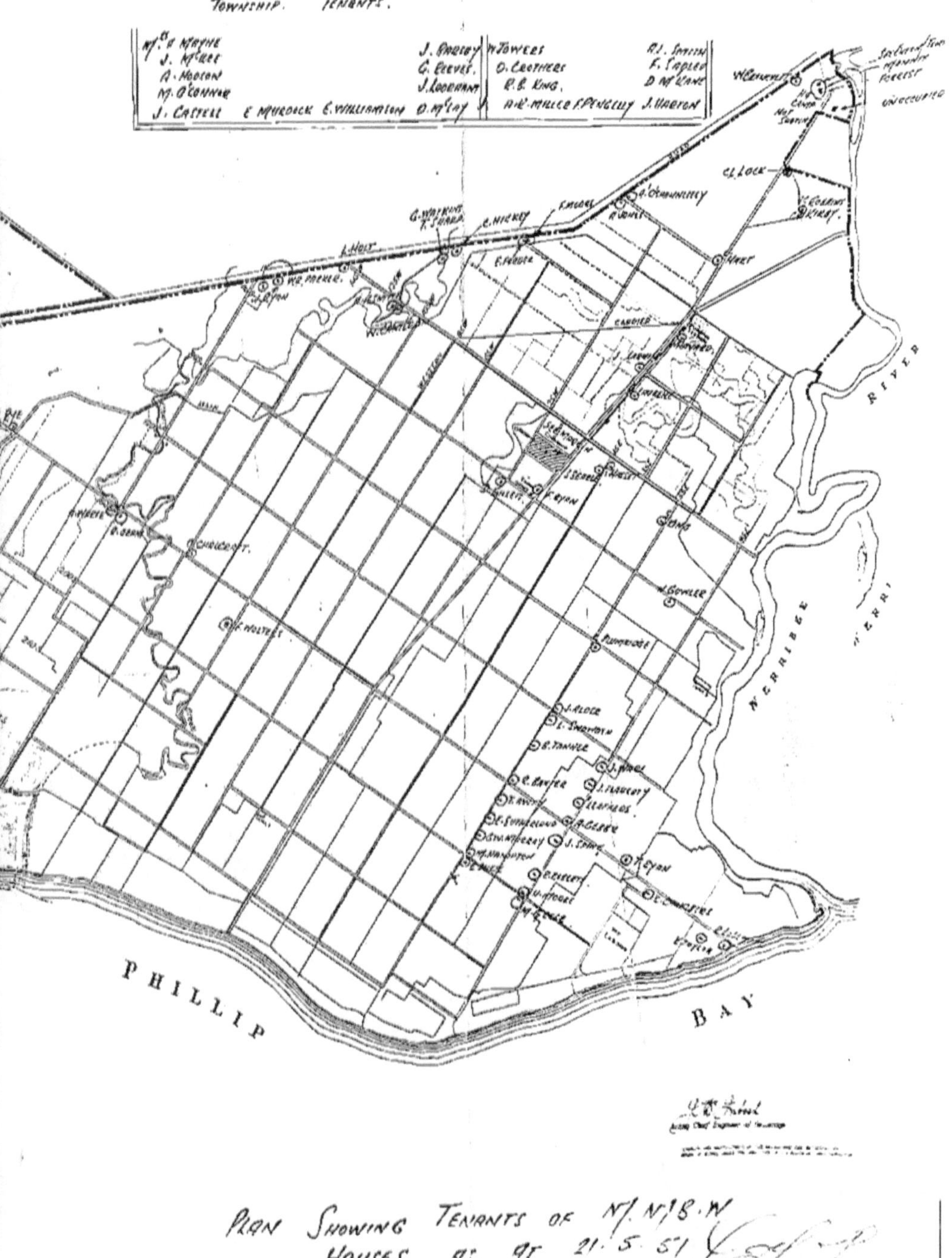
TOWNSHIP. TENANTS.
PHILLIP
BAY
WERRIBEE
RIVER
PLAN SHOWING TENANTS OF N.I.N.I.S.W
HOUSES AS AT 21.5.51

About the author

Dr Monika Schott is a Melbourne based writer and researcher. Life's intricacies and curiosities inspire her to write and give voice to stories that haven't been heard, particularly those of lost industrial communities and communities that have been isolated and segregated. Monika was shortlisted in the Ada Cambridge Writing Prize, has written several short stories, articles and various publications, and presents regularly at international forums. She's currently part of a research team uncovering the history, personalities and science of the State Research Farm in Werribee, Australia, where a small community once lived and worked. The site is of state heritage significance for scientific research and advancement of agricultural practices in Australia and illustrates a change from European agricultural practices to practices specific to Australia's climate and conditions. Monika will write the social history of this community as a next literary nonfiction and has begun writing *The jewel falls from the crown,* the sequel to *The faraway land of the house and two cows.* Visit www.monikaschott.com for more information.

www.ingramcontent.com/pod-product-compliance
Lightning Source LLC
Chambersburg PA
CBHW030821310726
48980CB00006B/587/J

* 9 7 8 0 6 4 5 4 7 5 4 0 1 *